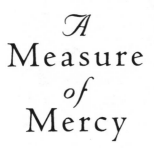

A
Measure
of
Mercy

Books by

Lauraine Snelling

Golden Filly Collection One *
Golden Filly Collection Two *

High Hurdles Collection One *
High Hurdles Collection Two *

SECRET REFUGE
Daughter of Twin Oaks

DAKOTAH TREASURES
Ruby • *Pearl*
Opal • *Amethyst*

DAUGHTERS OF BLESSING
A Promise for Ellie • *Sophie's Dilemma*
A Touch of Grace • *Rebecca's Reward*

HOME TO BLESSING
A Measure of Mercy • *No Distance Too Far*
A Heart for Home

RED RIVER OF THE NORTH
An Untamed Land • *A New Day Rising*
A Land to Call Home • *The Reaper's Song*
Tender Mercies • *Blessing in Disguise*

RETURN TO RED RIVER
A Dream to Follow • *Believing the Dream*
More Than a Dream

* 5 books in each volume

A Measure *of* Mercy

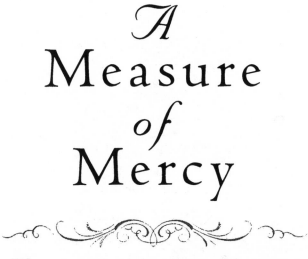

LAURAINE SNELLING

BETHANYHOUSE

MINNEAPOLIS, MINNESOTA

Published by Bethany House Publishers
11400 Hampshire Avenue South
Bloomington, Minnesota 55438

Bethany House Publishers is a division of
Baker Publishing Group, Grand Rapids, Michigan.

Printed in the United States of America

ISBN 978-0-7642-0727-3 (Large Print)

Library of Congress Cataloging-in-Publication Data

Snelling, Lauraine.
    A measure of mercy / Lauraine Snelling.
        p.   cm. — (Home to blessing ; 1)
        ISBN 978-0-7642-0726-6 (alk. paper) — ISBN 978-0-7642-0609-2 (pbk.)   1. Women medical students—Fiction.   I. Title.
    PS3569.N39M43   2009b
    813'.54—dc22

                                                                                2009025136

To all those creative people
involved in the creation and production
of the play *Bound for Blessing*:
many measures of mercy.

LAURAINE SNELLING is an award-winning author of over 60 books, fiction and nonfiction for adults and young adults. Her books have sold over two million copies. Besides writing books and articles, she teaches at writers' conferences across the country. She and her husband, Wayne, have two grown sons and a basset named Chewey. They make their home in California.

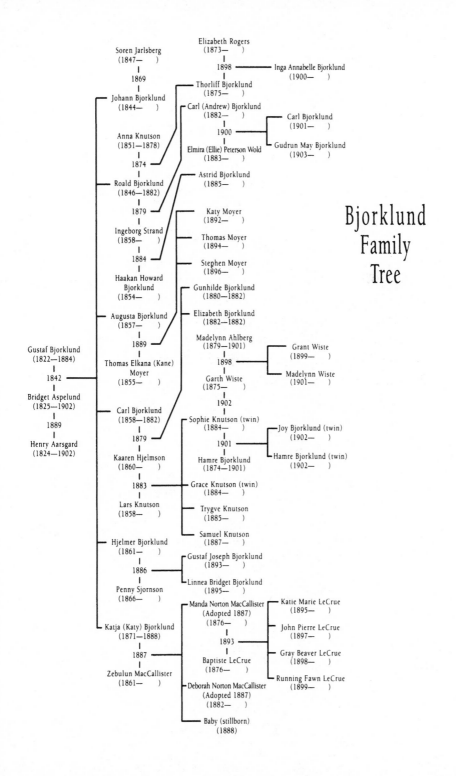

1

Go or stay." Astrid stared at the daisy in her hand and pulled off two petals. Sitting on the back porch, she was supposed to be hulling strawberries. But somehow that didn't work as well when one had life-altering decisions to make. She pulled another petal. "Go." And watched it drift down to the second of the three steps.

"You done with the berries?" her mother, Ingeborg, asked from the other side of the closed screen door.

Astrid shook her head. "Almost." She laid the daisy down and stood herself up, stretching her clasped hands above her head and twisting first to the left then to the right. The pull made her long for a good run across the fields. And that made her think of the old swing down by the river, where she and the others used to pump up to the sky until the day one of the ropes broke and one of the boys landed in the water. From then on they used it to swing out over the river and jump in. At least the boys did. The girls weren't allowed.

But she and cousin Sophie had leaped from the rope and never told anyone.

Maybe she should ask Sophie for advice. Maybe not.

"Here, I need a breeze for a while." Ingeborg handed her a tray with a plate of cookies and glasses of lemonade, ice chunks floating in it. Ever since they'd purchased the icebox from Penny's store—the Blessing Mercantile, the new name she'd given it—ice in the drinks was a common event.

Astrid set it on the table and sat in the chair to begin hulling. She could smell the fine perfume of strawberry jam cooking.

"I'm making biscuits for strawberry shortcake for dinner. That will make your far supremely happy." Ingeborg sat down, waving her apron to create a breeze. "Mighty still out here." She looked toward the west. "Could be rain coming. We sure need it."

They picked up their glasses at the same time, and Ingeborg drank a good part of hers. "All right, what is wrong?" She glanced over at the limp flower, now lying on the porch with several of its petals missing. "He loves me, he loves me not?"

Astrid made a face. "Now, who would I be thinking that about?"

"What, then?" Ingeborg, her braids fading from golden to silvered gilt and wrapped around her head crownlike, leaned toward her daughter, her voice full of love and concern.

"Same old thing. Do I stay here or go to Chicago for the surgical training?"

Ingeborg sighed. "I thought God would have made it clear by now, but one thing I've learned through the years, though He seems mighty slow at times, He is never late."

Astrid sipped her drink and nibbled on a ginger cookie. "These berries are for the shortcake?"

"Yes, so you might as well slice them too."

"Just us?" Since Jonathan Gould was living with them for the summer again as he learned to farm Dakota style, "us" included him.

"I think so. But what is left over we'll make into syrup for swizzles."

"And pancakes and ice cream and . . ." She smiled at her mother. Strawberries fixed any way were a favorite at the Bjorklunds'. "Feel that?" She tipped her head back to let the breeze whisper her neck. "But how do you know, Mor? God doesn't speak out of the bush anymore or in a thundering cloud. I need to know absolutely."

"Astrid, all I can tell you is that at the right time, God's time, you will know." She spoke each word precisely, softly, and yet with the conviction of steel holding them together and yet apart.

Astrid stared down at the daisy, all life drained out of it. When the time was right, she would know. How many times had she heard her mother speak those words through the years? Her answer was similar when Astrid used to ask why the sky is blue or how do the cows know when it is going to rain, or any number of other questions: "God made it so, and so it is." She'd known better than to ask again. At least for a while.

"Tomorrow I have my big exam with Elizabeth."

"I'll be praying for you."

"I know. To think she is putting me in charge of everything at the surgery for the day. I sure hope everyone is healthy around here."

"Then it wouldn't be much of a test, would it?"

"True." She set her glass back down with a click. "I'd better get the berries finished, and then I'm going to weed the garden."

"Put your sunbonnet on."

Astrid kept the groan to herself. She'd let it fall down to her back

11

like always. Sunbonnets were so hot, no honest breeze could even make it around those wide brims.

———

"ANOTHER ONE?" ASTRID looked up from cleaning the boy's wound. The easy day in the surgery was not turning out at all like she had hoped.

"An emergency." Dr. Elizabeth left the room in a swirl of skirt and apron. "Hurry!" She spoke firmly.

Astrid smiled at her young patient. "I'll be right back." She handed a gauze pad to the boy's mother. "Hold this on his arm, and I'll come back as soon as I can."

"Of course."

Astrid stepped into the hallway and across to the larger of the two examining rooms. She could hear several voices talking at once. Then a cry saturated with pain caught at her throat. Something bad had happened. As part of her physician exam, this was the day she was responsible for treating all of the patients who came to the clinic. No one had considered a serious accident occurring. She paused in the doorway. A man thrashed on the table while two others fought to hold him down. His teeth were clamped on the piece of wood someone had given him, yet he still sent one of the men crashing toward the wall.

Dr. Elizabeth glanced over her shoulder and nodded toward the other side of the table.

She wants me to take care of this? But I'm not ready, fired through her mind. Rather than turn and run like her heart screamed, Astrid stepped up to the blood-spattered table. The younger of the three men pressed a towel against the belly wound, his eyes wide as they darted from Dr. Elizabeth to Astrid.

Astrid turned to the pan to scrub her hands. "What happened?"

"He fell off the wagon onto a pitchfork that was stuck in the ground. The handle tore halfway through him."

Her heart hammering as if seeking exit, Astrid let the water run down her raised arms and took her place on the other side of the table.

"What would you do first?" Dr. Elizabeth asked.

How could she be so calm? Astrid sucked in a deep breath of air heavy with the scent of blood and something worse. "We can tell he is breathing all right, so settle him down with chloroform?" The words flowed in spite of her panic. "So we can do a thorough examination. Clear the clothing away from the site of the wound and check for other injuries."

"Right." Elizabeth lifted the towel just enough to look at the wound and laid it back down.

Astrid reached in the cabinet for the chloroform bottle, poured a few drops on a cloth, and moving swiftly, held it above the man's mouth so it didn't burn his skin. He gasped, his face relaxed, and his terrified eyes closed.

"Thank you. Now, if one of you gentlemen would take her place at his head and hold that bottle, I will tell you when to add a few more drops so we can keep him sedated."

"I will." The older man took Astrid's place. "This is my eldest son, Vernon. Doctor, please—I know this is bad—help God work a miracle."

Astrid heard a slight German accent in his plea.

"We'll do our best." Elizabeth felt beneath the patient. "You said the handle went halfway through?"

"Yes. Thank God it didn't go all the way. His legs work, as you saw. Arms too. But his insides are a mess."

Elizabeth looked to the younger man standing at her shoulder. "If you would go find my housekeeper and ask her to come in here, please? Her name is Thelma, and she's most likely in the kitchen." As he left, she turned to Astrid. "Go out and tell those waiting that we will be busy for some time."

Astrid flew out of the room, popped into the other examining room, where she had been before, and told the boy's mother that they had an emergency and she'd get back when she could. Several in the waiting room stood when they heard and said they'd come back another time. Astrid lifted down the earpiece on the telephone and asked the operator to ring the Bjorklund farm.

"What's wrong?" Gerald Valders, the daytime switchboard operator, asked as he put the call through.

"Terrible accident. Please call Pastor Solberg. We're going to need all the help we can get." She heard the phone ringing.

"Hello?"

Astrid calmed a little at the sound of her mother's voice. "Mor, come quickly. We need help. Bring your bag."

"I will."

Astrid hung up and returned to the examination room, now quiet but for the stentorian breathing of the man on the table. Thelma was helping cut away the man's shirt, her face even more wrinkled than normal.

"I called Mor," Astrid said.

"Good. I figured you would. The bleeding has slowed. Thelma, bring us a bucket of hot water and lay the instruments in the carbolic acid." She looked to Astrid. "Put on a surgical apron and scrub again. Sir? What is your name?"

"Baxter. We work on the bonanza farm across the river."

"Mr. Baxter, watch your son closely, and if he starts to blink or flinch, drip a couple more drops on the cloth."

"Yes, ma'am. You need my other boy?"

"We might." She addressed the young man who was once again at her shoulder. "Would you please wait in the hall. And if you are praying folk, please do so. We need the Almighty's help here." She closed her eyes for a moment.

After tying a kerchief over her hair, the color of aged honey, and donning the straight surgery apron that covered her from neck to ankle, Astrid lifted the instruments out of the disinfectant. She sucked in a deep breath, as the odors coming from the wound made her throat start to close, but kept moving. With the blood-soaked towel out of the way, the enormity of the wound made her glance up at Elizabeth, who was focused on the task before them. Astrid swallowed her question and began digging out debris, pieces of cloth, bits of wood, and bone where a rib had broken off. *Please, Mor, get here soon.*

Thelma kept handing the two women sterile cloths and mopping up blood and body fluids, along with the sweat from their foreheads.

When Astrid saw the tear in the intestine, she wanted to cry. How would they ever fight off the infection that would cause? She set her sorrow aside and slid her hand into the cavity to feel for more debris. "The handle bypassed the major arteries," she reported. Otherwise he would have never made it this long.

"Good girl." Dr. Elizabeth nodded. "Can you detect any more foreign substances?"

"Not big enough that I can find. How it missed his heart and lungs, I'll never know."

"Mostly stomach and intestine damage. We can suture those and then wash as much out as we can."

"Will we leave a drain in?"

"Yes. But take out as much damaged tissue as possible. You start with suturing the stomach wall, and I'll do the intestine. Thelma, we'll need several of the bulb syringes, and ask that young man out there to make sure there is water boiling. We're going to need more."

"How can I help?" Ingeborg stepped through the door.

"Thank God you are here." Elizabeth quickly raised her eyes toward her mother-in-law. "Pray while you clean and sterilize the instruments. If only we had a real operating room. Scrub up too in case we need another pair of hands."

"I've been praying. Gerald put out the call for prayer."

Astrid glanced at her mother. "Could you please get me a glass of water?"

"Me too," Elizabeth said. "How about you, Mr. Baxter?"

"Please." He nodded. "I just added three more drops."

"Oh, and please go finish bandaging that boy in the other room. His mother must think we have forgotten about him."

"I will." Ingeborg closed the door carefully behind her.

Astrid tied off another stitch and cut the thread. "His stomach is going to be lots smaller. So much of the tissue is damaged." She wiped the sweat from her forehead with the back of her hand. Trickles ran down her spine. They might have been at this for hours; she couldn't tell. She picked up another needle that Thelma had prepared and started again.

"There, last one I can find," Elizabeth said as she tied off a small bleeder some time later. "Let's irrigate."

Having just returned, Ingeborg put the stethoscope in her ears and listened to the man's chest. "His heartbeat is slow but steady. Lungs sound clear."

"That is truly miraculous." Astrid glanced up at Mr. Baxter to see a tear leaking down his cheek.

"Your son is very strong. But he's not out of the woods yet, not at all," Elizabeth warned.

"I know, but thanks to you he has a chance. I know about belly wounds. I've seen men die from them."

"Please, God, let this be one who makes it," Ingeborg said.

Astrid removed the last pad and dropped it into the bucket with the others. "Ready to close?" At Elizabeth's nod, Astrid looked to her mother. "You want to help?"

"Of course."

The three of them worked together as if they were quilting. They closed the peritoneum, repaired the damaged muscles, and finally stitched the layers of skin.

"He looks like a patchwork," Ingeborg said as she tied off her final stitch. "Please, heavenly Father, we have done our best. We thank you for giving this man life and strength, and we leave him in your mighty hands. Thank you for the wisdom you have given here and for the love you so freely spread on all of us. In your son's name we pray." The others joined her on the amen, along with another male voice.

"Ah good. You are here, John." The older woman smiled at their pastor, John Solberg.

"I've been out here praying for what seems like hours."

"That's because it has been hours." Elizabeth tipped her head back, stretching muscles too long tense. "Mr. Baxter, you did a fine job as our anesthesiologist. You can let your son come more alert now. The pain is going to be atrocious, so we will keep him sedated as much as possible for the first couple of days." She held a syringe filled with morphine. "This will help with the pain," she said as she inserted the medicine into his buttock.

"You will keep him here?" Mr. Baxter looked around. "Where?"

"We have rooms for such as this." Elizabeth checked the patient's pulse.

"Where do you want us to put him?" Waiting in the doorway, Thorliff Bjorklund looked at his wife.

"Let's use the bigger room. Mr. Baxter, my husband and our pastor are used to moving patients. They will show you how to assist them."

Astrid watched their patient. First his eyelids fluttered, and then he grimaced. "We better move him quickly. He's coming around."

The women stepped out of the room to give the men the space to do their job.

"This certainly shows our need of a surgical room with decent lighting and enough room to move about. Astrid, you passed today's examination with flying colors. Even without formal surgical training, I'd rather have you assisting me than any other doctor I know."

"It seemed as if the two of you could read each other's minds, you worked so smoothly together." Ingeborg leaned against the wall. "Astrid, how did you know what to do?"

"I guess I've memorized the pictures in *Gray's Anatomy*. But I can sure see the value of working on a real body." Now that it was over Astrid realized that, though physically she was tired, her mind was racing trying to process all the new information the surgery had given her.

"So has this convinced you to go to Chicago?"

Astrid thought for a moment. Elizabeth had been insisting she go for more formal instruction at the Alfred Morganstein Hospital for Women and Children. Since she already had so much practical experience helping at the surgery in Blessing, she would only need to go for the surgical training. If she could pass the tests on all the other required classes first. But Chicago was so far away! Yet working with Dr. Althea Morganstein, Elizabeth's own mentor, would be invaluable. Astrid knew her sister-in-law had taken her on with this plan in mind. She also knew Elizabeth would take it personally if Astrid didn't pass the rigorous examinations Dr. Morganstein required.

Astrid glanced at her mother and nodded. "Yes, I am certain."

Was that a whisper she'd heard or had God really spoken? Or just sent this test for her?

Ingeborg blinked at the moisture gathering in her eyes and returned the nod.

The trio followed the men into the larger of the rooms with beds on the first floor, the one they'd designated as the recovery room, and checked to make sure there was no blood leaking. When the young man groaned, his father took his hand.

"You rest easy, Vernon. The doctors are doing their best for you."

He thinks I'm a real doctor, Astrid realized. The thought made her smile inside.

"Do you want me to take the first shift?"

"No, I will." Ingeborg took her place in the chair. "You two go get something to eat and rest a bit. There are more people in the waiting room, but I told them it would be some time yet."

Astrid and Elizabeth swapped smiles. Doctors or not, sometimes mothers still took charge.

"Thank you, we will. After we clean up."

"Oh, and Thelma said to tell you she'd take care of the surgery. The soup is simmering on the stove, and the coffee is hot."

"Do you mind if I stay here for a while?" Mr. Baxter asked.

"You stay as long as you want. Have you had dinner?"

"No."

"We'll bring you a tray."

"Thank you, but you don't need to do that. I mean . . ." He lowered his eyes at the look Elizabeth sent his way. "I'd be obliged."

Astrid and Elizabeth found Thorliff and Pastor Solberg in the kitchen. "You want coffee?"

"We've not had dinner either," Thorliff said. "You want company?"

Elizabeth nodded. "Let's eat out on the porch, where it's cooler."

Fresh rolls waited on the counter in the cheerful kitchen, which was really Thelma's domain. She had geraniums blooming in the east window, white curtains with red trim, and braided rag rugs in front of the stove and the sink. The cushions on the oak chairs matched the red-and-white print of the tablecloth.

"Oh, this smells so good." Astrid inhaled the aroma of freshly baked rolls. "Operating rooms smell even worse than the milking barn in winter." She stopped at the sink, took off her bloodstained operating apron, dropped it in the tub of water set for soaking, and began scrubbing her arms and hands. "Scrub before we operate and wash up afterward."

"That young man needs a real scrubbing too." Thorliff took a platter of sliced meat and cheese from the icebox, along with a bowl of freshly washed lettuce leaves, and set them on a tray.

"That can be done later." Astrid stepped back from the sink so Elizabeth could wash up. She dried her hands and arms and used the towel to wipe her forehead and neck. Taking bowls down from the cupboard, she dished up the soup and handed the full bowls to Thorliff to set on the tray. When they were all seated around the table on the porch, they bowed their heads and let peace flow around them.

"Heavenly Father, thank you for the gifts of healing you displayed here today," the pastor began. "Thank you for willing hearts as we wait for you to finish what has begun. Thank you for the food before us, for this moment of rest. And, Lord God, whatever happens, we will give you all the glory. In your son's precious name, amen."

"Thank you. I cannot begin to tell you how much it means to me to know that you are out in that hall praying while we work on people like this one today. Between you and Ingeborg, you keep us sane." Elizabeth's lips curved in a deep smile.

Pastor Solberg smiled and nodded. "My privilege. So what is your prognosis on this case?"

"We've done what we can. Most people would say this one is impossible."

Thorliff took his wife's hand. "But, as Mor reminded me, with God all things are possible."

"And we have seen Him do the impossible before."

"That we have." Elizabeth glanced over at Astrid. "Are you all right?"

"I don't know. A wave of tiredness just rolled over me. I can hardly pick up my spoon."

"That's not surprising. Just make yourself eat and drink plenty of lemonade. It'll pass." Elizabeth did as she'd told Astrid. She turned to Thorliff. "What did you do with Inga?"

"She's out at Andrew's, playing with Carl. I took her there when I saw the man in the wagon. I knew you would be busy, and I didn't want her to see such carnage."

"Thank you."

Astrid drank half the glass of lemonade and buttered a roll, putting slices of meat and cheese and a leaf of lettuce on it. Her feet were aching, her back was whining, and her hands were shaking. Her eyes burned as if she had been crying—or would be shortly. Taking a bite of her roll, she ordered herself to chew. Elizabeth was eating her roll and laughed at something Thorliff said. Pastor Solberg nodded and joined in the laughter. All Astrid wanted to do was throw up what little she had eaten and cry herself to sleep. She'd made it through the worst surgery of her life. What was wrong with her now?

2

Ingeborg checked Vernon's pulse. Slow but steady. Amazed that he was doing this well after the surgery he'd been through, she sat down in the chair and picked up her prayers again. They felt tangible, like something she could hold in her hands. She closed her eyes, the idea of hands continuing like a gentle stream flowing through her mind. Only instead of her own hands, now she pictured God's hands, mighty and yet tender, holding this young man securely in His palm, His fingers gently stroking the inert body.

Thank you, Father. You bid us come to you, to bring you the broken of body and heart. Thank you that you promise to heal, to restore, to comfort. I ask peace for this child of yours—peace in his body and in his mind. Let him feel your presence, your great love. Father, I praise you and thank you for your never-ending love and mercy. You know all things, and you know his needs far better than I do. I thank you that we can trust you to do the very best. She leaned back in the chair, her praises continuing with each breath, each beat of her heart.

Please protect him from the infection that lurks from all the debris we couldn't find. She laid the back of her hand against his cheek and forehead. Still cool. *Thank you, Father.*

Dr. Elizabeth stopped in the doorway. "How is he?"

"Vernon is one strong young man. He is holding his own."

"Call me if you see any change?"

"I will. You look tired."

"Surgery like that takes every ounce of energy and skill. Thank you for your prayers, both for him and for us."

"God is in control."

"I know. Thank you for the reminder." Elizabeth brushed her hand over her forehead.

"Can you lie down for a bit?" Ingeborg asked, watching her daughter-in-law's face.

"I just sent Astrid up to lie down instead. She got a bit worn out. Not unusual for what she's been through. I remember reacting much the same. One time I fainted. Any surgery is grueling, but this was beyond anything even I've ever done."

"I'm not surprised. This was her first surgery inside a body, wasn't it?"

Elizabeth nodded. "She has stitched up many superficial wounds, set bones, and birthed babies. But having your hands inside the body of a living person is a whole different matter. I was proud at her willingness to put aside her discomfort and concentrate only on what needed doing." Elizabeth chuckled. "And she is just as amazed, I think."

Ingeborg sensed her patient moving before he actually opened his eyes. "Be still, Vernon. You are here at the doctor's. Your father went home to bring your mother in. All will be well."

Elizabeth crossed the room and stopped by the other side of the

24

bed, picking up his hand. "We are keeping you sedated so the pain will not be as severe. If you can understand me, please squeeze my hand." She smiled at the light pressure from his fingers. "Good. Go back to sleep now. You are in God's mighty hands."

He blinked, then closed his eyes and drifted off again.

Thank you, Father, that Elizabeth is acknowledging you more and more. Thank you, thank you. Ingeborg's mind filled with songs of praise and thanksgiving, lifting her spirit as well as her smile.

Elizabeth glanced over at her. "What?"

"I'm just thanking God for you and for all this that has happened. God is so merciful."

"Right now I need His strength, along with the mercy and grace."

"You have it." Ingeborg smiled at her.

"How do you know that?"

"Because I asked and you asked, and He says where two or three are gathered and agree, He will do it."

"Thank you both." Elizabeth drew in a deep breath. "I think I'll walk outside a couple of minutes before I go back to my waiting patients."

"Good idea. Fresh air is another of His gifts."

Elizabeth paused before she went out the door. "How is Haakan?"

"Stronger all the time. I can tell a difference in the strength between his two hands, but he says he can milk as well as he used to. Milking cows is good therapy for hands and arms."

"Good." Elizabeth yawned. "I'll be back in a minute or two."

We never have enough time to visit, it seems. Ingeborg's mind flitted to her strawberry patch. Next week she'd have the final picking. The season was early this year. They usually had strawberries in time for the Fourth of July. She'd just slipped back into praying when Thelma entered the room with a cup and spoon on a tray.

"I chipped some ice for the young man. A spoonful whenever he comes to will do."

"Thank you. I was about to come and get some for him to suck on."

Thelma nodded. "I will bring more later." She set her tray on the table next to Ingeborg. "Can I bring you something cold to drink?"

"That would be lovely, but I can come and get it."

"You sit there and put your feet up." She scooted the footstool over in front of Ingeborg. "Do you have your knitting?"

"No, I left in too much of a hurry to grab it."

"I'm making a dress for Inga. You could hem it if you like."

"I'd love to. Mange takk." Sewing for her little granddaughter and namesake always lightened Ingeborg's heart.

The young man groaned, and his fingers twitched on the sheet that covered him.

Ingeborg let the songs in her mind murmur aloud and watched as the lines in his face smoothed out. She felt his cheek again. Still cool.

Astrid, after tying on a fresh white apron that covered her from shoulder to ankle, stopped in the doorway. "Singing him to sleep?"

"It seems to help. Did you sleep?"

"Like a cat in the sunshine." She stretched and yawned. "Did Elizabeth mention that I got so shaky I could hardly stand?"

"That isn't surprising. The wonderful thing is that you were able to do what was needed. I've seen big men faint from far less. Elizabeth has told stories of nurses and doctors in training fainting in surgeries or having to leave because they were vomiting."

"The smell was horrible." Astrid shivered a little. "Worse even than when we burned the cattle."

"Because of the damaged intestines, but you persevered."

"You think helping butcher animals and chickens made me tougher?"

"Probably. Being out in the open air helps blow the stench away, not like in that small room." Ingeborg picked up the cup and held a chip of ice to Vernon's lips. "Try this," she said softly and smiled as he did so.

"I need to help Elizabeth with the other patients. I'll come back later so you can go home."

Ingeborg nodded and spooned another small chip into their patient's mouth.

Noise in the hallway caught her attention a bit later. A man's voice first and then a woman's.

"My son. I want to see my son." The mother's anguish swirled into the room ahead of a rounded woman with graying hair knotted in a bun. The lines in her face that bespoke hard work now slashed deeper with fear.

Ingeborg stood and motioned to her chair. "You sit here so you can be near him."

"Mrs. Bjorklund, this is my wife, Wilma. We came back as soon as we could." Mr. Baxter clutched his hat to his chest and stared down at his boy. "He is still alive."

"Yes, and he has swallowed some ice bits. It is there in the cup. He can have some every few minutes as long as he can swallow and keep it down."

The mother's tears dripped onto her son's hand as she clutched it to her cheek. She spoke in tear-seasoned German, but the tone sounded only of love.

Vernon's eyes fluttered open, and he stared into his mother's face, then turned slightly to look to his father. The faintest of nods welcomed their presence before he drifted off again.

"Can I get you anything? Something cool to drink?" Ingeborg asked.

Mr. Baxter shook his head. "Thank you. Perhaps later."

"I'll be back in a while. Call if there is any change or you need anything. The necessary is right down the hall."

"Not outside?"

"No. There is running water to wash with too. We all wash our hands to try to keep infection down. I can show you how to use it."

"Ja, that would be good." Mr. Baxter followed her from the room and down the hall. "This is most amazing."

"I know." Ingeborg opened the door. She turned the handles on the faucets, pulled the chain above the commode, and showed him the bar of soap and the hand towels. "Please wash and then show your wife how this works. We scrub our hands with brushes like the one there." She pointed to a brush on a glass shelf above the sink. *Please, Lord, let him not be offended.*

"Danke." He spoke his thanks with a slight bow, a look of amazement etched on his face.

Ingeborg headed for the kitchen and a cup of much needed coffee.

"You go sit on the porch, where there's a bit of breeze. I will bring the coffee." Thelma paused. "And the dress."

Ingeborg nodded, and out on the porch she sank into a rocking chair with thick red plaid cushions. A breeze lifted the tendrils of hair that had loosed themselves from the braids fashioned in a crown framing her face and neck. She let her head rest against the back of the chair and reveled in the cool air on her skin. A robin sang from the elm tree just off the porch. Swallows dipped and darted after bugs and brought daubs of mud to their houses in the eaves of the porch. Thelma set a tray on the table and the dress on a chair beside Ingeborg, then with a smile she returned back inside the house.

28

A plate of molasses cookies sat between a cup of coffee and a glass of lemonade. She started with the lemonade, holding the cold glass against her forehead and cheeks.

Inga's black-and-white cat mounted the steps and rubbed against her skirt, eyeing the birds as she mewed to be picked up.

"All right, come ahead." Ingeborg set her glass back on the tray and patted her knees. The cat didn't need a second invitation and leaped into her lap, bumping her head under Ingeborg's chin before turning around, kneading with her front paws, and curling in a circle. Ingeborg stroked the cat, enjoying the soft fur and the purring motor that started up with the first stroke. Smiling, she reached for the cup of coffee and a cookie. "Now if this isn't the life. Sitting here in the middle of the afternoon and ignoring all the work that needs doing." She eyed the pinafore with ruffles along the crossed straps and ties for the back of the gathered skirt. She knew the pink-and-white checks of gingham would delight her granddaughter.

When she finished the cookie and the cup was only half full, she picked up the dress, along with the threaded needle, and blindstitched the hem. The cat leaped lightly to the wide board that formed the ledge on the porch railing and prowled after the birds, the tip of her tail twitching as she melted into a crouch.

Ingeborg watched the cat between thrusts of the needle. "You better not let Inga see you hunting so close to the house."

"So, Mor, who are you talking to now?" Thorliff pushed open the gate and strolled up the walk.

"The cat."

"I see. Did Mr. and Mrs. Baxter arrive?"

"Yes. They are sitting with their son, so I came out here. You want some coffee or lemonade?"

"You sit still. I'll get it," Thorliff said when she started to get up.

For a change, Ingeborg settled back. She started to scold herself for being lazy but instead shrugged and chose to enjoy the moment of ease.

Thelma met him at the door with a duplicate tray of the one she'd brought Ingeborg. "You make sure your mother sits awhile longer."

"Look who's talking."

"Be that as it may. I wasn't working that surgery like they were and taking care of the young man." She raised her voice. "I took more ice chips in. Taking care of her son gives his mother something to do with her hands."

"Mange takk, Thelma. You are so wise. What would we do without you?"

A snort echoed the closing of the screen door.

Thorliff sat down in the other rocker. "Well, the paper is ready to send out. Samuel is taking it around town." He laid a copy on the table. "I brought you yours."

Ingeborg picked up the latest edition, smiling all the while. "Haakan will be happy to get this. He always looks forward to your paper arriving."

"He used to get the Grand Forks paper too. Doesn't he any longer?"

"He let his subscription lapse after the apoplexy. I should probably start it again."

"My interview with Keith, who runs the coal mine, is on the front page. I'm thinking Far might be interested in that. Perhaps we might want to invest in that venture, since it looks like a real boon to North Dakota." He shot his mother a questioning glance. "Not that we've recovered all the way from the hoof and mouth yet, but our bank has some money to invest."

"I know you'd rather buy more cows, but you and Far talk it over." Thorliff drained the glass of lemonade. "I'll go get Inga in a bit."

"Why not let her stay awhile with Andrew and Ellie? She and Carl always have a great time. After all, cousins need time to play together too."

"I'm not sure Ellie would agree with you. I think Inga gets Carl into all kinds of trouble."

"Like making mud pies in the rain barrel?"

"And putting a chair up so they could climb into the apple tree." Thorliff shook his head. "Andrew thought it was funny, but Ellie was sure they were going to fall and break their necks."

"Dressing the runt pig in baby clothes they took off the clothesline . . ." Ingeborg grinned at her son and shook her head. "She reminds me of Astrid when she was little."

"Astrid didn't get into everything like Inga does."

"We were all working so hard we hadn't time to watch her closely. So perhaps we didn't see some of the things she did. Besides, she had the twins to play with, and she and Sophie spent a lot of time being careful to watch out for Grace. Sophie was the one who thought up the antics."

"And she still does. Wait until you hear her plans for the Fourth of July celebration."

They heard a buggy pull sharply to a stop on the other side of the house. Someone else was in trouble. Andrew's voice brought her to her feet. "Mor, come help."

3

W hat happened?" Astrid met them all at the door of the surgery after hearing Andrew's voice.

"I think his arm is broken." Andrew held his son in his arms. "He fell off the ladder going up to the haymow."

Astrid touched the little boy's shoulder and arm that were held tight against his body by a tied-in-place flour sack dish towel. "The haymow?"

"I told them to stay out of the barn."

"Kitties." The word was barely discernable between sobs. Her nephew's round pale face tore at her heart.

"Come this way, and we'll see what to do." Astrid ushered them toward the small examining room. "What kitties, Carl?"

"There are kittens in the haymow." Andrew's voice deepened.

"We found them back in a corner when we were cleaning out the last of the old hay to get ready for the barn dance Saturday night."

"And Inga wanted to see them and dragged Carl along?" Grandma Ingeborg pursed her lips and shook her head.

"That's about it," her younger son agreed.

"Where was Maydell?" Maydell Gamble was visiting with Ellie again now that Dorothy was doing better. "I thought she was keeping an eye on Carl and Inga."

Andrew shrugged. "That seems to be a bit of a mystery."

"Lay him down there." Astrid pointed at the table in the middle of the room. She thought back to her last conversation when Maydell admitted she'd mostly been helping Dorothy with her children because she was hoping to see more of Gus Baard, but as soon as she'd shown up, he kept away. Usually Maydell's flightiness didn't ruffle her, but at the moment she could think of several things she'd like to do to Maydell, none of them comfortable.

When Andrew tried to lay his son down, Carl screamed and clung to his father with his unbound arm. Ingeborg leaned over his small body and stroked his face, humming one of his favorite songs.

"All right, Andrew. You sit in that chair and hold him." Astrid pointed to a ladder-back chair next to the wall. "Or do you want Mor to hold him?"

Shaking his head, Andrew sat down, holding Carl on his left knee so the wounded arm could be examined.

Astrid leaned over and whispered in Carl's ear. "You are Tante Astrid's big boy, aren't you?"

He nodded and tried to sniff back the tears, then buried his face in his father's shoulder.

"Carl, I need to find out what is wrong with your arm. I'm going to give you something to drink so you feel better."

Andrew stared at his sister, his face pale.

"Don't worry. It'll make him sleepy, and then we can help him more easily." She poured a bit of laudanum into a cup and added honey and water, then stirred it. "Here you go, Carl." She held it to his mouth, and after giving her a dubious look, he took a sip then drank the rest. "Honey can do all kinds of good things. You three wait here while I go find Tante Elizabeth."

As soon as she stepped out of the room, her mind flew back to the young man down the hall. How was he? She peeked in the door to see his mother and father on either side of the bed, Vernon sound asleep. What a day this had been, and it was only midafternoon. Leaving that room, she knocked on the closed door of the large examining room, obeying the command to come in.

"What do you think this is?" Dr. Elizabeth asked her immediately, pointing to two young girls who were covered in suppurating sores. The mother looked from Astrid to Elizabeth, then closed her mouth against what she'd started to say.

Astrid studied them without touching their skin. "Looks like poison ivy to me."

"And what do you recommend?"

"Baths in warm water with finely ground oatmeal, apply honey to the sores, leave the skin uncovered as much as possible so the air can dry the discharge." She turned to the mother. "Do you have rolled oats or plain oats at home to run through the coffee grinder?" At her nod, she continued. "That will help the itching. If you have some comfrey, grind that and make a paste to apply."

"I told them to stay out of the woods, but they had to learn the hard way."

"Do you know what poison ivy looks like?" Astrid asked the two weepy girls.

"We do now." The two girls looked at each other then at Astrid. "It was so pretty we made chains out of it to wear in our hair."

"I see." Astrid smiled at the mother. "Let us know how this goes. There are some other things we can try if need be. Soak all their clothes and bedding in hot soapy water. Anything they have touched wash with soapy water. They are highly contagious."

"Thank you, Doctors." The mother nodded to both Elizabeth and Astrid and herded the girls ahead of her out of the room.

Astrid had a strong feeling those two girls were in for more punishment than just how miserable they felt.

"You passed that one with flying colors. I'll get Thelma in here to scrub with carbolic acid. Let's go wash ourselves. That was the worst case I have ever seen."

"Are they new to the area?"

"Come from the Minnesota side like the Baxters. Good thing we have that bridge across the river now. The family moved here from someplace back East." The two joined at the basin and scrubbed hands and arms, then took off their aprons. "Just in case," Elizabeth added.

Astrid told her about Carl while they tied clean aprons on and entered the examining room. Carl lay sound asleep on the table, Andrew and Ingeborg standing on either side of him.

"Good, that is what I hoped would happen." Astrid smiled at her brother. "Did you try to set it?"

"No. That's what we have doctors for nowadays."

"You can work with animals but not humans, is that it?" Astrid teased her brother.

"That's right. Especially not my son."

With gentle fingers Astrid probed the arm, which was already swollen and hot. The break was halfway between wrist and elbow. "You hold Carl, and we'll do the traction."

Elizabeth nodded. "I'll take the wrist."

"Be ready for him to flail."

Andrew pressed against his son's shoulders with both hands.

"No, you lie across his body too. This is going to hurt."

Andrew gave her a funny look but did as she said.

"On three." Astrid gripped the boy's elbow and upper arm to steady it when Elizabeth pulled. "One, two, three." Elizabeth pulled, Carl let out a shriek, bucked, and nearly threw his father off. But the bone clicked back in place.

"I'll go get the ice." Elizabeth left the room while Astrid took a flat piece of wood with rounded edges from a shelf and began wrapping it in soft cotton. She laid it next to the arm, wrapped it in place, and folded a square of cloth into a triangle for a sling. When Elizabeth returned with small chunks of ice, they wrapped the ice around the boy's arm and tied the sling in place.

Sitting in the chair and holding his still son, who was once again asleep, Andrew nodded. "You two work well together."

"Thank you. I sure hope this is the last one of the day. You should have seen the cases of poison ivy we just took care of. My word, what a mess." Astrid studied her nephew, his long eyelashes feathering his round cheeks. "I'll send some laudanum home with you. I think when he wakes up, we should just wrap his arm to his body like you did to bring him in. Best for a little one like him."

"How's Vernon?"

"You know him?"

"I'd met him before. You think he'll make it?"

"I sure am praying so. All of us are." She shuddered. "That was the most awful . . ." She blew out a breath. "Why don't you take Mor home with you? She can take care of Carl. Both of them can use some rocking, and she can pray just as well there as here."

"I will. Tomorrow we are stringing more phone lines. I am now more convinced than ever how valuable that newfangled instrument is."

"That's it for the day," Elizabeth said as they watched Andrew carry his son back to the buggy and help Ingeborg settle the child in her lap.

"Other than Vernon." Astrid leaned against the wall. "Didn't I hear his father leave a while ago?"

"He had to go home to do chores." Elizabeth sank into a chair. "My daughter did it this time."

"Probably won't be the last."

"Poor little Carl. I should send Thorliff out to get her."

"No, let her help entertain Carl. She'll learn more that way. After all, you know it wasn't deliberate."

"Her disobeying Andrew like that was. He told her not to go to the barn."

"Maybe. Maybe he only told Carl, and he didn't share the information." Astrid thought to the times she'd been in trouble when younger. While she knew Inga deserved a punishment, she still wanted to protect her. As her far had said more than once, Inga could charm the birds out of the trees, let alone her little cousin, who did his best to keep up with her. Sometimes she forgot how young the two really were, the way Inga would interpret for Carl. She been talking since she was barely a year and a half. Her far said she was born talking.

Dr. Elizabeth dug her fists into her lower back and the aching muscles. "This has been some day. How do you feel about all the cases you took care of today?"

"Are you saying that you will still call this part of my final examination?"

"Yes, and you did remarkably well."

"Even though I overreacted? I don't think a doctor is supposed to fall apart."

"But that was afterward. And it was due to the adrenaline. Don't be so critical of yourself. I will always feel more secure when you are standing with me in a crisis."

Astrid stared at her for a long moment. "Do you feel insecure at times?"

"Of course."

"You mean that never goes away?"

Elizabeth chuckled at the look of consternation on Astrid's face. "Your mother would say that's what forces us to depend on our heavenly Father, and that's a good thing. Now, let's think about the schedule tonight for Mr. Baxter. I want his mother to sleep too, so let's go talk with her."

"Do you speak German?"

"A bit."

When the two of them entered the sickroom, Mrs. Baxter started from a half doze.

"Sprechen sie Englisch?" Elizabeth asked.

"Ein bisschen." The woman held her fingers close together to signal *a bit.*

Over the next few minutes Astrid watched and listened as the two tried to communicate. The agreement came when Elizabeth convinced the woman that among the four of them, including Mr. Baxter if he was able to return, they could all take turns caring for her son and that eating and sleeping were necessary for her too. She brushed tears from her eyes and clutched Elizabeth's hand.

"Danke schön."

Even Astrid knew that meant *thank you very much.* "We could call on the Geddicks for translation if Mr. Baxter can't be here," she said as soon as the idea popped into her head.

"That's a great idea," Elizabeth said with a nod. "They don't have a telephone yet, do they?"

Astrid shrugged. "I'll call and ask Gerald in the morning."

———

ALL WAS GOING according to plan during the night until Astrid came on duty at three o'clock. When Vernon shifted restlessly, she administered more morphine, but touching his skin made her heart sink. He was hot. *Infection must be setting in.* Much to the consternation of his father, who was watching over him at the time, she pulled back the covers and opened the window. "We have to cool him off."

"But he was shivering and cold, so I covered him."

"I know. That is the way of this. You start sponging his face and neck, and I'll go soak a sheet in cold water." When she came back the mister was doing as she'd said, but when she started to remove the sheet, he grabbed the edge.

"Nein, this is not proper."

Astrid stared at him. What did proper matter at a time like this? "But I am a doctor."

"You are a young woman. I will change the sheets." He took the wet bundle from her and waited.

Astrid shook her head. "Before you put the sheets on him, lay a towel across his, his . . ." She sought the best word so as to not offend. "Below his waist." She gestured at the same time.

"I will do that." He waited for her to leave the room.

"Who does he think worked on that young man's body yesterday?" she muttered as she leaned against the hall wall.

An outside door opened, and Pastor Solberg entered. "How is he?"

"How do you always know when to come?"

He shrugged. "I guess God tells me. But we all know these next hours are when life ebbs the lowest. Your mother and I have spent many of these dark hours of the morning praying and pleading for

God to heal, to bring the patients through this time." He paused. "Why are you in the hall?"

"His father wouldn't allow me to change the sheets, said it was not proper."

John Solberg stared at his feet, trying to hide his grin. "I have a feeling you will hear this often in the years ahead. Lovely young women—especially unmarried ones—are not easily perceived as doctors."

She rolled her eyes. "Thank you for the compliment, but he is going to have to get used to my being here. Vernon, er Mr. Baxter, is running a fever."

"That was to be expected, considering what he's been through. So now we do all we can and trust God to do the rest."

"I'll go bring a tub of water here to make it easier."

"Let me do that. You go check on your patient."

Astrid nodded and knocked on the door.

"Come in."

Mr. Baxter finished laying a wet towel across his son's forehead.

Astrid glanced up to see that the window was closed again. Surely this man knew better than to keep a sickroom closed up? But then, why should he? So many people still believed that fresh air brought in the vapors, that frequent bathing weakened the body. After all the old wives' tales she had read in her medical studying, she was grateful that new studies had proven so many of them wrong.

She crossed to open the window. "Please, the fresh air will help us cool him. And if he gets cold, which would be a blessing right now, we will close it and add covers."

The man sighed and nodded. "I s'pose you know best."

"Thank you." Astrid laid the back of her hand against the young man's cheek. Cooler but still hot. She felt the sheet, and wherever it touched his body, it was already dry. She fetched another sheet from the linen closet in the hall and dunked it in the tub, leaving it dripping to put over the other sheet. If they changed only the top one, propriety would be maintained.

———

DAWN WAS PINKING the sky when Mr. Baxter said he needed to leave to do chores at home.

"That is all right. There are enough of us to care for him. Do you have a telephone in case we need to call you?"

"No. But I will come back."

"Get some sleep first."

He shrugged, squeezed his son's shoulder, and headed out the door, fighting to keep Astrid from seeing his tears.

Pastor Solberg brought in a wet sheet. "Any improvement?"

"No. But I don't think he is any worse." Mutterings from the patient drew her back to his side. "He's been delirious off and on."

Mrs. Baxter entered, tying the ends of her head scarf at the base of her neck as she came. "My husband?"

"Left to do chores just a few minutes ago," Astrid said, speaking slowly and clearly.

"Ah, chores." She nodded her understanding.

"We are keeping your son wrapped in cold sheets to keep his fever down." Astrid pointed at the sheets.

"Looks like we are through the worst here, so I will be on my way. Can I bring you anything?" Pastor Solberg stopped at the doorway.

"Thank you, Pastor."

"Call me if you need me."

"I will."

A bit later Thelma brought in a breakfast tray for Mrs. Baxter. "I have yours ready in the dining room," she told Astrid. "Doctor and the mister are eating now."

Astrid nodded. "I just changed the sheets again, and Mrs. Baxter helped me, so now she knows what to do." She turned to the woman. "You eat now and drink your coffee. I will come back later." Astrid raised the bell on the small table by the bed. "Ring this if you need anything." Another nod.

Astrid followed Thelma out the door. She'd made it to the dining room when a wave of exhaustion nearly slammed her against the wall. Sinking into a chair at the table, she laid her head on her crossed arms.

"Are you all right?" Elizabeth asked.

"I will be. I didn't know we had waves like that in North Dakota."

"Eat what you can and then head for bed. Doctors have to be careful not to wear out too." Elizabeth heaved a sigh. "And thank you for letting me sleep."

"She needed that," Thorliff said, patting his wife's hand.

Astrid thanked Thelma for the cup of steaming coffee and propped her elbows on the table so she could hold it. Proper or not, sometimes elbows helped keep one going. "What else can we do for him?"

"Nothing that I know of. Try to get some nourishment into him, keep the pain as low as we can, pray he is strong enough to fight the infection." Elizabeth jotted a note down on the pad she kept beside her. "I'm going to consult with Dr. Morganstein and ask if there is anything else we can do."

"Good." Astrid stared at the scrambled eggs and toast on her plate. After swallowing three bites she laid down her fork.

"Go to bed before you fall sleep in your chair. Can you make it up the stairs?"

"I'll help her." Thorliff stood and came around the table. "Come on, little sister. Bedtime for you."

Astrid stumbled up the stairs, held upright by his strong arm. She fell across the bed, asleep before her head hit the pillow.

———

LATE AFTERNOON SUN slanted across the floor when she woke, her body demanding relief. After using the necessary, grateful anew for the indoor plumbing, she washed her face, combed her hair, and bundled it into a snood. A glance in the mirror reminded her that her apron was dirty, so she threw it into the laundry chute and made her way downstairs. In the kitchen Thelma handed her a cup of coffee.

"I was about to come check on you."

"Sorry, you should have woken me up."

"You'll be needed again tonight. His father is with him now."

"How is Vernon?"

"Young Baxter is weaker. They keep changing the sheets. I took them ice chips, and we wrapped some in a towel and put it at the back of his neck."

"Maybe we should put him in a tub of cool water."

"Maybe there is nothing more you can do—but wait. And pray."

Astrid stared at the housekeeper, sometimes nurse. "Are you giving up?"

"Up to you and the doctor."

Astrid squeezed her eyes shut. *I hate giving up.*

————

VERNON SLIPPED AWAY with the morning star two days later. His mother and father washed the body, loaded it in a wagon, and took their boy home to be buried next to their church.

Astrid struggled against the tears, fighting to contain the anger that waged war within her.

"We did all we could," Elizabeth said softly, tears puddling her words.

"It's not right. I trusted that God would add His healing to what we did. Mor prayed—we all prayed—and he looked to be getting better, and then he died. Was God not listening? Mor, Far, Pastor Solberg—they all say God is love and He cares for all of us. So why did He let Vernon die? His parents prayed. I don't understand." She stomped out a counterbeat. "If there was no hope . . ."

"Why did we try?" Elizabeth said as she studied her protégée.

"What could we have done differently?" Astrid spun around as if the words had finally penetrated her diatribe. "Yes! Why did we try? Why did we stitch the intestines back together? Fight through all that blood?"

"Because as doctors we have to try."

"No, not all doctors do. I've read about cases from the Civil War. Some of the wounded they left by the railroad tracks. They tried to save the ones they thought they might have a chance with. Belly wounds were always the worst." Astrid stared out the window, tears now streaming down her face.

"Maybe we should have just shot him and saved ourselves all the agony," Pastor Solberg said from his chair in the corner.

Astrid spun around, her jaw nearly on her chest. She tried to sputter an answer but could make no sense of it. "Why? Just answer one simple word: *Why?*"

"There is no answer. At least none that I've found."

Astrid stomped across the room, slamming the palms of her hands on the window frame. She clenched the wood, her nails digging into the paint. Words erupted, inner fire burning her mouth. "Not fair! It makes no sense. A good son like that! I hate this." She pounded the wall in time with her words.

"Ah Astrid, all I know is that God knows best. I have to trust Him because I know no other way to live. He is my God. Jesus is my salvation. He is and was the same for that young man who now resides with Him. Would you wish him back here?" He waved a hand around the sickroom, the pile of sheets, the smell of death. "In spite of anything and everything, I choose to trust, and that is the only way I can get through all this mess called life."

Astrid stared at the man she'd respected all her life. "Is there nothing else?"

"Not as far as I can see."

"Well, I think this is more rotten than the wounds." She spun around and stormed out the door. What ever made her think she wanted to be a doctor?

4

July 1903

L et's go get some ice cream." Sophie Knutson Bjorklund Wiste
laid a firm hand on her cousin's arm.

"Where are all your children?" Astrid glanced around looking for
the twins, who were just learning to walk, and Garth's son and daughter. For someone who hadn't thought much of motherhood, Sophie
had her hands full with the boardinghouse and four children.

"Deborah is taking care of them, and I'm taking care of you.
You've not even answered my telephone call." She pulled Astrid toward
the door of the surgery. "You might want to take off your apron."

Astrid looked over to Elizabeth, who was smiling. "You go. As you
can see, we have no one here in the waiting room at this moment, and
I have no appointments written down." She raised a hand as Astrid
started to object. "And you do not need to study right now. Go!" She

pointed toward the door, dramatically flinging her arm out. "And enjoy a break."

"Well, you don't have to get all official on me. I'm going. I'm going. You know Sophie never gives up. She'll nag me until—"

"Until you come along like a good girl." Sophie, who had bossed both her twin sister and her cousin since they were tiny, held the door open.

"You're letting in the flies." Actually Astrid was grateful for an escape. These last few days it had been difficult to concentrate, let alone pretend she still wanted to continue her studies. But she knew even if she decided against going to study under Dr. Morganstein, she could still use the experience Elizabeth gave her. Besides Mor always insisted that they not make drastic plans when upset, and so far, since Vernon's death, she hadn't calmed enough to think clearly.

"Then hurry."

"What's the rush?"

"There's someone I want you to see."

"Who? Sophie, what is the matter with you?" Astrid clutched the top of her head. "I don't have a hat on. I can't meet anyone." She dug in her heels so that Sophie had to stop or let go. "Is this someone male or female?"

"I'm not telling."

"You have a hat on. You are all dressed up. I am wearing my work clothes and no hat!"

"You look just fine." Sophie grabbed her hand again. "Come on!"

Letting Sophie have her way was a lesson Astrid had learned when they were little girls and inseparable, always traipsing across the small pasture separating their two houses. Why try to change years-long patterns? She let Sophie pull her along, no longer resisting but not making it easy either. As they neared Rebecca's soda shop, she heard laughter, a man's laugh but not one she recognized. The female laughing was Rebecca. She grabbed a post to the overhanging porch roof and jerked Sophie to a stop.

"Who is it?"

"You'll see."

"No I won't, because I am not going one step farther until you tell me." Astrid had her own brand of stubbornness, and she knew Sophie recognized it.

Sophie, her sky-blue dimity dress swirling about her ankles, glared at her. "The ice cream is my treat. Come on."

"Sophie!"

"This is someone you almost met several years ago, and now he has come back to town. I think you should welcome him back. That's only polite, you know."

"Sophie, I will get you for this. Just you wait." Astrid tried to turn and head back the direction she came from, but Sophie caught her arm.

"Please, just say hello and—"

"Well, hello!" The deep timbre in his voice, his wide smile, and flashing dark eyes caught her attention like none other.

"Astrid Bjorklund, I want you to meet Joshua Landsverk. Several years ago, he sold his cows to your mother and his land to your father, and went back to Iowa. Now he's returned to Blessing."

"I . . . I'm glad to meet you." So tall she had to look up, he had an ice cream soda in one hand and wore a smile that wrapped itself around her heart and gave a tug. Had she dreamed of this man, or why did he look familiar?

"Me too. I saw you the day I met with your mother. You rode off to get your pa. You were wearing a blue calico dress with a white apron with knee prints from where you'd been kneeling in the garden."

"Ah, hello. Welcome back to Blessing." *How do you remember all that? Are you visiting, passing through, come back to stay?* The thoughts darted through her mind like an evening flycatcher diving for insects. *Where have you been? Why are you here? What is the matter with me that my heart is racing?*

"Do you like strawberry?"

She blinked at the question. "What?"

"Strawberry sodas?" He handed her the one in his hand. "Or I could get you another flavor. I haven't touched this one. I mean . . ." He glanced at Sophie. "Am I being too forward?"

"Not at all, Mr. Landsverk. We love strawberry sodas around here." She nudged Astrid with a discreet elbow. "Miss Bjorklund, or rather *Dr.* Bjorklund, needed a break."

Astrid's heart tried to skip out her chest, but she sucked in a deep breath along with an order to settle down. "No, I mean, ah . . . yes. I do like strawberry sodas."

"Mrs. Valders said they are fresh strawberries."

"Mrs. Valders?" Astrid caught her gaffe. She still had a hard time thinking of Rebecca as Mrs. Valders. That title belonged to her mother-in-law, the woman who for years had tried to rule the town. "Yes, they would be fresh. Rebecca always uses the best of everything in her shop." Talk about inane. When would her usually quick mind kick into motion? She glanced down at the soda in her hand. She tried to hand it back to him, but he shook his head and took a step backward.

Sophie broke the lengthening silence. "Good seeing you again, Mr. Landsverk. I need to get back to the boardinghouse. Let me know if you need anything. We try to take good care of our newcomers here in Blessing."

"Of course, Mrs. Wiste." He touched the brim of his hat, but his gaze never unlocked with Astrid's.

Astrid sucked on the straw in the soda glass. Strawberry flavor exploded on her tongue. She could feel a smile stretching her cheeks. "This is really good."

"Let's go get me one, and then we can sit here and catch up on the last few years." He held out his bent arm, and she put her hand through the crook as if she'd been doing so all her life.

Good thing the other Mrs. Valders wasn't here or she'd have spread the news that Astrid was talking so familiarly with a strange man at the soda shop. She thought of backing away, but her hand felt comfortable against his arm. Together they entered the shop, dim inside after the bright sun.

"Astrid, hello. How do you like the new soda?" Rebecca, formerly Baard until she married Gerald Valders a couple weeks earlier, grinned at her friend from behind the counter.

Astrid glanced at the glass forgotten in her hand. She drank from the straw. "It's very good. I take it you've met Mr. Landsverk?"

"I have." She nodded up at their guest. "Would you like a strawberry soda for yourself? Or some other flavor?"

"Strawberry will be fine."

Astrid swallowed and let out a breath she'd held so long it was crushing her lungs. She could listen to that voice all day and not get tired of it. Deep baritone, not a bass, with a bit of Iowa twang or accent. Norwegian? Possibly, but not like others she knew.

"So, what brings you back to Blessing?" Rebecca asked as she filled the glass with fizzy soda water.

"Some unfinished business." He nodded at Astrid. Accepting his glass, he paid Rebecca and turned to leave. "I'm sure you'll see us often."

Us? Who did he mean by *us*? Had he brought a wife and family along? That wouldn't be surprising. What was surprising was the lump in her throat at the thought of his being married. *Now stop this, Astrid Bjorklund. You've not seen this man in three years, and then only from a distance. Would you begrudge him happiness? What kind of a woman are you?*

He set his soda on the white-painted table and pulled one of the two wire-backed chairs out for her to sit down. The touch of his hand on her back sent shivers clear to the soles of her feet and up to the highest hair on her head.

She hid behind her soda glass, forcing small sips past the lump. *I have to know.* "So, are you bringing your family out to show them where you used to live?"

He stared at her with a line between his eyebrows. "My family? My folks have no desire to come out here and aren't really pleased that I left. Pa was hoping I would stay there and keep working on the homeplace." A silence stretched.

So why didn't you? Look at him, silly, what is the matter with you? The voice sounded amazingly like Maydell telling Rebecca how to get a man interested in her.

"I guess I just wasn't cut out to be a farmer. I'm hoping to find another kind of work here."

She could feel his gaze touching her hair, her chin, her hands. When she glanced up from under her lashes, she was right. He was looking straight at her—not smiling but with a look that could only be titled tender. Astrid swallowed. And closed her eyes. When she looked again, he was leaning back in the chair, sipping his soda and still smiling. She must have been mistaken.

"When did you get here?" Surely that was a safe question.

"On the morning train. I took a room at the boardinghouse. That's when I talked with Mrs. Wiste. Does she really have four children? I mean, when I left you were all young girls still in school, and now she is married with four children."

"Sophie had twins, and her new husband already had two children." She didn't give him the long story of Sophie running away with Hamre and being widowed. That wasn't hers to tell.

"And the boardinghouse?"

"When my grandmother and her husband died, they deeded the boardinghouse to Sophie." Her straw gurgled on the bottom of the glass.

"Would you like another?"

"No thank you. I . . . I should get back to the surgery in case I am needed."

"Sophie, er, Mrs. Wiste said you are in training to be a doctor?"

Or was. The thought brought back all the sorrow of the last few days.

"What is it? All of a sudden you went sad." He leaned forward and raised his hand as if he were going to touch her cheek.

Tell him. Don't tell him. The inner argument picked up again. "I . . . something happened in surgery a few days ago. It made me wonder . . ." She paused and looked up to see sympathy in his eyes.

"Blessing is fortunate to have doctors here in town. So much has changed since I left. The flour mill, new houses, the new building for the bank, telephones. I was surprised when I went into the mercantile and Mrs. Bjorklund remembered me."

You would be hard to forget. Astrid found herself struggling to breathe normally. "I remember she was so pleased that you came in and paid your bill before leaving town. Some others hadn't, I guess. She and her kids just came back to town a few weeks ago, and then her husband, Hjelmer, joined them a week later. There are lots of stories about what has gone on in Blessing."

"All good, I hope."

"Not necessarily." Astrid pushed back her chair. "I need to get back." *No you don't,* her heart chastised. She picked up her glass and stood. "Thank you for the soda."

"I'll take those to the counter and walk you back."

"We are having a barn dance on Saturday if you'd like to come," she said when he returned and they started walking.

"Sophie already invited me. She saw my guitar and mentioned that I might like to play. I hear you have a great piano player now."

"Yes, Jonathan Gould. He's here for the summer. He's attending agricultural college in Fargo this fall. He and my cousin Grace are good friends."

"Mrs. Wiste's twin sister?"

"Yes. Grace is back East teaching at a school for the deaf."

He stopped walking for a moment. "It must have taken a great deal of courage for her to leave Blessing."

"Yes. We were all surprised she went, even Grace herself." As they walked along the road, she pointed out the houses and who lived in each one. "See, more changes in Blessing." When her arm brushed his, she caught her breath. Did he feel that too? Like when one walked on the rugs in the winter and got sparked by touching another person? Only this time it felt good. No, *exciting* was a better word. Every time she looked up, he was looking at her.

When she mounted the stairs to the surgery, he touched the broad brim of his low-crowned hat. "I'll see you tomorrow night, then?"

"Yes."

"Good." His smile made her feel warm all over.

She opened the screen door and went inside before she turned to watch him go whistling down the walk. Jaunty. Confident.

"Now, that is one handsome man." Elizabeth joined her at the door. "You leave with Sophie and come back with a man. Not a bad exchange."

"Elizabeth Bjorklund, the things you say sometimes." Right then Astrid wished for a fan. She could feel her face and neck flaming. "His name is Joshua Landsverk. He used to live here."

54

"I see." Elizabeth removed her apron and tossed it in the laundry. "Thorliff brought the mail. We have a letter from Dr. Morganstein. You want to read it?"

"No." Astrid felt the anger rising in her again.

"No?" Elizabeth turned to her with a worried expression.

"You read it to me. Out on the back porch. It's a bit stifling in here."

As they passed through the kitchen, Elizabeth asked Thelma to bring cool drinks out to the porch, where they took both of the rocking chairs, a round wicker table between them. Elizabeth drew the letter from her pocket.

"Did you hear Grace is coming home?" Elizabeth asked.

"Of course. I was surprised she didn't come with Jonathan, but he said she had some things she had to finish up at the deaf school first."

"Oh. Well, so much for surprises." Elizabeth looked up from the envelope when Thelma set a tray on the table. "Thank you. Would you like to join us?"

"No, I'm right in the middle of baking for the dance tomorrow night. You want we should take two chocolate cakes, or one dark and one light?"

"Two chocolate. You make the best chocolate cake." Astrid reached for her glass. "And please put the fudge frosting on one."

"I will do that. Anything else?"

"Mor says we are frying chickens tomorrow," Astrid added. "You want to come help?"

"No, thank you. I draw the line at butchering chickens. Too much blood."

Elizabeth stared at her retreating housekeeper and then at Astrid, and the two of them fought to hide their giggles. Thelma was not one to be funny. With all the blood Thelma cleaned up out of the surgical rooms . . . They laughed again, well aware of each other's thoughts.

"I'll practice my surgical skills on eviscerating and cutting up chickens."

"Are you all right after our last surgery?"

Astrid paused. *Should she tell her?* Instead of answering she just shrugged.

Elizabeth drew the paper out of the envelope.

"My dear Elizabeth,

"What a blessing it was to receive your letter. I so look forward to working with Astrid, or shall I say Dr. Bjorklund? I have a feeling that her coming here is not strictly necessary, but I am sure there are things we can teach her. I understand your concern that she be allowed to study a cadaver. I well remember the hours you spent in the dissecting room. I want you to know that we have improved the ventilation since you went to school here.

"Our next rotation begins the first week of September, but I recommend she comes in August to have the time needed in the anatomy hall—the sooner the better. Also, we will need several days for her to take all the written exams so that I can see where her strengths and weaknesses lie.

"Mrs. Issy Josephson, who has aged considerably since you saw her, inquired about you and your practice the other day. We still meet weekly for tea, along with several of our other benefactors. I do wish you could come along and meet with all of them. As you know, the more they believe in you and see firsthand your successes, the more they will donate to the hospital. Attending events like this are very important for long-range planning.

"Again, I so look forward to meeting your protégée. Let me know when we can expect her.

"Sincerely and with great joy,

"Dr. Althea Morganstein"

Elizabeth laid the letter on the table, set her glass on it to weight it down, and looked across the table at Astrid. "Why are you shaking your head?"

Do I tell her? "Do we have to make a decision right now?"

"No, but soon. You aren't having second thoughts, are you?"

"You said it wasn't absolutely necessary that I go to Chicago."

"And it isn't. I just believe that is the best plan. Especially after all the work you have done here. You are gifted, Astrid, and this will improve your skills."

So more patients can die? Astrid pushed the thought away as she slid back her chair. "I need to go home, get back to the farm to help Mor." She stood up and walked down the stairs. Looking back over her shoulder, she added, "We can talk later. You and Thorliff are coming to the dance, aren't you?"

Elizabeth hesitated as if she wanted to say something more but then grinned. "Wouldn't miss it. Besides, we have to bring all the chocolate cake you asked Thelma to make. You want to take the buggy home?"

"No. I'll walk. It is cooling off some." Astrid opened the gate of the picket fence, waved once more, and strode down the street that would connect with Bjorklund Road, as everyone now called the road leading out to the Bjorklund and Knutson farms. Cutting across the fields would be faster, but she didn't want to fight the barbed wire that fenced off the pasture.

Walking gave her plenty of time to think. Picking up a stick, she slashed at the weeds along the graded road. Maybe thinking wasn't such a good idea after all. Taking a whack at a thistle, she chose to ignore the dilemma of getting more formal medical training in Chicago and instead let herself think about the man with the sodas. Dreaming about Joshua Landsverk was far more fun. For a while she'd been sure again that going to Chicago was the best thing for her. And then Vernon Baxter died. Would more training on her part have kept that from happening? Or did God just decide not to help out?

5

Ingeborg stopped in surprise. "I thought you were still sleeping."
Astrid looked up from her perch on the wide board that topped
the low wall of the back porch. "Thought I'd watch the sunrise." She
shook her head slowly. "No, I just couldn't sleep." Her thick night braid
of wheat gold hair hung over her shoulder. While she had dressed in a
loose summer shift, she'd added a faded to near white apron over it.

"I'll have the coffee ready by the time the sun breaks the
horizon."

"I started the stove."

"Oh, I thought it was Haakan."

"No, I was adding wood to the first flames when he headed for
the barn, Jonathan right behind him." Astrid leaned her head against
the porch post. "Can you sit here with me a moment? Look at those
colors." She pointed toward the eastern horizon.

Ingeborg joined her daughter but remained standing. She stroked Astrid's hair. "Even those few clouds make the sunrise more beautiful, just like they do the sunset." She inhaled the sweetness of the honeysuckle vine that was sending pea green tendrils up the strings to the hooks so as to provide shade for those retreating to the porch in the heat of the summer. The summer room, Ingeborg preferred to call it, since they shelled peas, snapped beans, hulled strawberries, hand-sewed garments, and shared lemonade or coffee there. The rocking chairs and the steps were favorite places to work and catch any breeze that deigned to pass through.

The yellow climbing rose that matched the one by the front porch was already covered with buds, the bees hovering, seeking the first sip of nectar.

"Would you like to talk about whatever is keeping you awake?"

Astrid tipped her head back to look into her mother's face. "What if I don't want to do surgery? Ever again?"

"Not go to Chicago?" Ingeborg studied her daughter; the decision to go had been so difficult for her.

Astrid nodded. "Why go? After all we did, Vernon died anyway."

"And that woman who you fought so hard for, she died too. And yet you say you love helping babies into this world."

Crossing her arms over her bent knees, Astrid rested her chin on them. "I didn't think of that."

"As you've heard both Elizabeth and me say, we do our best and leave the rest in God's hands."

"But God didn't save Vernon."

"No, He took Vernon home." Ingeborg gently pressed her daughter's cheek into her side. "Life and death are His provenance, not ours."

"Then why do we try to save lives?"

"Ah, my dear, the questions you ask. There are no easy answers." Ingeborg stared at the gold rim just breaking the horizon. A rooster crowed, a cow bellowed, as if both of them thought that waking the sun was their personal assignment. Birds twittered in the cottonwood tree, whose arms now shaded the house.

"God's Word says that we are all given different gifts, all of them for blessing the body of Christ. By helping someone feel better, I feel as if I am walking in His shoes. Jesus went around healing the sick, restoring sight to the blind, and making the lame walk again. He showed His love through those events."

Astrid waited while a tear meandered down her cheek.

Ingeborg realized she had never spoken like this with Astrid before. "He calls us to be like Him. The greatest gift of all is love. Even though sometimes it is not easy. And He calls us to be close to Him. I feel the closest when I help that baby take its first breath, and when I close the eyes of someone who has passed on to glory. Life and death—all part of who we are—along with everything in between. I believe He calls you to use those same gifts, and now it is your job to learn to use them to the best of your ability."

"You want me to go to Chicago?"

"If that is where He wants you to go."

"But what about inside of you? Do you really think and feel I should go?" Astrid turned her head to stare up at her mother.

"Ah, Astrid, no mother wants to send her daughters or her sons off to some distant place, but if God calls you to do that, His calling is far more important than my feelings." She paused and allowed herself to imagine life there without Astrid. A tear matched that of her daughter. She inhaled the morning freshness and let it out on a sigh. "I want you to come back with all your new knowledge and be here to help Elizabeth. I want us to build a hospital that will make life better for many others around here." She paused and smiled. "Guess I have all kinds of wants."

"I hate to leave all of this." Astrid swept her arm out to include the houses, the farms, her town, her people.

Ingeborg stroked her cheek.

"Do I have to go?"

"No. You need to seek His face so He can guide you."

"I'm not very happy with Him right now." Astrid wrapped her arms around her middle, as if holding a pillow.

"I know. I've been there too, and the sooner I let go of what was making me angry, the sooner I felt safe and loved again." She kissed the top of Astrid's head. "It is a fact that God is happy with you. He rejoices over you with singing."

"How do you know that?"

"Because He said so." She kissed her again. "I'll bring the coffee out."

"I'll come help." Astrid stood and hugged her mother close, then arm in arm they entered the kitchen.

As Ingeborg poured the water into the coffeepot, she let her prayers rise with the steam. *Father, only you can tell my daughter what you want her to do. Please make it clear and heal her hurts. And mine if she leaves.* This was one of those times when she was sure she heard Him chuckle.

"All will be well" floated like a happy breeze around the kitchen.

Instead of taking their coffee back out to the porch, Ingeborg stirred eggs and flour into the sourdough batter she'd started for pancakes the night before. Astrid brought the ham from the wooden icebox that now resided in the kitchen corner and began slicing off pieces to fry for the men. That done and the ham beginning to sizzle, she moved the frying pan toward the back of the stove.

"I'll go feed the chickens and see if there are any eggs yet."

"Watch out for the speckled hen. She's setting and is meaner than a wounded badger. Like to tore my finger off the other day."

"She's getting old. I thought she'd probably go in the stew pot this winter." Astrid picked up the lard bucket of vegetable scraps they kept for the chickens. "Need anything from the well house?"

"Bring in that jug that has a red stripe. Your far will love having sour cream on his pancakes."

"Any chokecherry syrup?"

"Down in the cellar."

Ingeborg paused to watch her daughter swoop the cat up in her arms, hug and pet her, then set her down, grab the scraps can again, and head on out the door whistling. Ah, the resilience of youth, stumbling over a decision one minute, then whistling the next. "Astrid, you have no idea how much I will miss you. You make my heart sing." Her whisper joined the others heading for heaven and a heart that always hears.

By the time the men came up from milking, breakfast was ready to be put on the table, including a bouquet of sweet peas Astrid had picked from the garden. She set the flowers between the cut-glass creamer and the sugar bowl, which either sat in the middle of the table or on the windowsill for the sun to sparkle it.

Now that summer had arrived, the men washed outside at the bench set up with basins of water and soap; towels hung from hooks along the side of the house.

"Betsy stuck her foot in Haakan's bucket," Samuel crowed on entering the kitchen.

Ingeborg glanced at her husband, who both nodded and shook his head. "You can't let your mind wander with that one." He rubbed the youngest Knutson's head as he passed by. "From now on, you get to milk her."

The sixteen-year-old shrugged, his blue eyes dancing. "No matter. She likes me. I bring her corn from the garden." They'd been thinning corn the day before.

"Leave it to you." Lars nudged his son with his elbow. "Always charming the ladies, be they two-footed or four."

"He'll get lots of practice tonight at the dance." Haakan smiled at Trygve, the older Knutson son. "Just like you."

Trygve ducked his head, a telltale blush brightening his cheeks.

Ingeborg glanced over to see Jonathan watching the byplay. He'd told her once that the teasing that went on at the farm never happened in the home he grew up in. She often felt sorry for him, for in spite of his family's wealth, they didn't seem very close to one another. He grinned now, obviously enjoying himself.

Samuel crowed and Andrew laughed along with the other men as they all sat down at the table for Haakan to say the blessing. At the amen, the pancakes, ham, fried eggs, and applesauce disappeared as if carried away by a tornado. Ingeborg brought another platter she'd kept warming in the oven and handed it to Jonathan, her hand resting on his shoulder as she did the others.

His smile always warmed her heart. Though reared in New York City, the second son of a wealthy family, he fit in here as if he'd been part of Blessing all his life. "When is Grace coming home?" she asked.

"This afternoon. She sent a telephone message last night. She was able to catch an earlier train." The glow that lit his eyes told of his delight. While he and Grace were not formally engaged, everyone knew it was only a matter of time, since he'd already spoken to Lars about marrying his daughter.

"Good for her. What a nice surprise."

"I know. She said not to tell anyone, but since no one here would blab—" He stared at Samuel, who was known to not keep a secret very long.

"Who would I tell?" Samuel raised his hands in the air, trying to look innocent.

"Oh, Sophie, or Dr. Elizabeth, or—"

"They're not everybody. They're family."

"I rest my case."

Chuckles danced around the table. Teasing Samuel was always good for a laugh, until he managed to turn the tables and get even.

Astrid thumped her younger cousin on top of his head as she set another platter of meat on the table. "Just save a dance tonight for me, Romeo."

He grinned up at her. "I heard that new guy will be on the guitar tonight. Sophie said he likes you."

Astrid thumped him again. "How you have time to pick up all the gossip, I'll never know."

Ingeborg watched the cousins tease each other and noticed the slight blush on her daughter's cheeks. The dance tonight in Andrew's barn might indeed be interesting.

———

THAT EVENING AFTER the chores and supper were finished, Astrid and Grace sat out on the back porch, catching up on their news. They'd decided earlier to get dressed together, as they used to. Since the men had all gone to move the piano from the schoolhouse, the girls could sneak in some time together.

"Don't you miss Blessing terribly?" Astrid asked, holding a glass of ice water to her cheek.

Grace nodded and spoke carefully. Signing was far easier for her than speaking. "I do, but not so much with Jonathan in New York. Fall will be hard with him in Fargo."

"You could always come home early, you know."

"I know, but I agreed to another year, and I do love teaching there. The house and grounds are so lovely, with big old trees and formal flower beds."

"Well, we could do the flower beds, but somehow the trees won't grow fast enough to become big and old."

Grace smiled. "So you are going to Chicago?"

Astrid took a sip of water so she didn't have to answer right away. "I was so sure finally, and then after our patient died, I . . . I just don't know. Mor says God will lead me, but He doesn't seem to be very clear on this."

"Maybe you need to just keep moving forward and let Him open or close doors as He sees fit." Grace used her hands to sign at the same time, as if her feelings couldn't be said fast or firm enough with only her mouth. "He sure did for me."

Astrid set her chair to rocking, nodding with it. "I haven't said no, so perhaps I should just go ahead. I won't die of homesickness. After all, it is only six months."

"When would you leave?"

"Mid-August."

"We'd be leaving about the same time, then." She picked up her glass for another drink. "Let's go change, and I'll fix your hair if you do mine."

"Maybe we can braid ribbons in. I have new ones up in my room." The two made their way upstairs, where they had hung their dresses after pressing them.

"You better hurry," Ingeborg called up after them. "I told Andrew we'd come and finish setting up the tables."

"We will." They slipped out of their calico dresses, and after hanging them on hooks along the wall, Grace sat down on the bench in front of the dressing table and shook her hair loose from the snood she'd bundled it in for the trip.

Astrid picked up the brush and began brushing, her fingers working any tangles out as she brushed.

"Oh, that feels so good. I don't think anyone has brushed my hair since you did it last."

"You don't get together with the other teachers like we used to at our girl parties?"

"No. I'm the youngest on staff, and some of the others are married. My closest friend is Olivia, and she wears her hair short."

"Like I saw in the magazine?"

"Yes. She says it is much easier to care for."

"Well, she misses out on brushing, then." Laying down the brush, Astrid divided the hair, picked up a blue ribbon, and began braiding it in with the hair. When finished with the braids, she wrapped them in a figure eight at the back of Grace's head and pinned them in place. She handed Grace a hand mirror. "What do you think?"

"Beautiful. You want yours the same?"

"Of course. Just like we used to. Remember when Sophie cut her hair in a fringe?"

Grace nodded. "Only Sophie. But now many women are wearing a fringe or wrapping their hair around a rattail and wearing it poofed up in front."

"I tried it, but I didn't like it."

When they descended the stairs, Astrid in blue dimity with white daisies and Grace in yellow with darker ribbon trim, they found Ingeborg packing the last of the food in the boxes and baskets, ready to load the wagon.

"You two look like flowers right out of the garden," she said, handing Astrid a basket. "Put this right behind the seat."

SOMETIME LATER, INGEBORG surveyed the barn to make sure everything was just right. Fried chicken filled the white-dotted, blue-enameled roasting pan sitting in the middle of the table. So many platters, bowls, and plates covered the table that the white sheet could only be seen down the sides. Desserts covered another table. Both tables were made of long boards held up by sawhorses. Chunks of ice floated in a tub of red punch, along with fresh strawberry and lemon slices.

"It looks great," Kaaren Knutson said, stopping beside her dear friend and sister-in-law. They both watched the musicians tuning up at the piano, which had been hauled over from the schoolhouse and drawn by pulleys up the ramp to the haymow through the big front door. "I feared they'd drop that piano for sure."

"If you want something done right, ask those men of ours. They'll do it every time."

Lars had his fiddle out of the case and was tightening the strings. Haakan was putting the gut bucket together: an old washtub turned upside down with a rope running from a hole in the washtub up to the end of a rake handle. Plucking the rope and moving the rake handle gave the different tones.

Since Joseph Baard died, they'd not had a guitar at the community events. Tonight Joshua Landsverk was already causing the young girls to twitter. Ingeborg's gaze roamed the laughing crowd. Where was Astrid?

Finally she located her helping Ellie with baby May. Grace had Carl in her arms and was watching Jonathan at the piano. Elizabeth usually played for the parties, but tonight she and Jonathan would trade off so both could have more fun. The smile he sent to Grace brought a lump to Ingeborg's throat. The two were so in love it lit up the entire haymow. And such an unlikely pair. He, though having a wealthy New York family, now wanted to farm, and she, who never wanted to leave Blessing, was now teaching at a prestigious school for the deaf in the East and loving it. Yet they planned to return to Blessing and expand the school for the deaf that Kaaren had started all those years ago into something larger and finer.

Thank you, Lord, for Mr. Gould, who took me under his wing all those years ago and has been our benefactor ever since. Father, you have put so many wonderful people in our lives. Her gaze roved those gathered here to celebrate. All ages were here, from the babies like Dorothy's newest to those going gray, like Haakan and Mr. Valders. Family and friends as close as family, and of course some of whom she was not quite so fond. Although she had to admit Hildegunn had definitely been softening since her son's recent marriage.

She chuckled to herself, then turned as someone called her name. "Coming." She joined Astrid, who was smiling up at a young man who did indeed look familiar.

"Mor, you remember Joshua Landsverk," Astrid said. "He sold you some cows a few years ago."

She felt a click in her mind. "Of course. I knew you looked familiar. Welcome home to Blessing." Interesting that Astrid had not mentioned this visitor before, for that surely was a look of interest in his eyes when he smiled at her daughter.

"Thank you. It does indeed feel like home."

"You are planning on staying?"

He nodded. "I'm hoping there is work of some kind waiting here for me."

"He says he doesn't want to go back to farming," Astrid said with a slight wrinkling of her nose, as if anyone could think there might be something better than farming.

"Well, there is plenty of other work around here. You might want to talk with Hjelmer when he and Penny get here. Between Hjelmer and Thorliff, there is always something going on."

"Did I hear someone mention my name?" Thorliff stopped beside his mother and looked at the newcomer. "Don't I know you?"

"Ja, I am Joshua Landsverk. I once owned land south of town."

"Of course." Thorliff eyed the guitar strung over Joshua's shoulder. "I take it you are going to join our musicians?" He clapped Joshua on the shoulder. "Good for you. Make a place here for yourself right quick."

"He's looking for a job," Ingeborg said with a smile at the dark-eyed man.

"Good. Let's talk after church tomorrow. Right now I have to make sure Inga doesn't lead some of those other young ones on a merry chase." He glanced at his mother. "Invite him for dinner tomorrow?"

"To be sure. Please come." Interesting how Astrid was trying to act so uninterested in the man beside her. Ingeborg thought back to whether Astrid had ever met Mr. Landsverk. Unlikely, since she'd only seen him that once before he left for Iowa. Life was never boring. That was for sure.

"Thank you for the invitation. I'd be delighted to come."

Ingeborg had to stop herself from rolling her eyes. He might be talking to her, but his eyes were talking to her daughter.

6

What is the matter with me?

"He is handsome; that's for sure," Sophie said, stopping at Astrid's elbow.

"Who?" *Silly, you know who she is referring to. You haven't taken your eyes off him all evening.*

Sophie nudged her with an elbow. "You know who I am talking about. If he's not playing his guitar, he's dancing with you. I've heard several comments that he's not asked anyone else to dance."

"Oh." Astrid wished for a fan. Surely the sun was burning her skin in spite of it being after nine—and inside the barn. The setting sun was tinting the horizon from lemon to azure as the eye traveled upward. Maybe she'd gotten a touch of sunburn during the day.

"You can see that Grace and Jonathan are besotted. Love is just flying through the air." Sophie looked besotted herself. In love with *love* is what came to Astrid's mind, not that she knew much about love between a man and a woman, other than what she'd seen with her mor and far.

"How come Maydell is dancing with Toby?" Astrid asked her friend.

"She wants to make Gus jealous."

"From the look on his face, it's working. Someone better warn Toby."

"Oh, he knows what's going on. Toby's no fool."

"I wish he'd find someone." Remembering Sophie's comment, Astrid jerked her gaze away from Joshua, who was laughing at something someone had said.

"You mean Toby or the man you keep looking at?"

"I do not."

"Astrid, this is Sophie you are talking to." She turned to smile at the man who stopped beside her. "Yes, I'd love to dance with you."

Astrid smiled inside. Even Sophie's voice changed when Garth came up. Although they'd been married almost a year now, they still acted like newlyweds a good part of the time. Sophie was married; Grace was spoken for or engaged—even if not officially yet—Rebecca was married, though only a couple of weeks ago. Ellie and Andrew had been the first to marry, so that left only her and Deborah of their group. Oh, and Maydell, but she was a latecomer. Astrid frowned. Her feelings toward Maydell were still a little prickly after Carl's broken arm. And now she was trying to stir Gus up, not realizing Toby could get hurt. Or someone could get hurt. When was Maydell going to start acting like a grown woman?

And I'll soon be leaving. Or will I? The thoughts intruded again, as they had for the last days. *Will I or won't I go to Chicago?* At a tap on her shoulder, she turned to see her cousin Samuel grinning at her.

"You said you wanted to dance with me."

"That I did." She held out her hand. "Thank you for asking." They took their places in one of the squares, and Lars announced the dance, "Texas Star." The musicians swung into the tune, and Mr. Valders called, "Swing your partner do-si-do." One had to pay attention to the caller, even if you'd been dancing this one for years, or you might make more than yourself stumble. Astrid laughed at something Samuel said as he claimed her for a partner again after they'd moved in opposite ways around the circle. At sixteen, Samuel was no longer one of the children, but not really one of the adults yet either. But he was her favorite of the male cousins.

The dance ended with everyone laughing and puffing. A movement at the dessert table caught Astrid's attention. There was Inga taking cookies off a plate and handing one to Carl, who was getting a lot of attention with his broken arm strapped to his body. The two ran giggling over to the side and sat down against the wall to enjoy their booty. Astrid glanced around to see where the parents were. She saw Andrew and Ellie talking with Mr. and Mrs. Aspland, so newly arrived in Blessing from Minnesota. Since there were no babies around, someone must have taken them up to Andrew's house, where they would be laid out like cordwood on one of the beds with an adult watching over them. Oh yes, Tante Kaaren was missing. She loved being with the babies.

Astrid swayed slightly as the music slowed to a waltz.

"May I have this dance?"

Even his voice gave her the shivers. "Of course." She stepped into Joshua's arms and laid her hand on his shoulder. "You play so well." They moved together in the pattern, one hand warm at her waist, his other holding hers gently.

"Thank you. You suppose that will help me be welcome here?"

"Oh, I think you needn't worry. The people of Blessing always welcome those new to the area."

"You have to admit, I'm not exactly new."

"True, so then welcome home."

"You're the second person to say that."

"Really? Well, I guess that's part of Blessing."

"And the people who live here."

"Well, without the people, we wouldn't have much of a town."
Astrid Bjorklund, can't you think of something more brilliant to say?

"True." Joshua swung her in a circle so that her hand clutched his shoulder.

"What brought you back here?"

"It's a long story. Someday I'll tell you."

"Oh." *Who taught you to dance? This is heavenly.* "Do you have any brothers and sisters?"

"Yes. I have one sister, Avis, who is the oldest, and two brothers. I am in the middle of my two brothers. Avis was, or rather *is* not happy that I left. She wanted me to marry her best friend and settle on the farm next to that of my folks."

I'm glad you didn't. She barely caught the thought before it became words and made it out of her mouth. "I'm sure they miss you." There, that was far more proper.

"Perhaps."

She tilted her head back to look up at his face. Was that unhappiness she saw in his eyes? Possibly, with such an enigmatic comment. She watched as his face cleared and he smiled down at her.

"Will you be in church tomorrow?" he asked.

"Unless we have a medical emergency. It has happened more than once."

"I heard about the young man who died."

Astrid blinked. One more reminder. "Yes." Even to her ears her voice sounded curt. Who would have been filling him in on the news of Blessing? Most likely Sophie. What else had she told him? What a blabbermouth. Ignoring the argument that wanted to take over her mind, she nodded up at her partner, enjoyed one more turn, and as the music stopped, stepped out of his arms.

"Thank you." His voice sneaked in past the guard on her mind and made itself at home.

She nodded and turned at the sound of a male voice, raised in what surely sounded like anger.

"Toby Valders, you stay away from my girl." The frown on Gus's face matched the tone of his voice.

Toby stepped back, his hands raised. "We were just dancing. Since you weren't here, I . . ."

Astrid almost laughed at the glint in Toby's eyes. For certain he knew what he was doing, and Gus had fallen right into the trap. She nudged Grace, and the two grinned at each other with a slight nod.

"I . . . ah . . ." Maydell stamped her foot as her fists slammed into her waist. She glared back at him. "If I am your girl, and I'm not saying for sure I am right now, then you better act like I'm your girl and not go off with the fellows, smokin' and doin' whatever out behind the barn."

"I wasn't smoking. What's the matter with you?"

Astrid saw a couple of the men moving closer to the two of them.

Maydell narrowed her eyes and stared right at him. "How am I supposed to know I am your girl?"

"Well, because I told you so."

"That was weeks ago."

"That's telling him, Maydell," someone hollered from the sidelines.

Gus glared at her, but the glare had lost its impact.

"Show her who's the boss," someone else said.

"Then we better be getting married before you make a fool out of both of us." Gus grabbed her hand and started across the barn floor.

Maydell started to resist, but then as his words sunk in, a grin lit her face. "Why, Gus Baard, you finally got it right." She waved to a crowd that was beginning to laugh and clap.

Astrid groaned. Leave it to Maydell. She was getting her wish, although it was doubtful she'd ever live it down. At least from the look on Mrs. Valders' face. One might think of apoplexy when watching her. Astrid glanced around. Toby had managed to disappear, either as planned or for protection.

"Can you believe that?" Deborah asked as she joined Astrid and Grace.

"Did he really say what I thought he did?" Grace signed and spoke both, her voice seeming a bit rusty.

Astrid nodded and rolled her lips to keep from laughing. "Leave it to Maydell."

"How long before the wedding do you think?" Deborah signed too. All of them had learned to sign years earlier when Kaaren learned and taught the community. She turned to Grace. "How's school going?"

"I love teaching there. I never thought I would be happy away from Blessing, but I am." Her smile made the others smile back and follow her gaze as it located Jonathan talking with several of the men.

"He's working mighty hard here." Astrid leaned closer to Grace and signed like they used to when trading secrets without ever saying a word.

"Jonathan always works hard. He convinced his father to let him go to school in Fargo, and that was a big accomplishment." Her pride in him made Astrid grin.

"Has he learned to sign well enough?"

"To get by. You should sign with him this summer."

"I will. I hadn't thought of that. You know, with you gone we don't sign as much. One day when one of the deaf students came in, I was sure glad I knew how to do it. Dr. Elizabeth called for me immediately when she needed to tell him something to do."

"With all the new people coming into town, the school will need to offer classes to those who want to learn." Grace's speaking could not keep up with her signing. "If the deaf school grows like we are dreaming it will, there will be many more deaf people in the area. Mrs. Wooster, a benefactor from New York, says that families will move here to be by their loved ones. I know it happens that way where I am teaching."

Astrid watched Grace's hands fly and thought about what she was saying. What if there were surgeries that could help restore hearing? Would Dr. Morganstein know about that? Dr. Elizabeth had told her of places that were specializing in different therapies. Was there one for ears and hearing?

She felt him behind her before she heard his voice.

"May I walk you home?" While Joshua spoke low and close to Astrid's ear, the others stopped talking and grinned at her.

"Of course you may," Deborah answered for her with a wide smile. "Shame it is not farther."

Astrid could feel her face flaming. She glared at Deborah, which earned another burst of laughter from her friends. "I can speak for myself, you know."

"Well, go on, then. Answer him."

Even Grace was laughing. Having a choice between pouting and joining in the laughter, Astrid chose the latter. "Just wait. You'll be the brunt of all this one day, and we'll see how you feel."

"All right, what is going on over here?" Jonathan asked as he strolled up to those laughing.

"Walking home. That's what." Astrid grabbed Grace's hand. "You and Jonathan can come too."

"We can't go yet. We have to lower the piano down to the wagon and drive it back to church. We need all available young men. The old ones said it was our turn."

"The old ones?" Haakan echoed from right behind Jonathan, who flinched and rolled his eyes.

"I didn't mean that the way it sounded." Now it was his turn to be laughed at, and they all took him up on it.

"We 'old ones' will show you young ones how to move a piano. Come along, both of you."

The girls watched and cheered as the piano was lowered down the ramp to the wagon, where the young men climbed aboard and headed for the church. There they would unload it and get it ready for the next morning's service.

The unmarried girls waved good-bye and walked home together, laughing and teasing as they headed to the Knutsons' farm for the night.

"I think that was one of the most fun barn dances we've had," Deborah said later as they prepared for bed.

"Gus will have a hard time living down that scene."

"How long before they'll be married, do you think?" Grace signed.

"If Maydell has any sense, she'll tell us tomorrow that they're getting married next week." Grace and Astrid fell across the bed laughing.

"You think so?" Deborah sat cross-legged at the foot of the bed, brushing her hair.

"I do. Before he changes his mind." Astrid wiped a tear from Grace's cheek.

Giggling, the three tied ribbons around the ends of their night braids, blew out the lamp, and crawled under the sheet. A blanket lay folded across the bottom of the bed in case the night cooled down.

In the quiet Astrid signed to Grace's hand. "I'm so glad you're home. I really missed you."

Grace curled up close like they did when little girls, only now without Sophie wiggling.

"Me too," she signed back. "Long talk tomorrow."

Maybe Grace could help her understand how not to miss Blessing if she went to Chicago. *If* she went. The ifs murmured her to sleep.

Astrid woke to the sound of heavy footsteps on the stairs. Onkel Lars had stayed late. She rolled over on her side, careful not to push Grace off the edge. Walking home with Mr. Landsverk would have been interesting, but was she ready for more complications in her life?

————

JOSHUA WAS WAITING at the steps to the church when the Knutsons and their extra passengers drove up the next morning. The Bjorklunds arrived at about the same time. Joshua tipped his hat to Ingeborg in greeting and smiled at Astrid. "May I sit beside you in church?"

"Ah . . ." She glanced at her mother, who nodded. "I guess so." No man had ever asked to sit next to her like this. But when they shared a hymnbook and his full baritone harmonized with her alto, a thrill raced up and down her spine, then sparkled off her fingertips. Surely the entire congregation was singing better because of his voice.

When it was time for the sermon, Pastor Solberg stepped forward and gestured to a man who was sitting in the chair next to him behind the pulpit. "Today I would like to introduce a missionary friend of mine, the reverend Ted Schuman, who is serving in Kenya, Africa. He will bring us not only the message for the day but a report on his mission there."

Astrid had trouble concentrating on the beginning of the sermon with the warmth of Joshua's arm right next to hers. But the speaker caught her attention when he quoted Jesus' words from John's gospel: " 'Lift up your eyes, and look on the fields; for they are white already to harvest.' " He went on with a quote from Matthew: " 'The harvest truly is plenteous, but the labourers are few.' " After a pause where he looked around at all the faces in the congregation, he softened his voice. "The harvest is indeed ready, but the laborers are terribly few." He continued with stories of his life in Africa, of the native people who had come to faith in spite of their old beliefs, and the witch doctors who fought to destroy the light the white man preached.

He closed his sermon by saying, "If God is calling you to serve Him as a missionary in foreign lands, please hearken to His call. We so desperately need help, especially those with medical training."

His eyes seemed to bore right into her own. Astrid swallowed. Surely he didn't mean her. She didn't even want to go as far away as Chicago. *He couldn't mean me. Lord, is this really you?*

7

J oshua felt a huge weight leave his shoulders as he sat next to Astrid in the service. She had not refused his slightly impertinent request to sit with her. Maybe his impulse to return to Blessing was right and not crazy, as he'd been wondering, although he'd been pretty sure of that when his heart about jumped out of his chest as soon as he saw her again. He tried to compare the young girl he'd tried to forget with this Astrid sitting beside him. *I stayed away to give her time to grow up, and now I'm back and she didn't seem to be troubled or irritated by my attention. Then suddenly she became distant, like in a trance.*

What happened? What was that speaker talking about? Africa. Joshua had tuned him out, conscious only of the girl next to him. His concern for her blotted out the remainder of the service. But even after the benediction she didn't move until Joshua cleared his throat.

"Miss Bjorklund?"

Astrid blinked. She stared at the seat back in front of her, then up at Joshua. "What did you say?"

"Astrid, are you all right?" Mrs. Bjorklund's voice came from the other side of her, but she continued to stare as if on the far side of the valley and only echoes came to her. "Astrid!" Her mother spoke sharply this time.

Astrid nodded and slowly rose. She looked toward the pulpit and then turned slowly to the guest speaker at the doorway beside Pastor Solberg, greeting all the people. Joshua studied her, feeling a frown between his eyebrows.

"Did you ask me something?" She looked up at Joshua with a slightly dazed expression.

"Yes, I did, and I'll ask it again. Are you all right?"

When Mrs. Bjorklund laid her hand upon Astrid's wrist, she turned to smile at her mother. But it was an odd smile, like one painted on a wax-headed doll.

Ingeborg kept her voice low and comforting. "Astrid, is something wrong? You are not acting like yourself."

Tears filled her eyes. She shook her head and shoved past Joshua, heading for the side door. She seemed to be trying to avoid speaking to either Reverend Schuman or Pastor Solberg. Joshua had no idea which or why, but she was definitely upset. He hesitated for just a moment and then followed her, walking silently alongside her, matching her stride for stride. She sniffed and sniffed again. He handed her a precisely folded white handkerchief.

As she accepted it, a shudder went through her. Tears coursed down her face, and sobs wracked her chest. Planting one foot in front of the other, she seemed to keep time to something she alone could hear. And then he heard her say, "Not me. Not me. Not me."

Joshua kept silent and kept pace. All he could think was to take her in his arms and comfort her, protect her from whatever was bothering her. But he didn't. He kept his arms at his side, his muscles rigid with the effort. He'd come all this way to find her again, and now this was happening. What could be wrong?

Lord, if I were a real praying man, I would most certainly do that now, but I've not bothered you with much for some time. So if you don't want to listen, I understand. But if you are really the God that Pastor Solberg and the other man talked about, the God my mother told me about, please hear me and help this young woman. I don't know what to do. Did I come too late? Is there someone else? What happened to her in that service? She was fine before, friendly, and seemed happy to see me. And now she can't quit crying. Throwing propriety over his shoulder, he stepped forward, turned, and let Astrid bump into him so he could put his arms around her. No one should have to cry alone when suffering, as she obviously was.

Wishing he could do more but with no idea what to do, he held her and let her tears soak his shirt. She clung, fists clenching his shirtfront. When the storm slowed somewhat, he could finally make out what she was saying.

"I don't want to. Please, I don't want to." Sobs continued but now they were intermittent.

"Don't want to what?"

"Go to Africa. I don't want to go to Chicago even, but I really don't want to go to Africa." Gulps punctuated her words, breaking the thoughts into pieces that he tried to string together to make sense.

"Who said you had to go to Africa?" He hoped she could hear him but realized he sounded as confused as she.

She used his handkerchief to mop her face and blow her nose, but the tears dripped on. When she looked up at him, all he could see were diamonds and sapphires sparkling in her Bjorklund blue eyes. If he hadn't been positive he cared for her before, he was a goner now for sure.

He cupped his hands around her face and used his thumbs to wipe away the tears. "Astrid, please, all is well. You do not have to go to Africa. You don't have to go anywhere you don't want to go."

She sucked in a staggering breath and closed her eyes, resting against his warm chest. "Oh, my goodness." Obviously appalled at her behavior, she stepped back.

Immediately, Joshua felt struck by how much he'd rather she stay where she was.

"Please forgive me. I . . . I'm sorry. Oh my. What will people think?" She rolled her eyes, then mopped them again. "I'm in for it now."

"In for what? In what?" If he thought he was confused before, this was not helping.

"Standing here in your arms. Behaving like . . . like . . ." She couldn't seem to find the right words, and an errant sob caught her throat. She turned and started again for home. After a few paces she muttered. "You must think me deranged or something."

He shrugged. "Nope. That hadn't entered my mind." He gave his voice a lighter, almost teasing tone. "Should it? Enter my mind, that is?"

Astrid sucked in a mighty breath and blew it all out. "I hope not." She brushed tendrils of hair back from where they stuck on her now drying cheeks and adjusted her hat. Hearing the horse and buggy clip-clopping behind them, they turned and stepped to the side of the road. It wasn't just her mother and father, but several other buggies too and wagonloads of people going to the Bjorklund house for Sunday dinner.

Haakan *whoa*'d the horse, and the buggy eased to a stop. "Your mother was worried about you."

Ingeborg gave his arm a push and *tsk*ed. "Would you like a ride?"

"I'll be all right, Mor. Don't worry. We'll see you at the house." She glanced up at Joshua, and he nodded back to her. They turned and kept walking as the others passed them. Her cousins didn't even make teasing comments. Their faces showed their concern.

Thorliff and Elizabeth were the last to drive by, and he stopped his horse. "Get in."

Astrid shook her head. Joshua couldn't resist a smile. His own attempts to boss his younger siblings often had the same effect.

"Please, Astrid, join us so we can talk," Elizabeth said, leaning forward. "Inga is with the others."

Astrid heaved a sigh. "You needn't make a scene of this. I can explain my behavior."

Thorliff's eyebrows met his hatband. "Something sure hit you hard. I remember one time when I tried to outrun some demons. It doesn't work. Just gives you an aching chest and blisters on your feet."

"I didn't run."

"Close to it. But if you would rather walk it off, we'll meet you at the house," Elizabeth said.

"But—I—" Thorliff gave his wife a husbandly look.

"We'll see you at the house," Elizabeth finished, at the same time giving him a poke in the side.

Astrid rolled her lips together, and Joshua could see she was fighting back another wave of tears.

The breeze blew the dust to the south so they didn't have to choke on it. Instead, they walked together wrapped in a silence that felt as comfortable as a well-washed quilt.

A meadowlark clinging to a goldenrod loosed his song in notes of joy that Joshua was sure he could see sparkling in the sun. Dewdrops still outlined a spider's web in dots of glitter, a prism of golden rays.

"Thank you," Astrid said.

"You are welcome."

"I suppose you want to know what happened."

"Only if you want to tell me." Joshua wasn't sure he wanted to break this peaceful silence they had back.

"Not sure if I want to, but . . ." The silence stretched for several paces. They could hear Barney barking, welcoming everyone home. "You know when Reverend Schuman said God was calling people to come serve in Africa?"

"Yes. Missionaries always say that. Several came to the church near the farm in Iowa, and they always needed more missionaries in Africa, China, India, everywhere. They also needed money to help their missions. So I gave some."

"He said they need those with medical training. It was like he was staring right at me and talking right to me."

"I see." Joshua struggled to find words so as not to offend her, but he really hadn't been listening too closely.

"Thank you for coming with me—and sharing your handkerchief." She held up the soaked and crumpled bit of cloth. "I'll wash it for you."

He smiled at her. "That's not necessary."

"You don't think I'm crazy?"

He shook his head. "Not at all." How could he? He still wasn't really sure what they were talking about. He was just happy to see her smiling again.

As they neared the steps of the Bjorklund farmhouse, one of Pastor Solberg's daughters called to her from the front porch, "Astrid, where are the jacks?"

"I'm coming." She clapped her hand on her hat to keep it from blowing off and dashed up the walk, taking the three stairs in a leap.

She'd chosen the hat that morning in the hopes of looking like a proper and attractive young lady to the man beside her. And then all this happened. *Oh, fiddle. There went my young lady image. Guess he is seeing the real Astrid Bjorklund today. Crying my eyes out one minute and leaping the stairs the next. What will he ever make of this?* But when she glanced back at him over her shoulder, his smile was definitely not condemning.

Inside she found the jacks and told the girls to take them out on the porch so others could play if they wanted. She and Grace spread the tablecloths on top of the tables the men had set up under the cottonwood tree so the food could be brought out.

Grace hugged her and then signed, "What happened at church? Are you okay?"

Physically or mentally? A song from childhood whispered through her mind. *Here am I, send me.* A song about Samuel. God called his name in the night. Surely God hadn't called her name today. Surely she was making this up. She shook her head, trying to shake her thoughts away.

"Not sure," she signed back. "I'll explain later." She might crumble into small pieces if she did so now. Or melt into a puddle of tears again.

What if that was God calling her? But what about being needed right there in Blessing, North Dakota? All the plans and dreams for the new hospital, serving others—surely that was what God was calling her to do. *I'll go to Chicago if you want, but please, not to Africa.*

"When are your cousin and her family coming from Norway?" Astrid heard Mary Martha Solberg asking Ingeborg as she came back to the kitchen.

"Either tomorrow or the next day, as far as we know. We'll just keep meeting the train until they get here." Ingeborg handed Astrid a platter with sliced ham. She hesitated for a moment and gave her daughter a long look.

"Well, if you need more room, we could sleep a couple at our house," Mary Martha said.

"Thanks, but we have the rooms at Kaaren's to use until the students come back in the fall. We should be able to get a house built for them by then."

Astrid held the screen door open with one foot while Grace carried out one of the crockery bowls. Everyone brought food for meals like this, so it was more a case of getting it set up than anyone cooking all night, although her mother had set a pot of beans to baking the evening before. She looked around to see where Mr. Landsverk had settled and saw him talking with Hjelmer and Thorliff. Inga was sitting atop her father's shoulders, which meant she'd gotten into something again.

Trygve and Samuel were tossing the ball to each other by the well house. The baseball game would start as soon as the food disappeared. A thought ripped through her heart. When she went to Chicago—*if* she went to Chicago—she'd miss all this. Let alone if she went to Africa. *Please,* she pleaded, *I don't want to go to Africa. Stop that,* she reminded herself. *Remember, God let young Mr. Baxter die. Why would He listen to you bellyache about not going to Africa? Besides, if you are mad at Him, how can you ask for anything?* That would take some thinking on. Pastor Solberg and the reverend Schuman had appropriated the rocking chairs on the back porch and seemed deep in discussion. She caught a word or two as she went by. Was he trying to talk Pastor Solberg into going to Africa? Slowing down, she caught a few more words. It sounded more like a plea for support. The Blessing Lutheran Church had always sent money for missionaries as part of their tithe. She could remember putting her pennies into a can marked *Missionaries.* She and all the rest of the Sunday school contributed, and some of the quilts the women made went overseas too.

"But we have a mission field a lot closer," she heard Pastor Solberg say. "The Indians on the reservation need far more help than we give them."

"There's never a lack of the poor to be helped," the other man added. "Jesus said the poor would always be with us, and He wasn't making up a story."

Astrid felt a glimmer of light reach into her heart. Maybe it wasn't the place but the service she had responded to.

As soon as the food was all set out, Ingeborg held Inga up to ring the triangle. The little girl held the straight bar with both hands and swung it around. When she dropped it, it missed her grandmother's toe only because of some fancy stepping.

"Sorry, Gamma. It fell."

Astrid had to turn away so she wouldn't laugh. Leave it to Inga. She grabbed the little girl. "You come sit with me."

"Good." She leaned close to whisper, one that could be heard clear to the barn. "Can we have chocolate cake first?"

"No, sorry."

She'd just filled their plates and sat down when Mr. Landsverk took the seat beside her.

"Care if I join you?"

Astrid smiled. "Not at all."

"My pa sitting there." Inga glared at him.

"Sorry, kitten, this man is company. You be nice to him."

Inga put on a very fake smile. "You can sit over there." She pointed to an empty place on the bench on the other side of the table.

Thorliff scooped up his daughter. "You come sit with Ma and me, Miss Queen Bee."

"But, Pa . . ."

"Too bad." He set her plate on the table. "You can sit on my knee."

Astrid looked to the man beside her. "So goes life in Blessing. Miss Queen Bee, as her father calls her, would rule her kingdom with a golden scepter."

"She's a pretty smart little girl. I heard her tell the little boy with the broken arm that when he gets big she might marry him."

"That's her cousin Carl. If she'd not talked him into climbing the ladder to see the kittens in the haymow, he would not have a broken arm."

"Who are the two boys who were playing catch?"

"The older is Trygve and Samuel the younger. They are Grace and Sophie's brothers."

"I'm surprised Sophie, or rather Mrs. Wiste, isn't here."

"You can call her Sophie. She'll be along. She makes sure everything is done properly at the boardinghouse before she leaves on Sunday because that is Miss Christopherson's day off. Once they get here, Inga will have older cousins to play with. That always makes her happy."

"All right if I sit here?" Penny Bjorklund asked as she sat down on Astrid's other side.

"Of course. You and I never get a chance to talk. You remember Mr. Landsverk?"

"Very well. Good to have you back in town."

"I've heard the best thing that has happened lately is that you and your family have returned. From Bismarck, is that right?"

"Yes, and grateful every minute for coming home. Bismarck is a great place, just not a good one for this family. I saw you talking with Hjelmer. Did he talk to you about the windmills?"

Joshua nodded. "I guess I start tomorrow. He said there are three wells to be dug and four windmills needed."

So he was going to stay. Astrid felt a wave of joy run down her back to her toes.

"Sounds about right. He's got some repairing to do on the machinery first. I do hope you're a good mechanic."

"Well, I've repaired plenty of machinery on my father's place."

"Not much different I am sure. Astrid, when do you leave for Chicago?" Penny asked.

"*If* I leave for Chicago, you mean."

"Oh, I thought . . . I mean . . ."

"Depends on who you talk to: me or Dr. Elizabeth." Astrid looked up from studying her plate. "I'm just not sure I want or need more formal training."

"And what does Tante Ingeborg say?"

"You know what she says. 'Ask God and He will tell you what He wants you to do.' I remember when you were so frustrated about leaving Blessing. She said the same to you."

Penny nodded. "And I am still wondering if we didn't hear correctly or if God really did want us in Bismarck. And if He did, why?"

"Maybe it was so you would appreciate home more." Kaaren laid a hand on Penny's shoulder as she leaned over to fill the coffee cups.

"How come you're doing that? Let me help." Astrid started to stand.

Kaaren pressed down on Astrid's shoulder. "Finish your dinner first. This way I get to find out what's going on around here. Like overhearing bits of conversation here and there. Delightful."

"You mean you are eavesdropping?" Astrid made a horrified face. "After all those years of telling Sophie and I—"

"And *me*."

Astrid rolled her eyes. Once a schoolteacher, always a schoolteacher. "After all those years of telling Sophie and me that eavesdropping is not polite." Astrid faced Joshua. "Back in the early years of Blessing, Tante Kaaren and Mor started the school, and Tante Kaaren was the teacher. She's the one who taught all of us to sign so that Grace would have people to talk with. Eventually it led to the school for the deaf."

"And I can't wait until Grace comes back here permanently to teach. What a thrill that will be." Kaaren moved on up the table, filling coffee cups and chatting with everyone as she went.

"Someday I want to be like her," Penny said with a sigh.

"She and Mor always seem to know what to do."

"I know."

"What if I hear wrong? About what God wants me to do?"

"Like perhaps us with Bismarck?" Penny paused, staring unseeing at Astrid. "I guess God figures out a way to make it all right again. I think Hjelmer is far more content now with Blessing, now that he had a taste of living in a city somewhere else, working for someone else. And if it took our moving there to help him learn that, it was worth every minute and every tear."

Astrid blew out a sigh and gave Penny a hug. "I hate to make mistakes."

"Don't we all?"

Samuel stopped behind them. "Mr. Landsverk?"

Joshua turned to answer. "Yes."

"Would you like to join our baseball game? We play out in the pasture as soon as everyone is finished eating. Most all the men and boys play."

"And the girls cheer," Astrid added.

"Will you be cheering?" He smiled down at her as gently as he had when she'd cried all over his shirt.

At the look in his eyes, she could feel her cheeks growing warm. "Yes. I'll be there." *After I have a talk with Reverend Schuman,* she suddenly decided.

8

Interesting to feel pulled two ways. One part of him wanted to go with Astrid whether she had invited him or not. The other was pleased he'd been invited to play ball, and he headed for the field with the Knutson boy, whichever one he was, Trygve or Samuel? Joshua definitely had trouble telling them apart. He stared after Astrid, striding purposefully across the yard. Not strolling but pounding the grass with her heels. Was she angry?

"Have you ever played baseball?" Thorliff asked as he stopped beside him.

Joshua nodded. "The town near my pa's farm has two teams. I usually played first base or pitched."

"Good. You can be on our team."

"How are the teams chosen?"

"Used to be the men against the boys, but now we just choose up sides. It's more fun if we are fairly evenly matched."

Joshua shot one more look after Astrid and walked with Thorliff to the game. The diamond was marked with gunnysacks filled with sawdust on the bases and a worn holey rug for home plate.

"What do you use for a backstop?"

"The catcher just better not miss. Makes for a sure home run if he does. We've been talking about putting in a real field over at the school, backstop and all. Somehow building houses seems more important than a backstop."

"You're on our team," Trygve called from the pitcher's dirt mound.

"Nope, sorry. We got him," Thorliff answered.

"But I asked him first."

"Too bad. I brought him over." Thorliff glanced at the man beside him, a couple of inches taller than his own six feet. "With arms as long as yours, you ought to be able to catch about anything. You say you can pitch?"

"Not the best but adequate."

"Good. We flip a coin to see which team is up first."

With the arrival of two Geddick boys, the teams were full. Thorliff and Trygve joined the others at home base to flip the coin. Trygve called heads. Tails came up and he groaned.

"Thorliff, you always win."

"Only when Hjelmer is on my team." He looked around at the players. "You all know Joshua Landsverk?" When the Geddicks shook their heads, he introduced Joshua, and the others said their names. "Okay, let's play ball." He assigned the batting order, and the rest of them went to sit in the shade of the barn to wait their turn. "You have to watch out for cow pies," Thorliff told Joshua, "though we try to clear them away from the playing field. A bit sloppy if you slide into a base through one."

And me in my best clothes. Do most people go home to change after church? He looked around. Seems like they did or brought work jeans along.

Haakan sat down beside him. "Glad to see we have a new player."

"You don't play?"

"Used to but had a bit of a medical problem this winter, and my docs say I have to take it easy. I could do outfield fine, I think." He tipped his head to the side. "I take it you've played before?"

Joshua told him what he'd told Thorliff. "Who is that playing second base?"

"That's Gerald Valders. He was on duty at the telephone exchange, so he couldn't come to the dance last night. His brother, Toby, is playing for us."

"Telephones, eh? They have 'em in town at home, but Pa drew the line there. Said he didn't need any such newfangled machines to eat up what little he makes."

"Plenty of folks feel that way until there is an emergency. Then they realize telephones can save lives."

The crack of bat on ball grabbed their attention. With a line drive right over second base, Hjelmer charged toward first base, rounded it, and headed for second.

"Here, here!" Samuel leaped for the throw and missed tagging Hjelmer by mere inches.

"I'm safe!" Hjelmer yelled, getting up and dusting off his hands. "Good try there, young man."

Samuel glared at him. "I'd a had you if you'd stood up."

"That's why I slid." His reply made the others laugh.

"What brought you back to Blessing?" Haakan asked Joshua.

I can't tell him I couldn't get his daughter out of my head. "I got tired of farming." He paused, wishing he could tell the whole story, but now was neither the time nor place. "I remembered liking it here until the grasshoppers ate my harvest and the blizzard near to froze me to death. So I came back, hoping there might be other work here besides farming."

"That was a hard year for many folks."

Can't tell him I was going back to see if I could talk Fiona into changing her mind either. Needless to say, she hadn't, but that might have been because she was married to someone else by then. Romance hadn't been easy for him.

"So you're going to work for Hjelmer putting up windmills, eh?"

"Looks that way." Joshua picked a blade of grass and tossed it away. "I've always liked putting things together." He watched one of the Geddick young men take a stance with the bat over his shoulder.

"There's plenty of work around here for any enterprising man. Blessing is growing far more than we ever dreamed." He raised his voice. "Come on, Geddick, hit that ball."

Joshua reminded himself that no matter how much he wanted to see how Astrid was doing, he needed to stay here with the game. After all, if he wanted to live here, he needed a job and friends. Or there would be no possibility of getting to know Astrid.

"Strike one," yelled the catcher when Geddick stood there and took the pitch.

"Come on, that looks—"

"Strike two."

"Come on, Heinz, you can do it. Don't let him buffalo you," Hjelmer yelled, leading off second.

Trygve spun and fired the ball to second base. Samuel caught it and ran after Hjelmer, who was now sprinting for third base.

"Tag him, tag him," the outfielders shouted.

But Hjelmer slid out from under the tag and stood up safe.

"You cheated!"

"No I didn't. You just didn't run fast enough. In this life you gotta be ready for anything." Hjelmer dusted off his pant leg.

"Ain't that the truth," Haakan muttered under his breath.

Joshua turned to look at him. The man now wore deep lines from the sides of his nose to the commas of his mouth. His eyes were more sunken, the robust strength that Joshua remembered no longer there. He seemed to clamp and open his fist as a reflex action. Whatever had happened to him? While he looked older, he still seemed in good health. Joshua nudged Thorliff. "Why don't you ask your pa to be umpire? You know, call the strikes and foul balls?"

Thorliff stared back at him, then gave a slight nod and leaned around him. "Pa, why don't you go out there and be the umpire. Then we'll have a fairer game." When Haakan ignored him, Thorliff leaned over and poked his father to get his attention. "How about you go out there behind the batter and play umpire?"

Haakan nodded. "Not a bad idea. I think Geddick is getting a bad rap." He stood and raised his arms. Play stopped. Thorliff stood too. "Pa's going to play umpire out here, so Trygve, you better be more careful how you pitch."

"Yeah, don't hit your old onkel, or you'll get to milk all the cows tonight."

Trygve groaned. "One more thing to slow down the game."

"That's what you think." Haakan went to stand behind the batter and snugged his fedora down on his head. "Let's go."

Trygve lobbed one in.

"Ball two."

"Hey, he already has two strikes."

"Yes, and it should be ball three, but I was giving you the benefit of the doubt."

Trygve heaved the next one in. Geddick swung, caught it, and the ball sailed out into left field. He ran to first, then second, and Hjelmer ran home.

"You're up next," Thorliff said, motioning to Joshua.

Joshua hit it on the first pitch, the ball arcing up and away. The two fielders ran back and still the ball kept on going. Geddick ran toward home plate, with Joshua steamrolling after him.

"Oh, blast." Lars, who was playing outfield, kicked the ball out of the fairly fresh cow pie and let it roll in the grass to get it cleaned up.

"Two more points—we're three ahead." Thorliff clapped the two runners on the back. "And it's still the first inning. Joshua, you can play on my team anytime."

"That was an accident. I've never hit like that before."

"That's what being back home where you belong does for you."

Joshua stared at Thorliff. Was this really home, or was he here only because of Astrid? "I'll have to think on that." He sat down next to Hjelmer and watched the game while he wondered where Astrid was. Other women had come out to watch the game but not her.

"Hi there, Astrid," Pastor Solberg greeted as Astrid mounted the steps to the porch. He turned to his guest. "This is Miss Astrid Bjorklund, our resident doctor-in-training."

"How do you do, sir."

"Very well." The reverend Schuman smiled, yet his eyes seemed tired. Or maybe he was weary in general. He cleared his throat. "I saw you in church."

She watched him clear his throat for the third time. When she thought about it, he'd been doing that during the service too. "May I ask you a few questions?"

"Of course." He motioned to the empty chair beside him. "Why don't you sit down while we talk."

"I'll leave you alone, then." Pastor Solberg started to stand, but the pleading look Astrid sent him settled him back down in the rocker again. "I guess they can play ball without me for a change." He leaned forward and, resting his elbows on his knees, clasped his hands. "What is bothering you?"

"How do you know something is bothering me?" The question slipped out before she could clamp it off. That didn't sound very polite.

"Ah, Astrid, how many years have I known you?"

"All my life."

"Then shouldn't I be able to sense unrest when I see it?"

Astrid glanced at the other man watching her. He cleared his throat again.

"It's about something you said, Reverend, about needing those medically trained workers in Africa."

"We need people like that desperately. You have no idea how severe the crisis is there. Jesus calls us to heal the sick."

"But what about here? Doctors are needed here too."

"I'm sure they are. Do you feel God is calling you to be a doctor?"

"In most ways I already am one. I've been in training for over a year and working for Dr. Elizabeth for two or three years. My mother was the one everyone called for medical help before Elizabeth moved here. I thought I wanted to be a nurse, but I've decided to become a doctor and will be taking more intensive training."

She stared at the man and watched his Adam's apple bob again. What was wrong with his throat? "But I don't want to go to Africa."

"Who said you had to go to Africa?"

101

"I thought you were speaking right to me."

"Then perhaps I was. Sometimes God works that way."

"But I don't want to go to Africa. I don't even want to go to Chicago. I want to stay here." Tears threatened again. *I will not cry. I will not be a big baby.* How embarrassing. "How do I know if this is God calling me?"

"You ask Him."

"But what if it is Him?" she asked in barely a whisper.

Reverend Schuman leaned forward. "Then you have to make a decision—to go or to stay. What I usually find is that if it is God, He will keep calling you. Remember Samuel? He said, 'Here am I, Lord.' "

"At least he didn't have to go to Africa."

Pastor Solberg chuckled. "There's my Astrid."

"He was given a rather large assignment, though. But it didn't happen until God had trained him for the job. He will lead you step by step, and if you follow those steps, you will know what His will is. You also check what you hear against the Scriptures. How did God call people?"

"He struck Paul blind."

"True. How did He call the disciples?"

"He said, 'Follow me.' But they could see and hear Him. Jesus was a real person and went up to them and told them what to do."

"True. We have to listen both inside and out. But He will make His will clear to us."

Astrid sighed and leaned back in the chair, setting it to rocking with one foot.

"Does that answer your questions, young lady?"

"I have one other."

"What's that?"

"How long have you had the problem with your throat?"

Solberg rolled his lips together, glanced at the surprised look on his friend's face, and burst out laughing. "She's like her mother, direct and observant, without an ounce of coyness in her."

Astrid waited for him to answer.

He squirmed a little in his chair, almost like a child who's had to sit too long. "Why?"

"Because if you haven't done so already, you need to have it looked at. Something isn't right."

"Do I come to see you or Dr. Elizabeth?"

"Dr. Elizabeth. Shall I put you on the appointment sheet for ten o'clock in the morning?"

"I think that would be fine."

"Good." Astrid stood. "Thank you."

"Know that we will both be praying for you to follow God's leading. Would you like the three of us to pray now?" Pastor Solberg touched her sleeve.

Astrid hesitated. What if someone saw them? *Don't be dumb. What does that matter? People get prayed for a lot around here, and you don't mind it in the operating room, in fact you count on it.* "Yes." Now it was her turn to clear her throat.

"Why don't you sit back down, and we'll each put a hand on your shoulder."

Astrid did as asked, her own hands clenched so tight her fingers cramped. Her shoulders felt the warmth of their hands, and she blinked and swallowed. Right now, all she wanted to do was run to the field and join those she could hear shouting and laughing. Why couldn't she leave well enough alone and ignore what she thought she heard?

Even the twittering birds in the cottonwood tree fell silent.

Pastor Solberg led off. "Heavenly Father, I thank you for this young woman you have given to me to shepherd all these years. I rejoice in all the gifts you have given her: gifts of service, of healing, of love and encouragement. She is such a blessing to us all, and we thank you for Astrid Bjorklund." He paused, his voice deepening. "Lord, she is your daughter and you have a purpose and a plan for her life. Please make it clear to her what you have in mind, so clear there is no room for doubt. And then give her the grace to follow your leading."

After a bit Reverend Schuman joined in. "Lord, we know that you want us to understand your Word and your guidance, for you have said so over and over. The Word says you speak in a still small voice, but there are many instances in your Word where you spoke clearly and with great precision. We ask you to do that for Astrid. Of those to whom much is given, much will be expected. I know that you will use her in a mighty way wherever you send her. And, Father, thank you for the privilege of this moment, of our meeting. We will give you all the glory for what you will accomplish. Thank you. Amen."

Astrid wiped the tears that she'd not known were dripping and blinked again. Heaving a belly-deep sigh, she looked up. "This reminds me of confirmation."

"It is kind of like that. One more step forward in the path He has chosen for you." Pastor Solberg patted her shoulder. "The Lord will bless and keep you."

She nodded. "I think I know that part."

"The rest will follow."

"Good. I don't have the proper clothes for Africa right now." As she stood again to leave, the men joined her. "You coming to watch the game?"

"Wouldn't miss it."

When Astrid reached the field, she leaned up against the barn by her mother. "Who's ahead?"

"We are."

"So you've taken sides?"

"This time." Ingeborg clapped and shouted, "That's the way." She turned to look at her daughter. "You all right?"

"I think so. At least for now. But I still don't really want to go to Chicago, let alone Africa."

9

The next morning Hjelmer looked up as Joshua approached. "So when can you come to work?"

Joshua stared at Hjelmer, who was studying the bent blade for a windmill head. "Right now. That's what you said."

"Good. Grab that end of the blade, and we'll heat it up enough to bend it easily. You ever worked with metal?"

"As in . . . ?" Joshua grabbed one blade, and Hjelmer picked up the one next to it that also had a slight bend.

"Forge?"

"Some. I can do the basics."

"Machinery repair?"

"I can take things apart, hopefully figure what's wrong, either fix them or buy a new part and put them back together. What I don't know, I learn quickly." Together they walked toward the glowing forge, where Mr. Sam was pounding a new edge on a plowshare.

"You ever drill a well before?"

"Dug one but not drilled."

Hjelmer cleared off a bench and hefted a flat bar of cast iron. "We'll heat this blade then lay it on the workbench, place this iron bar on it, and clamp it down. Don't have to heat it much."

Joshua watched as Hjelmer set up the process. Was this all? "You asked me when I can start work, but you didn't say what I'd be doing." *Or how much I'd get paid. Should I ask or just prove to him all I can do?*

"Depends. I'm not really sure. I sell farm machinery as well as repair it, drill wells, and sell and install windmills. Mr. Sam runs the blacksmith for me. More farms used to have their own forge, but not many do anymore since we are farming with more machinery. I need a man who can fill in wherever needed. I imagine one day we will be selling and repairing automobiles here too." He cocked his head. "You ever driven one?"

Joshua shook his head. "Pa would have nothing to do with all those newfangled contraptions—that's what he called them."

"Does he have a tractor?"

"Nope. But he did buy a two-bottomed plow, a mower and a rake, and discs. He still seeds by hand. He has only a half section, so he hires someone for threshing. He might invest in a corn seeder if the harvest is good this year, but that's what he has sons to do."

"Bet he's going to miss you." Hjelmer sighted down a blade and laid it on the to-be-repaired pile.

"Both of my brothers are still there, so he didn't mind my leaving." *Much.* He wondered if his father wasn't actually relieved that the troublemaker was gone. Joshua pumped the bellows a couple of times, then pulled on heavy leather gloves, worn black and smooth through all the smithing. Using two pairs of tongs, he held the blade over the forge, moving it slowly back and forth, then laid it on the metal bar on the bench. Laying the other bar on top of it, he set a clamp in the middle, and Hjelmer set another. With the third one in place, they stepped back, studying the blade.

"That should do it."

When they finished that, Mr. Sam heated the plowshare again. "You ever pounded out one of these?"

"Pa always did that. He could put a fine edge on about anything."

"You want to try this?"

Joshua grinned. Finally the chance to do a blade himself after years of watching.

"Go ahead. Do it. Can't do another windmill blade till that cools down."

Joshua straightened out his grin. The older man moved with the grace of a dancer, heating the metal, pounding it, knowing just when to stop one and start the other. His father had moved like that, but there hadn't been any bantering in his shop. If you had time for frivolity, you weren't working hard enough. Going home again had been a mark of failure against him, yet his father wanted his sons there. Joshua never had been able to figure the man out. But he had taught his sons to be good workers, and now one of them was away from home working for someone else.

"You wants to try it?" Mr. Sam's invitation brought him back to the forge in Blessing.

"Yes." Joshua pumped the bellows until the iron glowed white hot again, lifted the steel blade to the anvil, and using a medium-weight iron hammer, honed a fine edge on the plowshare. Then he dunked it in the bucket of water kept for cooling iron.

"You foolin' wid ole Sam?"

"No, why?"

"You said you din't know much about sharpening plowshares. That was good as any I seen done."

"You had it nearly finished. You did the hard part."

"Good decision, boss. This man be a big help."

The three worked for the next couple of hours until dinnertime, when Lily Mae, Sam's daughter, brought three meals over from the boardinghouse. She set the covered plates on the picnic table under the tree behind the general store and brought out three cups of coffee from the kitchen where Rebecca and Gerald lived.

The men washed their hands at the pump and sat on the bench seats.

With Linnea, Hjelmer's daughter, close to her heels, Rebecca brought them a pitcher of lemonade filled with ice.

"Thanks." Hjelmer leaned forward and made a funny face at his daughter, setting her giggles in gear.

Joshua glanced at Hjelmer. "There is still ice in the icehouse?"

"Ja. They put in plenty more since so many have iceboxes now. Before you know it, we'll have a machine here that makes ice year around. Penny and I get information all the time on new inventions." Smiling proudly, he continued, "Years ago, Penny sold the first sewing machines here, started a whole new way of life for the women in Blessing."

Hjelmer's son, back to being called Little Gus, ran across the yard. "Pa, can I go swimming with Samuel at the river?"

"It's pretty cold yet."

"Is that a yes or a no?" He glanced over his shoulder, fidgeting from one foot to the other. "Please?"

"Did you ask your mother?"

"No, she's busy."

"Did you finish weeding your rows in the garden?"

"Yes."

"Why don't you go fishing instead? Fried fish would taste mighty good."

"P-a-a."

"Oh, all right. But take your fishing pole just in case. Samuel's a good fisherman."

"Thank you." The boy ran to the back porch of the store, grabbed a pole with hook, line, and bobber and headed for the river, his bare feet slapping up puffs of dirt as he ran.

"I remember those days." Joshua took a bite of his sandwich and chewed slowly. He hadn't had many chances to go fishing. Work on the farm was always more important. *If I ever have a son, I want him to be able to go fishing. I want to take him fishing.* He stared at his sandwich. Where did thoughts like that come from?

They'd just finished eating when Thorliff walked around the corner of the store. "Hjelmer, your house will be in tomorrow. The letter just arrived. Don't know why they didn't use the telephone."

"That's great news." Hjelmer paused a moment. "But we're not ready."

"Right. I've got Toby and Heinz working over there. Can you come too?"

"Sure. The three of us will be right over." Hjelmer looked at Joshua. "I take it you know how to use a hammer."

"Somewhat."

"Somewhat, like setting that edge on the plowshare?"

"We built a machine shed and a shed addition on the barn. Oh, and a new silo and corncrib."

"I see." He turned back to Thorliff. "Be there right away."

"Glad to have you along," Thorliff said to Joshua. "We have a good team."

And I don't have to milk cows. Joshua finished his sandwich and emptied the glass. "I'm ready any time you are."

"You have any tools?"

Joshua shook his head. "Do I need to buy some?"

"No. We have plenty. Sam, can you bring a file to sharpen the saw blades?"

"Where is your house going to be?"

Hjelmer turned and pointed to a lot two blocks over with mounds of dirt. "That's it. We've poured the exterior walls and set the drain, and we're ready to build the center support wall."

"I've not worked with concrete before."

"Don't worry. You'll learn."

As they approached the building site, Hjelmer pointed to two eight-foot posts made from a single tree trunk. "Going to use those to support the upper floor. We'll set them on concrete pads, which we need to frame and pour. Then we'll run a beam from the back wall, across the posts, and to the front."

"I see. You want me to start on the pads?"

"That'll be fine."

The afternoon flew by as the men worked to get the basement ready to begin framing the lower floor and walls. Joshua wrapped a bandanna soaked in water around his neck and pulled his wide-brimmed hat more securely down on his head. The errant breezes didn't make it into the cellar.

Measuring, cutting boards, and nailing the forms together kept his mind too busy to think about what his new pay would be or to wonder what Astrid was doing. Although when he stopped to get a drink of water from a jug covered with soaked burlap, he remembered the good feeling her cheering for him had caused. Even while he was running the bases, he could hear her yelling his name. The game had picked up in intensity when the women and girls had arrived to root the teams on. Thorliff's team had won by four runs—eight to four, not a bad score. This game had been more fun than those at Winding Creek, the town closest to his father's farm. There he was always under the cloud of his father's criticism. After all, he should be working, not playing. And baseball? What a colossal waste of time, his father thought.

The people of Blessing seemed to know how to work hard yet play and have a good time too. Back in Iowa, Sundays had been for worship and thinking on one's sins, not for enjoying a huge family get-together, playing baseball, and eating ice cream in the afternoon.

He hung the cup back on the hook and returned to making his form. That done, he poured the concrete and troweled the top of it before stepping back. With three iron bars imbedded in the concrete and sticking straight up to be fitted into the posts once the concrete was dry, they could proceed.

"Looks good to me. Let's go measure and cut those posts." Hjelmer pulled his handkerchief from his back pocket and mopped his face. "Sure is getting hot."

"You're just not used to manual labor yet," Thorliff said, clapping his uncle on the shoulder. "Just soft. That's all."

"Who do you think shoveled out a good portion of the basement?" Hjelmer held up his hands. "No more summer hands for me. I've got calluses to prove it."

As the sun was starting to set, they put their tools away and headed for home. "See you here at seven o'clock tomorrow," Hjelmer called.

Joshua raised a tired hand in acknowledgment and kept on walking. He needed a pair of leather gloves; that was for sure. He climbed the steps to the boardinghouse and pulled open the screen door. Fragrances of fresh bread, sizzling meat, and fresh coffee drew him into the dining room, where Miss Christopherson pointed him toward a seat.

"Your supper will be right out. I was beginning to wonder what had happened to you."

"I got a job with Hjelmer Bjorklund. We'll start putting up his new house tomorrow after it comes in on the train." He sat down, looked at his hands, and quickly stood again. "I'll be right back. Need to wash off some of the grime first." When he returned, a plate of sliced roast beef, potatoes smothered in brown gravy, and string beans with bacon waited at his place. Two slices of bread and butter covered a plate beside the other, and a full coffee cup finished it off.

"This looks wonderful."

"Thank you. I'll tell Mrs. Sam." Miss Christopherson glanced around the room. "You're about the last one to be served, and there's plenty more where that came from."

"Thank you." Joshua tucked into his meal, polishing off that plate and one more before he decided he was full.

"Too full for chocolate cake?"

"Yes, no, I ah . . ."

"I'll get it."

He watched the woman, no longer young but not yet old, scurry back to the kitchen. He knew she wasn't the waitress, but she made sure he got plenty of food every evening and at the other meals too if he showed up.

Waiting for his dessert, he leaned back in his chair and let his gaze wander the room. A family of four sat at one table finishing their supper, the two children, a boy and a girl, sitting perfectly still, sneaking glances at other folks. The parents ate without a word. Something like meals had been when he was growing up. His mother never ate a meal with the rest of the family but served everyone. If there was anything left, she ate it after the others were finished. Smaller children were definitely seen but not heard.

Several drummers shared another table, laughing at something one of them said. He'd heard that many spent the night in Blessing just to have a good meal at the boardinghouse. News traveled on the railroad and brought new people to town. Like him. But the railroad hadn't been the calling card for him. Maybe he should invite Astrid to have supper with him there some evening. He knew that even in his mind he should be calling her Miss Bjorklund, or even Dr. Bjorklund, but somehow it just didn't happen.

"Enjoy your cake." Miss Christopherson set the plate on the table and refilled his coffee cup.

"Oh, I will. Thank you."

"Can I get you anything else?"

He shook his head. "But thank you."

"Have a good night." She left and he watched her check on the other two tables, her graciousness bringing smiles to several, even to the little girl and boy.

After supper Joshua made his way upstairs and down the hall to his room. He sat on the freshly made bed and pulled off his boots, setting them under the edge of the mattress. Washing his hands had not been enough. He gathered up his towel, soap, and a set of clean clothes and walked down the hall to the bathroom, claiming it in use by putting the *Occupied* sign on the outside of the door. How his mother would love having hot and cold running water at her house.

He turned on the faucets in the claw-footed bathtub and finished undressing while the water deepened. When he sank down into the water, his sigh rose with the steam. This was surely a bit of heaven come down to pleasure a body. He sniffed the bar of soap. Even it smelled good. Life in Blessing was "some good," to quote his sister, Avis. Shame he'd waited so long to come back.

Now all he had to do was convince Astrid—Miss Bjorklund, or rather Dr. Bjorklund—that he was the man for her. But why would a doctor want to be married to a nobody like him? Should he even try? How would she be both a wife and a doctor? Although Thorliff and Dr. Elizabeth seemed to manage. Maybe he needed to rethink his expectations.

10

T*hey're coming. They're coming.*

The song danced through Ingeborg's mind as she and Haakan drove the wagon toward Blessing and the train station. Her cousins would be arriving today. She was so excited since receiving the telegram last evening that she'd hardly slept. All those years ago she'd taught Alfreda how to make cheese and take care of the cows up at the saeter, the high mountain cabins where the young women and girls spent the summer pasturing the milk cows in Norway.

It was up there that Freda, as they all called her cousin, had fallen and broken her leg. The fall had left her with a permanent limp, and Ingeborg with the guilt that she'd not done a better job in setting the leg. They should have sent her home to someone with more experience.

"What is it, my Inge?" Haakan asked softly.

"So many years since I've seen her."

"Ja, that is true. But I am sure she is feeling the same nervousness. As you say so often, all will be well."

"Uff da, there you go, turning my words back on me. Why do they sound so much better and wiser if I am saying them instead of listening to them? Or do I mean it the other way?" She tucked her arm through his. "She has wanted to come for a long time."

"I know. Shame her husband never wanted to come. Making a good living is so much easier here. He might still be alive if he had."

"You call what we all do easy?" She stared at him, purposely widening her eyes to look shocked.

Haakan chuckled. Just the response she'd wanted.

"Would we have had all this were we still in Norway?"

Ingeborg slowly shook her head as she let her gaze rove the fields, some with wheat and others with corn, all swaying in tune with the breeze. Cattle grazing in other fields, her cheese house, the big barns. "God has given us so much." She shook her head again. "But there is something missing, you know. Something that will indeed make Freda homesick."

"The mountains?"

"Ja, she always loved the mountains. And here the land couldn't be flatter. As if God rolled it out with a giant rolling pin."

Haakan patted her knee. "Leave it to you to think of something like that. Shame we don't have the soddy any longer. She could have her own house, then."

Ingeborg nodded. The last big flood in 1897 had floated away Metiz' cabin and washed out all the soddies in the area because the walls were made of sod blocks cut right out of the prairie. "There is plenty of room at our house. And Solem, her married son, and his family can stay over at Kaaren's until school starts again."

Haakan *hupp*ed the horses into a trot when they heard the train whistle floating up from the south. "Someone could stay in the cook wagon too, you know. At least until harvest."

"Are Mrs. Geddick and her girl going to cook for you again this year?"

"Far as I know." He stopped the horses at the hitching rail and wrapped the reins around the whipstock. Stepping down, he turned to help Ingeborg use the wheel spokes as steps. "We should have put a bench in the wagon. It would make it easier for her to sit."

After flipping the tie rope around the rail, they left the horses and strolled onto the heavy planks that formed the platform. Ingeborg slid her hand through the crook of her husband's arm. "Thank you for coming with me."

He patted her hand. "I wouldn't have missed it."

Ingeborg stared into his eyes, no longer the intense Bjorklund blue but still like chips of sky come down to smile at her. Even after all these years, the love that shone in them set her heart from a walk to a trot, and his smile kicked it into a gallop. She fanned herself with the other hand. "My, but it's gotten warm, don't you think? I should have brought a parasol."

Haakan stared at her for a moment and then chuckled. "Do you even have such a thing? I can't remember when I saw you bring it out last."

"You don't mind that your wife doesn't have milk-white skin?" She batted her eyes, making him grin even wider, and raised her other hand to her cheek. "Why, I declare, I didn't use my buttermilk poultice this morning."

"Your what?"

"Astrid and Elizabeth were talking about ladies using buttermilk soaks to keep their skin white and how important *Godey's Lady's Book* said it was to keep the sun off our skin so that women would be more attractive."

Haakan leaned closer so she could hear him over the hissing and shrieking train. "And what did *Godey's Lady's Book* say about women wearing britches?"

"Haakan Bjorklund, you know I gave those up at your request all those years ago and never looked back."

"Never?"

"Well, not too often." She swatted him on the arm. "You behave yourself. You don't want to scare poor Freda off now with tales that should be forgotten."

"As if I would ever do that."

Ingeborg took a step forward when the conductor placed his stool on the platform. Two drummers stepped off first and headed for the boardinghouse. A young man helped his wife down and set one of his children down beside the mother. Were these Freda's children? Ingeborg tugged on Haakan's arm to move forward.

The conductor helped another woman down, this one gray and gaunt, her gloved hand covering her mouth in a coughing spasm. Another young man handed out several valises, and the conductor set them on the landing.

Ingeborg stared at the family, then sent Haakan a questioning look. He nodded and they moved forward.

"Freda?" Ingeborg cleared her throat and raised her voice. "Freda Brunderson?"

The woman turned slowly as if fighting off heavy weights. "Ja." Her voice broke, and she coughed again, leaning against the shoulder of the younger man. When she could speak, she whispered, "Ingeborg?"

Ingeborg crossed the remaining distance and put her arms around the old woman, speaking her greeting in Norwegian. "Welcome, my dear cousin, to Blessing." She cradled the now sobbing woman in her arms.

Haakan extended his hand to the older son. "Hallo, I am Haakan Bjorklund."

"Ja, takk. I am Solem Brunderson. This is my wife, Anna, my younger brother, Gilbert, and my children. Thor is the oldest, and the little one is Signe."

Haakan shook hands with the men and nodded to the woman, who clutched her daughter to her side. Even with her shawl covering, her advanced pregnancy was obvious.

Solem switched to Norwegian, apparently having used up his English in the greeting. "Please to forgive us. We have all been ill on the voyage, and the train trip was not much better. Mor seems to have fared the worst, but then she wore out taking care of all of us."

"I am surprised they let you through the inspection in New York."

"Ja, we were afraid too. But Mor turned worse after we got on the train. Your letters proved to them that we would have work and a home."

"I'm sorry, folks, but you are going to have to move away from the train. We are ready to depart."

"Our baggage?" Solem again spoke in Norwegian, but the conductor pointed to the stack of luggage unloaded off the baggage car.

Haakan caught Ingeborg's gaze and nodded. "Let's take your mother to the wagon first and get her settled with the children; then we can return for the trunks."

Freda clung to Ingeborg, but after three steps she began to collapse. Haakan caught her and started to lift her in his arms, but Ingeborg shook her head. "Two of you would be better." She motioned to Gilbert, who seemed the healthiest of the lot. He stepped forward and locked arms with Haakan to form a chair for his mother to sit on. When she had both arms wrapped around their shoulders, they lifted her and made their way to the wagon.

I should have brought blankets and quilts. Ingeborg studied the empty wagon bed. *If only she had told me . . .* But that had nothing to do with now. "I'll get in first, and then I can hold her." Using the wagon wheel spokes, she climbed into the wagon and propped her back against the front wall. Gently they settled Freda next to her, then handed the children in. "You might find it easier to sit on the wagon seat," she said to Anna.

"Nei, Mor." The little girl started to cry. From the tear streaks on her face this wasn't the first cry of the day.

Solem ignored the child's crying and handed her and his son in to Ingeborg also. "Now stay there," he said softly in Norwegian. "We'll be back."

Thor clutched his sister's hand and huddled into the opposite front corner of the wagon. Anna turned on the wagon seat and smiled down at him. "This is good. We will be home soon."

Ah, home. Lord, help these poor waifs settle in here. Ingeborg leaned her cheek on the top of Freda's head. The heat smote her. "How long have you had the fever?"

"It started on the train. She couldn't keep anything down, like on the ship." Anna winced to the point of shutting her eyes.

"Are you all right?"

"I hope so, but . . ."

"But . . . ?"

"This baby might be coming early."

"How early?"

"Three weeks, a month." Anna shifted on the seat, stifling a groan.

"When did the pains start?"

"During the night. I thought it was left over from the sickness on the ship."

"Can you see the men coming?"

"Ja, I think they have everything."

"Good. We'll take you right to see our doctor." She glanced back at Freda. "Both of you."

"But we cannot . . . do not have . . . I mean . . ."

The horror on her face spoke her thoughts clearly.

"You are not to worry about anything right now. You think on the baby and let us take over the rest. The doctor is my daughter-in-law."

Haakan and the men drew a cart up to the wagon and hefted one of the trunks from one to the other.

"Haakan."

He set a satchel in and turned to Ingeborg. "Ja?"

"We need to go by the surgery. Anna is in labor, and Freda is burning up." Just then Signe leaned forward, gushed vomit over her grandmother's skirt, and burst into wails.

"We'll hurry." They finished loading. "Leave that cart where it is, and let's go. Solem, you sit up here with your wife."

The three blocks to the surgery felt like a mile as the wagon jolted up the street. Ingeborg ignored the mess on Freda and tried to comfort Signe, as did her brother. With the dust filtering up from the turning wheels, Freda started to cough, turning into gags with the violence of it.

"Here, you tie the horses." Haakan jumped from the wagon and, pushing open the gate, ran up the walk. He leaped the steps, his boots thundering on the porch.

Astrid threw open the door. "Far, what's wrong?"

"One's having a baby, and the other is coughing." He leaned against the doorframe to catch his breath. "Do you have a stretcher?"

"You sit down." Astrid pointed to a chair. "We'll take care of all this." She turned back, called for Thorliff, and grabbed the stretcher they always kept folded in the corner by the door.

Thorliff and Thelma caught up with her as she started down the steps. The three of them got to the wagon, where Gilbert had already lowered the tailgate.

"Take Freda first," Ingeborg ordered. "We'll bring Anna. Walking is good for her anyway." She ignored the weeping children for the moment and helped settle Freda on the stretcher so that Thorliff and Gilbert could carry her into the house. Solem helped his wife climb down and kept her from falling as another spasm doubled her over.

"Mor!" the little girl cried. "Mor."

Astrid looked at her mother. "You take them, okay?"

"Ja, and those contractions are coming closer and closer." Feeling a wetness on her arm, she glanced at the boards. Water dripping from the seat above. "Her water broke. I'll be in to help immediately. Come, children. It's all right."

"Signe is sick," Thor said.

"I can see that. Come along now." She held out her hand, and after a second he reached for it.

"Signe, we're going into the house now," Ingeborg said in Norwegian. The words felt odd somehow when said out loud. She had become so used to speaking her native language only in her thoughts. "Come."

Ingeborg stepped down from the wagon and took the little girl in her arms. "Shh, all is well." This time the eruption went down the front of her summer dress. And if she was seeing right, there was blood in it. *Dear Lord, you know all things. Give us wisdom to do what is best for these poor people. We're depending on you to make them well and whole again.* The smell assaulting her nostrils said the child had more problems than a queasy stomach.

Haakan met her at the steps. "You want me to take her?"

"No. No sense anyone else getting dirty. Did Elizabeth say where to take her?"

"No. There are a couple of patients already waiting in the examining rooms. They are putting Freda in one of the recovery rooms and Anna in the other."

Lord, this is one of those times when I remember how much we need a hospital here. If more than two patients, we don't have room. She carried Signe down the hall and sat down in a chair with the little one on her lap. "Run water in the bathtub, will you, please? We'll start there."

Haakan nodded and opened the door into the downstairs bathroom. When he shut it with a stammer, he caught Ingeborg's questioning look. "It's busy."

Ingeborg swallowed a smile. Poor Haakan. A woman must have been in there. "She'll be out in a minute, I'm sure." Rocking and crooning, she stripped the clothing off the little girl and dropped the foul-smelling shift on the floor.

Thorliff came out of the bedroom, followed by Gilbert, and closed the door behind them. "Elizabeth said to ask you to come in as soon as you can," he told Ingeborg.

"I'll get this one in the bath first." She stood when the door to the bathroom opened, and Mrs. Magron tiptoed out.

"Has something terrible happened?" she whispered, her eyes darting around at the sounds from behind closed doors.

"Our visitors from Norway arrived, and they are sick. Could you please watch this little one in the tub while I check on my cousin Freda?"

"Of course." Mrs. Magron turned back to the bathroom and turned the handles on the tub, and the water gushed in.

Thor stood beside her, his eyes as round as silver dollars. "Are you magic?" he asked in Norwegian.

Ingeborg and Mrs. Magron chuckled and set little Signe down in the water, only to have her scream more.

"She's afraid of so much water," her brother said.

"I see. Would you like to get in too? That might make her feel better."

Thor's eyes still wide, he nodded.

"This is Mrs. Magron, and she is going to stay with you while I go check on your mor and bestemor. You can use that stool to climb into the tub as soon as you get undressed." Ingeborg dipped a towel under the water and wiped down as much of her dress as possible.

"You want I should throw their clothes in with them?"

"No. We'll wash those later, but thank you for helping." Ingeborg edged toward the door and slipped out as soon as Signe changed to a whimper.

Dear Lord, help us, she silently pleaded as she heard a groan turn into a cut-off scream from the room where Anna suffered in the midst of delivering her baby.

11

W ater's already broken," Anna panted around a contraction. "I know." Astrid glanced at the man beside the bed, his wife's hand strangling his. "Have you assisted before?"

He looked as if he were struggling with her words, then as understanding came he shook his head, fear widening his eyes. "At home the midwife sent me to the barn."

"I see. Well, we do things differently here. If you do as I say, you can be a big help." She laid her hands on the burgeoning belly, then placed her stethoscope on it. She could hear the baby's heart racing. Her throat dried immediately. "Anna, can you hear me?"

She nodded.

"We are going to get you undressed and into a nightgown. This baby looks to be in a mighty big hurry. You've already had two children?" Another nod. "Both normal births?"

"She lost one once, our first," the man explained. He knew his English, Astrid saw, but she would need to keep her words simple.

"Thank you. If you help me, this will go faster."

He nodded and began unbuttoning his wife's dress. Between the three of them, and in between contractions, they got Anna undressed and into a loose gown.

"Now, if you will take off your boots and sit with your back against the headboard, we'll position Anna with her back against you." Astrid used her hands to show him what she wanted him to do and then glanced up to see his eyes close. He sucked in a deep breath and bent to untie his boots.

While he did that, Astrid checked to see how far Anna was dilated. "How long have you been having the pains?" Astrid switched to Norwegian, making it easier for Anna to understand.

"They started during the night but got worse the nearer we come to Blessing." She spoke a combination of Norwegian and English.

"Ja, well this baby wants to come pretty soon. So, Solem, you sit behind her like I showed you." She glanced at the man's face again, whiter than the sheets on which his wife lay. "You're not going to faint on me now, are you?"

He shook his head, teeth clamped on his bottom lip.

"Ohhhhh." Anna cut off what threatened to become another scream.

"Anna, if you need to scream, you go right ahead."

"The children . . ."

"The children are fine. Don't worry."

"Signe, she's been sick too." He shook his head. "We were all sick. It was a terrible crossing. Even the sailors said so."

"All right, we'll keep the children here." She caught herself almost praying. If only Pastor Solberg would show up. She wondered if anyone had sent for him. While God didn't seem to regard *her* prayers, He listened when her mother and her pastor prayed. Another thought had crossed her mind, but she'd not pondered on it. Because there had to be a God. The Bible said so, and she'd seen too many prayers answered to doubt that part. He just didn't seem to listen to her.

But right now she sure needed someone to help her. She studied her patient while keeping her eyes veiled. Anna lay collapsed against her husband, the last contraction having taken all her strength. As labors went, she'd not been at this one terribly long, but the time from when the water broke until the baby crowned had been hard labor, and with the last stretch of time, nothing more had happened.

"I'll be right back."

"Don't leave us." Her husband looked as if he might leap off the bed and go running out of the room.

"I need Dr. Elizabeth."

Anna groaned as another massive contraction jerked her body upright in spite of her husband's helping arms. Her groan escalated, rising to a scream that she muffled by clamping her teeth. The grimace sent a shiver up and down Astrid's spine. She checked to see if the baby was crowning, and when nothing had happened, she tore out the door.

Taking a deep breath to calm herself lest she scare other patients, she knocked on the other bedroom door and peeked in.

"Don't come in," Elizabeth ordered. "This might be contagious."

"But I need you."

"Ingeborg, you keep cooling this woman. I'll be right back." Elizabeth motioned to Astrid to back up. "What is going on?"

"Nothing. Anna is in full labor and not dilating any further. The baby hasn't crowned yet."

"I see. You've checked for position?"

"You mean internally?" Astrid clamped her teeth on her bottom lip.

"Yes." Elizabeth clipped the word.

Astrid shook her head. *I can't*, her mind screamed.

"You've done it before."

"I . . . I know. But . . ." Astrid looked down at her hands. Not since Vernon's surgery. *I touched him inside, and he died.*

"It's coming!" Solem shouted.

"See, you worried too soon."

Astrid headed back into the delivery room. The baby had not only crowned, but one more push should free it. Astrid gasped at the blue skin. As the baby slithered out, she saw why. The pulsing cord was wrapped tightly around the baby's neck.

Astrid reached for a scalpel to cut the cord, but what if the mother bled to death? Was the baby dead already or in extremis? Both Mor and Elizabeth were contaminated. She slid her fingers under the cord to take the pressure off the baby's throat and pushed on his chest at the same time. *Breathe, baby, breathe. God, help me. What do I do?*

"What's wrong?" Anna gasped.

Fingers flying, Astrid found two lengths of string and tied the cord in two places before cutting between them. Each moment seemed like an hour, as if she were standing up in the corner and watching rather than in blood to her elbows and a blue baby in her hands. With the infant freed, she tipped him upside down and smacked his feet. Then pushed again on his chest. *Breathe! God, please make him breathe!*

Regowned and scrubbed, Dr. Elizabeth entered the room, taking everything in at a glance. She called out the door, "Thelma, warm water—now!"

"The cord . . ."

"I can tell. We'll swish him in warm water. Sometimes that works. Breathe for him. Cover both his nose and mouth and force the air into his lungs." While Astrid did that, Elizabeth massaged Anna's now flaccid belly with one hand, and with the other she packed sterile cloths between her legs to staunch the blood flow.

When Thelma brought in a tub of warm water, Elizabeth said, "Take over here for me so I can help Astrid."

Anna groaned again, and the afterbirth flowed out onto the soaked pads, along with too much blood.

"Swish him a couple times, then breathe for him again. See, his color is improving."

No it's not. He's not responding at all. Tears streaming down her cheeks, Astrid did as she was told. Swish and breathe. One puff, two. *Please, baby, breathe.*

But he didn't.

She held the little body to her chest, wishing she could fill him with her breath. Her tears dripped on his still face.

"Can I hold him?" Anna weakly raised her arms, her voice broken.

Astrid laid the little body on his mother's chest. "I'm so sorry."

Solem sniffed, his tears dropping down onto his wife's head. He laid his hand on the baby, his other arm clutching Anna. "He's so perfect. He can't be dead."

"Here, Astrid, keep packing and massaging while I go for some medications," Elizabeth ordered.

"You want me to get them?"

"No, I better."

Astrid took over while Thelma cleaned up the room, dumping the pail of soaked pads and bringing another stack of clean ones from the cupboard. *It's all my fault. I should have known. If I'd done the internal exam, I would have known. Why, dear God, why did that baby have to die because of me?*

Elizabeth came back in the room and held a cup to Anna's mouth. "Drink this. I know it tastes terrible, but I had to hurry."

Anna gagged but got the liquid down.

"Good, now you rest while we get this bleeding stopped. I think it is abating already." Elizabeth put the cup beside the bed. "Mr. Brunderson, I think you can move now if you want to."

"I'm fine. I help Anna. . . ." Solem's eyes moistened, but no tears fell.

Anna leaned against her husband, and together they held their baby.

He looked up at Dr. Elizabeth. "We should not have come. That awful voyage killed our baby."

"No, this could have happened anywhere. We don't know why, but it just happens sometimes. You can't blame yourselves or the circumstances." She looked directly at Astrid. "This is no one's fault. You could not have done anything differently to keep it from happening. I hesitate to say this, but we do know this baby has gone back to his heavenly home. You will see him again when you get there."

"If we get there." Solem shook his head. "You can't be certain of that, you know. You just do your best and hope."

Could that be true? Astrid paused, wanting to say something but unsure. What if Pastor Solberg was wrong? But what about the Bible verses she had memorized all these years? *For God so loved the world, that he gave his only begotten son, that whosoever believeth in him should not perish, but have everlasting life.* Others ran through her mind. The Bible never lied. God's Word was truth. She'd said that at confirmation. "Is Pastor Solberg here?"

"Yes, I saw him in the hall."

"Good." Astrid stepped out the door. Sure enough, there he sat, his eyes closed but his lips moving. He wasn't sleeping.

"Pastor Solberg?" she called softly.

He heard her and hurried to her.

The tears spurted again. "We . . . I . . . The baby died."

Pastor Solberg gathered her in his arms and held her, his soft murmurs sounding much like her mother.

"Please." She stepped back. "They need you."

He nodded and entered the room.

It was all she could do to follow him through that door. All she wanted to do was run away, far away from the smell of blood and a silent baby held by two sobbing parents. She found the anger she had brought under control raging upward again.

———

THAT EVENING, WITH Anna sleeping in her room and Freda fighting against the fever in the room next to that, Astrid and Elizabeth sat out on the back porch, letting the evening breeze dry the perspiration that soaked their clothing and drained their spirits.

Once Elizabeth determined that there was no contagion, they sent the two brothers and Thor with Haakan. Signe was at last calm and asleep on a cot near Freda. She still had some fever but not as high as her grandmother's. They all sighed with relief when Elizabeth determined the blood Ingeborg saw came from a cut in Signe's inner lip and not from the chest.

"Astrid, there was nothing else you could have done."

"I didn't do an internal exam." *I put my hands in Vernon's body, and he died. Now I couldn't touch Anna, and her baby died.*

"You would have felt the head and known that the baby was in the proper position for birth. He wasn't breech. You wouldn't have found this."

Astrid heard the words Elizabeth spoke, but the ones in her head screamed louder and drowned out all reason.

The crickets picked up their evening melody, joined by the whine of mosquitoes. A dog barked off in the distance, probably singing at the haunting whistle of a freight train heading north and then west.

"Discuss this with your teachers at the hospital. They'll have better answers than I do."

Astrid heaved a sigh. "I think my going to Chicago would be a waste of money."

"You let me decide that. After all, it is my money," Elizabeth snapped and then sighed. "We are all very tired. I truly understand what you are going through, both with medicine and your faith."

Astrid leaned forward to argue but then dropped her hands.

Elizabeth continued. "It's always harder near the time of decision, but think about this. How can more training *not* help? It makes us better equipped to win more often. It's only for six months, September through February. Take this opportunity, and if you are still struggling afterwards we'll talk then."

Too tired to argue, Astrid changed the subject. "Do you want first watch, or do you want me to take it?"

"Ingeborg said she'd stay until midnight. Then she'll come and wake you. I'll take the three o'clock."

"She's not going to die, is she?"

Elizabeth snorted. "Only God knows that, but I don't think so. For a while I was afraid of cholera, but I talked with young Mr. Brunderson, and he said there was no mention of cholera on the ship, or they would not have been allowed to dock. Typhoid would have been handled the same."

"Pneumonia?"

"Probably the results of dysentery of some type. The way the shipping companies treat their passengers in steerage is beyond reprehensible. Crammed together like they are, it's a miracle more people don't die in passage. Did your mother ever tell you about her voyage?"

Astrid shook her head and brushed away a blood-thirsty mosquito. If the breeze were a little stronger, it would drive the pests away. "I'll ask her sometime. She doesn't like to talk much about the hard times, you know. Just that God lived up to His word and brought them through."

"Thorliff has shared all his memories with me. Your mor and Tante Kaaren are indomitable women. I don't think I could have ever lived through all they did and on top of that be such godly women."

"Mor says we are all becoming that."

"Well, today was surely one of those dark valleys. But He brought us through."

"But the baby died." The words lay between them.

"You have to let it go, you know. This is God's problem, not yours. No matter how learned we become and how hard we try, life and death are always His province. You do your best and leave the outcome in His hands. Your mother taught me that. She says God taught her."

Astrid pushed herself to her feet. "I'm going to bed. Can I get you anything?"

"No, thank you. Good night. Make sure you come wake me at three."

"Of course."

"If the crisis comes earlier, ring the bell."

Which crisis? Astrid wondered as she climbed the stairs. *The patients' battle or mine?* And she couldn't ask Mor—not now. She hadn't seen that look on her mother's face since they lost all the stock. As she tumbled across the bed, Elizabeth's question ticked in her mind like the downstairs clock. Was it the medical training she didn't want to go toward or the flashing dark eyes she didn't want to say good-bye to again?

12

The clacking train wheels hauled her closer and closer to Chicago.

"Supper is being served in the dining car." The conductor paused beside her. "You are Dr. Bjorklund, are you not?"

Yes . . . no? What? "I am Miss Bjorklund, ja, er yes." Elizabeth had warned her that to those outside of Blessing, she was not yet a doctor. Her certificate would come from Dr. Morganstein on the completion of her studies in Chicago. If she managed to complete her studies there, that is. Every day since Vernon Baxter died, she'd questioned whether becoming a doctor was the purpose of her life. And then Anna's baby died too.

"I have heard good things about you. The folks of Blessing are indeed fortunate to have two capable doctors in such a small town. Farther west doctors are few and far between."

Please, not another mission field. The day before she left, she'd received a letter from Reverend Ted Schuman in Africa. He'd managed to include another plea for her to listen to God's calling, and if He wanted her in Africa, there was need of her services. The stories he told. The thought of all the travel needed to get to his mission was scary enough, let alone the horrors of the medical needs there. She stared out the window to see shallow rolling hills planted in wheat or miles of tall green corn. For one used to pancake-flat land, this was some different. As were all the towns. Grain elevators dotted the land crisscrossed by railroad tracks and roads. Tall oak and elm trees shaded houses, while every barn had a silo to store the chopped corn.

The closer they drew to Chicago, the tighter grew her dread. She should have stayed home where she belonged. While Elizabeth had planned to come with her, she had two babies due any day, and one of the mothers was ensconced at the surgery to keep her off her feet. And since Mor was still nursing Freda and Anna, they decided that Elizabeth was needed more at Blessing. Which left Astrid with far too much time to think.

Astrid tried studying one of her textbooks—anything to keep away the dark monster that seemed to have taken up residence just on the periphery of her vision. She was sure that if she turned her head quickly enough, she would see it and would be devoured by its slathering jaws. She'd never known such fear and doubt, and the worst part was she'd not been able to tell anyone about it.

The black dots on the page danced before her eyes, making her feel nauseated.

She thought back on the going-away party her friends had organized to give her a happy send-off.

"After all," Sophie reminded her, "you'll only be gone a few months, and you'll be so busy the time will fly by." She dropped her voice to a whisper. "And I'll make sure that no one tries flirting with Mr. Landsverk."

Joshua Landsverk, the first man Astrid had hoped would be more than just a friend. After all, she had plenty of male friends, but this one was different. This time her heart picked up speed every time she saw him, and now she understood why Ellie had never considered anyone but Andrew and was willing to wait for him for years if necessary.

Surely the look in Joshua's eyes when he smiled at her meant he felt the same way. The girls teased her about him, and even Thorliff mentioned what a good, dependable man he was.

She'd tried to insist she should stay and help Mor, but she said Freda only needed time to get strong again and Anna the same. Rest, North Dakota sunshine, and good food were all they needed to give God time to work the healing Mor was sure was happening.

For the first time in her life, Astrid didn't feel she could talk out her turmoil with her mother. How would she understand that God refused to hear Astrid's prayers? And so she had given up praying. He had let two of her patients die when she'd been fighting to save them. A young man with his adult life right in front of him and a baby who never had a chance at life at all.

"Next stop, Chicago. Everyone will be disembarking there. About fifteen minutes to Chicago." The conductor stopped to answer a question from the people several seats ahead of her. Outside the dirty window were houses right next to each other. As the train drew closer to the station, the buildings rose taller, some for housing, some factories. Brick walls blackened by years of soot, iron steps down the outside of some of the buildings, wash hanging on lines strung between buildings. Did people actually live in these filthy places?

How will I bear this? Six months. Surely I can put up with anything for six months. I will be so busy at the hospital, I won't have time to be homesick. That's what Elizabeth promised. Maybe I'd be better off in Africa. But that would mean saying good-bye to Joshua forever. It was hard enough this time. He had smiled and said he would be there when she returned. Nothing more. No pledges. But he seemed to care, or was that just hopeful feelings on her part? She clasped her hands against her roiling stomach as the train screeched to a stop at a huge station. When she stepped off the train, the smells of coal smoke, engine grease, and hot metal assaulted her nostrils. Walking with the other passengers down the long wooden platform, she kept her eyes on the person in front of her. Surely evil hid in the dark spaces above them capped by a roof.

Dr. Morganstein's letter said for her to go to the main depot entrance, that someone would be there holding a sign to meet her. He would take care of getting her luggage and take her to the hospital. He who? She felt like clapping her hands over her ears to muffle some of the cacophony that assailed her. This was worse than harvest. At least when they shut the steam engine down, quiet reigned. Not here. The majority of the crowd moved toward glass doors with multipaned windows that arched upward for two stories, so she let the force carry her along. It was a good thing someone else was getting her trunk, because she had no idea where to go for it.

Hoping for fresher air once she made it outside, she found the heat, humidity, and smells were equally as bad, if not worse. Pigeons fluttered about on the sidewalk, pecking at bits on the concrete and flapping away from hurrying feet. Perspiration trickled down her spine and neck. Where was the fan she'd brought on Elizabeth's recommendation?

Look for the sign with my name on it. The thought jerked her focus up from the sidewalks. Had someone been waiting inside for her? She stared around, trying to locate her driver. Someone bumped into her and mumbled something that did not sound like an apology.

She eased her way back toward the wall and out of the main stream of traffic. No one was holding a sign that she could see. She turned and pulled open a door to return to the inside of the station. Would she be reprimanded for standing on one of the wooden seats with a curved back?

Why did I ever come to this place? She thought to the envelope in her reticule that contained money and instructions on how to get to the hospital should some unforeseen circumstance keep her driver from retrieving her. But what about her trunk? *I want to go home.* Tears burned the backs of her eyes and made her nose start to run.

Astrid Bjorklund, pull yourself together! Sniveling never did anyone any good. If Grace can travel all the way to New York by herself, and she can't hear, what do you have to bellyache about? Now, just sit yourself down on one of the benches and give this some thought. Taking out her handkerchief, she dabbed at her neck and in front of her ears. *And find your fan. That's right. Sit down, take a deep breath, and find your fan.* She did as she ordered and, with the slight cooling from the moving air, thanks to the fan, considered what to do.

An elderly man with gray hair curling at his collar came through the door, catching her attention. He held up a sign with *Bjorklund* written in large black letters. A wave of gratitude washed over her so powerfully she slumped against the seat back. She was saved. When he swung her way, she raised her gloved hand to catch his attention. *He looks about as relieved as I feel grateful,* she thought as she stood and picked up her carpetbag and book bag. He crossed the marble floor and bowed slightly.

"Miss Bjorklund?"

"Yes."

"Please forgive me. There was an accident in the street, and I had to go out several blocks around it. I thought sure I had left early enough. Have you been waiting long?"

"No. I am just glad you are here." She pulled a ticket from her reticule. "This is for my trunk. I didn't know where to get it."

"You weren't supposed to. You wait right here, and I'll fetch that. You have only one trunk?"

"Yes, sir." She indicated the two bags at her feet. "And these."

"Good. I'll be right back." He started off and turned back. "Pardon me, miss, my name is MacCallister. Most everyone calls me Mac."

"Yes, sir, Mr. MacCallister."

"Just sit down and be comfortable. I know that traveling makes one weary."

Astrid did as he suggested. With this worry gone, she watched the other travelers in peace. And what an unending stream to view. Everyone from tiny babes in arms to small children to an old man in a chair with wheels and a robe over his knees paraded by. She'd seen pictures of wheelchairs in catalogs, but they were more astonishing in real life. No one in Blessing had a baby buggy either, but she saw several in the crowd. A young mother with a crying baby sat across from her, while a small girl, index finger in her mouth, clung to the woman's skirt. When a man came, he scooped the little girl up in his arms and strode off, hardly waiting for the wife to gather the baby and follow.

How rude. He could have taken one of the woman's carpetbags at least. Astrid glared at the disappearing man, definitely not a gentleman, and took her gaze elsewhere. Only a few minutes had passed when MacCallister showed up, followed by one of the luggage handlers, Astrid's trunk balanced on his right shoulder.

"I have a conveyance outside. Let me take those bags for you, and we'll be on our way." He led the way, and within minutes they were loaded and driving down the street, dodging traffic—human, horse-drawn, and machine.

Astrid fought to take it all in, but the sights and sounds were too overwhelming to be absorbed in one trip. The trolley car seemed to have the right-of-way. While she'd seen Hjelmer's automobile in Blessing, and Elizabeth had talked about purchasing one, it seemed every third person owned one here. And they were all driving them at once. Sometimes closing one's eyes was the better part of defense.

Though Mr. MacCallister called over his shoulder the identities of all the landmarks she saw, it was too much to take in. The old fable of country mouse in the city most certainly fit her. To think that Elizabeth had talked of Chicago with delight and had promised Astrid good memories and great adventures. The best adventure would be to turn tail and run back home.

"Here we are," MacCallister said at long last. He stopped the horse in front of a cut-stone building that reached three stories into the air and was really two buildings joined together. City grime blackened the stone walls, but the name, *Alfred Morganstein Hospital for Women,* cut in the stone above the double-glass doors, still stood out. Underneath it were the words *Under his wings you will find refuge.* Astrid recognized that as being part of a familiar psalm, and hoped it would calm her fears. Refuge. This hospital was indeed a place of refuge. Elizabeth had said so. The ten steps up to the door were divided in two by a wider step protected by a railing on either side. A concrete ramp angled out from one side and, after an L-shaped turn, ended at the front door also. Off to the side, a portico, with an *Emergency Entrance* sign hanging from it, covered a driveway wide enough for a horse-drawn ambulance.

MacCallister climbed down from the high seat, opened the side door, and raised his hand to assist her in stepping out. "This might be the last of courtesy you'll receive for a while, so you'd best enjoy it. Once inside, you'll find everyone is too busy to wait on manners. You go on up the stairs, and I'll bring in your trunk."

Astrid did as he said, trying to blow out her terror with a breath on each step. By the time she reached the top, she sucked in a final breath, held it, and then let it all out. She straightened her spine, firmed up her jaw, and pulled the door open.

"Can I help you, miss?" said a woman from behind a desk in the vestibule.

"I . . . I'm Astrid Bjorklund, here to attend training."

"Oh yes, Miss Bjorklund. Doctor said to let her know as soon as you arrived." She stood and came around the battle-scarred wooden desk. "I'm Mrs. Hancock. I'll show you the way."

A woman's scream from somewhere down the long hall gave Astrid a start.

"We have several women in heavy labor," Mrs. Hancock explained. "Sometimes it gets a mite noisy around here. Especially when it is a full moon. More babies born then than at any other time." She took one of Astrid's bags and motioned to her to follow. "Did you find that where you came from?"

"We didn't usually have more than one birth at a time, so it would be hard to say." She was already learning that Mrs. Hancock might appear elderly, but keeping up with her was something else.

She stopped in front of a closed walnut door and tapped before opening. "Miss Bjorklund has arrived," she said as she sailed on in, ushering Astrid right after her. Astrid caught a glimpse of tall windows hung with plain white drapes pulled to the sides. They proceeded through another door at the order to "Come in," and Astrid caught her first glimpse of Elizabeth's hero, Dr. Althea Morganstein, sitting behind a cherrywood desk big enough to serve dinner for eight. White hair crowned a face whose lines deepened with her smile. She rose and came around the desk.

Astrid felt she should curtsy as in the presence of royalty. This was *the* Dr. Morganstein, by whom legends were created, according to Elizabeth. She extended her hand to meet that of the doctor, who then clasped her other hand over Astrid's.

"Ah, my dear, I have been looking forward to this day for a long time." She looked Astrid up and down, smiling and nodding all the while. "I feel as though I've known you for the last several years. Did Elizabeth tell you how I tried to keep her here? She would have made a fine teacher." She chuckled. "Well, I guess I will find out what kind of a teacher she is."

Or what a terrible student I am. The thought sucked the joy out of the moment. *I have to do well, for Elizabeth's sake if not my own.* This was not a new thought but likely the one that forced her to get on that train in spite of her insides screaming that she should have stayed in Blessing, that something terrible would happen if she left.

Dr. Morganstein drew her over to sit in one of the wing chairs, while she took the other. "Now, tell me how your trip was."

"Fine. Longer than I thought it to be."

"Your first time away from home?"

"Yes, ma'am. I thought to go to Grand Forks, but Elizabeth insisted I come here. She said there was nowhere else I would get the training I need."

"I am glad she still feels that way. Our program here has changed in the years since she graduated, but I can guarantee you will have plenty of surgery time. I have set up your exams to begin tomorrow morning, right after breakfast. Mrs. Hancock will show you to your room. You will be sharing with an older woman who is finished with her surgery rotation and will be starting obstetrics. I hear you've had plenty of experience with that."

Astrid lowered her eyes and nodded, forcing her fingers to quit twining themselves together and laid them in her lap.

Dr. Morganstein leaned forward and covered Astrid's hands with one of her own. "We all suffer when we lose a baby, but we must let go, knowing that the child is now with almighty God and there was nothing more we could have done."

But what if there was? Astrid clamped her teeth together and made herself nod, as if she agreed. "I take it you've spoken with Elizabeth since I left home?"

"I have. She is very concerned about you. Much like a mother hen with her first chick leaving the nest."

Tell her. She ignored the voice.

"Oh my, Mrs. Hancock, why didn't you remind me? I said we'd have tea as soon as Astrid arrived. Be a dear and ring for it, please. And you must join us. Astrid needs to feel she has someone here she can talk to."

Within moments a tea tray arrived, and Mrs. Hancock poured.

Astrid took her cup and saucer, allowing one lump and milk. "Thank you." As she lifted the cup to her mouth, the fragrance of Ceylon black tea made her inhale again.

"Ah. There is something relaxing about tea," the doctor said, "while coffee just propels one to get going and keep on. Today we'll have tea, and I'm sure you'll learn where the coffeepot is kept refreshed around the clock."

Dr. Morganstein set her cup in its saucer. "Now, tell me about little Inga. From what I hear, she is a bit of a handful."

"We sometimes call her Queen Inga because she likes to run things, especially her father. My brother is enthralled with his little girl. She gets her cousin Carl in so much trouble. He even fell in the barn and broke his arm. She forgets he is younger and not quite as capable as she. When we need a laugh, we go find Inga. The other day I found her reading a book to him."

"She can read already?"

"Not really, but she knows the story so well, it seems she can."

At a knock at the door Mrs. Hancock rose and hurried out.

Dr. Morganstein sighed. "Another emergency, I suppose. They try to keep me from rushing out to help these days, and I know there are sufficient doctors around to cover things, but . . ." She shook her head slightly and used the tip of her lace handkerchief to dab at her nose.

Settling herself a bit straighter, she took in a deep breath and focused back on Astrid. "Enjoy your first day here, my dear. Starting tomorrow, Dr. Barlow, one of our instructors, will show you around. Your uniforms will be in your room, and you will be referred to as Dr. Bjorklund. There are ten in the surgery rotation with you. Elizabeth said that although you've done surgeries, you have not dissected a cadaver. Since that is the best way to learn the intricacies of the human body, we will make sure you get adequate experience in that. It is in the first year's curriculum, so you will be working with our new students. We have a young man here who is a bit older but comes from your part of the country. He is half Sioux and half white and insists that his name is Red Hawk. I insist that he be called Dr. Hawk.

"I have set aside an entire week for you to go through all the exams. I know this will take tremendous effort on your part, but if there are areas in which you need more classwork, we will attend to those, along with the surgery rotation. Do you have any questions?"

Astrid shook her head. What would they do if she just slipped out and returned to the station and took the train home? She hid behind her teacup, swallowed the last drop, and set the cup down. She could not disappoint Elizabeth like that, no matter how uncertain about her future she was. If she couldn't handle it all, it was best to find out now.

13

BLESSING, NORTH DAKOTA

I miss Astrid."

The sheets flapping on the line held no answer. Ingeborg felt like shouting to the heavens, *Lord, bring my daughter home safe.* But she knew Astrid was where she was supposed to be—wasn't she? Sliding the last clothespin over the end of the folded sheet, she picked up the clothes basket and returned to the house, stopping with one foot on the bottom step. Why was she so fluttered about this? Flustered was the proper word, but she felt she was like the sheets, snapping in the wind. Were it not for the clothespins, she'd go fluttering off, whipped and tossed by the wind.

"Lord, I thank you that you are my wire, my post, and you are pinning me in place. Let me cling to you, for you are never changing. You send the sun and the wind, the birds and the butterflies. Thank you for all the land you have given us." She shaded her eyes with her hand and searched the fields in the distance to see where the men were finishing the haying. Wheat rippled like waves in the wind, the color changing from green to yellow and on toward gold as harvest approached. A shimmery light green kissed the oat fields as the grain started to head out, leading toward the yellow to come.

Off in the distance one of the high-stacked hay wagons neared Andrew's barn, ready for the hay to be swooped up into the haymow. Haakan said they'd have to start stacking hay outside because all the other barns were already full.

Surely they would have a letter from Astrid any day now. After all, she'd been gone a week.

"Ingeborg, would you like me to make the pies for supper?" Freda asked from the doorway.

"If you feel up to it. I have one more load to rinse and wring, and then the washing will be finished."

"You keep babying me like this, and I'll turn into a fat toad."

"I doubt that. The canned apples are down in the cellar. I checked and the strawberries are done for."

"The raspberries made wonderful jam. I thought with all the eggs we could make a jelly roll for a treat and use the skimmings."

"What a wonderful idea."

The ringing telephone made Ingeborg climb the rest of the steps and enter the house. The stove heat smacked her in the face when she opened the screen door. Crossing the kitchen, she lifted the earpiece from the wooden box that hung on the wall.

"Hello."

"Ingeborg, this is Elizabeth. Thelma is making meatballs for supper, and I thought you could all come here before the town meeting."

"I'll ask Haakan when he comes in for dinner. I don't see why not.

We're mostly talking about the hospital proposal and plans tonight, aren't we?"

"As far as I know. Thorliff has some rough plans drawn up, and I've prepared a report on how many cases we've handled through our surgery and how we see the need for a full-service hospital. Or at least the beginning of one."

"I know we discussed it at the last quilting meeting. So many don't want to take on any more debt, but with the flour mill doing so well, we can funnel those monies into more community services, like the hospital."

"I think Thorliff is going to suggest that those who want to could buy bonds."

"Really? He didn't mention that here."

"He was talking with somebody somewhere who said his community had done that."

Ingeborg rubbed her chin. "We've come a long way."

"We have. I'm hoping we can encourage a dentist to come to town too. Office space at the hospital might be a drawing card."

"Ah, my dear, you do dream big."

"Well, if Kaaren's school grows the way we think it will," Elizabeth said, "we'll need more services here to take care of people."

"I know. But remember, it wasn't that long ago that I was the only person here with any medical background at all."

"You could look at it this way: See what I started."

Elizabeth's chuckle made Ingeborg laugh. "Uff da, such goings on."

"We do live in exciting times. Anna didn't come for her appointment."

"Anna doesn't want to come for anything. Any suggestions?"

"We have to get her out."

"Kaaren sent the children over to Ellie's," Ingeborg said. "All Solem can talk about is going back to Norway."

"How can they afford that?"

"They can't. And Freda has no desire to go back."

"Have you heard from Astrid?"

"No." *But I have a bad feeling, and I don't know why. Lord, still my heart. I know you can take care of her in Chicago too.*

"She'll be okay. Althea would contact me if she thought something was wrong."

"Ja, I know. You want me to bring anything for supper?"

"No, we'll be fine."

Ingeborg said good-bye and set the black earpiece back in the pronged holder. How quickly they had become dependent on this new instrument. Thorliff had a crew out planting telephone poles so that all the farms could be connected to town and each other. The switchboard, run primarily by Gerald Valders, had filled so they'd put in a new panel. The men were talking about one day needing a second person on the switchboard. Deborah had finally agreed to take one of the daily twelve-hour shifts, and while Mrs. Valders could fill in, they really needed another person part time. Who'd have ever thought they would have more jobs than people to fill them?

She turned and told Freda to skip the pies and go ahead with the jelly roll. They would use the leftover gingerbread with applesauce for dinner. Back out on the porch to finish the wash, she marveled at how fast she could get the wash done these days. Thanks to Penny, who'd brought in washing machines like she had the Singer sewing machines and made all the women's lives easier. No more rubbing one's fingers raw on the scrub boards. She lifted the last of the work pants from the rinse water and carefully fed them into the wringer with one hand while turning the crank with the other.

"How about a cup of coffee?" Freda asked from the doorway.

"That sounds good. Let me hang these first, and then I'll drain the rinse water onto the roses." A hose connected to the bottom of the square tub could be opened and none of the water wasted. Not that she'd ever wasted any, carrying all the used household water out to her flowers and the garden when it needed it. So far this year they'd had just enough rain. She turned the spigot and hoisted the clothes basket up on her hip. Nearly eleven already, and the men would be in at twelve or when they heard the clanging triangle.

How she loved wash day when the sun shone. The wind dried the clothes about as fast as she could hang them, larks trilled from the fields or swooped and dove overhead, scattering notes like iridescent flower petals.

Nothing smelled better than linens and clothes right off the line.

"What did Dr. Elizabeth say about Anna?" Freda asked in Norwegian, since her growing English vocabulary was not sufficient for nonessential words yet.

"She's concerned," Ingeborg said as she sat at the table.

"Anna needs to take care of the children she has and her husband. You are all being too soft on her."

Ingeborg sighed. "The children are well cared for."

"True, but not by their mother. Since Grace came home, she has taken over all the children."

"She does love the little children. She says younger ones like ours here are so much fun after all her school-age students. And these can hear, so she gets more practice in speaking."

"I do not know how she has learned to talk. I didn't know deaf people could learn to do that."

Ingeborg took a sip of her coffee and a bite out of her applesauce cookie. "I know. She has worked so hard."

"And Anna . . ." Freda shook her head. "I know she had a bad time. I lost two or three babies through the years. You are sad, but you get up and keep going." She stared out over the fields. "To not like it here, I do not understand either her or my son. They will never have anything like this in Norway."

"Does Solem really want to go back, or is he wanting to do that for Anna?"

Freda shrugged. "Who's to know? He does not want to talk to me about it. Does he think I forced him to come with me? I thought I was giving him a gift, a new life with a chance to own land."

"Has he thought of going farther west to homestead? There isn't much land left to buy around here."

"The only money he has is what he has earned here. As you know, that trip took everything we could save." She propped her elbows on the table, her round face crowned by a circle of braided hair, concern carving deeper lines from nose to the corners of her mouth and between her eyebrows.

Ingeborg remembered her as the laughing girl from their summer weeks in the high mountain meadow saeters, where they took care of the cows and turned the milk into cheese.

"Does Gilbert feel the same too?"

"No, he loves it here. As do the little ones. I will cut the curds this afternoon on that last setting of milk. You want the whey for the hogs?"

"Ja. The chickens like it too. And Andrew will take home some of the full cans for the animals at his place."

"I am so amazed at all you have managed to do in the years since you left Norway. If only my husband had been willing to come when you wrote so long ago."

"God has indeed blessed us, but it has never been easy. I sometimes dreamed of going home, especially when the wind was howling like wolves in a blizzard. When we lived in the soddy, I thought of Mor's snug house, with the animals sheltered right below us, not across the yard in the barn. You wait. This winter the men will again string ropes on posts to get to the barn without getting lost."

"Uff da. You have written of those, and I found it hard to picture. You realize your letters were passed around for everyone in Valdres to read, not just our family but anyone who visited. Johann Bjorklund kept the family land, but it can barely support him. I think he is sometimes tempted to sell out and come over too."

Ingeborg shook her head. "All this talk of winter makes me shiver, even in this heat. I'll make dumplings for the stew when I bring in the dry things." She smiled at her cousin. "Back to your worry about Anna. I have an idea."

———

THAT NIGHT AFTER the town meeting, Haakan yawned and stretched as they prepared for bed. "That hospital won't happen overnight, you know."

Ingeborg *tsk*ed as she pulled her nightdress over her head. "Nobody believes it will." Sitting herself down on the edge of the bed, she unplaited her hair, running her fingers through the wavy strands, then picked up her brush and started her one hundred strokes.

"It will cost more than they are estimating, even if we do most of the work ourselves."

"Like a barn raising, you mean?"

"Ja, with all of us donating our labor to assist a building crew. None of us have the training to put up a building like that. We'd have to hire an overseer."

Ingeborg nodded. Haakan really believed in the hospital, but he always had to work through things in his own time and way. Talking it over with her seemed to help. "How would it be so different than building a barn? Two stories but with many rooms on two sides of a hall instead of one big one for the haymow?"

Haakan flipped back the sheet and lay down, locking his hands behind his head. "I hate to see us go into debt for this building. We did for the flour mill, but we knew that would bring in revenue from the beginning. This is far more expensive, and who can afford to pay the prices they will need to charge the patients in order to pay for the building?"

"You have a point there, and you said it well at the meeting." She put down her brush and rebraided her hair in one loose plait. "Not to change the subject, but has Solem mentioned anything about his wife?"

"No, not a word. But I can tell something is weighing on his mind. He's a quiet man, but he's frowning much of the time."

"Well, be ready. We are going to take Anna outside whether she wants to or not."

"You'll carry or drag her?"

"If it comes to that."

Haakan rolled onto his side and patted his wife's shoulder. "Leave it to you, my Inge. Anna doesn't have a chance."

Ingeborg listened as Haakan slipped into sleep, a little puff coming on every exhale. *Lord God, I have to believe this idea comes from you, so I ask you to go before us and prepare the way. Give us the right words, the love that can come only from you. Please heal her heart and fill her with love for the two children she has.* She reminded herself to call Pastor Solberg in the morning and then tumbled into the well called sleep.

————

AFTER BREAKFAST AND calling Pastor Solberg on the telephone,
Ingeborg sprinkled the clothes that were to be ironed that day while
Freda cleaned up the kitchen. Today was Kaaren's turn to fix dinner
for the men, so after mixing and kneading bread and setting it to rise,
she poured two cups of coffee.

"We are going over to Kaaren's to get Anna."

"Get Anna?" Freda's eyebrow lifted.

"That's right."

The clop of trotting horsehoofs brought her to her feet and the
window. John Solberg was dismounting to tie his horse at the gate
to the fenced yard. After all these years, Haakan and Andrew had
fenced in the yard to protect her flowers from marauding cows; not
that they got out often, but one cow could decimate the tasty flowers
in minutes, and what it didn't eat, it stomped.

"Good. I figured he'd come."

"Ingeborg, what are we doing?"

"Come and see."

The three of them walked across the small pasture, as they called
the stretch of field between the two houses.

"Care to enlighten me on how we are going to do this?"

"Put her in a chair and carry her, if we have to."

"Down all those stairs?"

"That might be enough to get her up, don't you think?"

"She is so weak." Freda rubbed the top of one finger and tongued
her lower lip.

"I know. That is why we have to get her out in the sunshine."

Like an advancing army they strode up the steps of the Knutsons'
house and into the south-facing door of the school wing.

Kaaren met them with Samuel, who at sixteen was fast growing into man size. "I've been praying this works."

"What do we do if it doesn't?" Freda asked.

"We aren't even considering that."

They marched up the stairs, continuing the advance into the bedroom where Anna lay curled in bed, the shades drawn at the window.

"Anna." Ingeborg shook the woman's thin shoulder.

Anna mumbled and blinked bleary eyes.

"You must get up now and come with us."

Anna shook her head. "No. Go away."

Please, Lord. Ingeborg glanced at the unused chair by the window, then back at the bed. While picking up a corner of the bedsheet, she nodded and kept nodding as she indicated Kaaren, Samuel, and Pastor Solberg to each do the same. On three, they lifted the corners, worked their way closer to the now whimpering woman, and hoisted her off the bed.

"No! No!" Anna's shriek was too weak to carry even to the bedroom door.

Out the door they went and, with the men in front, carried her down the stairs and out onto the porch, where the porch posts sent shadows and the honeysuckle vines lent a sweet fragrance. A cot stood waiting, padded with a feather bed and a stack of pillows.

Gently they settled Anna on the cot, and Pastor Solberg took the chair closest to her head.

Anna had not ceased shaking her head, one bony fingertip touching her cheek. She lay curled in on herself, like the newborn she had lost.

Ingeborg brushed away the tear that leaked down her cheek. *Lord, I know this is for the best, but . . .*

"Can I go now?" Samuel asked.

"Yes, thank you, son. Before you go, though, would you make sure the woodbox is full? We have beans to can today after dinner." Kaaren glanced at the others. "I thought we could snap beans while we visit."

"Of course."

"Everyone gather round and let's pray." Solberg laid his hand on Anna's head, and the others did the same. In spite of Anna's attempt to shrink into the bedding, each found a place to lay her hands, and they closed their eyes.

Ingeborg inhaled the nectar of honeysuckle and exhaled, letting her tight shoulders drop back down where they belonged. So far, so good. Pastor Solberg's words danced with a robin's song, carried aloft by the sun, which peeked between the leaves that whispered a lullaby.

"Heavenly Father, we thank you for this glorious morning and for this place of healing. Thank you for Anna and her family and the care you have taken of them and us. Thank you that you have said to come to you all who are weary and heavy laden, that you will give us rest, not only for our bodies but for our souls. And Lord, Anna needs your comfort and healing. She has been grievously wounded, and we are fearful that without your healing grace, she will slip away. Her husband needs her here, as do her children. So we ask for your mighty hand to beat back the terrors and bring healing to her heart, mind, body, and soul. Fill our dear Anna with your love, your comfort, and your peace."

One whimper followed another.

Ingeborg picked up the prayer. "Breathe strength into her body and break the dam of sorrow that is holding Anna captive. Free her, Lord God, as only you can do."

Another whimper punctuated the gentle silence.

"God, I don't know how to pray like this." Freda choked on her words.

Ingeborg laid her other hand on Freda's shoulder and rubbed gently.

"You're doing fine." Pastor Solberg's voice wove baritone into the morning symphony.

Freda lifted her apron to mop her tears.

Lack of words did not a silence make as they basked together.

"God, forgive me," Freda prayed, gulping between words. "I thought I was doing the best for my family."

"God's Word says, 'If we confess our sins, he is faithful and just to forgive us our sins, and to cleanse us from all unrighteousness.' So, daughter of the King," the pastor pronounced, "you are forgiven, in the name of the Father and the Son and the Holy Ghost."

All three women were using their aprons as mops.

Ingeborg glanced down at Anna's face. A slight smile fluttered her lips. Her body had loosened bone by bone so that one hand lay open instead of clenched in a fist.

"And everyone said amen."

And they did, blinking and sniffing.

"I'll bring out the tea." Kaaren patted Anna's hip and floated back into the house.

An hour later, amid the snap of beans and gentle conversation, Anna started to cry. Single tears leaked first and, with the release, built into an outpouring of the sorrow, hurt, anger, and fear that had been dammed inside since she held her dead infant. The women took turns mopping her face, holding her, and murmuring comfort as if she were a child again.

Ingeborg sent her silent praises heavenward as she snapped beans, took her turn with the grieving woman, and watched Freda's amazement at what was happening. She had yet to learn that when one prayed for someone else, God frequently tiptoed in and healed the praying heart also.

When Anna finally fell asleep, this time her face smoothed free of the lines that had fought to become a permanent part of her, Ingeborg motioned to Freda, and the two of them strolled back across the field.

"Well, I never." Freda shook her head gently, as if not wanting to disturb the new thought and experience she'd just gone through. "Are you sure this God you all love so and serve is the same one we had in Norway?"

Ingeborg chuckled. "I am sure. Perhaps we have learned how much we need Him because of the hardships we have endured here. And we have Pastor Solberg, who has taught us what grace really means. We just saw God's grace in action. No matter how often I see Him work in marvelous ways, I am still amazed. And grateful."

"Ja, grateful. Thank you. I think my Solem will be much more content now."

"I hope so." *At least he will have his wife back if what we experienced is only the foretaste of what is coming, which I have all faith that it is. I wish Astrid had been here to be part of this.* That thought surprised her. Did Astrid need healing too?

14

Joshua stared at the metal blades lying on the ground, fanned around the central gears of the windmill head. They'd drilled the well, thanks to the horse-powered auger, and the frame itself was halfway up. Raising the top would be the final stage.

"Hey, Joshua," Trygve called down from the top of the ladder, "we're ready for the next batch."

Joshua waved and nodded. Ever since they'd rigged up the pulley system, carrying the lumber to the next level had been easier. While they were building with wood as yet, Hjelmer was talking about building out of steel soon. As someone had told him, Hjelmer was always trying out the latest inventions. Joshua looped the chain around the pallet that held the braces he had already cut to fit, tested it to make sure it was solid, and led the team out to pull up the load. The pulley and chains creaked and groaned as if someone were torturing them, and the load lifted into the air, swaying some with the motion. He watched as they unloaded it onto the boards that had been laid across the struts and then he backed the horses to lower the wooden pallet. Until he'd come up with this rig, they'd been carrying the wood up the ladder. The man on the ground had sawed while another one had nailed.

For safety's sake he banished all thoughts of Astrid from his mind while working. And since they worked until dark in the long evenings, the only thinking time he had was on the trips back and forth for supper and sleep. That's when thoughts of Astrid took over. She'd been right when she'd said she probably wouldn't have time to write much. He'd received a note from her a few days after she arrived in Chicago, and that was it.

The woman at the farmhouse clanged the iron triangle, signaling that dinner was ready. Gilbert Brunderson and Trygve slid down the ladder, their feet barely touching the treads.

"One more level, and we set the machinery," Trygve said, wiping his forehead with a grimy handkerchief.

"I think we should bring Mr. Sam out with us to do that," Gilbert said. "Four pairs of hands will come in right handy."

Joshua nodded. He'd been thinking the same thing. The head on this windmill was heavier than the others due to the longer blades.

"My neighbor off to the south came by and admired the mill," the farmer told them, his hands shoved in his overall pockets as he eyed the windmill.

Joshua nodded for him to continue. "Does he want me to come by and talk with him?"

"Wouldn't hurt none. His well went dry last summer. Can't get too deep hand digging." He led them to the washbasin set up on the porch. When they'd finished cleaning up, the men headed indoors, where the wife had the food dished up.

"Have some more," the missus said when the plates were nearing empty. "I got more on the stove."

The men nodded, and the bowls and platters made it around the table again. Sometimes one ate more because the food was so good, but sometimes one did so to be polite. This place was not like the boardinghouse or the Bjorklunds'.

"Thank you, ma'am." The men took turns saying the words before they headed back out. Stepping out onto the porch, they drew their hats tighter down on their heads and pulled leather gloves from their rear pockets.

"Lookin' mighty fine," the farmer said from behind them. "Matilda is making noises like now we can pipe water into the house too. Ain't that the craziest thing?"

"They sell hand pumps for the house at the mercantile in Blessing. Running water would make her life a lot easier."

"What would she do with all the extra time? Leastways she won't have to crank it up out of the well no more."

Joshua and Trygve swapped looks. *Why, she might have time to cook better food,* Joshua thought but kept his comments from his face. One thing certain, when he had a wife, he planned to make sure she had house machinery like men had farm machinery. Or like the drill press back at the shop in Blessing that had an engine to run it.

That evening the crew left a bit early since they wanted to hoist the head first thing in the morning when they were all fresh and had another set of hands. He'd thought to ask the farmer if he wanted to help them but thought the better of it. From the looks of the farm and the house, the man lacked some in work habits.

"Pa would have something to say about that fellow." Trygve slapped the reins, and the team picked up a trot.

"Your pa sets a mighty fine example," Joshua said. "No places cleaner and prettier than the Knutsons' and the Bjorklunds'."

"Andrew's too," Trygve added. "Someday when I get married, I'll do like he did. I think. But sometimes I dream of homesteading myself. Maybe head to western North Dakota somewhere. I've heard about the Badlands, and I'd like to see them." He turned to Gilbert sitting in the wagon bed. "You ever thought of going west to homestead?"

Gilbert nodded. "Ja, I think on it."

"Be smart like those first Bjorklund brothers were and make sure you have someone to start out with. From the stories you told me, the two working together made a mighty big lot of difference." Joshua looked over at Trygve.

"Ja, you get Mor and Tante Ingeborg talking about the early days, and it's hard to believe what they went through. Both their husbands dying like that. Mor said she wanted to die too, but Tante Ingeborg wouldn't let her. You know what the winters can be like here."

"That's one of the reasons I don't want to be a farmer, especially not here. But the grasshoppers took my father's crop in Iowa last year, so there is always something, no matter where you settle." Sometimes Joshua felt bad that he didn't speak Norwegian. While Gilbert tried to follow their conversations, he most likely missed out on a lot.

"You know, I was thinking. We could set up the cook shack for a place to sleep when we get farther away from Blessing. We wouldn't have to camp under the stars or drive so far back each day." Trygve braced his elbows on his knees, the lines loose in his hands. "They'll be using that for harvesting pretty soon."

"True. Maybe it is time to build another one."

Joshua looked over his shoulder to the young man riding beside him. "You have a good head on your shoulders. I'll mention it to Hjelmer. Or you can."

"Who's going to help you after harvest starts? You know I'll be going with the threshing crew."

Joshua shrugged. "No idea. It all depends on if we have more to do."

"Oh, Onkel Hjelmer will be bringing back lots of orders."

After they started drilling this well, Hjelmer had left on horseback to call on farmers. He had pictures drawn of the new windmills, and a photographer had taken pictures too, so he could show the real thing in action with cattle drinking from a full watering tank.

"I hope you are right."

"Mor says he has the Midas touch."

"Oh." He remembered hearing about King Midas in school but didn't remember much. Joshua thought about asking, but he brushed it aside. "What else has he done?"

"He used to be a gambler and won all the time."

"No one wins all the time."

"Maybe not, but when he won, he won big. Tante Penny made him promise to not gamble anymore."

"So he went into farming? Huh, that's the biggest gamble of all, and most of the time you have no recourse." His brother and the grasshoppers came to mind. The weather, the hoof and mouth that nearly wiped everyone out all over the West.

"No, he's worked on the farms, but he's never cared much for farming. He apprenticed as a blacksmith, Mor said, in New York City before he came west. He likes to work with new inventions, new ideas, things like that." Trygve nodded over his shoulder. "Like the windmills. He had an automobile for a while but said that was more for those living in bigger towns. We didn't have gas to run it nor roads to run it on."

Joshua tucked all the information away for future thinking. He'd had a feeling from the first that he and Hjelmer had a lot in common. He had a couple of ideas of his own that he'd tried talking over with his brother Frank, but he was too hardheaded or just plain proud to use an idea from a younger brother, especially one who let his mouth get away at times. Perhaps what Pastor Solberg spoke on was true for him too. That God put people in places at certain times for certain things. What was it he'd said? Joshua lifted his hat and scratched his head. The words danced in, darted out, and brought others with them. *For such a time as this.* He'd been talking about Queen Esther from the Old Testament.

But he'd applied it to each of those sitting in the congregation, fanning themselves in the heat. Something else he'd said. Words did the same, only this time they played ornery and refused to join up. Something about a plan. But how did that fit with Astrid so far away? Or was that his own plan and not God's?

They trotted up to the livery and handed the team and wagon over to young Solberg, who'd been hired on to take care of the animals since Mr. Sam had all he could do with the blacksmith shop.

Trygve waved as he and Gilbert jogged off across the fields toward home. They'd leave again before sunrise. He should have stayed in town. Ah, to have the energy of the young. Joshua snorted at himself. Here he was, not even thirty yet and thinking Trygve, at nearly eighteen, was so much younger. He set off for the boardinghouse whistling. Perhaps there would be a letter from Astrid. Now, that was something to pick up his pace for.

"You have a letter. I put it in your room," Miss Christopherson answered his greeting with the news, accompanied by a smile.

"Thank you." Joshua took the stairs two at a time. Surely it was from Astrid. In his haste he fumbled with the knob and nearly burst through the door. He could tell from across the room that the handwriting was not Astrid's. He flung his hat toward the coat tree and crossed the room.

Only Frank wielded a pencil like he was drilling a well. With foreboding weighing his shoulders, Joshua sat down on the edge of the bed to read. Of the family only his mother wrote to him.

> Dear Joshua,
>   I write this with a heavy heart and sadness. Our mother went to be with our Lord last week, Monday. She was fine in the morning, but when Pa went to the house for dinner, she was lying on the floor. It must have been her heart, although none of us knew anything about a bad heart. I don't think she did either.
>   We buried her in the churchyard the next day.

Rage ripped through him. *No one called or even sent a telegram. They could have given me a chance to make it back.* He could have caught the train. What felt like a scream came out as only a moan, thanks to his clamping his teeth so tight his jaw cramped. He forced himself to return to the letter.

> With the heat and all, there just wasn't time for you to get here, so we decided to not go into town to call but write. I told Pa I would do this for him.

Joshua laid the letter aside and went to stand at the window. His mother was gone. She wasn't that old, not even fifty. He counted out the years. Forty-eight. Her birthday in June made her forty-eight. His father was ten years older, and they'd always assumed he'd go first, since he had trouble sometimes with his breathing. His mother had said she would come visit him as soon as he had a house. He'd told her she needed to come for the wedding, when the time came.

The moisture in his eyes leaked halos around the gaslights that dotted Main Street, something else new that had come to Blessing while he'd been gone those three years.

"Gone. Lord, I can't believe it." He blew his nose. A tap at the door caught his attention. "Yes?"

"Will you be coming down for your supper?" Miss Christopherson's gentle voice questioned.

"Ah yes. I'll wash and be right down. Th-thank you." He left the letter lying on the bed and, taking towel and washcloth from the bar on the side of the washstand that now did duty as a nightstand since the running water had come in, walked down the hall to the washroom. What he really wanted was a bath, but that would wait until after he ate. They were so good to keep a meal hot for him as it was. He washed hands and face, ignoring the wounded eyes that caught one glance before he thought to shield them.

He heard several men laughing in the cardroom, where they often suggested that a bar would be advantageous. But Mrs. Wiste stood firm. They could play cards, and there were plenty of spittoons throughout the room, but she would not sell liquor nor could they drink in her establishment. Also, if they smoked, it had to be outside on the porch. If they wanted to stay here, they had to abide by the rules.

He made his way between the tables to the one that had become his. A basket of rolls with a pat of butter sat waiting for him, along with a glass and pitcher of iced tea.

"Your supper will be right there," Miss Christopherson said from the door to the kitchen. "It is almost warm enough."

He nodded his thanks and pulled out the chair. How his mother would have loved this room with starched white tablecloths and napkins the same. A small blue vase held a single rose bloom, and all the food tasted as good as hers, including the pickles.

"Ah, Ma, I wish I'd insisted you come to visit. You could have enjoyed a few days without taking care of anyone." He wasn't sure he'd said it aloud, but he felt someone beside him and looked up.

"Your letter was bad news?" Miss Christopherson held his plate in both hands.

He nodded. How did she figure that out? He heaved a sigh and motioned for her to set the plate down in front of him like she always did. "My mother died last week." There. The words were out, somehow making the news a reality.

"Oh, I am so sorry." She laid a gentle hand on his shoulder. "Can I get you anything else?"

"No thank you. I guess I thought my mother would live forever."

"This was sudden, then?"

He told her the gist of the letter. "And it's all over. Life goes on." He'd only glanced at the remainder of the letter. Looked to be other family news. Things his mother usually wrote, always ending with *and one day, I hope you'll come home again, at least for a visit, and bring your bride with you.* One time he'd told her about Astrid and how he thought on her so often. She'd said she'd pray for them, and he knew she had.

Who would pray for him, for there to be a *them* now? And was it even possible? Astrid had barely spoken to him when she'd told him she was leaving for six months. No warmth, no tears, just basic facts. He'd wanted so much to ask if she really wanted to go, but it seemed like she was holding herself together with twine. After all this time he could wait another six months. Not that he had much choice if he loved Astrid.

15

SEPTEMBER 1903
CHICAGO, ILLINOIS

Passing the tests when she first arrived soon became the least of her worries. Now that the term had officially started, the subtle animosity coming from the other students was something else. And dreaming of Blessing. No matter how often she reminded herself that her banishment was only for six months, something inside refused to believe it. Add to that the insidious nagging thought—would Joshua really still be there when she finally did get home? She pushed his face to the back of her thoughts before tears came again. She paused outside the door to the lab, where she'd been assigned a cadaver with Dr. Red Hawk. The name didn't surprise her. She had been told he was half Sioux and half white. What bothered her was his barely suitable civility. She'd heard that Indians didn't like to talk a lot, but still he could be polite. He wasn't uneducated, since he'd been accepted into the program here.

If only she could dissect her half of the body when he wasn't there. But they were supposed to help each other. She'd heard other students laughing and sometimes telling macabre jokes in the cadaver lab. But most of the other students were female. She knew her mother would say that God had a purpose in all that was happening to her. And she should keep her eyes on Him instead of the situation.

Easier said than done. She clasped the handle and turned. The smell of formaldehyde made her eyes burn as soon as she pulled open the door.

"Glad you could make it," Red Hawk said with one raised eyebrow.

"I'm not late."

"Oh, pardon me. Guess I got here early."

Shocked that he had spoken that many words in a row, she ignored him, opened her kit, and laid out her tools: scalpels, forceps, paper, sharpened pencils to take notes with, and most importantly, the text-book that contained all they needed to know. She and Dr. Hawk were still working on the legs.

Two other female students tried to stifle their chuckles when they came through the door but didn't quite make it. The instructor glared at them from the front of the room.

"Thank you for bringing him out." Astrid knew her voice sounded as stiff as she felt. The first one to arrive always went into the cold room and wheeled out the gurney that held their cadaver. Since she had rounds with Dr. Franck just before this class, she was never the first one here. Dr. Franck was another reason for her hesitation. He'd made his opinion quite clear. She should not have been given the privilege of the six-month surgical rotation without having been in a classroom situation the same amount of time as the others.

With the mistakes she was making, he was probably right, not to mention those she had made on the entry examinations. She had known the answers, but she couldn't bring them to mind on command. All she'd wanted to do was vomit and run back to the first train heading west. There would be no joy in telling Elizabeth her scores, but at least she had passed.

She closed her eyes for a moment against the burning and opened them to find Red Hawk staring at her across the sheet-draped corpse. If he made one more disparaging comment, she would . . . she would . . . She had no idea what she would do other than what she did. Squaring her shoulders, she slipped the apron over her head, tied it, and picked up her scalpel. Today she would be working on the muscles and nerves surrounding the knee.

Several minutes of cutting and writing notes had passed when she said, "There is something on this one that you might want to see." She caught herself in surprise. Why on earth had she said that? Because that was the way they were supposed to act whether he chose to cooperate or not.

"Thank you." He came around the end of the gurney to where she was pointing.

"Scar tissue?"

"A lot. He was severely injured at one time, and it looks like it healed without any medical assistance. I can't see how he walked on it."

"Maybe that is why the muscles are so much more developed in the other leg." They had puzzled on that the day before, but Red Hawk had stopped her from summoning the instructor. "We had a brave in our tribe who dragged one leg after a horse fell on him. The boys teased him."

His stark comment forced her to look at him. Thick dark hair flopped on his wide forehead. Were he home on the reservation, she

175

was fairly sure his hair would have been long and worn in plaits. Not that she really knew that much about the Sioux tribe, other than what she'd learned years ago from their friend Metiz, but long hair on the men seemed pretty standard. His square face and what appeared as sunburned skin set him apart from the others. This was the first comment he'd made about anyone back home. Maybe there was hope after all.

Together they excised to the bones, which looked nothing like the pictures they'd ever seen of a knee. Calcification made the components nearly unidentifiable. They looked at each other and nodded. She raised her hand to catch the instructor's attention.

"What is it?" he asked.

"You might want to look at this knee."

He made his way between the gurneys. "Excellent." He clapped his hands. "Gather around here. We have an abnormality."

Abnormality? Astrid mentally shrugged. In her mind an abnormality was something the patient was born with. She quickly jotted the word down to research later and stepped back to let their instructor take her place.

"What do you see here?"

"A knee that was injured severely," Red Hawk answered promptly, "and the body built calcium around it to compensate."

"Good. What had you seen on the body prior to this?" He looked to Astrid.

"Scar tissue on and under the epidermis."

"Anything else?"

"Had I seen him walking, I'm sure he either favored or dragged this leg. Perhaps used a crutch or cane."

"But since you couldn't see him walking, anything else?"

Panic clawed at her throat. She took a deep breath. "The musculature on the opposite leg was greatly increased, most likely compensating for the injury."

"And you did not draw that to my attention?"

"No, sir."

"In spite of the fact that all anomalies are to be mentioned?"

"I'm sorry, sir." *Red Hawk, this is your doing.* If only she could melt into a puddle and slip out under the door.

Her breathing sounded loud in the silence, as if everyone else had turned to stone.

She'd learned her lesson from someone else's previous error. Making excuses did not help. Just take the upbraiding and be more careful in the future was the gist of one of their study group's late night discussions. The only one she'd been to so far. But then, she'd only been there for sixteen days, not that she was marking the days off on the calendar.

She glanced at Red Hawk from under her lashes to see him studying the floor, the sheet, looking at anything but her.

This isn't fair, her insides screamed. But Pastor Solberg's voice responded. *"Who said life was fair? The sun and the rain, they both fall on the just and the unjust. As does the blizzard and the drought."*

"Have you anything to say for yourself?"

She shook her head. "No, sir."

He looked around, catching everyone's gaze. "What is the first rule of medicine?"

"Do no harm," they all chanted back.

"And the second?"

The silence stretched.

Astrid searched through all the rules she'd learned. Did *Thou shalt not kill* apply here?

"Come now, you've seen it written on the boards before."

Festina lente, make haste slowly, floated through her mind, but she'd not seen it on the board. But perhaps it had been on the board before she came. She'd have to ask someone else.

Their instructor shook his head. "I expect you all to have looked it up and be ready for an exam tomorrow."

Astrid gulped. She knew all the material. Why did her stomach tie itself in figure eights?

"On the skin and everything below the knee." He strode back to his desk and took his seat, glancing up to find them all staring at him. "Back to work. You're wasting time." He nodded at a raised hand. "Yes, Dr. Smith."

"Does that include the knee?"

"I said everything below the knee. How would I test you on something you have not completed yet?"

The exhalation of breath was room wide.

Astrid stared at the malformed knee before her. Nothing in it matched any of the pictures or diagrams she had studied before. She glanced over to see Red Hawk following something—a nerve path?—that she couldn't even see. What could she do? Think, Astrid, think. Ask the instructor for assistance? Ask Red Hawk if she could learn from his work? Run screaming back to her room? Throw her things in a suitcase and . . . ?

You promised yourself you would not think of leaving again. Choose to think of something else. The commands might as well have been shouted down a well, echoing but never working.

"You have fifteen minutes to clean up and put your things away. Make sure you clean your instruments thoroughly. Are there any questions?" Without even glancing to see if some hardy soul raised a hand, he returned to his writing, the pen scratching across the paper.

Knowing that the lab would be open in the evening for those who wanted more time, Astrid tucked her pencil into the slot for it and closed her writing pad. Taking her instruments to the sink, she washed them off with soap and water, and then washed her hands.

"Are you coming back tonight?" Red Hawk whispered.

She nodded. What else could she do?

"Good. Me too." He covered their cadaver with the sheet and unlocked the wheels of the gurney to push it back to the assigned slot in the cooler.

When the bell rang, they filed out of the room without a word, walking slowly until the instructor went ahead of them.

"So what is the motto on the surgery hall?" one of the older women asked the others.

"First do no harm," Astrid said.

"But then what could be the second?" They all looked at each other, shaking their heads.

"I was hoping someone else remembered it. That man makes me forget my name, let alone medical information." There, she'd said it.

"Oh, me too. He glares at me, and I—"

"He doesn't know how to smile," someone added.

"As if he is doing us a favor by permitting us to sit at his feet and learn from his sculpted lips." The derision on the first woman's face matched the spoken words.

The jumble of comments as they made their way down the hall and stairs made Astrid smile. For the first time she felt part of the group, even if she hadn't been able to remember at the right time. She wasn't the only one feeling so out of sorts.

As they went their separate ways, she headed for the room she shared with one other woman—Elyse by name, Dr. Davidson by title. Elyse would graduate in May, with one more rotation after this one. They hardly saw each other because Elyse worked the night shift on the obstetrics floor for this rotation.

"Dr. Bjorklund!"

Astrid stopped in the act of opening her door at the call. "Yes?"

"We have an emergency surgery, and you've been ordered to scrub up. Operating room four."

She started to ask a question but nodded instead. "I'll be right there." She set her books on the table she used as a desk and hurried down the stairs, her hand slick on the stair rail. She'd observed several surgeries and birthings, but this was the first time she had been ordered to scrub. Would she be assisting or observing or what? The questions kept time with her feet slapping the stairs.

In the scrub room she soaped her hands and arms, standing next to Dr. Whitaker, who was doing the same.

"Glad you could come."

"Thank you, sir. What are the symptoms?" She blinked. Was she being too forward?

"Elevated temp, pain, and tenderness in the lower right quadrant."

"Appendicitis?"

"Looks that way. Hope we get it before it ruptures."

"Yes, sir."

"Have you done one like this before?"

She shook her head. *And I've not gotten that far in anatomy either.* But in her mind she could see the diagram of the little thumblike organ. If enlarged with infection it could burst and send peritonitis throughout the patient's abdomen. "No, sir."

"Ever opened or closed?"

"Yes, sir. Both. But not with this diagnosis." She dipped her hands into the carbolic acid and let the liquid run down her raised arms. One of the nurses held a surgical apron ready to drop over her head. She turned so that the strings could be tied. Another pulled a white cap over her hair, tucking in the strands of hair that fought to fly free.

"Just do what I tell you."

The internal butterflies banged against her rib cage instead of flying in formation. She'd not been in an operating room like this other than on tour and observation.

"The patient is ready, Doctor," the head surgical nurse said, intoning the vitals.

"Good." He nodded to the nurse holding the ether cone. "Proceed."

Later, when he dropped the swollen but still intact body part into the basin, he caught Astrid's gaze. "Would you like to close?"

She agreed to, well aware what a privilege he was giving her as new as she was. Why was he? Her work to this point hadn't been of the quality to attract his attention. Dr. Morganstein had told her she would be starting with simple things like broken bones and repairing injuries. She stepped forward, staring into the open incision. Her mind flipped back to the day she'd fought to clear all the debris from Vernon's abdomen. This was far different; all the organs were lying where they belonged, the blood flowing in the proper vessels, not leaking like a sieve. She took a deep breath, exhaled, and took the threaded needle the nurse offered her. At least she could sew a fine seam, thanks to her mother and all the hours of practicing ties and knots.

"Make sure you don't pull the sutures too tight. You get more scar tissue that way. Adhesions can be very painful and sometimes necessitate further surgery."

"Yes, sir." She closed the peritoneum, then loosened the retractor so the muscles could return to their proper positions. Working through each derma layer, she was able to forget the doctor and nurses who were watching her, as well as the students likely observing in the balcony above. Her knees were shaking by the time she tied off

181

the last suture and stepped back. At home she would have done the dressings too, but here there were other staff members to do that.

"You did well." Back in the scrub room, he dropped his mask so she could see his smile. "I could tell you've applied a fair number of sutures before."

The simple compliment made her eyes burn. "Thank you." *Thank you, God. Thank you, Mor. I finally did something well again.* And she'd been correct in the diagnosis.

"You remind me of Dr. Bjorklund. You have that same fierce dedication she had."

"Still has. She made sure that I studied all the basics, including all her texts from here. She's a hard taskmaster."

"Yes, well, we'll see how much more we can add to your fund of knowledge and experience."

Astrid thanked him again and returned to her room to change clothes. She was soaked from the skin out, not realizing until they were done how hot it had been in the operating room. Outside, Chicago broiled in a summer heat wave, making the hospital much like a kitchen during canning season. If only she had time to take a shower. But a sponge bath would have to do. Her stomach grumbled, reminding her that breakfast had been hours earlier.

She had another class in twenty minutes. She scooped up the letter standing next to her lamp and tucked it into her pocket to read while she ate. At least there would be bread and cheese or something set out in the dining room for those who couldn't make the scheduled mealtimes. Guilt nagged her down the hall. She'd not written home since the first letter to let them know she'd arrived safely. How would she ever fit in everything she had to do to finish this rotation in six months? Why had Red Hawk let her take the blame for his mistake? More importantly, how was she going to work with him without confronting his perfidy?

———

ASTRID FELT THE crinkle of her mother's letter, still unread, when she hung her apron on one of the hooks on the wall. She pulled it out and puffed her cheeks in a sigh. How could she be so tired she didn't even have the energy to read a letter from home? Moving quietly so as not to disturb her roommate, although Elyse was sleeping so hard a fire bell wouldn't penetrate, she slipped her nightdress over her head and tiptoed out the door, down the hall to the community washroom. There she slit the envelope open and removed the two sheets of paper, covered front and back with writing.

"Oh, Mor, I can't do this." Without reading a word, she stuffed it back in the envelope, used the necessary, and returned to her room. Her eyes ached from the formaldehyde, and her legs hurt from standing at the gurney for so long. But she knew the cadaver's leg and foot from the knee down. Red Hawk had not appeared, so she'd used his side for her study. Surely she would dream of bones and muscles tonight.

16

BLESSING, NORTH DAKOTA

J oshua slipped the guitar strap over his shoulder and strummed a couple of times, then adjusted the tuning pegs and fingered the strings again. That sounded better.

Jonathan Gould hit a C chord on the piano, and Joshua tuned again, right along with Lars on the fiddle. When they were in agreement, they nodded to Pastor Solberg on the gut bucket, and the four started off the fall dance with "Blow Ye Winds, Blow." Blessing folk continued to arrive at Andrew and Ellie Bjorklund's barn, both on foot and by wagon, leaving their covered dishes at the tables set up for that purpose and joining the dancing.

Joshua wished he could quit watching the newcomers, always thinking how much more he would enjoy this if Astrid were there. If he'd been afraid he'd lose interest in her with her gone like this, he now knew without a doubt that she was the one for him.

Jonathan was in the same boat. Here he was getting ready to leave for Fargo in a few days, and Grace had already gone back East. She'd been offered additional teacher training and was taking advantage of it.

Pay attention, he told himself when he missed a beat. But all he could think of was whirling Astrid around, holding her in his arms for a waltz, enjoying her laughter. One of the many things he loved about her was that she knew how to enjoy herself. And help others around her have a good time too.

Sophie, or Mrs. Wiste, caught his eye and gave him a tiny wave. He nodded and smiled back. No one could resist smiling at Sophie. The way Garth smiled down at his wife made Joshua wish for Astrid even more.

Watching Mr. and Mrs. Bjorklund dance by, he knew he wanted to be like them. Both showed glints of white in their blond hair and encroaching lines on their faces, but it was obvious they loved to dance and they loved each other. *Think on something else, Landsverk. All this seeing love is making you jealous.* He glanced over to the table with the tub of punch. Some of the younger children were pouring and giggling. Interesting that over in the fenced-off corner, the cousin Anna was watching over the little ones who were still awake. He didn't see her husband anywhere.

When he saw Gus and Maydell two-step by, he almost chuckled, remembering a previous dance when she had sort of forced Gus into a marriage agreement. Last he'd heard, the wedding would be after harvest. Everything here revolved around the farming calendar. Tilling, planting, haying, harvesting . . . a fight all the time to keep the weeds down and praying for the right weather. Even if he didn't want to farm, when one was working with farmers, the same seasons applied. He thought about Hjelmer's house and how there would be so few to finish the interior when harvest took the bulk of the men away.

"Let's take a break after this number, shall we?" Lars suggested a few tunes later. "I'm drier'n a water hole in August."

"Sounds good to me."

Lars raised his voice. "This is the last dance for a while, folks. Maybe the ladies would like to open the food table about now."

"You could have given us a warning," some female called back.

"Why, that would be too easy, now, wouldn't it? All right, we will play one more number so you have time." He glanced to his fellow musicians. " 'Little Brown Jug'?" At their nods, he tapped his foot four times, and away they went again.

Since the people let the musicians go through the line first, Joshua had a plateful of food in his hand when the elder Mrs. Valders stopped beside him.

"I'm sorry to hear about your mother," she said.

Surprised, he nodded. "Thank you. She would have enjoyed a party like this."

"We are fortunate to have so many good musicians here in Blessing. Dr. Bjorklund is very talented on the piano too. I think she was relieved when Mr. Gould volunteered to play."

"Oh, really?" The things one learned at a party.

"Well, I'd best see to making more punch. Hot night like this, everyone's extra thirsty."

"That's for sure." He raised his cup. "I really appreciate my share." He took his plate over to where benches had been set up and sat down to eat.

Toby sat down beside him, his plate heaped. "You heard from Hjelmer?" He picked up a piece of fried chicken and took a bite. "Ah, Thelma over at the doctor's sent this chicken."

"How do you know that?"

"She makes the best fried chicken in town. Mrs. Sam from the boardinghouse comes a close second. Don't know what they do different from the others, but they do. Mrs. Bjorklund makes the best bread. Just ask Thorliff."

"Back to your question. Nope, I haven't."

"Figured you would by now. Penny said anything?"

"About what?"

"If he's sold any more windmills. I figured you're about done with the one south of here."

"We are. Trygve goes out with the threshing crew Monday."

"They'll start with the Knutson place, then the Bjorklunds' and the Baards'. I used to work that crew until Thorliff got so busy building. You need a job, we always have one for you."

"Thank you. If he does come back with more orders, which I'm sure he will, I'm going to need some help myself. I'd like to start building a house too."

"You better get on Thorliff's list." He nodded as Trygve sat down cross-legged in front of them. "What you doing hanging out with the old guys when all those cute girls are giggling for you?"

Trygve rolled his eyes. He looked up at Joshua. "You know we talked about building a sleeping wagon?" Joshua nodded. "Well, I talked to my pa about it, and he said he was sure Hjelmer would pay for it. We can build it in our machine shed after we return from threshing."

"When is harvest done here?"

"We're usually done by now, but with the cool and wet summer we had, we're behind schedule. We do all the locals and then go west to thresh for others. We've been going to many of the same farms for years. Andrew stays home to take care of the livestock and chores, and Samuel would rather do that too. I like helping Pa with the big machinery. When that steam engine and the threshing machine chug down the road, people sit up and take notice."

"What do you pull it with?"

"The steam engine has wheels. Between the two, it looks like some kind of monster coming down the road. We set up and farmers in the area bring their wagonloads of sheaves of wheat to be separated."

"That's the way my father does it. He says the machinery is just too expensive for most farmers to purchase." But then his father thought everything was too expensive. He expected his sons to work for nothing and to be grateful for the privilege. Sometimes he still wondered why he had returned home when he left Blessing, but he knew. Fiona. Fickle Fiona. Now he wished her and her husband all happiness, but that had taken a long time. Seeing Astrid again had helped him forget Fiona. For a moment he wondered how Pa and the others were getting along without his mother there to feed and take care of them. Who was tending her garden and putting up the produce? His brother's wife had enough to do with her own house and children.

He brought himself back to the conversation. Both Trygve and Toby were looking at him. He'd missed something all right. "Sorry, you made me think of my father's farm. What did you say?"

"Just more about threshing. I take it you aren't interested in going on the crew."

"Nope. I'd rather put up windmills any day."

Lars strolled over and stopped behind his son. "You about ready to start in again?"

Joshua nodded and finished the last of his potato salad. One thing for sure, the cooks around there were superb. He glanced over at the table of pies and cakes.

"They'll set out the desserts at the next break. Grab yourself another cup of punch before they run out."

They tuned up again and started the next set, this time a square dance with Haakan as the caller. The dancers wove the patterns at a pace that would make anyone puff. When they finished, everyone clapped and headed for the punch tub again.

189

"Hey, Joshua, I heard you singing on Sunday. You ever do any solos?" Lars asked.

Joshua shrugged. "Sang sometimes in church."

"Well, how about that. You know 'Shenandoah'?"

"Of course."

"Can you play and sing both?"

Joshua shrugged again and nodded. Actually he enjoyed singing, but he wasn't about to volunteer. Some practice time would be good, but he knew that song well.

"Hey, folks, we got a treat in store for you tonight. Mr. Landsverk here is going to sing for us."

The crowd hushed and looked toward the musicians. They played a few bars as an introduction, and Joshua picked up with "Oh Shenandoah, I long to hear you. . . ." He picked his guitar instead of strumming, the notes rippling out like sunlight on river water. When he finished, a silence greeted him.

They didn't like it. The thought died in birth as one person started to clap, and it became contagious. He looked over to see Ingeborg wiping tears and Mrs. Knutson doing the same. He guessed they liked it all right.

When they took their next break, Pastor Solberg came up to him. "I knew you had a good voice, son, but that tugged right on the heartstrings. We'd be honored to have you sing for church some Sunday, if you would like."

"I'd like that." And just maybe his mother would be able to hear him sing again. She was the one who gave him a love of music and started him playing the guitar.

"Thank you."

Ingeborg handed him a plate with both chocolate cake and chocolate cream pie. "I saved some for you."

"Thank you. My favorites."

"I know. Perhaps when people get tired of dancing, we could all do some singing. Would you mind leading?"

"My pleasure, ma'am."

Later, as they sang, people picked up the harmonies, and when one song was finished, someone else would start up another. They went from "She'll be Coming Round the Mountain" to "Bringing in the Sheaves," from "Buffalo Gals" to finish with "Simple Gifts." As the final note faded away, a silence full of peace picked them up and carried them home.

As one of the children said, "That felt just like church, Ma, don't you think?"

"More like what heaven will sound like, I expect."

Lars clapped a hand on Joshua's shoulder. "Well, you can't beat an evening like this anywhere, I don't think. Thank you for taking part."

"Thank you for asking me. I nearly forgot how much I love playing and singing."

"I don't think you need to worry about that happening. Not now. See you in the morning."

Joshua returned to the boardinghouse and sat down to write to Astrid. If she had been there to enjoy the evening, it would have been as close to perfect as he could dream.

And that's just what he told her.

You haven't been gone all that long, and all I know for certain is that we are all looking forward to you returning home to Blessing, but me most of all. I am beginning to see why you love Blessing so much. This place is truly blessed. That's about all I can say about it. I hope that all is well with you, that you are learning all that you need and want. I know I don't write very much, but I think of you often.

He wanted to write *I think of you all the time*, but that really wasn't quite proper. He signed his name, *Yours most truly, Joshua Landsverk.* Climbing into bed, he threw even the sheet off, warm as the night was. He locked his hands behind his head and stared into the darkness, gratitude welling up so all he could say or think was "Thank you."

If only his mother were still alive so he could write to her about the evening. Was life like that, always a sorrow to reduce a joy? Or did joy overpower the sorrow?

17

CHICAGO, ILLINOIS

When Astrid woke at a rap on the door, she thought she'd just fallen asleep. "Yes."

"Time to get up."

"Thank you." She glanced across to the other bed, now empty. Talk about dead to the world. She must have been sleeping like Elyse had been when she came in. She dressed quickly and brushed out her hair while hurrying to the washroom. At least there was a sink available. When she'd washed and brushed her teeth, she braided her hair on the way back to her room and wrapped it in a figure eight at the base of her skull. At least that way she'd not have to fuss with it later in case she had to don a surgical cap again. "Got to" would be more appropriate than "had to." Bless Dr. Whitaker for inviting her to assist.

She'd just sat down with her tray when one of the nurses called from the doorway. "Dr. Bjorklund."

"Yes."

"Dr. Whitaker asked me to find you. He wants you to meet him on the surgical floor in ten minutes."

"Thank you. I'll be there." Astrid shoveled in her oatmeal, spread jam on her bread, and was thankful the coffee wasn't so hot that she couldn't down it without getting burned. Bread in one hand, she set her tray on the counter and headed out the door. Good thing she'd grabbed her stethoscope on her way out of her room, along with the pencil and small pad of paper she'd stuck in her pocket.

"Good morning," Dr. Whitaker greeted her. "You will be doing rounds with me today. Dr. Franck has been so informed."

"Thank you, sir." Hers was not to question why, she reminded herself as she nodded.

"We'll start with our appendectomy of yesterday. Did you check on her last evening?"

"Yes, sir."

"Good. While that wasn't within your responsibilities, I'm pleased that you took the initiative and showed such concern. How was she faring?"

"She was groggy and complaining of pain, but that would be normal with that type of surgery. I checked her chart, and saw a new prescription for pain had been ordered. I waited while the nurse gave it to her, and then she went back to sleep. There was no sign of elevated temperature, and her pulse rate was strong although a bit fast."

"And you notated your observations on the chart?" He picked up the chart as he asked.

"No, sir. I was not assigned to do that." *And I've heard stories of how some physicians resent another doctor treating their patient.* "Besides, you had already written the same findings half an hour earlier."

A smile tickled the lines radiating from the edges of his eyes. "When you check on her through the day, feel free to write your observations on the chart. If you are going to be assisting me, I want you to be involved in all aspects of caring for my patients."

Had she heard right? Assisting Dr. Whitaker. Elizabeth's other hero. And according to her, the best surgeon in the world. "Ah, well, thank you, sir. I mean . . ." *Stop! You sound like a ninny.* She huffed out a breath. *Please, Lord, don't let me make any more stupid mistakes.*

After they had seen the rest of his patients, he motioned her into the office behind the nurses' station and sat down. "I have a couple of questions for you. Please, be seated."

She sat on the edge of the chair. Now what was happening?

"I've read all your essays and exams prior to coming here and your list of patients cared for in Blessing. I was surprised that you didn't score higher on the exams administered here. Do you have anything to say about that?"

Astrid swallowed. How to answer? She sucked in a deep breath and clamped her fingers together. "I knew the material, but I just couldn't pull out the answers to write them down at the time."

"In other words, you froze. Or have you always had a problem with written tests?"

"No, sir."

"You have not only assisted, but according to these files, you were the primary physician on several cases from birthing babies to setting broken bones and removing a bullet. You have had more medical experience than anyone your age I've encountered before."

"Thanks to Dr. Elizabeth, er Dr. Bjorklund. She wanted to make sure I was trained sufficiently not to embarrass her when I came here."

His eyes crinkled again. "That sounds like Dr. Bjorklund all right." He stared into her eyes. "Do you usually panic when under duress?"

"No, sir. Just since—"

"Dr. Bjorklund, your dissection class is about to start." A voice came through the open doorway.

"You go on. We will continue this discussion later." He stood and picked up the stack of charts. "In your spare time, you will want to acquaint yourself with all these patients. We have two surgeries tomorrow morning, starting at seven. One a muscle repair and the other abdominal. And I am on call for the ER, so you will be too. Go and breathe deeply so you do your best on this exam. Dr. Franck is a stickler for punctuality, as well he should be."

"Yes, sir. Thank you, sir." Astrid hurried up the stairs and down the hall. Running was not appropriate, but it sure would be helpful.

This time she would not succumb to the fears that rode her. *I have a heart of love and a sound mind.* Where did that come from? Of course, from one of her memory verses from Sunday school. *For God hath not given us the spirit of fear; but of power, and of love, and of a sound mind.* She prayed as she entered the room, *Lord God, I most certainly do need that sound mind. Please keep the fear away.*

She took her seat just before Dr. Franck turned from the blackboard. "Good of you to join us, Dr. Bjorklund." The slight twist he put on her title made her swallow. She swallowed again and sucked in a deep breath. *Sound mind, sound mind, sound mind.*

He removed the cloth he'd draped over the other blackboard. The list of ten questions made someone groan. At least it wasn't her. She read down the list. Yes, she had studied all that. Yes, she had seen it all on the cadaver too. Now to write. *Please, Lord, I know this might not be important to you, but it is to me. Please help.*

She paused a moment before her pencil hit the paper. Had she prayed like this before the other tests? Her mother would say God was trying to teach her something. But what? More lessons? She made herself breathe deeply and leaned her neck from side to side.

Once she began writing, her pencil flew across the paper, the words pouring from somewhere inside faster than she could write them down. She finished the test, including the question titled for extra credit. When she reread her answers, she could hardly believe it. She sounded just like the textbooks. Had she really memorized all the information like that? She made a couple of small changes and stood to take her exam paper to the instructor. As she walked up the aisle, his eyebrow rose. He took her paper and glanced down through the answers, nodding as he went. "You are dismissed, then, Dr. Bjorklund, for today."

One of the other students brought her papers forward. He glanced down. "You might want to work some more on question five. You have plenty of time."

"Thank you, sir." The young woman returned to her seat.

Astrid forced her feet to walk sedately back to her chair. She picked up her things and walked out the door. In the hall the skip and jump burst loose, and she added one spin to the dance. Finally a good test. *Thank you, God.* She said it again in a whisper. Had she been at home, she would have gone out and shouted to the blue bowl of North Dakota sky. *Thank you, God.* He did listen to her prayers after all, not just her mother's. She started down the hall, refusing to get trapped again in questions about the death of Vernon and the baby. Perhaps there were indeed no answers there. Like her mother often said, some things we'll only learn in heaven.

Glancing at the watch she wore pinned to the chest of her apron, she hurried back to her room and sank down on her bed to read her mother's letter.

My dear daughter,

How I miss you. How we all miss you, including Inga, who asks when Tante Asti is coming home. I know you are up to your eyebrows in work there. I hope you are learning all that you can and that when you write, you will take time to sleep more than to write to us. We are all praying for you.

It looks like harvest will begin next week. As always now we are praying that the rain will hold off. And as always, your far is restless for it to begin. He says that the sooner we start, the sooner he can get home again. I wish he would let the younger men do it all, but you know your far. If I said that to him, he would be mortally offended. So I pray and rejoice that he is so much improved. He still tires more easily than he used to, but he is healthy, and that is all that matters.

The girls had a party for Grace before she left for New York. I wish she could have stopped in Chicago to see you, for both your sakes. The girls all said they miss you and are sending prayers up for you.

Inga got Carl in trouble again. He tries so hard to keep up with her. That's like a spring breeze trying to keep up with a tornado.

Anna is pulling out of her depression. She and I talked again the other day, and I told her what I had experienced all those years ago. Why is it that so often a good cry and a shoulder to cry on are as therapeutic as most medications? I know that getting her out in the sunshine was the first step toward healing.

Mr. Landsverk came for dinner after church on Sunday. He is doing well with the windmill business. He and Trygve are talking of building a little house on wheels like the cook shack for when they go beyond the range of returning home at night. He received a letter that his mother died, and I know that was a shock for him.

I better close now. The bread is ready to be punched down, and Freda is out picking beans again. We are having a bumper crop, for which I am so thankful. I think we'll do leather britches again. We didn't have enough last year. I'm going to let the last pickings dry on the plants so we have more dried beans too. God is blessing us with such bounty. I know He is taking care of you.

Love always from your mor

Astrid wiped at the tears that trickled down her cheeks. Instead of going down for the stack of reports, she took out pencil and paper. Even just a note would be better than waiting for time to write a letter.

Dear Mor and all those I love in Blessing,

Please share this, as my time to write is nonexistent. I finally took an exam that I didn't panic over. I did like I used to at home. Thank you for your prayers, and I am thanking God that He answered mine.

I was asked to assist Dr. Whitaker. Elizabeth will be thrilled with that news. I am astounded, considering my bad scores and mistakes. The thought that a mistake on my part could endanger another person's life didn't used to plague me like this. I didn't think about it. I just did what I knew needed to be done.

I need to go read charts. I love you all and am so looking forward to returning home to Blessing and seeing you.

Dr. Astrid Bjorklund.

P.S. I love signing my name that way. Is that prideful? I hope not.

She'd just finished putting a stamp on the addressed envelope when a knock came at the door. "Yes."

"Dr. Bjorklund?"

"Yes, come in."

One of the nurses peeked in the door. "Dr. Whitaker needs you in the ER."

"I'll be right there." She dropped her letter off at the desk as she flew by. "Please see that gets in the outgoing mail."

"I will."

Astrid grabbed an apron off the line of hooks beside the door to the emergency room and, after making sure she had her stethoscope and pad and pencil, tied the apron strings as she walked in.

"He's over here." A nurse beckoned from one of the curtained cubicles. She held the curtain back for Astrid to enter.

"Notify the charge nurse that we need an operating room immediately," he said, glancing up at Astrid.

The nurse hurried out of the room. "Hold this for me." He nodded at the other side of the gurney and the patient.

A young boy lay on the gurney, both legs smashed beyond recognition. Astrid took the strings of the tourniquet and finished tying it off. The flow of blood ceased.

"I'm going to have to amputate both legs. There is nothing I can do to repair such destruction."

The woman standing with the boy hid her eyes with one hand, her groan preceding the shaking of her shoulders.

"He fell under the wheels of a dray," Dr. Whitaker muttered to Astrid.

Astrid had to swallow the acid from her stomach. Such terrible wounds. Why wasn't he in school, where he would have been safe? She turned at another groan from the woman and caught her as she fainted.

"Get her out of here."

Another nurse jumped to his bidding.

"Give him another whiff of ether. He's coming around."

Astrid picked up the cone and the bottle to administer the anesthetic.

"The operating room is ready," a nurse said at the doorway.

"Good. Let's go." He stepped back, and two orderlies took the head and foot of the gurney and wheeled it out while Astrid and the doctor headed for the scrub room.

"Have you done an amputation before?" he asked.

"No, sir."

"We're going to have to take both legs off above the knees, which condemns this lad to life in a wheelchair. He probably lives in one of the tenements with flights of stairs that he will not be able to manage, even with crutches, if he can somehow learn to use those. He'll most likely end up a beggar on the streets."

Astrid fought the tears that his words brought.

"That's if we can keep gangrene from setting in and taking his life."

Would dying be preferable to a life like that? The thought made her want to vomit. Was this another side to doctoring she'd not considered?

18

The grate of saw on bone lasted two lifetimes.

Astrid held steady to administer more anesthetic if the doctor asked, but every particle of her being screamed "Run!" She willed herself home to the fall, when they would soon be cutting wood for the stoves, but there was no way she could convince herself that was what was going on.

"Are you all right?" one of the nurses asked under her breath.

"I will be." Astrid gritted her teeth and bent her knees slightly. She'd read that could help keep her from fainting. She'd never fainted during an operation before, but then she'd never heard bone being cut before either.

The boy stirred beneath her fingers, and she snapped back to the hot lights and heavy air.

"Another drip, stat." The doctor's voice cut through the remaining fog.

With more drops of chloroform, the boy sank into unconsciousness again.

"Dr. Bjorklund."

"Yes, sir."

"Let the nurse take over your job. I want you to observe and assist me with this."

"Yes, sir."

Maybe it was the fumes floating upward that were causing her to be woozy. The nurse took over, and she stepped to the opposite side of the table.

"You see that I had to remove the bone high enough to where I had good skin to work with. Also to bone that was not injured." He glanced across at her, and she nodded, recognizing the long flaps of skin that he indicated.

"One of the greatest trials for an amputee is the pain of bearing the weight on the artificial limb, so this way we cushion the stump as much as possible. Sometimes double amputees decide to use a four-wheeled flat board, propelling themselves with their hands. Others choose a wheelchair. This boy is young enough that he might adapt to crutches. Now, we fold this one under first, then cover it with the front flap and stitch around it. This is a technique developed during the Civil War when so many of the wounded lost a leg or foot." He handed her a threaded needle and picked up another for himself. "You start on that side, and I'll start on this."

When they finished, he asked for water for those in the room. "We don't need any dehydration problems or fainting for any of us." He looked to those assisting him. "If you need to step outside for a moment, now is the time to do so, before we start the second leg."

Stepping outside was only a prelude to what Astrid ached to do.

Her entire insides screamed at her to run. Run all the way back to Blessing. Or at least down the street to a small park she had located on one of her few walks.

"All right. Let's begin again."

A nurse removed the dressings on the second leg, equally as damaged as the first.

"You will assist in cleaning out the debris." He nodded to Astrid. "Excise the tissue to healthy tissue."

Astrid removed bone splinters and bloody bits that she didn't bother to identify.

"Suture any blood vessels so that we can release the tourniquet." As they cleared the operating field, he continued. "We will make the cut on the bone here."

Astrid forced her eyes to remain open, constantly ordering her mind and hands to obey. When she inhaled, the heavy odor of blood clogged her nostrils. Before she could compensate, her knees buckled, and the light went out.

She came to sitting on a bench, one of the nurses holding her in place with a hand on the back of her head, forcing her head down. She coughed and choked on the fumes of the smelling salts held near her nose.

"What ha . . . ?" She added a groan as she realized where she was. "I fainted?"

"You aren't the first nor will you be the last." The nurse let her sit upright. "Get your head down again if you feel faint."

Astrid leaned her head against the wall behind her. "I think I'm going to be sick."

The nurse handed her a basin. "You aren't the first. Next time you'll get through just fine."

If there will be a next time. "But I've assisted on I don't know how many surgeries. Why this now?"

"The heat, the length of the operation, and most likely fatigue. All those things. Dr. Bjorklund, this is not the end of the world, or your medical career." Her voice firmed up as she spoke. "I've nursed more students, both doctors and nurses, through things like this. Have you ever done an amputation before?"

Astrid shook her head but stopped as even that slight motion caused her stomach to send up warnings.

"Ohh." This time she gave in to the retching. When she finished, the nurse handed her a wet cloth.

"Wipe your face. Breathe deeply, and when you can, stand, wash up, and go lie down in your room for a while. We'll call you if necessary."

Astrid did as ordered, not that she had much choice. "Thank you."

The nurse rose. "One day you'll be coaching some other hapless student through this same thing. Next time you'll do better."

If there is a next time, she thought again. Mortification weighed like a suit of armor, dragging at her shoulders and clanking about her ankles. She emptied the pan and rinsed it out at the sink. Then, after removing her operating room garb and stuffing it into the laundry bin, she made her way to her room and collapsed on her bed. Surely this was what failure felt like.

————

LATE THAT AFTERNOON, she found herself outside Dr. Franck's office door. The idea had come to her when she woke from a dead sleep, afraid she'd slept through afternoon class, evening rounds, and supper. But instead, she'd only missed dinner, and her stomach didn't feel much like food anyway. Since today was not an anatomy class day, she'd not seen this teacher for two days. While he'd probably heard of her ineptitude, she knew she needed to talk with him. She raised her hand to knock and let it fall to her side. Why ask? He'd only say no and most likely make fun of her besides. She started to turn away but something made her grit her teeth and knock on the door.

"Come in."

Fully understanding how a mouse might feel with its foot in a trap, she pushed open the door and stepped inside. The only item on his desk was the book he was reading. All the other books were shelved, and every paper must have been in the place assigned it because no paper was visible. How did he do it?

"Yes, Dr. Bjorklund?" Clipped and to the point.

"I . . . I have a request." She'd started to say *favor* but changed the word.

He nodded for her to continue.

She swallowed the lump in her throat that threatened to choke her. "In the dissecting of the cadaver, do we ever do an amputation?"

"No."

"Then how does one learn to do the procedure?" she asked him respectfully.

"Have you ever sawed wood?"

"Yes, sir."

"It is much the same. Primarily, you need a freshly sharpened saw."

Her insides quivered at the mention of the instrument. She sucked in a fortifying breath. "Would . . . ah . . . could one do an amputation on the leg of the cadaver?"

He stared at her. "You would want to do that?"

"Yes, sir." She swallowed again. "I fainted this morning in the operating room. Dr. Whitaker had asked me to assist with a young boy who had fallen under a dray, and his legs were destroyed." Tears burned behind her eyes, but she blinked and raised her chin.

"I made it through the first leg."

"I see."

Surely that wasn't a twinkle she detected in his eyes. "I understood from your admittance papers that you have performed a number of surgeries with your training doctor."

"Yes, sir. But no amputations. Mostly birthings." *Why, oh why, did I ever think this was a good idea? Because this is why I came to Chicago. That's why.* The argument in her head made her hands twitch to cover her ears.

"I see."

Is there nothing else you can say? She heaved a sigh and turned toward the door.

"Where are you going?"

"It is obvious that you are not willing for me to experiment like this. Thank you for your time."

"I said nothing of the kind. If you truly believe in what you see as necessary, then you must have the backbone to see it through."

Hope shot from her heart to her head. She spun back to face him.

He was leaning back in his chair watching her. "We have an extra cadaver at the moment. I believe that I will do a demonstration in tomorrow's class and give everyone an opportunity to use the saw on a real bone. You are dismissed."

"Thank you." She exhaled again. *And perhaps you will allow me to do more after the others have left, if I ask. I do have the backbone. It's my stomach that seems to be the problem here.* She felt the door click behind her. While leaping down the stairs would not be professional in the least, she still felt like doing so, along with giving a whoop or two. Instead, she made her way down to the children's ward and stopped to check on Benny, as she'd come to know his name by carefully filling in his chart with all the vital signs and observations.

His eyes fluttered open when she checked his pulse and listened to his heart.

"I hurt."

"I know. I'll get you something more." She patted his shoulder. Seepage through the bandages covering the stump of his right leg concerned her. She felt his forehead. Warm but not hot. "If I bring you some soup, do you think you could eat it?"

He nodded, his eyes shadowed by the pain.

"I'll be right back." She left his chart at the end of his bed and stopped at the nurses' station. "Please give Benny another spoonful of the laudanum and honey mix, and I'll bring up some chicken soup for him."

"He refused to eat earlier."

"Was he awake?"

"Off and on."

"Has he had any visitors? Like a mother or father?"

She shook her head. "I have a feeling he is one of the homeless children who live on the streets. We get many of them now that we've opened the hospital to care for children as well as women."

"But there was a woman who brought him in."

"She didn't stay around, so we are assuming she was not a relative."

"So there are children out there with no one to feed and care for them?"

" 'Tis a disgrace, it is."

Astrid stared at the nurse. "I've read about such things but somehow never thought it was real."

"Oh, it's real all right."

"So who will care for him when he leaves here?"

"He'll go to the poor farm or the orphanage. He might be a runaway from either place already."

Astrid chewed on the side of her lip. "I'll be right back. Please give him the pain medication right away." The nurse nodded. Astrid headed for the kitchen, her feet clacking out her frustration down the hall and the stairs. What was this world coming to that children lived on the streets? *Toby and Gerald did.* The thought stopped her like a glass wall. No wonder they'd hopped a train, hoping they'd find something better farther west.

When she returned with a mug of chicken broth with a few mashed noodles in it, and a spoon, Dr. Whitaker was examining the boy. She waited at the foot of the bed.

"I see you ordered more morphine."

"Yes, sir. Also a spoonful of laudanum with honey."

"Good. I was about to do the same, to be given as needed. I will leave you in charge here. The dressings need to be changed in the morning. If he begins to run a fever, what will you do?"

"I will sponge him with cool water, force liquids, and lay cold wet sheets over him if need be. At home we've used ice chips wrapped in cloth at the neck and placed the patient's hands in cold water. Usually we could use a tepid bath, but with his legs like this, they shouldn't get wet."

"Very good, Dr. Bjorklund. May I add one more thing?" He studied her. "I always pray for my patients. I believe God is the Great Physician."

"Yes, sir." If only Mor were here. She would pray, she and Pastor Solberg. But they weren't here, and so far God had not answered her prayers for healing in the past. Why should He start now? *Remember the exam.* The thought caused more consternation. Did God pick and choose which prayers to answer and ignore others?

She put the inner discussion aside. "And, sir, I want to apologize . . ."

Before she could finish he waved her to stop but smiled as he left the room.

After supper she checked on Benny again and then returned to the dissecting room to pull her cadaver out of the cooler. Red Hawk met her as she locked the gurney in place.

"I had hoped to be here before you." His glare said more than his words.

I was hoping you wouldn't come at all. What could she say? Sorry? No, that made no sense. Why was he so . . . so rigid? No, that wasn't the right word. But it was more than unfriendly. "Oh" seemed the only answer appropriate. Why was he polite, almost friendly, at times and then harsh or even rude at others?

"You've gone ahead of me."

"Yes." *Why does it matter?* she wondered. She laid out her instruments, wishing she had a saw and the permission to use it.

They both went to work, he still on the leg and she up to the abdomen.

"You are going ahead of the rest of the class."

"I know." She studied the diagrams in her textbook. While she'd assisted now on two abdominals, she'd not had time to study each organ. Perhaps if she had known the abdominal cavity more fully, she'd have been able to save Vernon.

As clearly as if she were standing right behind her, Astrid heard her mother say, "I do the best I can with what I have, and I trust God to supply the healing."

Trust God. Her mor made that seem so easy. But it wasn't! What about the times God didn't heal? Like with Vernon. Like with Anna's baby. And what about Benny now? Was God going to turn His back again? Or was it all her fault?

She finished the abdomen and then returned to the leg she had

211

mostly completed, locating and tracing the nerves. Such small tissue to have such impact on the body working correctly.

But visions of a small boy falling beneath the iron-shod wheels of a loaded dray wagon kept getting in the way. Where would a small boy who was a double amputee go to heal and begin a new life? If only she could send him home to Blessing. Surely someone there would take him in.

"Are you feeling ill again?"

She stared up at Red Hawk, who was looking at her, waiting for an answer. "I'm not sick." The light dawned. "You've heard?"

"I'd say probably everyone knows."

Astrid stared at him. It was humiliating enough to have it happen, yet to be the brunt of gossip and snickering—what could be worse?

"Nurse reminded me I was not the first to faint nor likely to be the last." She tried on a grin, thinking it more along the line of a grimace, but at least it wasn't tears.

"She's warned us all as we take the surgical rotation." He jotted some notes down on his pad.

"You've already gone through the surgical?"

"The first one, but there are three or four I think."

"I see." But she didn't. Were they designing a special rotation just for her? And if so, why? She glanced up at the clock on the wall. She'd been here for two hours already. "I need to go check on my patient."

"I guess I'll put this away—again."

"Thank you." She studied him for a moment, deciding to ignore the *again*. She had gotten the gurney out. Just because he was being rude again didn't mean she should be. *A soft answer turneth away wrath.* The verse in her mind stopped her. *Why* was always the question. Maybe he was as homesick as she was?

Her curiosity chewed on the matter as she climbed the stairs to the children's ward, where the lights were dimmed and voices hushed.

She heard a child whimpering, realizing as she drew closer that it was Benny. "What is it?" she said gently as she stroked his forehead.

"My legs. My legs hurt so bad. And my foot."

The legs yes, but the foot? He had no foot. Was this the phantom pain she'd read about? "I'll get you a drink." She poured a glass of water and squeezed three drops of morphine into it, then held it to his mouth, lifting his head so he could drink. When he finished, he stared at her through bleary eyes. "Are you an angel, miss?"

Astrid sat down on the edge of his bed. "No one's ever called me an angel before, but if it makes you feel better . . ." She let the thought hang and laid the back of her hand along his cheek. Still warm but not more so than before. "Go to sleep now."

He nodded, a smile touching the corners of his mouth and impossibly long eyelashes drifting closed.

Tomorrow they would get him cleaned up. She'd be back to check on him in a couple of hours. "Call me, please, if he worsens," she asked the nurse on duty.

"I will."

Astrid returned to her room just as her roommate was closing the door on her way to her shift.

"There's a letter for you. I left it on your pillow."

"Thanks." By the masculine handwriting and the return address, she knew it came not from Blessing but from the missionary in Africa. "Oh, Lord, just when things were starting to settle down. All I want to know is if this is really your call—or not."

Heaving a sigh, she opened the envelope and pulled out the single sheet.

Dear Dr. Bjorklund,

Greetings from Africa and all of us here at the mission. I pray daily for God to help you in making the decisions ahead of you, that you may hear Him clearly. Should you find that you are called to Africa, you will need to first attend a missionary school for several months. I have a good friend in Athens, Georgia, who is dean of the missionary school there. I can send a recommendation to him if you decide to go there.

Our good news is that our church building, which is also the school, much like the early families did in Blessing, is now completed. One day we hope to even have a wooden floor, but for now we rejoice. We use the hut we used to use for school now as our medical clinic. There is a visiting doctor, a man who covers hundreds of miles, calling on villages such as ours.

We are sharing the gospel, as we are called to do, and I am learning the language. I wish I learned as quickly as my children do. Hearing the children sing "Jesus Loves Me" in three different languages makes me think what heaven will be like.

I do hope and pray that you are enjoying your schooling and perhaps even have had some opportunities to see a bit of Chicago. As you no doubt know, Moody Bible Institute is in Chicago. I was privileged to attend there for a year. I'm sure the school has grown since I was there. This must be a day for remembering. One of my men here said he was homesick for heaven, an apt reminder for every day.

Blessings from the mission field,
Rev. Schuman

Astrid smiled as she folded the thin paper and put it back in the envelope. The letter had traveled for a month, according to the date. And he'd said he was near a big town that had railroad service. *Homesick for heaven.* The line made her realize she wasn't as homesick for Blessing any longer. She'd not had time to be.

19

BLESSING, NORTH DAKOTA

This harvest seemed longer than any other. It probably just seemed longer because they got such a late start due to the cold and wet summer.

Ingeborg stared out the window. An early frost turned to strewn diamonds in the rising sun. Good thing she'd been paying attention and covered the tomato plants and the cucumbers. She'd been hoping for a few more pickings, and now the weather would most likely turn warm again. Indian summer, one of her favorite times of the year. Canning was winding down. They had yet to dig the carrots and other root crops to store in the cellar—some in sand, others, like the potatoes, in bins.

If only Haakan were home. Granted, they had more places to thresh this year, the reason for his prolonged absence, but sometimes rationality had nothing to do with feelings. No matter that Freda still lived with them, she missed Haakan. And Astrid. Maybe that's why this year was harder—the holes were larger. She tried to push back the concern that still simmered in her for Astrid. There was something beyond the strain of her studies, but she couldn't read between the brief lines Astrid managed to send home. "Lord, you know, so please keep her heart," she prayed.

She heard Andrew whistling on his way to the barn. She'd seen him striding across the fields, his dog at his heels. Staying home from the threshing crew was always his choice, and a good one it was. Someone had to take care of the home chores. The cows always needed milking and the other animals needed to be fed. Once it really turned cold, they'd be butchering hogs and the steers now kept in the corral and fed extra grain to fatten up for slaughter.

She rubbed her elbows, feeling the chill from the partially opened window. She always hated to close up the windows and lock the storm windows in place until spring.

The rattle of the stove lids told her Freda was up and starting the fire.

"Uff da, I'm getting lazy lately. Freda is spoiling me rotten." She turned from the window, and after pinning her braided hair into a coronet around her head, she donned a clean apron and joined her cousin in the kitchen.

"It froze last night. I should have realized you would know better than I about the weather here. Yesterday was so warm and beautiful, I can hardly believe the change." Freda slid the last stove lid back in place and adjusted the damper.

"I didn't get the zinnias covered. I'm sure they're drooping, along with the marigolds. Neither of them tolerates frost."

"Would the seeds still be good?" Freda took the bread knife from the drawer. "I thought fried egg bread sounded good for today."

"That'll be wonderful." Ingeborg dumped the used coffee grounds into the bucket for the garden. Even the chickens didn't need coffee grounds, but her roses loved them. After filling the pot halfway with water, she set it on the stove and measured in the ground coffee. Since they didn't need to make breakfast for the men, Andrew went home to Ellie and the children, George McBride went back to his shop at Kaaren's, and the two boys from the deaf school had breakfast there, as did Samuel. Two years earlier they had built a separate house for George and his wife, Ilse, who helped Kaaren run the deaf school. Besides helping with the farming, George taught woodworking skills to the boys from the school.

The cat meowed at the door and, when Ingeborg opened it, trotted in carrying a dead mouse. She laid it on the braided rug in front of the stove and looked up at Ingeborg.

"So you are bringing me a gift, are you?"

The cat chirped in response.

"Well, I thank you, but you may eat it." She nudged the dead body closer to the cat. She would have sworn the cat shrugged before picking up her prize and going behind the stove for her breakfast.

"She's a good hunter, that one."

"I know. But since she seems past the kitten-bearing years, she brings her offerings to me. One day the mouse was not dead, and we chased it all over the kitchen before she caught it again."

Freda shuddered. "Never have cared much for mice, especially not in the house." She made a face. "Dirty things."

"Astrid used to catch them and wanted to keep one for a pet. She fixed a cage out of wire screening and fed it oats out of the feedbox. Along with bits of cheese."

"In the house?"

"For a short while. One day the cat tipped over the cage and dispatched the mouse. I talked her out of getting another."

With the bread, dipped in beaten eggs with a bit of milk

added, sizzling in the pan, the kitchen began to smell like morning. Ingeborg set a jar of raspberry syrup on the table along with a bowl of applesauce.

"I used the last of the sour cream for the cookies yesterday. That would have been good on the bread too."

"At home we used lingonberries."

"I know. Here we have Juneberries, chokecherries, and the berries we grow in the garden."

Freda dished the fried slices onto two plates she'd heated on the warming shelf and set them on the table. "Will you say grace?"

Ingeborg nodded. She bowed her head and let the kitchen noises settle her. The steaming teakettle, a piece of burning wood breaking, the cat now purring her contentment, a rooster crowing, all part and parcel of her mornings, all things to be thankful for. She started to say something else but switched to the Norwegian tradition. "I Jesu navn . . ." The two women finished the age-old words together and smiled at each other at the amen.

"A piece of home." Freda spread the butter on her toast then added the syrup.

Ingeborg looked up at the sound of boots being scraped at the boot brush nailed to the porch floor.

"I brought you a bucket of milk," Andrew said as he set the metal bucket on the counter out of the cat's way. "I didn't run it through the separator. You heard anything from Far yet?"

"Thank you. Just the letter you brought over two days ago."

"I thought he might telephone."

"I'd be surprised if very many farmers out West have telephones yet. Would you like some breakfast?"

"No, thanks. Ellie will have mine ready." He looked to Freda. "You need some muscle power in the cheese house today?"

"I do. Takk for asking." Freda nodded at him.

"I'm taking a shipment in to the train today, all those you crated yesterday. You need anything from the store?" Ingeborg held her cup with both hands, elbows resting on the table.

"I'll ask Ellie." He headed for the door. "I'll be back right after I eat."

Freda watched him go. "Such a fine young man you raised. Well, all of them." She nodded. "You can be proud."

"Thank you. I give God all the glory. He has blessed us so mightily."

Freda mopped up the last of her syrup and sighed with pleasure. "I hope the men are eating well too."

"They have to be, or Mrs. Geddick will know the reason why."

"How she can take such pleasure in cooking in that little bitty wagon is beyond me."

"She loves to feed men. Haakan often says that she can turn little into so much." Ingeborg got up and brought the coffeepot over to pour refills. "I need to catch up on some correspondence, so I'll be ready to go by eleven or so. If you need anything, the list is on the counter. Just add to it."

"Do you have any yarn you have spun finer for a baby's sweater?"

"I might have some left. Look in that cupboard behind the spinning wheel. Why?"

Freda leaned closer. "Anna thinks she is pregnant again."

"This is wonderful. Why are you acting like it is a secret?"

"She hasn't told Solem yet."

"How can she? He's been gone for six weeks." Ingeborg smoothed her napkin with her fingertips. "Such wonderful news. If I don't have any yarn left, we can buy some at the mercantile. Penny carries a variety of yarns now that so few people have sheep anymore." She stopped at the look on Freda's face. "What is it?"

219

"She's so afraid she might lose this one too. That's another reason she's not told anyone."

"How many times must we tell her, the cord around the neck like that is rare. Sometime the baby must have turned wrong or some such. It was not her fault."

"You know that and I know that, but she worries."

"We have to get a house built for them, that's all there is to it."

"I could go live with them, then."

"But why? Are you not happy here?"

"Of course I am happy. This is a dream come true, but I have this yearning for land too. I've been thinking that maybe we need to go farther west so we can homestead like you did."

"But does Solem want to do that? Or would he blame you for another decision that he is unhappy with?"

Freda heaved a sigh. "Sometimes I think I should have been a man."

"Well, I'm going to run that pail of milk through a strainer and set part of it for the cream to rise. We'll be needing to churn again in a couple of days. If you want my opinion, I say you should stay here, where you have family and friends. Homesteading is terribly hard work, and you are no longer a young woman, let alone not having a husband who dreams of land." She pushed herself back from the table. "Leave these dishes. I'll do them after a bit."

After straining the milk through a clean dish towel, she set two shallow pans in the pantry for the cream to rise and poured the remainder into a jug and set it in the icebox. No longer did she have to keep everything out in the springhouse to keep cool. Penny had talked her into buying an icebox shortly after she returned and started restocking the store.

SEVERAL HOURS LATER, after running out to take the covers off
the garden, and with the crated cheese wheels in the back of the wagon
and her lists in hand, Ingeborg drove into town. Leaving the crates
at the train station to be shipped to her customers, she tied the team
in front of the Blessing Mercantile, although most of them called it
Penny's store.

The bell over the door announced her arrival, and Penny came
through the door from the kitchen, her face blooming into a smile
when she saw who it was.

"Ingeborg, I was beginning to think you were mad at me or
something the way you never darken my door."

"Oh, fiddle, you know that's not possible." Ingeborg inhaled the
fragrances of the store: leather from boots and harnesses, including the
tooled saddle that hung on the rack on the wall, kerosene for lamps
and lanterns, the oil that coated various tools to keep them from
rusting, starch and dyes, waxes for cleaning and candles, herbs like
sage and thyme hanging in bunches from the bare rafters. "It always
smells so good in here now that it is back to normal." She shuddered
remembering what the false Harlan Jeffers had done to the store.

"You must be smelling the molasses and ginger that went in the
cookies I baked this morning. Surely you have time for a cup of
coffee."

"I was beginning to think you'd never ask." She handed Penny a
list. "Let me go get the mail first and leave my other list at Garrisons'.
No one made it to town yesterday."

"You want me to start filling this?"

"If you like." Back out on the boardwalk that edged Main Street
from the store to the grocery store and Rebecca's soda shop to the
building that housed the bank, the post office, the barbershop, and

the telephone switchboard, then the boardinghouse across the street, Ingeborg waved to Rebecca, sweeping the walk in front of her shop.

"If I don't get going, I'll be in town all afternoon."

"Have you heard from Astrid?" Rebecca asked.

"No. Perhaps today."

"Come by for coffee."

"I'll stop on my way back," she promised in spite of her good intentions.

Mrs. Valders looked up as the door opened. "Ingeborg, how good to see you."

"Thank you. I feel like it's been months since I came to town. You'd think I lived twenty miles out or something." Sometimes she was still shocked at the pleasant turnaround Hildegunn was working on. Ingeborg started to slide her outbound mail into the slot but stopped when Mrs. Valders said to bring it to the counter.

"I've the mail all ready to put in the mail pouch. I'll add yours before I take it to the station." She did so while she talked. "I almost came out to your house last night with your mail since no one came to town. You have a letter from Astrid." She handed the mail across the counter. "You want Kaaren's too?"

"Of course. Anything for Freda or Andrew?"

"Andrew's farming magazine is here. That young man sure keeps up on the latest things, doesn't he?"

"That he does." Ingeborg slit open the letter from Astrid, knowing full well that Mrs. Valders was as curious about the news as anyone. That was the way of letters. Everyone got to share the news. She pulled out the single sheet of paper and glanced down at the sparse writing.

"She didn't write much," Mrs. Valders said, leaning over the counter.

"No. But she says all is well and she has been assisting in the surgery. Her classes are interesting, but her favorite is dissecting the cadaver that she shares with a young man from South Dakota named Red Hawk."

"An Indian? And a dead body?" Mrs. Valders' mouth hung open, her voice squeaking on the word *body*.

Ingeborg kept from laughing out loud by clearing her throat and continuing on as if the postmistress had not spoken. "She doesn't think too highly of Chicago. Says it is dirty, smelly, and windy." She folded the page and tucked it back into the envelope. "That's what I remember of that city too. We were so grateful to get back home. She says to tell everyone hello." She glanced up to see shock still freezing Hildegunn's face. She didn't mention Astrid's cry for help. What was she to do about the letter from Africa? Was God really calling her to be a medical missionary there? How was she to know for sure?

"I'll be back after today's mail comes in."

"Yes, of course."

As Ingeborg left the post office, she ached over Astrid's questions. *Lord, I don't want her to go to Africa. Aren't there plenty of people here who need her help? If she goes to Africa, I'll never see her again. How can I give her wisdom when I have none to give?* She knew she should be saying "Not my will but yours, O Lord," but right now she couldn't. She hurried by Rebecca's shop and into the store before she collapsed in tears.

"Ingeborg, what is it?" Penny asked after one look at Ingeborg's face.

"He asks too much."

"Who? What are you talking about?"

"God." She choked on the word, tears bursting like spring freshets leaping down the mountains in Norway. Handing Penny the letter, Ingeborg dug in her reticule for a handkerchief.

"Come, let's go back to the kitchen. I'll put water on for tea."

Ingeborg followed Penny through the doorway and sank down in a rocking chair.

Penny read the letter as she filled the teapot. "No, Astrid can't go to Africa. We need her here. Surely there must be another way. Surely."

"But if indeed it is God calling her?"

Penny shook her head. "Please forgive me, Lord, but I pray you have something else in mind. We need Astrid here."

"More than they do in Africa?" The two women stared at each other through tear-filled eyes.

20

CHICAGO, ILLINOIS

I believe the crisis will be tonight."

Astrid stared at the doctor, who peered at her over his glasses. She and one of the nurses were taking turns changing the quickly drying sheets and encouraging Benny to drink. They had moved him into a smaller room so they could care for him more easily. If she closed her eyes, she could almost believe she was at Elizabeth's, and Mor and Pastor Solberg were praying out in the hall. If she closed her eyes, she might not wake up again—for hours.

She looked away so the doctor wouldn't see the tears pooling and about to overflow.

"Dr. Bjorklund, you have to understand that we humans can only do so much. You've done all you can and—"

"And we will keep doing so as long as it takes." Speaking around the lump in her throat was difficult.

"I was going to say that you have to depend on our heavenly Father to finish the job, be it here or in heaven."

"I know that. I've been praying for Benny all along." She didn't add that God didn't seem to listen to her prayers for healing all that much. But she didn't know what else to do. Praying was so ingrained, as were the Bible verses she'd memorized through the years, that they just happened. If only she could talk to Pastor Solberg.

"What about the rest of your patients?" he asked.

"I . . . I've seen to all of them."

"I know you have, but if you are so tired you collapse, what will happen to them?"

"I suppose someone else will take care of them." She lifted the cloth from Benny's forehead and felt the ice pack under his neck. The ice was nearly melted—again.

"We can do that here, but what about later, when you are the only doctor around and everyone depends on you?"

"But how can I leave him?" The cry was wrenched from her by unseen hands.

"You make sure there are others that can and will do what you are doing right now, and you come back to check on him. I know this sounds stern and unfeeling, but you are here to learn all that you are able, and we are here to both take care of our patients and to teach young people how to be the finest doctors they are capable of becoming." He turned to the nurse. "Is there someone to take her place?"

"I will get another nurse to relieve her."

"Thank you." He turned back to Astrid. "Now you go get some sleep. I will leave orders for you to be called when and if the crisis occurs. You are due in the OR at seven thirty in the morning, and you will have had breakfast by then."

"Yes, sir."

He ushered her out of the room ahead of him. "Good night, Dr. Bjorklund."

Just before falling on her bed, she prayed one last time. "Lord God, please heal this little boy." Asleep on the next breath, she heard nothing until she felt someone shaking her shoulder. She sat bolt upright. "Yes?"

The smile that greeted her made her blink. "Benny is sleeping peacefully. The fever broke. There is no sign of gangrene in either stump. Go back to sleep so you can do your job in the morning."

"What time is it?"

"Four or so. Good night."

"Thank you, God, thank you." A tap at the door at six o'clock started her day. She peeked in on Benny before heading to scrub. He was still sleeping, his breathing natural, his skin normal. Dare she hope that God really had answered her prayer? Dare she doubt? That thought made her blink. What would Mor say? Her face would be beaming, and she'd be singing "Praise ye the Lord" and thanking Him over and over.

"So be it," she whispered, and all the while she scrubbed she kept time with *thank you, thank you, praise His holy name.* She felt like shouting it and dancing around the room, but instead she raised her arms and let the water run off her elbows. Benny was sleeping, a healing sleep. No longer sliding away.

After three surgeries in a row, one for an arm with a compound fracture, another for a stab wound, and the last a torn leg, she finished her rounds and then dropped in to see Benny awake and eating the soup a nurse was feeding him. He smiled at her.

"You the angel?"

"No, I'm the doctor. You didn't get to see the angels this time around."

"But I saw you."

"She was here much of the time. Dr. Bjorklund is her name." The nurse held the spoon to the boy's lips.

"Lady doctors?" His eyes widened.

"There are more and more of us." Astrid nodded at the child. "I'll see you later." She paused. "By the way, how old are you?"

"Six."

"You're missing school."

"Don't go to school."

"Why—?" She caught the nurse shaking her head. "I'll come by to see you later, then."

Sitting with her elbows propped on the table in the dining room, she could hardly hold her head up to drink the much-needed coffee. Why was this more tiring than caring for patients with Dr. Elizabeth? Of course, at home she didn't do three surgeries in a row. Her thoughts went back to Benny. Not in school, a street child, but now one with no legs. She knew two boys who had run from New York, street boys like Benny, and ended up in Blessing. Gerald and Tony Valders. Who in Blessing might be willing to help this child? Wooden legs and crutches. It would not be easy. But there he would be loved, and he could go to school.

"Dr. Bjorklund." The call came from the doorway.

Astrid drained her cup of coffee and, grabbing a sandwich off the tray, headed for the door. Time to think seemed to be an unknown commodity here.

"We have a woman who's been in labor for twenty-four hours. Someone brought her in and then disappeared."

"In the ER?"

"For now. We want to move her to Obstetrics, but all the other doctors are busy right now."

"What's her pulse?"

"I don't know. They just sent me to get you."

Astrid stopped at the sink to wash her hands and then followed the nurse to a curtained cubicle. The woman on the table stared at her through exhausted and fear-filled eyes.

"I'm Dr. Bjorklund. What is your name?"

The woman closed her eyes and gritted her teeth. "Uh . . ." She panted till the contraction passed. She muttered a name in a language other than English.

Astrid turned to the nurse. "Do you understand her?"

"I think she is speaking Gaelic. An Irish immigrant, maybe." She wiped the woman's sweaty forehead. "And no, I don't understand Gaelic either."

"Has she had other births?"

"I don't know."

"Does anyone here speak Gaelic?"

The young nurse shrugged. "I've been on the floor for only a couple of weeks. I don't know."

"Talk about the blind leading the blind here." Astrid laid her stethoscope against the woman's extended belly. "The baby's heart rate is accelerated." She lifted the drape and checked for dilation. "What information do we have on her?"

"I can go check. All I know is she's been in labor for more than a day."

"Go." Astrid tried to keep her voice steady. Panic wouldn't be helpful, that was for sure. She smiled at the young woman. "I'm going to examine you to see what the problem is." She dipped her hands in the basin of carbolic acid and shook them out, then laying one hand on the abdomen, she explored the birth canal with the other. What she felt was not a smooth little head.

The woman groaned and thrashed her head from side to side. She tried to sit upright.

"Don't be afraid." Astrid kept her voice soothing but firm, smiling into the terrified green eyes. Surely if she'd had other children she wouldn't be so frightened.

"There's no one out there waiting for her," the nurse said as she returned. "Admitting said two men half dragged her in, then hightailed it out again. Nurse thought maybe she is a lady of the night."

"A what?"

"A prostitute, Doctor." She looked around as if she'd been caught cursing.

Astrid blinked. So sheltered had her life been in Blessing. She'd not learned the term until she came here, where the hospital served the dregs of humanity. "So that means she's not seen a doctor or possibly even a midwife?"

"Sometimes when the midwife can't help, they send the women here."

"Well, if they'd do that earlier, it would sure help." She checked the baby's heart again. "We're going to lose this one if we don't do something different and soon. Call an orderly so you can hold her down while I see if I can turn the baby. It's either breech or posterior presentation." Astrid tried to remember the stories her mother had told of the babies she'd birthed through the years. Cesarean was an option but a last resort. How could she turn the baby?

An older nurse came in with one of the orderlies, who waited by the door. "Sean here speaks Gaelic. Tell him what you need."

"Thank you." Astrid told him and waited while he talked with the woman.

"First baby. She doesn't want to die."

"That makes all of us. Tell her I am going to examine her again and she has to lie still or you will hold her down."

He translated while the three of them took opposite positions. "Ready."

As soon as the contraction passed, Astrid tried again. When she closed her eyes to concentrate more fully, she could hear her mother once saying, *"We had the woman get up on her hands and knees, and I was able to turn the baby."*

"All right. Here's what we are going to do. We're going to turn her and help her to her hands and knees, then you all will hold her there while I try to turn the baby."

The nurse gave her a questioning look but nodded.

As they rolled her over, the woman screamed like an animal caught in a trap. The orderly kept talking with her as they forced her to kneel, even though she was so weak she couldn't hold the position by herself.

Dr. Barlow pushed aside the curtain. "Do you need help?"

"Someone rub her back. See if we can get her to relax." *God, help us.* "Hold her up!" The woman screamed again, the cry fading into faint groans.

Astrid got her hand into position again. *Please don't let us lose her either, God, please. I can't stand another one dying.* The next contraction threatened to cut off the circulation in her arm, but the baby turned, and Astrid gave a yelp of joy when she felt the head in the birth canal. "We got it. Turn her over. Sean, you brace her against your chest and let's get this baby into the light. Tell her to push now. Scalpel."

The baby had blue fingernails, toenails, and lips when he slid into her hands, but even so, he wailed at the shock. The nurse laid him on a blanket on his mother's chest. "Here you go, dearie. A fine son."

Astrid ignored the tears streaming down her cheeks. When she heard one of the nurses sniff, she knew she wasn't alone.

"Well done, Doctor." The older man patted her shoulder. "Come and talk to me when you get her cleaned up."

Astrid nodded. Her attention, now focused on cutting the cord when it stopped pulsating and letting the nurse take over on that process, focused back on her patient to stop the bleeding. "Here, massage her belly," she told the young nurse in training as she packed soft cloths in place. "We can help the uterus contract that way and expel the afterbirth. Here it comes." Another contraction delivered the remaining tissue.

The older nurse stopped beside her and spoke under her breath. "I'm going to scrub as much of her as I can while the others care for the baby. She is filthy."

"Do you get many like her?"

"No. Most don't get pregnant. There are ways to prevent it, you know."

"I heard what I thought might be an old wives' tales and that the Indians know of a way."

"Don't know about the Indians, but—"

Thinking she might want to explore this subject further, Astrid tucked it away in her mind and turned back to check on her patient. How could anyone be so dirty? Did she not have access to clean water? She checked her patient's pulse and smiled down at her. "They'll bring your son back to you as soon as he is cleaned and dressed. We're going to move you to the ward now."

She shook her head.

Wishing Sean were back, Astrid listened to the weak voice tell her something that seemed very important to the patient.

"I wish I could understand you." Astrid turned back to the nurse. "I'll check back later. Let me know if there is any change. Make sure she gets some soup and . . ."

The nurse was nodding.

"Sorry. You know all that. Thank you for helping."

"I'd not seen something like that done before. I was sure we were on our way to the OR." The older nurse *tut-tut*ted almost like Mrs. Valders when she didn't quite believe something.

Benny was sleeping again when Astrid stopped by his bed. The

chart said he'd eaten dinner and taken his medications, his temperature was slightly elevated, and the doctor had ordered the dressings
be changed in the morning. She left him and continued her rounds.
When she had only half an hour until class, she dropped by the dining
room for a cup of coffee and a handful of cookies. Sitting down at
the table, she took her pad of paper and pencil from her apron pocket
and started a long overdue letter to Joshua.

> Dear Mr. Landsverk,
>   Thank you for your letter. I'm glad to hear you are enjoying
> building windmills. That certainly is a job that makes life easier
> for your customers. They must be very appreciative.
>   Life here at the hospital is extremely busy. It makes me wonder
> how we will ever have a real hospital in Blessing. The operating
> rooms here seem to be busy all the time. I assisted with a little boy
> who fell under a dray wagon and lost both his legs. Such terrible
> things happen on these city streets. How I long for the open air
> and quiet life, although that's not how I thought about it when
> I lived there.

She paused and rubbed her chin with the pencil. What else could
she tell him? About dissecting the cadaver? He'd probably be morti-
fied. The woman who'd finally given birth? One did not discuss such
things with a person of the opposite gender. *Sex* was another word
never used.

I will add to this later. It is time for my afternoon class. She stuffed
the pad and pencil into her pocket, stopped by her room to pick up
her text and notebook, and headed up the stairs to the third floor,
where the classrooms were located. For a change she was the first one
in the room.

She dug into her other pocket for a handkerchief and found the
letter from the missionary in Africa. She removed the sheet and read

it again. *Lord God, is this from you? One minute I think it is, the next I'm sure it's not. Or is it just that I don't want to go to Africa? I want to go home to Blessing, the sooner the better.* She thought of crinkling the whole thing and tossing it in the wastebasket.

"You're here early," Red Hawk said as he sat down beside her. "A letter from home?"

"No, from Africa." She folded the letter back up.

"Africa? The so-called dark continent?"

She thought a bit. Could she talk with him about something this important? Or would he go into his mocking, cutting responses? "Do you believe in God?"

He looked at her for a moment before answering, "I believe in the Great Spirit."

"Does your God talk to you?" She squirmed a little at his concentrated gaze.

"In visions and through the elders." He paused. "I do think you and I believe in the same God."

"So you read the Bible?"

"Some. My mother did, which is why she named me Isaac, although I prefer Red Hawk. What does this have to do with your letter?"

Astrid paused for a moment. Why was he being so forthcoming this time? She wanted to hear more of his story, but for now she had to finish. "I will explain, but do you believe God calls us to different services?"

"I believe He brought me here to learn to be a doctor so I can help my people." He glanced over his shoulder when he heard someone else entering. "If that is what you refer to as a calling, I guess I do."

"Before I left home, I heard this man talk about his mission in Africa. He said they needed medical missionaries and looked right at me. Now he writes to me telling me more and encouraging me to come to Africa." How amazing it was to be talking with him like this, as if they weren't just students across a cadaver.

"I see. Had you ever wanted to go to Africa?" His mouth twitched just a fraction as if he were trying not to smile.

She shook her head. "Not in the least. I am a homebody. We are dreaming of building a hospital in Blessing, and I'm to be one of the doctors there."

"Unless you go to Africa?"

She nodded. "Why do things have to get so complicated?"

As Red Hawk leaned toward her to answer, another student stopped at her side. "I hear you may have saved a woman's life today, and her baby. Where did you get such an unusual idea?"

"My mother has been helping birth babies and caring for the sick in our area. I remembered her telling about an experience like that."

"Have you also done a cesarean?"

"No."

She saw Red Hawk shut down into his impassive look again. Could he be jealous of her medical experiences? She kept herself from staring at him, willing him to come back. One of these days she'd just ask him.

"All right, Doctors, let us begin." Dr. Franck tapped his pointer stick on the desk. "We are here to learn the human anatomy, not discuss personal things."

Astrid pushed her letter back into her pocket and opened her textbook. A letter from Africa, and a letter to a man whom she thought she was interested in getting to know better. His letter had been brief to the point of being stilted, more a note than a letter. And now she couldn't find anything to tell him about. She rubbed her forehead. And heard the instructor call her name.

She looked up. "Yes?"

"If you would like to join our class, we would be most appreciative." The bite in his voice told her she'd not been paying attention.

"I'm sorry. Could you please repeat your question?" Maybe she needed another cup of coffee. Maybe what she really needed was answers. *Remember Benny.* The thought floated through, distracting her from the question again. From the look on the instructor's face, she'd better focus on what was going on—right now. She braced for another line of sarcasm. What had he asked her?

"Just say yes," came a whisper from Red Hawk.

"Yes, sir."

"Good. I'm glad you decided to join us."

She knew better than to be distracted in this class. Dr. Franck believed women should be in nursing but should not be qualified as doctors, and here she was, playing right into his hands. What had he been asking her? She jotted a note to remind herself to ask Red Hawk. And thank him for his help. Honey instead of vinegar. Would it work?

21

BLESSING, NORTH DAKOTA

I think my wife is ready to hang me out on the clothesline."

Joshua raised an eyebrow. He didn't blame Penny for being disgusted. Perhaps downright angry if she'd not heard from her husband any more than he'd said. "You were gone a long time. Even I began to think something had happened to you."

"No telephones down around there. Sure makes me appreciate some of the things we've developed in Blessing. I'm thinking we should be selling telephone systems and installations. There's going to be a boom there."

Nodding, Joshua took a swig of his coffee. He and Hjelmer were sitting in the dining room at the boardinghouse, supposedly discussing where he would be putting up the next windmill. "So where do we go to next?" And it better be soon; the weather might not hold much longer.

"I have two orders south of Grafton. That's all we'll get done this fall, I'm afraid. I'll work with you on those. I don't see any sense in doing another trip like the one I just took. By the way, here's your pay." He handed Joshua an envelope. "Sorry I didn't get it to you sooner. We'll set it up next time I leave for Penny to pay you regular like. I really didn't think I'd be gone so long."

"Thank you." Joshua looked at the details about the upcoming orders. "They both paid a deposit?"

Hjelmer nodded. "That way we can be sure they won't change their minds. I have the specifics for each one too."

"Clear down to Valley City. That brings up an idea Trygve had." He nodded his thanks to Miss Christopherson, who refilled their coffee cups.

"More cinnamon rolls?"

Hjelmer handed her the plate. "I have sorely missed the good cooking here in Blessing. No wonder this boardinghouse is so famous."

"Coming right up," she said with a smile. "Do you need anything else?"

Both men shook their heads and returned to their discussion. "That Trygve, he has a good head on his shoulders. What's his idea?"

"That we build a wagon like the cook shack the men take threshing. Small stove, cupboards, and beds for two or three men."

"You know, I saw pictures of hammocks that they use for the crews in ships. They're made of canvas and can be hung against the wall until night. Leaves the center free for cooking and such."

"We could carry our tools in outside boxes, some materials on top or side racks."

"You ever see a gypsy wagon?"

Joshua shook his head.

"I remember one year they came through here, a whole flock of 'em. I asked if I could see the interior. They used every inch of space. I think that's where Haakan got the idea for the cook wagon. That or a chuck wagon like they use on cattle drives." He took out a pencil and paper and began sketching. "One of these days there will be plenty of roads and automobiles driving them. I read that one company is now working on what they call a truck. Has a wagon bed for hauling things." He smiled at Joshua's snort of disbelief. "No fooling. You know, once we get these two windmills finished, we can build this wagon during the winter. We can use Lars's machine shed, I'm sure. Not enough space at the livery or the smithy."

"So when do we leave?"

"Soon as the rest of the parts get here. I'll order them today."

The fragrance of warm cinnamon rolls preceded Miss Christopherson like an invitation. "I brought you fresh coffee too." She set the plate on the table. "Thorliff, er . . . Mr. Bjorklund, phoned and asked if you were here. He's on his way over."

"Good, thanks."

A minute or so later Thorliff dropped two copies of the *Blessing Gazette* on the table. "Thought you could catch up on the news." He pointed to the headline. "James J. Hill's second ocean liner, the *Dakota*, will carry two thousand passengers when completed."

Joshua glanced at the article. "Guess all the railroads weren't enough for him."

"He's one smart businessman, that's for sure." Thorliff turned to Hjelmer. "So you finally decided to show your face again."

Hjelmer chuckled. "Spoken like my favorite nephew." He pointed to the plate of cinnamon rolls. "Have one of these. Maybe it will put you in a better mood."

"My mood always improves after the printing is finished. There's something about a new issue that still gives me a thrill." He smiled at Joshua. "You want to come work for me and become my press operator?

Give me more time to do the writing and layout. Just getting to be too much for one man."

"I thought you were going to go weekly."

"I would if I could find someone dependable to work for me. Thinking of putting an advertisement in some of the regional papers."

"If you concentrated on the paper and didn't try to run a construction company at the same time . . ." Hjelmer started.

"If my partner would stay around and help me instead of off traveling half of North Dakota . . ."

Sometimes Joshua wasn't sure whether the two were teasing each other or if Thorliff really was disgusted with his uncle. "You going to have any houses to sell this winter?"

"No. The two we're finishing are already spoken for. Then we have Hjelmer's. Why? You want one?"

"I do. You think we could get a basement dug and poured before winter sets in?" Joshua felt like looking over his shoulder to see who'd said that.

"You going to be here to do it?"

Joshua glanced at Hjelmer, who half shrugged. "We'll be setting two windmills starting next week."

"Where?" The men chatted awhile longer and finished off the rolls before Thorliff pushed back his chair. "We have a lot for sale if you want to go look at it. Fastest way to build is to buy a Sears and Roebuck house. We can all put it up. Like you said, get the cellar dug and poured before the ground starts to freeze."

Hoping his stomach would quit bouncing around, Joshua took a deep breath. Did he have enough money to begin such a thing, let alone finish it? While he'd been putting everything he earned into an account at the bank, staying at the boardinghouse took a hefty chunk of what he made.

Thorliff paused. "You know, if you are concerned about money, you can talk to Valders at the bank. You have an account there, and that means you are eligible to apply for a loan."

A loan. He'd never in his life borrowed money. His father had only done so once, and he'd never quit hounding his sons to not do the same. But then, his father never put his money in a bank either. Living in Blessing was far different from living in Iowa.

"If you want to look at it now, I can take some time to show you." Thorliff gave a nod over his shoulder.

Joshua glanced at Hjelmer.

"We're finished for now. Go look and then join me at the smithy. Mr. Sam and I have something we're working on."

Within the hour Joshua had measured out the lot with Thorliff, and they'd shaken hands on the deal. He could put half down and pay the rest as soon as he was able. If he helped on the construction crew this winter to finish off the houses they had roughed in, he could pay off the rest.

He walked into the bank, withdrew most of his savings, and walked back to Thorliff's office to sign the papers. When he left, he owned a half-acre lot in the township of Blessing in the state of North Dakota. Or at least he owned half of it, with a commitment to pay off the rest. As soon as he possibly could. He huffed out a deep breath. There would be no more slack time. He thought to the invitation he'd received to play at a dance in Grafton. They'd offered to pay him and his train fare. Now he knew for sure he would take them up on it—and look for other opportunities.

He folded the pictures and floor plans for the Sears and Roebuck houses that Thorliff had loaned him and put them in his shirt pocket. He'd study them tonight. Which one would Astrid like? Her name had been in the back of his mind all through the negotiations and transaction. He wanted a house of his own to bring his wife to, to raise a family. And he wanted that wife to be Astrid. The more he thought about it, the more certain he was he'd made the right decision, in spite of what his father would say. What would Astrid think if he wrote to tell her about the lot and the house? He sighed. Writing letters was not one of his talents. As soon as he picked up a paper and pencil, his mind skidded to a stop like a stubborn mule. His sister Avis had chided him about that, saying his letters were so brief she wondered why he wasted a stamp. But he'd promised to write. What kind of a man was he to let a small thing like writing a letter bring him to his knees? Tonight he would write the letter. That's all there was to it.

Conviction in hand, he headed for the smithy. What was Hjelmer up to now?

Sometime later the ringing of the church bell brought everyone out of the buildings on the run, scanning the horizon for smoke. Johnny Solberg galloped his horse down the street. "The threshers are home! The threshing crew is home!"

"Who rang the bell?" Mr. Valders demanded.

Johnny pulled his horse to a stop and stared down at his horse's neck. "Sorry. I did. I thought everyone wanted to know." He pointed to the south. "See, there they are."

The smokestack of the huge steam engine belched enough black smoke to make one think there was indeed a fire or a monster clanking its way to Blessing.

"How did you see so far?" Mr. Valders continued his inquisition.

"I was up in the bell tower sweeping out the bird droppings, and I saw it. Pa said I should let everyone know."

"Did he say ring the bell?"

"Well, no, but he said I could take Boone and come tell you all.

242

He said to apologize for ringing the bell too. I'm sorry if I scared all of you."

"Just remember, that bell is to announce noon church services or a fire."

"Yes, sir."

Since it would still be awhile before the ponderous behemoth arrived in town, folks returned to their activities, and Johnny trotted his horse back to school, where he belonged.

———

THAT NIGHT AT the boardinghouse, Miss Christopherson announced that there would be a party Saturday night at Andrew and Ellie Bjorklund's barn to celebrate the end of harvest. Everyone was invited. She stopped at Joshua's table. "I know they are hoping you will bring your guitar and join the musicians."

"Of course. Who's going to play the piano, or are we doing without?"

"Most likely Dr. Bjorklund. It would sure be easier if they had the party at the school, but of course the barn is bigger in case it rains." She nodded to his coffee cup. "You want a refill?"

"Thanks, but I think not. I better go practice for a while. I don't play often enough." *That is something I intend to change,* he promised himself. *I need to talk to Thorliff again and see how I can fit other work in.* Thinking on how much money he owed was turning his supper into a rock in the bottom of his stomach.

———

THURSDAY EVENING, AFTER having attached blades to the heads for the next windmills all day, he ate as fast as possible, took a lantern,

243

and headed for the lot that now belonged to him. The night before he had decided which house he wanted to order, so now he paced off the ground, pounding in pegs for markers. Once that was finished, he strung string from peg to peg, and then taking the shovel he'd brought with him from the smithy, he shoved the point into the ground and slammed it deeper with his foot, grateful for the thick soles of his boots, which took the impact. He started on the north side of the site and worked his way from peg to peg, tossing the dirt well beyond the string.

The chill wind turned his sweat icy cold, but the digging kept him warm enough. He mopped his forehead when he stopped to lean on the shovel. Digging was not something he did regularly. He'd even let Trygve dig the anchor holes for the windmills they'd set. In spite of the heavy leather gloves, his palms burned and his fingers cramped. When the lantern flickered low, he hefted the shovel over his shoulder and returned to his room to fall onto the bed exhausted.

ON HIS WAY to work on Friday he glanced over to the mounds of dirt. Good thing he'd have more time on Saturday. They were only working at the smithy until noon. If the rest of the parts and the lumber came in today or Saturday, they'd head to the farms on Monday morning. The first farmer had agreed to feed them and let them sleep in his barn.

"Come on over to our house for supper tonight," Hjelmer invited later that afternoon.

"No thanks. I need to get more digging done."

"You have to eat."

"Miss Christopherson is going to keep something aside for me. I was hoping to get a good part of the cellar dug before we leave."

———

THE BAD THING about digging was that his brain wasn't needed, so thoughts of his brother floated through his head. Even though he'd not wanted to stay on the farm, he resented the way Frank took over and treated Aaron and him like hired hands without pay. His brother's officious attitude ate at him like chiggers from a summer lawn digging under the skin. If he never saw his pa again, he wouldn't mind. The fear that he was starting to be like his father had driven him from the farm—both times. He knew now he never should have gone back. He'd tried to close his ears when Pastor Solberg talked about forgiveness and how critical it was to not carry grudges. Far as he was concerned, he wasn't carrying a grudge, he was burying it under mounds of dirt.

———

RIGHT AFTER DINNER on Saturday he headed for his someday house, shovel and gloves in hand. He'd been digging for about ten minutes when he looked up to see Trygve and Haakan, both carrying shovels, stepping over the string that marked the eastern boundary.

"Thought you might like some help."

"But . . . but . . . I can't pay you."

Haakan's eyebrows tickled his hatband. "Son, you have a lot to learn about living in Blessing. Here, we take care of our own."

Trygve winked at Joshua before digging the first shovelful. "Besides, we got to save your hands for tonight. We need your guitar."

Take care of our own. The comment stayed with him. Had he

proven himself to Haakan? He'd detected some coolness back when he'd asked if he could court Astrid. He figured it was because he was a stranger. And Astrid was the man's only daughter.

————

THAT NIGHT AT the dance as Dr. Elizabeth plinked out the notes, he and Lars tuned up their instruments.

"I see you started on your cellar." Always a doctor, Elizabeth nodded toward him. "How are your hands?"

"Oh, just a blister or two. It's the rest of me that's sore. Haven't dug this much in my whole life. Back home, my younger brother got to dig the drainage ditches. And our house was already built."

"Don't let those blisters get infected."

"I won't."

Lars nodded and drew the fiddle bow across all the strings, the signal they were ready to play. He tapped his foot. "One, two, three, four." And they swung into a rollicking polka, with couples taking the floor and others clapping from the sidelines.

At the first break, Gus Baard, with Maydell Gamble by his side, stood up as soon as the music ended. His cheeks were red enough to light the room.

"Go on, boy, what you got to say?" someone called from the back.

Gus started to talk, choked on his words, and shook his head. Maydell nudged him in the side.

"I . . . ah . . . we . . . um." He sucked in a deep breath. The words tripped over each other. "You all know I asked Maydell to marry me, and—"

"Ja, that was at the last dance." The comment sent chuckles flitting around the people.

"Well, she said yes, and we were going to get married right after threshing, but now we decided to get married right after Christmas, and we want you all to come."

"Well, I should hope so." Pastor Solberg led the clapping and cheering. "Let's pray the Lord's blessing on these two young people and on the food that's about to be served." As the quiet fell, he raised his arms. "Lord God, we thank you for this evening, for the good times we have and for all the good things you have given us. We ask for your blessing on these two young people. Teach them how to love each other and build their coming marriage on your strong foundation. Bless the food so lovingly prepared for us, and protect us all from the attacks of the enemy. In Jesus' name, amen."

"Food's on," Penny called. "Save a place for the ice cream that Rebecca and Gerald are providing."

Since the musicians were invited to go first, Joshua filled his plate and sat down on one of the benches.

"Mr. Landsverk?"

He turned to see thirteen-year-old Johnny Solberg on the bench beside him. "Yes?"

"I . . . I wondered . . . I mean, well, my pa said I should ask you."

Joshua waited a moment, taking a bite out of the drumstick he'd picked up. "Ask me what?"

"You know how I want to play the guitar and you said you would teach me come winter?" The boy's eyes pleaded more than his words. "Could we maybe start now rather than waiting for winter?"

Joshua thought about his house and all the work it would take. He chewed carefully. Shame he had to say no. He started to decline, and then a thought hit him. That's what his father would do, saying that what Johnny wanted wasn't important, only building the house counted. Joshua shook off the thought. "Of course we can start now. When would you like?"

"Pa said maybe for a while after service on Sundays?"

Nodding, Joshua set his chicken bone back on his plate. He wiped his hands on a napkin and extended his right. "I'd say that's a very good idea." They shook hands. "Now, do you have a guitar?"

"Pa said I will get one if you will teach me."

"You let me know when you have it, and we'll meet at the church like you said."

"Thank you." Johnny ducked his head.

"You have to promise to practice."

"I will." The boy leaped to his feet and ran off to tell his friends.

Joshua looked up to see Pastor Solberg smiling and nodding at him.

During the next break Joshua was standing by the punch bowl drinking his second glass when he heard two women talking. Recognizing Mrs. Valders' voice, he started to walk away, but the mention of Astrid caught his attention.

"And you know, Astrid is spending a lot of her time with a young half-breed from the Rosebud Reservation. Red Hawk is his name."

"Well, I—"

"The same place she wants us to send our quilts and supplies to. You mark my words, there will be trouble here."

Joshua set down his glass and strolled back to where the instruments waited. Spending her time with an Indian? His Astrid? How could she?

That night he dreamed of home the first time since he left. He probably should write a letter, let them know he was doing well. One of these days.

The fragrance of frying bacon drew him out of bed.

Red Hawk was surely an Indian name. Why would a worthless Indian be at a hospital in Chicago? Was he studying there too, or did he just work there? So many questions and no way to get answers. Should he write and ask Astrid? What were the women talking about? Sending quilts and supplies to that reservation? Indians. That was one area his pa had been adamant about. And rightfully so.

22

NOVEMBER 1903

Ingeborg stared out the window into a world of swirling white. A blizzard already and it was only the first of November. This promised to be a long winter.

She turned back to her letter writing. For some unknown reason she missed Astrid more today than at any time so far. Now to write to her without wailing about how terribly quiet the house was, how she already missed the warm days, how she hated the thought of the winter darkness. She rubbed her sweater-clad elbows and added wood to the fires in both the kitchen and the parlor. Was it time to hang the heavy curtains over the arch from the kitchen to the parlor and over the door to the stairs?

Finding herself pacing the floor between parlor and kitchen, she stopped in front of the kitchen stove and pulled the coffeepot to the front, where the heat felt good. "Stop this!" she ordered herself, speaking out loud to get her own attention. Shame she had sent Freda over to help out at Kaaren's, since they'd caught up with their chores in the cheese house. Kaaren had several children home in bed with the grippe. Both Ingeborg and Elizabeth had been over there making sure it wasn't something worse. Freda was most likely helping with the wash that with all the bed changing would have soon become overwhelming.

"Just because you are alone for the time being, you can't go around feeling sorry for yourself." She knew she could make a telephone call, something that had yet to become habit, and check to see how they were doing. She knew that sitting down with her Bible would calm her too. She also knew that praising God in spite of what seemed bleak was the best antidote of all, so she chose to pull out the ingredients for ginger cookies.

"Now, Lord, I thank you and praise you for butter and eggs and flour," she said as she set them on the counter. "Thank you for wood for the stove, for the heat in here, for this snug house." Her thoughts flew back to the sod house, where the snow had drifted under the door until Haakan put in a doorsill and they padded around the door with a strip of coyote hide, tanned with the fur still on it. It seemed appropriate that they used the things of the land to protect themselves from the weather that fought to devour them or drive them away.

She caught herself humming as she stirred the dough with a wooden spoon that Andrew had carved for her years earlier. "Lord, I thank for you for my children, all so healthy and hardworking." She prayed for each of them and moved on to the grandchildren. Inga loved eating gingerbread men, so Ingeborg took out the cookie cutters and the raisins for eyes, nose, mouth, and buttons. Carl would eat the raisins first and then start at the feet, but Inga always giggled and ate the head first, waving her decapitated cookie in the air, crying "Look at my cookie" before taking another bite. Talk about liking an audience, her oldest grandchild most certainly did.

Hearing the men kicking the snow off their boots as they crossed the porch, she slid the first pan of cookies into the oven. Haakan liked the round ones best, dusted with sugar, so that's what went in first. The blizzard tried to blow them through the door and follow them in, but Haakan turned and put his shoulder against the wooden frame to force the door closed.

"Good thing we put up the ropes last week." He took the broom to finish sweeping off any remaining snow, including from Andrew's shoulders. Every year they pounded in posts and strung ropes from the house to the well house and on to the barn, just for instances like this. Wandering off and getting lost in the white and windy world was far too easy and had happened to more than one person they knew.

"Another thing to praise God for." Ingeborg smiled at her husband and son. "Cookies will be out in just a few minutes."

The wind blew itself out sometime during the night. Ingeborg woke to silence. Ah, blessed silence. No banshees wailing at the corners of the roof seeking entrance through the smallest crack. She curled next to Haakan, spoon fashion, and rejoiced in the quiet, his strong body, and the comfort of their goose down–filled feather bed covered with the quilts she had so lovingly made. Ah, so many things to be thankful for. The most obvious being grateful the north wind had abated.

Haakan's hand clasped the one she'd curved over his ribs. "God dag."

"Ja, it will be . . . it is."

"Still snowing?"

"I haven't been up to check. I hate to leave our warm bed."

He rolled over and kissed her forehead. "I know the wind is hard for you."

"Ja, it tries to bring back bad memories, but I think I finally outsmarted it. When the wind howls, I sing louder."

"Ah, my Inge, such a treasure you are."

She dug into his ribs. "You just want me to get up first and start the stove."

"I stoked it during the night, so it shouldn't be too bad."

"You were up, and I didn't even know it?"

"You were sleeping so sound the roof could have lifted off."

She loved the teasing note in his voice. In the summer they never took a few moments like this. The workload was too pressing, and the daylight hours never lasted long enough. Throwing back the covers so the cold hit him too, she dug her feet into the fur-lined moccasins Metiz had made her years before and drew her wool robe off the bed post. Laughing at his mumbled accusations of meanness and cruelty, she shoved her arms into the sleeves and tied the belt as she crossed the floor to the doorway.

"Coffee before you head to the barn?"

"Please. And wake me in half an hour."

Humming, she removed the lids and rebuilt the fire in the kitchen stove. He was right. There were plenty of glowing coals, and the temperature in the room was more chilly than cold, another benefit of the passing wind. She took a spill from the jar on the warming shelf and lighted the kerosene lamp always kept trimmed and ready on the shelf behind the stove.

The cat peered at her from her box between the stove and the wall, yawning and stretching her front legs, claws extended.

"Looks like everyone is sleeping in." Ingeborg left the kitchen and stopped in front of the woodstove in the parlor. The isinglass windows glowed faintly, their pink-orange hue an indication the coals there were still burning. Leave it to Haakan to take such good care of them, not that they needed the stoves burning all night.

When she brought Haakan his coffee, he patted the bed beside him. "So is it still snowing?"

"I think so, but short of going outside, it is too dark yet to tell for sure." She sipped from her cup. "I've been thinking."

"Uh-oh."

"What if we were to get on the train and go see Astrid?"

"Chicago is a ways away."

"I know how far it is." She ran her finger around the rim of the cup. "I know we could telephone the hospital too, but when would she have time to talk with us?"

"If we went there, how would she have time to see us if she can't take time to use the telephone?"

"Well, if she were to telephone, we'd not have to catch anyone else up on the news, that's for sure." The two chuckled over the rims of their cups.

"Ja, as they say, these are party lines." He nudged her knee, cocked on the bed so she could be facing him. "What's for breakfast, wife?"

"Maybe nothing if you can't pay serious attention to what I said."

"I figured you were just dreaming." He drained his coffee cup and heaved a belly-deep sigh. "But dreams are necessary for living at times." He threw the covers back and felt for his slippers. "I think by next winter we will have indoor plumbing. What do you think?"

"You mean the hand pump in the kitchen is not enough?" She'd felt the installation of the red hand pump in the dry sink was a miracle in its own right. Cold as it could be, keeping the water line from freezing was going to be difficult enough.

"No. I want a biffy and a bathtub like they have at the boarding-house. No more thunder mugs under the bed." After buttoning his wool shirt, he shoved his feet into his wool pants and pulled down the cuffs of his long johns, then stood and hoisted his suspenders over his shoulders.

Ingeborg watched for a moment, as always observing to see if he favored his right side. No sign that she could see, and she knew better than to ask. "Well, I better restoke those fires and get going on the biscuits. How about some redeye gravy over the biscuits? We are about out of ham, you know."

"I know. Surely it is cold enough now to butcher. We'll prob'ly have a warm spell after this."

"Good." She smiled and sent her husband out in the dark that still only showed a faint horizon. Surely they didn't have to milk so early. After all, there was no field work to do today.

"Keep that coffee hot."

"I will." Humming, she set about turning the sourdough she'd started the night before into bread. While she could now purchase yeast at the grocery store, she still preferred the flavor of her own sourdough bread. It took longer to rise, but the fragrance of the sourdough starter flavored the entire house.

She'd just checked that the oven was hot enough for the biscuits when she heard boots thumping on the porch. She glanced at the clock. The men had not been gone long enough to finish the chores. Something was wrong.

"Ingeborg!" Haakan's voice.

She flew to open the door, her mind already going crazy with possibilities, the foremost that someone had been injured. "What's happened?"

Carrying something under his coat, Haakan pushed into the warm kitchen. "I . . . we found her in the haymow."

"Who?" Ingeborg reached for his coat. Inside, wrapped in his arms, she saw a child with dark matted hair, dressed in a skin coat, leggings, and mittens. "Is she alive?"

"Ja, so far." Haakan handed her to his wife. "At least she is breathing. We found her burrowed under the hay or she would have been frozen to death. She may be close to that anyway."

Ingeborg sank down into her rocker near the stove and began

unlacing the child's wrap. She pushed the hood back to see the child's face. Dark lashes feathered her cheeks. Matted hair had been braided but was now snarled about her head. She took off the fur-lined mittens and checked the child's fingers for frostbite.

Haakan knelt beside her. "What can I do?"

"Get the washtub and fill it halfway with tepid water." She held the child with one arm and began unlacing the knee-high fur-lined boots. All the garments were made of deerskin with the hair turned inside or, in the case of the mittens, rabbit skin for softness.

While she could hear Haakan doing what she had asked, her mind stayed with the child, a line of prayers girding them all. *Heavenly Father, help this child of yours. Whoever she is, you, oh Lord, know.* Checking the small toes, she found several turned white, but the feet seemed to be all right, what she could see through the dirt. The stink of grease and fire smoke mingled with urine as the child lay without moving.

"The water is ready. Feels cold to me but any warmer would be bad."

Ingeborg nodded as she let the child's clothes fall to the floor. She handed the little one to Haakan and stood to take her back, clutching her into the warmth of her body. "Get some towels and that small quilt off the stand in our bedroom." While she talked, she knelt beside the tub and lowered the inert body into the water. "We could make it warmer in here if you circle the chairs and drape the spare quilts from the trunk over them."

She kept one hand under the little girl's neck to keep her floating and gently rubbed the small body with a cloth. Haakan set up the chair circle in front of the stove, which cut off the drafts immediately.

"How can I help you?"

"I think you've done all you can. Now we wait. If the cold doesn't kill her, she might yet die of starvation. Look at this." Moving gently she scrubbed the stick-thin arms and legs. "Have they no food on the reservation?"

"We don't know she's from the reservation. I have no idea if someone brought her here, or she got lost in the blizzard."

"Was the barn door open?"

"No, and I don't know if it had been opened. I wasn't paying attention. I was just trying to get out of the cold myself. Andrew is the one who found her. I told the others to keep milking while I brought her to you."

"What do we have to dress her in? Other than blankets for now." A shiver rocked the little one, her ribs showing through the dark skin. "Good. She is responding. Put the towels on the oven door. Oh, my word. I need to get the biscuits out. They're probably burned to bits."

Haakan grabbed a dish towel, folded it, and opened the oven door to grab the pan of well-browned biscuits. "They'll be edible."

"Leave the door open. We can wrap her in the towels now, then in a quilt, and I'll sit here and hold her in the heat." When they finished, Ingeborg rocked the chair gently, cuddling the little girl all wrapped up like a baby in the quilt.

"I'm going back out to help finish milking."

"All right." She heard a mewling like a kitten's cry from the child in her arms. "Hear that?" Pulling back the quilt she watched as the girl's eyelashes fluttered. Another shiver rocked her, and her eyes flew open. She stared up at Ingeborg without moving, as if frozen indeed.

"It's all right, little one," she crooned softly. "You're all right. You're safe here."

The black eyes stared back at her, not moving, not blinking until another shiver wracked the little body.

"How did you get here? Where are you from? Who brought you?" The questions poured forth in the same mother croon Ingeborg had used with her own children and grandchildren and any other small children who needed her. She held the girl close, trying to give her all the body heat possible. Her own face wore the heat from the stove like sunburn, but she stayed in the gently rocking chair until the little girl's eyes drifted closed and she sighed to sleep.

Haakan found them in the same place. He stoked the fires before taking off his boots and sliding his feet back into his moccasins. "Andrew says he barely made it over. I told him he was nuts to try. We can't string a line that far, but we can handle the fifteen milking cows without him. Good thing we put the posts clear to Lars's. Although he said he could see plenty clear enough this morning, I think we should wait until daylight before milking during these winter months."

"The child was awake some. She still shivers once in a while but seems to be sleeping peacefully."

"What did she do?"

"Just stared at me like a wild animal that freezes so as not to be seen."

"That might well describe her. What will we do with her? Notify the Indian agent?"

"Why? We have plenty of room. She can stay here until someone comes for her."

"They probably think she died in the blizzard."

"No. For some reason I feel certain someone brought her to our barn."

"Well, why not to the house, then?"

"Afraid? Thought we might turn them away?"

"Aw, Inge, have we ever turned anyone away?" He set the skillet on the stove and retrieved the sliced ham from the table, where Ingeborg had started breakfast. With the ham sizzling, he fetched the eggs from the pantry.

"If you hold her, I'll make the breakfast."

"You hold her. I'll make the breakfast. If she sees another strange face, she might be frightened to pieces. Have you tried the telephone yet?"

She shook her head. "But no one has called either."

"I'm thinking the lines might be down. The blow last night was enough to take them down even without the ice on the wires."

He walked over to the box on the wall and lifted the receiver. Even after he spun the crank on the side, nothing happened. "Hello? Hello?" He hung it back up. "Out between here and town at least. Who knows about the rest."

"You going to make gravy?"

"I think I draw the line at gravy. Ham and eggs are plenty fine. Looks like we need to scrape the bottoms a bit on those biscuits." He cracked four eggs into the popping grease and used the turner to splash the ham juice on them.

"You do that like you cook every day."

"I learned a long time ago."

"Why didn't you ever say anything?"

"Why mess up a good thing?" He grinned at her. "You want to eat at the table or in that chair?" He took the plates down from the warming shelf, slid the eggs and ham onto them, and headed for the table.

Ingeborg leaned her head against the back of the rocker. *Lord, you sure know how to throw a curve into my day. Again I know you have a plan. Thanks for letting us be a part of that plan.*

Haakan came over and held out his arms. She put the sleeping child in his strong arms, stood, and leaned into them both. A child in their house. Only a visitor most likely but a child to love nonetheless. "Let's eat. If she wakes up, I'm sure she'd like something too." By the look of the little body, she needed a lot of good food. Were the rest of her people in such bad shape as she was?

23

Joshua stared out of the boardinghouse window at the heavily falling snow. There'd be no more well drilling for a while, and he could only imagine how deep the snow would be in his cellar before this quit. He blew out a sigh and shook his head. Here he'd been hoping to get the basement finished and the house framed in before the snow so he could work inside in the winter.

So much for good ideas. So much for earning enough money to pay off his lot. He shook his head and made his way downstairs to the dining room. At least he had food and a good roof over his head. What if they'd been on their way to do another well and windmill?

"Sure is nasty out there," Miss Christopherson said when he sat down at his table.

"How did Mrs. Sam get here to cook?"

"Well, we all spent the night here. That's what we do when it starts to blow from the north, although this is early for a storm like this. Do you want oatmeal first or bacon, eggs, and fried cornmeal mush?"

"I'll pass on the oatmeal this morning, thank you."

"Coffee coming right up."

"Is that cinnamon rolls I smell?"

"Sure is. I'll bring you one with the coffee."

As she hurried to the kitchen, he looked around at the few others gathered in the dining room. A family that looked like they were planning on heading west. He wondered why they had gotten off the train in Blessing. There wasn't any land around here for either buying or homesteading. The Bjorklunds and Knutsons bought up whatever came available. Two well-dressed men sat at another table. They obviously knew each other. Railroad men perhaps? Sure looked like businessmen. A drummer sat over against the wall. How many would still be here after the westbound train came through?

He ate his breakfast and returned to his room to stare at the snow-blinded window.

How long since he'd had a day with absolutely nothing to do? He mentally made a list. He could write to Avis. She would be pleased to hear from him. He could write to Astrid. Or he could write to Frank and see if there was any way to make things right there. Not that he wanted to, but Pastor Solberg's sermon series on forgiveness kept eating away at him.

If the snow let up he would go down to the smithy and see if there weren't enough parts to put together another windmill head. A draft sneaked under the window, nearly freezing his midsection. He slammed his fist on the top of the lower frame in the hopes of driving it tighter into the frame. It slipped some, and he cranked the latch closed. That helped, and he could roll up a towel or something to block the remaining draft.

Restless and feeling confined in his room, he took his writing kit and headed downstairs to the gathering room, where a fire roared in the fireplace and gas lamps cast a cheerful glow against the dim light coming from outside. Sitting in a chair at a table, he laid his supplies out and started with the letter to his sister. That would be the easiest.

He told her about his job, playing his guitar for dances and church. He knew she would be appalled at the guitar in church. Back in Iowa only organ or piano music was proper for worship. He told her about digging the basement for his house and that the blizzard was filling it in far more quickly than he'd dug it. He closed with a question.

> I am thinking of coming back for Christmas. Do you think I will be welcome there? Or have Father and my brothers pretty much washed their hands of me? It all depends on the weather, of course, if we can finish the cellar and frame the house. Depends on if winter is really here or we will have another warmer spell for a time.
>
> Please write. I miss you and I know you miss Mother. I am still in shock I think, almost pretending she will be waiting and glad to see me when I get there.
>
> Your brother,
> Joshua

Addressing the envelope, he overheard the two men talking. He realized they must be land speculators, buying land up in the West and then selling it again to those who wanted to still get in on cheap land. He knew that no matter what the monetary price of the land, it would cost them far more in sweat and heartache. He'd seen others already giving up and heading back East. He'd been one. What would life have been like if he had stuck it out here? There wouldn't have been the showdown between him and his brother. He should have been smarter, that was all. His father had planned for Frank to have the farm all along, just stringing him along to get as much work out of him as possible. He'd never planned on paying for that labor.

When Joshua realized his teeth were clamped and his fists clenched, he shook his head. Good thing he had put the remaining money from selling his land south of Blessing in the bank in Iowa so that he'd had some cash to bring north with him again. This time he would build a decent house, not even think about farming, and concentrate on building windmills and digging wells, something he enjoyed doing. When they released the gears and let the windmill spin for the first time, he felt like whooping himself. One more family had a well and a windmill to bring up the water. Seeing the water gush from a pipe into a stock tank or down a pipe to the house pleased him greatly. One woman cried when she used the hand pump to bring water into her sink for the first time.

There was something beautiful about seeing windmills silhouetted against a sunset or sunrise. It said there were people there who cared about the land and the life.

He took out another piece of paper but paused before writing when Miss Christopherson announced that coffee and cinnamon rolls were set out in the dining room if anyone was interested.

He was. He stopped at a window in the dining room but couldn't even see across the street. The wind was picking up again. Those two years in his shanty he'd nearly lost his mind when the blizzard closed him in like this. He'd strung a rope to the barn so he could care for his cows and horses, but the tar paper shack had been nearly useless for keeping the cold out. He got frostbite sitting right next to the stove. He'd finally glued newspapers to the walls to help insulate it.

"The westbound train will be in the station in fifteen minutes," Miss Christopherson announced a few minutes later. Sure enough, the two businessmen and the family all gathered their things and made their way to the door. "You just follow the fence, keeping close by it, and you cannot miss the station. You can get lost in the middle of the street if you don't." She bid them good-bye and Godspeed and pushed against the door with her shoulder to shut out the screaming wind demanding entrance.

"You think it is letting up any?" Joshua asked when she returned, brushing snow off her apron.

She shook her head. "Not at all. Can I get you more coffee?"

With two letters to leave in the box for the mail, he returned to his room after dinner and picked up his guitar. Here he'd been thinking there was no time to practice, and now with the storm blowing Joshua had plenty of time. He'd best be making good use of it. He was still trying to get the chording right on "The Old Rugged Cross" when he heard a knock on the door. After setting the guitar on the bed, he crossed the room to open the door.

Miss Christopherson had raised her hand to knock again but dropped it to her side. "I have a favor to ask."

He nodded. "Was I bothering anyone?"

"On the contrary. We were all wondering if you would be willing to play down in the kitchen so we don't have to sit in the dining room to hear."

The earnest look on her slender face made him smile. "I don't want to bother anyone."

"Oh, no bother. We could do some singing while we make supper. If you please, of course." She paused a moment. "I'm sure we could find a couple of cinnamon rolls to make it worth your while."

Joshua chuckled and shrugged. "Of course I can play down there, and it would probably be warmer than here too. I'll be right down."

"Thank you."

He picked up his guitar, a couple of picks, and what little sheet music he had, and made his way down the stairs, a rosy warm feeling clinging to his chest. He played while the staff cooked and laughed and sang along. Several other patrons drifted in, and what started out to be a dreary day turned into a party. Mrs. Sam taught him a couple of new songs that she said came from her people when still in slavery. As she sang them he fingered the chords, writing them down at the end so he wouldn't forget.

"How come you don't come to the dances," he asked during one of the eating times.

"I'm always either fixing food or cleaning up. Just don't work out, that's all."

And that was why they were never in church either, he surmised. "A voice like yours needs to be heard more."

Mrs. Sam rolled her eyes. "Pretty words don't cut no nevermind wit me."

But he noticed that she pushed an extra roll his way.

———

"WE HAVE TO have a name for her," Ingeborg said that evening.

Haakan glanced up from the table, where he sat with his Bible open and the kerosene lamp close enough to make reading easier. "She's slept all day?"

Ingeborg nodded. "I woke her to feed her some soup, and after eating what I fed her, she fell right back to sleep. Without ever saying a word."

"Perhaps she cannot hear."

"No, she can hear. The cat mewed, and she looked over to the stove."

"We can most likely get to town tomorrow, and I'll ask around, see if anyone has seen any Indians passing through."

"I keep thinking about Metiz and wishing she were here to help me." She pulled the coffeepot forward to the hot part of the stove. "Some days I still miss her so much the tears come. Metiz, and Agnes. I remind myself how blessed I am to have had two such wonderful friends, and I am grateful, but . . ." She huffed a sigh. "You want some coffee?"

"Do I ever turn down a cup of coffee? And perhaps some of that rhubarb sauce with a bit of cream?"

"I s'pose you'd like cookies with that too?"

"If that's not too much bother." His eyes twinkled in the lamplight.

"And all because I wanted a cup of coffee." She fetched the canned sauce from the pantry and the cream from the icebox she'd moved into the pantry by the window, where it was cold enough to not need ice. For years they had stored cream and eggs and things that spoiled in the screened box off the window and let Mother Nature keep things cold enough. During the winter, they didn't even need the outer box. The closed-off pantry sufficed.

"Chocolate or gingerbread?"

"Both."

Ingeborg chuckled as she dished up their rhubarb sauce and cookies. Haakan did like his cookies . . . well, all desserts. She turned from the counter to see two black eyes staring at her from the pallet by the stove. She smiled and nodded, but the child ducked her head. Putting extra cookies on the plate, Ingeborg carried the things to the table. "She's awake," she whispered.

Haakan turned to look and gave his wife a questioning glance.

Ingeborg returned to the stove and carried the coffeepot to the table to fill their cups. She picked up a cookie and brought it with her to set the coffeepot back. Then kneeling at the pallet, she held out the cookie.

The child's nostrils flared at the fragrance, much like a wild animal checking the wind.

"Here, this is for you." Ingeborg held it closer.

The little girl stared from the cookie to Ingeborg and back again before tentatively reaching for the goodie. She sniffed it, and then stuffed it into her mouth as if fearing it would be taken away.

"Well, that worked." Ingeborg brought two the next time, and the same thing happened, only now without the waiting.

"You better not give her any more," Haakan said softly. "It might make her sick. Too rich."

"True." Ingeborg rose and returned to the pantry, bringing back a jar of milk this time. She poured half a cup and took that over. It disappeared as readily as the cookies. "Well, she knows how to drink from a cup."

"I'm sure they have cups and plates or something similar on the reservation by now." His teasing tone made her smile back.

"Metiz said they used to drink out of tanned hides or a horn, sometimes vessels carved of wood." She looked down at her moccasins, made so long ago with such love and care by Metiz. "I wonder if the school that was started on the reservation is still going. Or if they have any medical help."

There had been talk of combining the small reservation to the north of Blessing with some others in western North Dakota, but nothing had come of that. While the churchwomen sent a barrel of quilts and used clothing to the reservation once a year, they'd not maintained close ties. Metiz had come south from the Winnipeg area, where there was a gathering of Sioux French-Canadian families—not really a tribe but a settlement.

How would they communicate with this child? Ingeborg dipped her cookie into her coffee cup, aware of the black eyes that watched her every move.

"You suppose she needs to use the pot?" Haakan, ever practical, asked.

"What do her people do?"

"Probably just step outside the tepee, or whatever, and squat."

Ingeborg nodded. "Lesson one, then. Goodness, think how long it has been since I potty trained a child."

"I say we bring Inga out here for a couple of days, and she'll take care of all kinds of training. You know how she loves to boss Carl around."

"That's not a bad idea."

"It's a good idea. I thought of it."

"But what if this little girl doesn't speak English?"

Haakan thought a moment. "I'll lay money on Inga."

Ingeborg cleared off their coffee things and extended her hand to the child. Black eyes stared up at her, but finally the girl stood and reached out with her own hand. Together they walked to the rocker, where Ingeborg sat down and tugged gently on the small hand. "Come sit with me." She patted her knees and held out both hands.

After hanging back for a bit, the little one stepped close to her knees and allowed Ingeborg to help her up into her lap.

"See, that didn't hurt at all. You can be comfortable here with me, and we'll rock a bit and maybe sing some songs."

The girl grabbed the arm of the chair when Ingeborg first set it to rocking gently, but soon she relaxed and a smile touched her face at the pleasant motion. Slowly she sank against Ingeborg's chest and heaved a big sigh.

Ingeborg matched the sigh. The stink from the black hair made her wish she had washed her, but at the time, getting her warm was about all she could do. She started humming and moved into singing "Jesus Loves Me." Following that with other songs, she let her mind wander ahead. *Lord, you knew she was coming to us, and now please let me know what I am supposed to do. Take her to the reservation? Keep her here in the hopes that someone will come for her? I know to do one thing, to love her. Somewhere her mother can't or is gone. Has she other family? How do we get her to talk?*

She felt the thin little body relax against her and her breathing even out. The most important thing was to keep her from any ill effects of her near to freezing.

"Where will she sleep?"

"I'm thinking of a pallet beside our bed. Do you think she would be warm enough there? Or she can sleep with us. What will Freda say when she comes back to see we have another guest?"

"I think Freda will be just like you, delighted to have a child to fuss over."

"I'm that obvious, eh?"

Haakan just smiled. "Well, for one thing, I hope you can get her bathed and her hair washed tomorrow. I'd forgotten the Indian smells of bear grease and smoke and who knows what else."

"I'm going to ask Kaaren if she has any clothes over there that might fit her. Your undershirt will do for tonight. Do I scrub her deerskin clothes like I do cloth?"

"Did Metiz scrub her things?"

"She did her wool and cotton things. How do we keep the deerskin from getting stiff if I wash it?" So many questions. Haakan took the sleeping child and laid her on the pallet by the stove so Ingeborg could stand. She let the cat out and retrieved bedding from the trunk at the foot of their bed.

Haakan banked the stoves while she folded a feather bed in half and laid it on the floor by the bed, then added folded sheets and quilts. She laid one blanket over the back of a chair by the stove.

When they were ready for bed, she wrapped the warm blanket around the little one and laid her in the middle of the well-padded pallet, tucking the quilts around her. Since her hair felt damp, Ingeborg brought a knit wool cap from the box by the door and put it over her head.

"There. Dear Lord, let her sleep peacefully, and keep those who brought her to us safe."

"Amen," Haakan said as he lifted the covers for Ingeborg to crawl under.

"We could put her in Astrid's room after Freda comes back. That way there would be someone upstairs with her."

"Very true. Good night, my Inge."

Sometime during the night, Ingeborg felt a little hand lifting the covers, and the girl crawled in bed with them, snuggling against her back without a sound.

Was trust built so easily? A couple of cookies, a warm place, and a lap complete with rocking chair?

24

When Ingeborg awoke before daylight, she picked up the sleeping child and nestled her back on her own pallet before heading for the kitchen to wake the fire in the stove. With the clatter of lids and the scrunch and thunk of wood, all morning sounds to her ears, she didn't hear the patter of two little feet and turned to see the little body, clothed in a droopy undershirt, climbing up into the rocker. The girl settled herself and leaned forward to get the chair moving, then stared at Ingeborg with a tentative smile.

"Well, good morning to you too." Ingeborg held out her hand. "Come, I'll show you the pot. You must be in misery by now."

The smile disappeared, and she ducked her head, at the same time sliding forward off the chair seat. When Ingeborg showed her the enameled pot behind the dressing screen, the child hoisted the shirt and sat down like she'd been doing so all her life. When she finished, she hopped up and looked at Ingeborg, who nodded and smiled.

Back in the kitchen, she found her clothes in a pile in the corner and sat down to pull on the leggings.

"No." Ingeborg shook her head. "They are wet and dirty." She held out her hand again and brought her back to the chair, leaving the clothing behind. The child glared up at her but climbed up in the rocker again and jerked it into motion, arms clamped across her chest.

Ingeborg sliced a piece of bread, added butter and jam, and handed it to the child.

She took it, dipped a finger into the red jam and licked it off, then attacked the bread.

"Slow down. No one is going to take it from you." Was food so scarce that people fought over it?

Ingeborg fixed the coffee and took a cup in to Haakan, the squeak of the rocking chair following her.

"She's up, eh?"

"Ja. Could you hear us?"

"I heard you and figured what was going on. She made it through the night without accident or incident?"

"I felt her crawl up behind me at some point. She's a pretty brave little girl. She's not happy right now because I didn't let her put her own clothes on. I'm going to call Kaaren and see if someone can bring things over."

Haakan pondered a moment. "Did you check her head for lice?"

Ingeborg flinched. "I didn't think of it. Oh, ick." Her scalp felt itchy at the thought. "I will. Scrubbing with kerosene will not be easy. It stings and stinks both." She left the room and fixed another slice of bread to distract the child while she lifted and parted her hair. Sure enough. Lice. Now she'd have to strip the bed and wash all the bedding this morning. Why hadn't she thought of that last night? The easiest thing would be to cut her hair short to make it easier to wash.

Crossing to the telephone on the wall, Ingeborg cranked the handle. She turned to smile at Haakan. "It works today." His shrug said he was as surprised as she was. When she heard Rebecca's voice saying "Number please," she knew something was wrong. Gerald usually took the night shift and Deborah MacCallister the day. "Is Gerald suffering again?"

"Yes. The fever started yesterday, and the muscle cramping made him miserable all night. Dr. Elizabeth sent over some quinine—we had run out. He'd been doing so well, you know. We were hoping the malaria had gone away."

"From what I've read, it never goes away, but the episodes don't happen so often."

"That's not good news. What number did you want?"

"Knutsons', but first where was the break in the line? We had no phone yesterday."

"You'll have to ask Thorliff. I'll put you right through."

Ingeborg listened for the ringing. Kaaren picked up on the third.

After the greeting Ingeborg continued. "We have a guest here who needs some clothes. She's about six or so, I would say. Small for her age."

"Where did she come from?"

"The Indian reservation, I think. But someone must have brought her here. Andrew found her burrowed into the hay, or she surely would have frozen to death. She slept all of yesterday, and the phone was down, as you probably know."

"I'll dig in the trunks for something and send one of the boys over with them. The milkers have already left." Kaaren paused a moment. "What are you going to do with her?"

"What can I do? The hardest thing is she's not spoken a word, so we don't know if she speaks English or not."

"Uff da. Mine can't hear. You have checked for that, right?" At Ingeborg's assent, she continued, "And yours doesn't talk. You don't even know her name?"

"Nothing. We only know that she is so skinny it makes you want to weep, but she's one tough little girl. She has lice." Ingeborg glanced over to where the rocking chair kept moving. "And she loves the rocking chair."

"What was she wearing?"

"Deerskin top, leggings laced to her knees, and moccasins with leg coverings with the hair side in. I have to figure how to scrub them too." Ingeborg paused at a click on the phone line. Who had been listening in? That was one thing about the telephone. You never knew who all would hear your news. Not that it mattered if others heard at this point.

Kaaren chuckled. "Well, the news is out now. I better get back to helping Ilse get breakfast on the table."

"How are your sick ones?"

"All on the mend. Why don't I send Freda back with the clothing? You might need help with the scrubbing."

"Good idea. Takk."

Ingeborg hung up and turned to see Haakan pulling on his boots. "Think of a name for her."

"You want me to tell Andrew?"

"I guess. It doesn't really matter. Someone was listening, and I'm sure the entire town of Blessing will know by ten."

"If it takes that long." He pulled his wool winter hat with the earflaps down on his head. "Keep the coffee hot."

Ingeborg brought the washtub back in and filled the boiler with water to heat. She could feel the dark eyes watching her as she moved about the kitchen, stirring up oatmeal for breakfast and slicing bread to be dipped in beaten eggs and fried. As the fragrances permeated the kitchen, she returned to the bedroom to get dressed, turning to find the child right behind her, as if she didn't dare let her out of sight. She exchanged her robe and nightdress for the layers of clothing needed to keep warm enough. Wool stockings, flannel drawers and camisole, padded woolen petticoat with another over it and then her wool serge skirt and a sweater over her waist, finishing off with an ankle-length apron.

All the time she kept up a running monologue describing what she was doing and why, although she wondered why she did that. If the child did not speak English, she hoped the river of words sounded comforting. When the little girl shivered, Ingeborg returned to the kitchen, where it was warmer, to brush and braid her hair.

"Ingeborg, I'm home," Freda called as she opened the door.

"Good. Come over here, where it is warm." Ingeborg laid the brush down and divided her hair into three sections. "How was the walk? Did you use the lane or the path across the field?"

"I followed the path the milkers used. The sun is trying to break through the clouds." While she talked Freda unwrapped her long scarf and hung her outer things on the pegs on the wall. "I brought several sizes. She doesn't look very big."

"She's not." Ingeborg wrapped her braid around and around at the nape of her neck and pinned the coil in place. "There, that's better. Now, let's see what you have. After we finish breakfast, we are going to bathe her, and I'm thinking perhaps cut her hair to make it easier to wash."

"Lice, eh?"

"Not surprising. Kaaren has to delouse a child or two every year.

I know you've been washing bedding day and night, but we'll have to do that here too. Everything she might have touched, including our bed. She crawled in with us during the night. I never even thought of lice. All I could think was to get her warm again. She was so cold."

"Any frostbite?"

"Remarkably little. Some spots on her toes is all." Ingeborg laid the clothes on a chair where the little girl could see them from the rocker. "These are for you." She held up a woolen shift and shirt, along with knit woolen stockings. "Oh good, I was wondering how quickly I could knit her some."

When Haakan came in from milking, they sat down at the table.

"Andrew suggested we call her Emaline. I thought that was kind of pretty." Haakan bowed his head, and the others followed.

Ingeborg glanced up from under her lashes to see the stubborn look had returned to the child's face. If she thought sitting at the table was bad, wait until she had to endure the kerosene. *Lord, help us through this.*

"I think we should cut it." Freda shook her head as they studied the rat's nest that was Emaline's hair. Ingeborg was still debating whether they should give her an English name or perhaps call her Shy Fawn in honor of her heritage. But then the other children would probably tease her, so an English name would be better.

"I guess you are right." Ingeborg fetched the scissors from her sewing basket in the parlor. She handed Emaline two cookies, one for each hand, and lifted a hank of hair. When the sound of the scissors made the child whip her head around, the women sighed. This was not going to be easy.

Thunder settled on the girl's brow.

"You distract her," Freda suggested. "I'll cut. We can make it pretty later."

They developed a rhythm. Ingeborg held out a piece of cookie. Emaline reached for it, and Freda snipped off more hair. By the time they finished, both of them were shaking their heads. Now the hair no longer looked like a rat's nest but like something had been chewing on the black mass. Freda dumped the cutoff hair into the fire.

"Pew! Burning hair stinks something awful."

"Let's get the bath done. Some children enjoy the water. Maybe this won't be so bad."

Emaline liked the warm water, splashing and holding her hand up with the soap bubbles. Even when Ingeborg rubbed the rose-smelling soap into her hair, she didn't mind, sniffing the bar and nodding. But when they applied the kerosene, she scrunched up her face and let out a shriek that made the cat leap out of her box and slink off into the parlor. Ingeborg offered a piece of ham to distract her. Cookies would disintegrate into the water. They rinsed, soaped again to get the kerosene smell out, and rinsed some more. By this time all the fight had gone out of the child, and when they bundled her in warm towels and settled her in Ingeborg's lap in the rocker, Emaline curled into as small a piece as she could, without a whimper.

"I sure hope we got 'em all." Freda blew out a sigh. "I do not want to go through that again."

Ingeborg didn't remind her that it usually took at least two doses. Right now she just held the little one close and rocked gently, singing like she'd done the night before. She was glad they had few tangles to comb out, with her very short haircut.

The sound of boots on the porch caught their attention. Thorliff pushed open the door with a smile. "I hear you have company."

Ingeborg looked at Freda. "What did I tell you? Everyone has heard." She smiled at her son. "How about bringing Inga with you tomorrow? We're hoping playing with her will make our little guest talk."

"She hasn't spoken?"

"No. Only a shriek when we poured the kerosene on her head for the lice."

"Well, who wouldn't shriek?" He set a package on the table. "Thelma sent some things she'd made for Inga that are too big yet. See if they fit."

"Who told you?" Ingeborg asked, nodding to the sleeping child in her lap.

"Thelma. No idea who told her, but—"

"Coffee?"

"If it is hot. I told Far I'd be back out to the barn to discuss something with him. The clouds are still arguing with the sun."

"Good. I wasn't ready for winter to settle in yet." *And perhaps we can find out more about our little one if it clears enough so someone can ride out to the reservation.*

"I brought you a letter from Astrid." He handed the envelope to Ingeborg. "Care to read it aloud?" He nodded his thanks for the coffee that Freda poured for him.

"Of course." Ingeborg slit the envelope open and drew out the single sheet of paper. She glanced down the page. "Oh my. She has a little boy who had to have both legs amputated, and she is wondering if someone here in Blessing would be willing to take him in." She looked up to see Thorliff and Freda exchanging looks of astonishment. "This must be the time to take care of God's little ones, children that no one else seems to want."

———

WITH THE STORM gone, after breakfast Joshua waded through snow knee-deep in places and bare ground in others, depending on how the wind drifted it. Smoke rose straight above chimneys, and the warming sun sparkled the iced tree branches. One of the Geddicks waved to him from behind the team dragging the snowplow to clear the streets where needed. Penny was sweeping the porch of the mercantile.

"How'd you like our blizzard?" she asked.

"I didn't. Nothing to do at the boardinghouse but eat and drink coffee." He neglected to mention the party in the kitchen.

"Shame you couldn't have made it over here. I could keep ten people busy cleaning and building new shelves and display racks. Well, maybe not ten."

"Hjelmer out yet?"

"Oh yes. He and Mr. Sam are working on something over at the smithy. He's planning on you being there."

"Good. Do you have a big pad of paper I could buy and some more pencils?"

"How big?"

Joshua held his hands out about twenty-four inches apart.

"If I don't, I know you could get some from Thorliff. He sometimes has odd sized newsprint paper left over and gives it to the schoolchildren. Pardon me if I'm nosey, but what are you drawing?"

"House plans. Where I want changes from the plans from Sears and Roebuck's."

"I see. Did you get the basement all dug?" Penny asked.

"Nearly. Still a pile of dirt in the center."

"I think they are fixing something then going over to work on our house. I hear you were the star of quite a party at the boardinghouse during the blizzard."

281

"We did have a good time. Made the time pass right quick."

"Made me wish we were still living at the boardinghouse too." She leaned on the broom handle. "I can't wait for our house to be finished. The house we're renting is much smaller than our house in Bismarck. Made us feel closed in during the blizzard. I do hope we have more fall now before winter really sets in." She shook herself. "I better get this done instead of jabbering the morning away. And keeping you from working on my house."

Joshua touched the brim of his hat with one finger and headed for the smithy, where he could hear a hammer ringing on metal. One thing for sure, if you were looking for a place to get warm, the smithy was it. The fire glowed red-hot in the forge, changing to white as Hjelmer pumped the bellows. Mr. Sam held a steel bar by the tongs with one hand and set it in the middle of the hottest flame until it glowed red, turning to white. Then he laid the bar on the anvil and set to pounding it into another shape with the heavy hammer.

"What are you working on?" Joshua raised his voice to be heard over the roar of the forge and the clanging metal.

"Good morning." Hjelmer turned at his question. "Thinking on a way to get the grease to last longer on the windmill head so the men don't have to go up and grease 'em so often. There's got to be a way. You given any thought to this?"

"No. I've been thinking on the drill. I know the horses are easier since we got to have them along anyway, but what if we used a kerosene engine, something similar to what's on the washing machines Penny carries at the store? I'd bet the company makes all sizes."

"I thought about using a steam engine, but they're too big to be practical. Something I read . . ." Hjelmer narrowed his eyes trying to remember. "I think they're using kerosene engines to run the machines that make ice. You looked through a Sears and Roebuck catalog lately?"

"Nope, sorry." Joshua shook his head. "Been concentrating on their house plans."

"Think we'll order a couple of the catalogs. May be something in there we can adapt."

They left the shop a bit later and spent the rest of the day working on the interior of the house. Joshua nailed rough-cut two-by-quarter-inch strips on the walls so they'd be ready for the plaster later. One of the wise things about Hjelmer, he was always looking ahead. Like here they were running wire in the walls and ceilings for the day when electricity would come to Blessing. He knew there were electric lights in big cities, but gaslights were a new commodity in the country, where most people still used kerosene lamps. Joshua figured he would do the same. All he was learning on this house he could apply to his own. Indoor plumbing like they had at the boardinghouse, a furnace in the basement with heating vents and ducts to the rooms upstairs and down. He would give anything to be able to show his house to his mother. It would be a far cry from the tar paper shack he'd built out on his farm.

What would Astrid want in a house? kept coming to his mind. As he hammered away on the slats, he realized more and more how little he really knew about the young woman who was taking medical training in Chicago. One thing he did know, she had strong opinions.

"When you're done in here, come help me in the parlor," Toby Valders said from the doorway.

"Sure enough." He returned to his lath laying. Thinking of Astrid reminded him of the bit he'd heard about her and a half-breed from the Rosebud Indian Reservation. He had no idea where that was, but how did a half-breed qualify for medical training in

Chicago? After what the Indians did to his family, his pa never had a good word to say about them. He figured his pa was right on that count. Which brought him to more thoughts on his brother. He slammed a nail home with enough force to dent the piece of wood. He hit his thumb and finger with the hammer while holding the next nail.

He bit back a yelp and the stream of words his mother had never tolerated in her house by stuffing the wounded members into his mouth. When he calmed down enough to think, he heaved a sigh. Served him right. Maybe if he'd put to work the things Pastor Solberg spoke about, he'd not get so angry. Or maybe not.

25

CHICAGO, ILLINOIS

Astrid stared at the November calendar. In less than a month she would be halfway through her training in Chicago. Unless she chose to stay at the hospital for additional training. After she had successfully turned the baby in utero, Dr. Barlow had suggested just that. Her staying on.

"You will get far more experience here than you will in such a small place as Blessing." Sitting on the corner of his desk, he had removed his glasses and polished them with a handkerchief. "I believe you are a woman gifted with a keen mind and a natural sense of what is needed."

Astrid blinked and almost asked him to repeat himself. Surely he hadn't really meant what he said. "Th-thank you, sir."

"Your essay says that your mother is a healer. Is that right?"

Nodding, Astrid tried to remember what essay he was talking

about. It must have been on her entrance exam. She'd found it nearly impossible to remember what all she had written in those whirlwind hours.

"And you've learned all you could from Dr. Elizabeth Bjorklund? She was leaving here just when I arrived." He tapped the paper he'd picked up from his desk. "You are very young to have covered all this. Most of our students have been through college and now are in their third year here. Some will go on to internships either here or at other hospitals. That could be you." He waited, as if expecting her to answer. When she didn't, he continued. "If you could go anywhere, what specialty would you be interested in?"

She knew he wanted an answer now. "I . . . I don't know. I've not given that any thought at all. We, Dr. Elizabeth and I, were looking for more training in surgery, because she was sure medical techniques had changed in the years since she had been here." Other than the mission field. Should she tell him about that? "We hope to build a hospital in Blessing."

"Well, I strongly suggest you give my recommendation some serious thought. If you have any questions, feel free to come and ask. Dr. Morganstein concurs, and I know she is planning on talking with you too." He stood. "In the meantime, keep up the good work."

Astrid stood and nodded. "Thank you, Dr. Barlow. I'll do some thinking and praying on that." After she'd left the room, she had sagged against a wall in the hallway.

What a shock that had been. A good shock, but still . . . She pulled her gaze away from the calendar now and sat back down in a chair, her coffee cup on the table beside it. So many things to think about, and whenever she tried to spend time really thinking, she fell asleep. Praying was about the same way. She'd tried reading her Bible, and more than once found herself with her cheek on the pages when Elyse came into the room some hours later.

"Just follow the leading you know." How often had she heard Pastor Solberg say that? She eyed the bed. With the time she had before evening rounds, she could take a nap, write a letter, or study the book on hands she'd borrowed from the library. Opting to write to Pastor Solberg, she took her writing case out of the trunk under her bed and, propping her back against the wall, set pencil to paper. She didn't have time to fuss with pen and ink.

Dear Pastor Solberg,

    I have wanted to write and ask your opinion on a matter that is troubling me, and I believe now I am desperate enough that I cannot wait any longer. You and I had discussed the prospect that God might be calling me to become a medical missionary in Africa. You said at that time that God would make this clear to me. So far He has not, at least not in a way that I can understand. Yet the thought never goes away.

    If He is calling me, would I not begin to have a desire to go there? To feel some kind of peace about what's ahead? I know that worry is not of Him, and yet I find myself awake in the night, straining to hear His voice like Samuel did. But I hear nothing, and yes, I must confess, I am worrying over this. I still do not want to go to Africa, but I do want to follow God's will for me.

    Help me, please. Pray for this to be made clear. And please pray that I can wait for the answer, if that is what I am being told to do. I cannot afford to lose sleep, as our schedules here are busy, full to the minute, and I am getting so tired.

She stared at her letter. It sounded awfully whiney. A sigh puffed out her cheeks. Maybe she should just toss this in the wastebasket and start over. But when would she have time again? She leaned her head against the wall. Oh, to be able to just sleep until she woke up.

    I must close and join Dr. Whitaker on rounds. Greet everyone for me. I miss you all so, but not nearly as much as at first. Perhaps I am adjusting after all.

Sincerely,
Dr. Astrid Bjorklund

Without reading it again, she folded the letter and slid it into an envelope. Once the address was added, she pushed herself upright and, letter in hand, headed for the front desk, where stamps were available and the mail went out.

"Dr. Bjorklund?"

She turned at the call. "Yes?"

One of the nurses from the children's ward was hurrying toward her. "If you have time before rounds, could you drop by and talk with Benny? He's been asking for you."

"Of course. Have they found out anything about his home and family?"

"Not really."

"Has anyone been looking?"

"That is the job of the social services. We gave them the information." The older nurse shook her head. "You have to learn the system, you know. There are rules we have to follow."

Keeping her tone civil in spite of what she wanted to say, Astrid thanked the woman and finished her errand. Who wrote the rules? And wasn't that little boy more important than any stupid rules? Since Benny had been transferred back to the children's ward, she paused outside the door and made sure she was wearing a cheerful smile.

Several of the children greeted her when she entered the long room lined by beds on both sides. She stopped at the foot of Benny's bed and pulled his chart from the rack on the bed frame. According to what was written there, they'd been able to cut back on the pain medicine, and he was considered ready to be sent home if they could decide where to send him. She glanced over the chart to see him sitting against the pillow, arms crossed over his chest, staring at two children playing in the aisle.

Astrid sat down on the side of his bed and waited for him to look at her. When he ignored her, she tapped his arm. "Hey, Mr. Benny, how are you feeling today?"

"My foot itches." He still refused to look at her.

"I understand that. It's called phantom pain. It will go away eventually." She waited some more. If stubborn had a name, it could be called Benny. But perhaps that was what had kept him alive on the streets of Chicago.

"Are you ready to tell me your last name yet?"

He shook his head.

"Do you have a last name?"

He wrinkled his mouth but gave no other response.

"Benny, how are we to find someone to help you if you won't give us any information?"

A tiny shrug raised his thin shoulders.

She waited again, thinking and praying about what to do next. "Nurse said you were asking for me."

"You din't come this morning."

"I know, but I am here now."

"Not the orphan place."

Ah, so someone had told him he would be going there if they found no family. "Do you have any brothers or sisters?" She'd have missed the slight nod had she not been watching from the corner of her eye. She'd learned that she could get more information if she acted more disinterested. So he did have siblings. "Are you the oldest?" A barely perceptible headshake. "So you have a big sister. I always wanted a big sister, but I have two older brothers instead."

He looked straight at her, his gaze far older than any six-year-old she'd known.

"Bigger brother then?"

His eyes dimmed. "He died."

The whisper near to broke her heart. Tough as he tried to be, the hurt hadn't left.

Lord God, there has to be a home for Benny.

Send him to Blessing.

She'd heard that prompting before but had forgotten to bring it up yesterday as she'd planned. Of course. Someone in Blessing would take him if the hospital would send him there. She leaned forward and wrapped the little boy in her arms. *Benny, we are going to find you a home and a family. I know Mor would take you without batting an eye, but you need younger parents. You need brothers and sisters and cousins and a bed to sleep in and enough food to grow like you should.* All the time her thoughts ran rampant like a herd of frightened cattle, she rocked him gently.

If I were married, I'd take you. A vision of a certain broad-shouldered man with laughing dark eyes zipped through her mind. Joshua Landsverk was indeed interesting. *Pay attention here,* she chided herself. Who should she talk to in Chicago about her idea?

How she would love taking this little boy home to Blessing for Christmas. Could they keep him in the hospital that long? Would she get time off at Christmas like Grace had been able to from her school? Schools closed down for the holidays, but hospitals were most likely very busy. Another question to put to someone in charge.

"Benny, I have to go take care of other patients now. I'll come back later. Can I bring you anything?"

He lifted his head. "Cookies?"

"If I bring you a plate of cookies, will you share with the other children?" His emphatic nod made her smile. "I'll be right back." As she left the room, she was mentally counting how many cookies they would need. Someone was bound to say this would spoil their supper. Had she gotten herself in hot water? Perhaps sneaking him one would have been better.

But the cook down in the kitchen smiled back at her request. "I will send 'em up immediately, soon as we can count 'em out. Take them to Benny, is that right?"

"Yes, please. He's a six-year-old double amputee. Third bed on the right."

"Lord love the poor child. You go on about your business." Cook nodded toward a stack of cookies cooling on the counter. "Take one for yourself. Doctors always need a pick-me-up."

That evening after supper she found a note on her door regarding a meeting with Dr. Morganstein and some others at two in the afternoon, two days hence. They would be discussing possible plans for the hospital in Blessing.

Astrid stared at the note on Dr. Morganstein's personal stationery. They should have Elizabeth there, not her. But one of the reasons Astrid was in Chicago was to gain the training for the new hospital. Elizabeth would have liked to have taken time off to come, but she didn't feel she could. She folded the paper and slid it between the pages of her Bible. Time for another session in the dissecting lab with their friend Hank, as they had begun calling the cadaver. Perhaps Dr. Red Hawk would not be there tonight. They'd started the thoracic cavity in class earlier in the day. She really couldn't continue without him. She picked up her kit and headed out the door. If he didn't make it, she would go back to dissecting the hand. Amazing creation, the body. The human hands and feet had the highest concentration of individual bones. She mumbled the litany of the bones of the hand on her way up to the laboratory.

Red Hawk was nowhere in sight, so she had a peaceful time further dissecting the hand. Only one other pair of students was in the room, and their discussion made for comforting background noise that kept the darkness in the corners. After she put the cadaver away in the cooler, she left the room. Exhaustion didn't catch up with her until she was halfway down the worn walnut stairs and sagged against the hand-smoothed banister. Where had Red Hawk been? He knew they were having another exam the day after tomorrow. Or was it already after midnight? She kicked off her shoes and then fell into bed, clothes and all. When the knock on the door woke her, she forced herself to throw the cover back and sit up.

Thank you, Lord, for a real sleep for a change. She rubbed her eyes and stretched, then grabbed her towel and soap and staggered to the washroom. Maybe cold water would help more than hot.

———

THE NEXT AFTERNOON she arrived for the meeting dressed in a navy blue gored skirt with a lace inset waist rather than the uniform apron. Wearing her own clothes made her feel dressed up and lent a feeling of confidence, or that is what she told herself. Somehow the fluttering in her stomach didn't go along with her mind. She had braided her hair and pinned it in a figure eight from neck to crown on the back of her head. Stopping outside the door to take a deep breath, she took another and ordered her hand to stop shaking before knocking and obeying the invitation to enter.

Dr. Morganstein beckoned her to join the others at the chairs circled around a low round table draped in a gold embroidered damask cloth. The ornate silver service waited to the right side of the table in front of Dr. Morganstein. Plates of tea sandwiches, cookies, and jam tarts waited to be passed around.

Astrid's stomach rumbled, since she'd skipped dinner to get ready on time.

"Let me introduce you to the others," Dr. Morganstein said with a hand on Astrid's arm. "You have met my friend Mrs. Issy Josephson." Astrid nodded and smiled. Should she shake hands or curtsy? What was polite? "And this is her nephew Jason, who is in charge of the foundation the Josephsons set up to expand medical services into rural areas."

"I am pleased to meet you, Dr. Bjorklund. My aunt has told me much about you." His deep voice flowed like a peaceful river, and his smile reached his eyes, not just the polite kind that twitched the lips.

"Thank you." What should she say? "I am pleased to meet you too."

"And last but not least, Mr. Abramson, who assists our hospital in establishing new programs and services."

Astrid nodded and smiled at each of them, then took the chair that Dr. Morganstein pointed her to. "I wish Dr. Elizabeth Bjorklund could be here, since she is the one who will be in charge in Blessing."

"We will be talking with her again. In our conversation last night, she said you knew as much about her dreams for the hospital as she did." Dr. Morganstein lifted the tea server, and one by one poured the cups full according to the desires of those in the circle. Right now what Astrid wanted more than anything was a glass of water, but she accepted her tea, passed the plates of lovely food, and was careful not to take too many. No matter how ravenous she'd become, she would mimic the others and do exactly what they did.

"Rather than engage in a lot of social chitchat," Dr. Morganstein said when she'd finished serving, "Dr. Bjorklund, will you begin with describing the surgery as it is now in Blessing?"

Astrid set down her cup and folded her hands in her lap. After clearing her throat once and then again, she told them first how her mother had traveled to provide what medicine she could with the simples she used and the knowledge she had learned. "Then five years ago, when my brother Thorliff brought home his bride, Dr. Elizabeth Bjorklund, who finished her medical training here at this hospital, she and my mother worked together to care for the folks of Blessing and the surrounding area. The house Elizabeth and Thorliff built included a waiting area, two examining rooms, and two rooms with beds for birthings and recoveries. She always wished for a real surgical room, so they added extra lighting and a sturdy table to one of the examining rooms." Astrid knew she was speaking too fast, but the words kept coming, like the mountain creeks of Norway during spring thaw.

"It took awhile for people to ask for Dr. Elizabeth rather than my mother, but they soon learned, and Mor continued to assist Elizabeth when she needed her."

"I'd like to inject something here, if I may," Dr. Morganstein said.

"Of course." *I should have asked for questions, given others a chance to talk.* Astrid forced herself to ignore the inner turmoil and listen closely.

"Dr. Bjorklund realized early on that her mother-in-law is a gifted healer in her own right, and her simples of herbs and natural remedies could add a great deal to our own pharmacopeia. She has sent me lists of the products they used out there, and we have added many to our supplies here. I fear that as medicine progresses, we will lose track of natural treatments that have worked so well."

Jason Josephson leaned forward. "I am impressed with what Dr.

Bjorklund and your mother have accomplished in Blessing. Did you by any chance bring lists of treated cases, perhaps a daily log of patients seen?"

"Yes, Dr. Bjorklund has given me the information you are asking for. I will provide these to whomever you request."

He nodded and sat back. "Good."

Astrid breathed a sigh of relief. *Oh, Elizabeth, you should be here.*

Dr. Morganstein motioned for her to continue. "Can you tell us about your vision for the future?"

Astrid wet her lips and continued. "We have presented to the people of Blessing a plan for a building designed specifically for a hospital. The plan includes an operating theatre, birthing rooms, examination rooms, a laboratory, a kitchen, and offices for other services. We are hoping that we can find a dentist who will move to Blessing too. I was not at the presentation meeting because I was already here, but Dr. Elizabeth . . . er Bjorklund, said it went well. There's something you need to understand about Blessing. The people started years ago by creating a cooperative bank, and through that have built a co-op grain elevator, a flour mill, and a building that houses the bank, post office, barbershop, and telephone switchboard. Now we are asking them to invest in a hospital."

She watched the others nod and look to each other, whisper and shake their heads. Was Blessing so unique in its way of doing business?

"Who is on the board that makes the decisions?" Mr. Abramson asked.

"Everyone who has an account at the bank."

"There is no board of directors?"

Astrid shook her head. "Everyone is invited to vote. There are some people who always show up and others who don't bother."

"So who runs the daily operations of the bank?"

"Mr. Anner Valders. He is paid to run the bank." Astrid leaned forward. "You have to realize that Blessing is a small town, but it is growing like many of the towns in North Dakota."

Astrid had no time to even sip her tea while the two men threw more questions at her, usually with a look of unbelief at her answers.

"All right, gentlemen, please give this young woman a chance to breathe. Would anyone like more tea?" Dr. Morganstein smiled at Astrid. "Especially you, my dear. You've not even had a chance to finish your first cup."

"Thank you." While the others chatted, Astrid ate the dainty sandwiches, two tarts, and a cookie and nodded her appreciation when Dr. Morganstein refilled her teacup. Had she given the right answers? The best answers? What else would they throw at her? She looked up to see Mrs. Josephson smiling and nodding at her.

"You did well, Doctor. I should have warned you that my nephew turns into a barracuda when he gets excited about something."

Astrid knew that was a fierce fish, so she nodded back. After wiping her mouth with her napkin, she blew out a breath.

"I think we have all the information we need for today," Mr. Josephson declared after another long look at the other man. "I believe we need to make a trip to this town of Blessing and speak with the folks there. I'd like to do this before Christmas, if possible." He glanced at Astrid. "I understand you would not be able to attend due to your training here, but if we decide to proceed . . ." He slapped his hands on his knees. "Thank you for your time, Dr. Bjorklund. We'll be talking again."

Astrid said her good-byes and made her way to the door. Once in the hall she blinked and shook her head. Why did she feel as though she'd just been run over by a fire wagon pulled by six horses?

"Dr. Bjorklund, you are wanted in the scrub room. We have an accident victim in need of surgery." A nurse beckoned her to hurry.

Two hours later they moved the woman to a single room rather than the ward so she could receive extra care and observation for the following twenty-four hours.

"We need to keep her sedated," Dr. Franck said to the head nurse. "I want Dr. Bjorklund checking on her every two hours. Call her if she is needed."

Both Astrid and the nurse nodded their understanding.

Astrid skipped her usual time in the laboratory and went to bed instead, leaving instructions for someone to call her at eleven. She checked on the woman at eleven that evening and then returned at one and three the following morning. This time she loosed the bands holding the woman in bed since she seemed to be sleeping peacefully and stepped out the door to answer a question the nurse was asking. At the sound of something falling, she leaped back into the room. The woman lay on the floor, unconscious, blood flowing from a new gash on the side of her face.

"Why did you untie her?" the nurse questioned, horror on her face.

"Because . . . because she was sleeping so deeply, and I—" Astrid fought to figure out why she had done that.

"Doctor said she had to remain sedated. Did you not give her the dose of morphine?"

Astrid shook her head. *I thought you did that.* But she kept the thought to herself. Had she just not been thinking clearly?

Dr. Franck glared at her when he arrived. "Did you not understand the orders I gave? She was restrained for a reason. To prevent something like this from happening. If you can't follow orders, how do you expect others to?"

26

S omething is bothering you."

Astrid looked up to see Red Hawk studying her instead of their cadaver. "What do you mean?" What she really wanted to ask was "How do you know?"

"Well, you are frowning. Usually you delight in this, and you've been sighing. You are not usually sighing, so I figure something is bothering you."

His eyes looked black in the gaslights. Lately they'd been talking more. She'd gotten him talking about his people on the reservation and how he had worked to be able to come here. He'd said his people needed more teachers for both the adults and the children.

To tell him or not to tell him.

"And you have dark circles under your eyes, which means you are not getting enough sleep."

"Do any of us get enough sleep?"

His gaze never wavered.

She huffed a sigh and saw his eyebrow arch. "I have a decision to make, and I don't know which way to turn."

"How soon do you need to make it?"

"Before the end of training."

"Does it have anything to do with the letters from Africa?"

She nodded. She'd shared bits of one of Reverend Schuman's letters. She thought he would appreciate the need for doctors in Africa and might tell her if things were that bad on the reservation. "They need medical missionaries."

"The whole world does, including the west of America."

"I think God is calling me to go there." She stared at her hands, then looked up at him. "And I don't want to." There. She'd laid it out for someone else's consideration.

"Like I didn't want to come here, and yet I knew it was what I needed to do?"

"Possibly. Probably. What made you decide to come?"

"My people are dying of starvation and the diseases that come from that. My uncle is the medicine man, and he decided I would be the next one. He said the white man's medicine is stronger than his."

She'd never heard him talk so much at one time. The last few weeks he'd talked more, but this time he was letting her see a bit of his life. "I didn't know things were so bad on the reservations." Maybe they were becoming friends after all. Maybe her patience was paying off.

"My people need to be free, but that life can no longer be. We do not believe a man can own the land."

"Like my people do?"

He nodded and returned to his dissecting. So she did the same, making sure she was no longer sighing.

Wasn't there a difference between going clear around the world to a country that didn't want the missionaries anyway and coming here? And then getting to go home, which is what she had planned in the first place.

Maybe she would hear from Pastor Solberg one of these days, and he would have the answers for her.

————

THE HEAD NURSE stopped her the next morning when she was on rounds with Dr. Whitaker. "We have not been able to locate any family for Benny, so whether we want to or not, we will be forced to send him to the orphanage." The look in her eyes said she was no happier with this news than Astrid.

"Can't we keep him here long enough for him to try some prosthetics?" Astrid kept her voice low but inside she wanted to scream. There were two schools of thought among the staff. Should they provide wooden legs for Benny and crutches and see if he could manage them? Or should someone make him a flat wooden scooter with wheels that he would propel with his hands? A chair with wheels was another option.

"This won't be happening that soon. I just wanted to prepare you."

"Thank you." *Mor, you have to find someone in Blessing to take him.*

Later she asked Dr. Whitaker, "How long until Benny's stumps are healed well enough for him to try wooden legs?"

"I have ordered them, and we'll try next week. You do know I don't hold out a lot of hope for this?"

She nodded. "But he has to be given a chance."

"The best thing we can do right now is help him build strength

301

in his arms and chest. Crutches, a cart, any mode of mobility for him is going to require the use of his arms."

"I see. Do you know that he is crawling on his hands and stumps? One of the nurses was kind enough to sew some thick pads into his trousers so he could crawl that way without hurting himself."

"I saw that. He is one determined boy. It's why I hold out hope that we can help him somehow."

"What if we were to find a home for him somewhere else?"

"I don't see what harm that would be. You have something in mind?"

"Actually, I wrote to my mother in Blessing, North Dakota, and asked her to find someone there who would adopt him."

"It would be better than being a beggar on the streets of Chicago."

"There he would get an education and plenty of love. He's a bright little boy."

"With an abundance of street smarts. More than he should have at his age. You need to make that clear to those who might agree to help."

———

THAT NIGHT INSTEAD of going up to the lab, Astrid found a quiet place in the dining room and took out her writing kit. After thinking about what Red Hawk had said, she started a letter to the women of Blessing Lutheran Church in care of Mrs. Solberg.

I am writing this to all of you because I need your help. Well, not really me, but there are people in terrible need on the Rosebud Reservation in South Dakota. I know you've been sending quilts and clothing and food to the Indians northwest of Blessing, and I hope you don't quit doing that, but could you please find it in your hearts to do more? This winter will be terribly hard on people who are already weakened by lack of food, housing, and medical care. Please gather up what you can and have it shipped down there. I know God will bless you for being His hands to these people. As Jesus said, "Inasmuch as ye have done it unto one of the least of these my brethren, ye have done it unto me."

One of the daughters of Blessing,
Dr. Astrid Bjorklund

Without giving herself any time to think about it, she addressed the envelope so it was ready to send.

Next she wrote to the head of the missions school that Reverend Schuman had told her about, asking them if she were to come there, if she could do a two-year mission term to Africa rather than the customary four years. With that letter ready to send, she started one to Joshua.

Why was it harder to write to him than to anyone else? Not that she had written to many others, but she felt she had to pick and choose what to tell him. Perhaps if his letters to her were not so brief and stilted, she would feel freer to write about life at the hospital.

What it comes down to, she thought, *is that I just don't know him very well at all, and while I've heard of people getting to know each other through letters, this doesn't seem to be working.* She rubbed her eyes and tipped her head back and to the sides, trying to pull the tightness from her neck and shoulders. A day with no surgery had been unusual. She thought back to her time with Benny. She'd found him in the wagon being pulled by one of the other children.

"How did you get out of your bed?" she'd asked.

"I slid out."

"Didn't it hurt when your legs hit the floor?"

"Some. But I checked, and they don't bleed no more."

"What if we make wooden legs for you and teach you how to use crutches?"

He shrugged.

"It won't be easy, but you could get around." *Please, Lord, let it be so.*

"I ain't goin' to the orphanage." He clamped his arms across his chest.

"I'm working on something," she whispered, leaning closer to his ear.

His face brightened. "I could come live with you."

"You're going to have to go to school."

Now he frowned.

"You don't want to grow up ignorant, do you?"

"Ig-igrant. What's that?"

"You learn things like the meaning of words in school. You learn to read. You know how much you like it when someone reads to you." At his halfhearted shrug, she continued, "And you learn to do arithmetic. Along with so many other things I can't begin to tell you all of it."

"No orphanage."

"Then you better use the pull-up bar that the janitor is making for your bed. He said he'd have it here tomorrow."

He looked at her out of the side of his eye, a trick of his when he wasn't sure what she was asking.

———

THE NEXT AFTERNOON Benny's bed was at the center of a group of giggling children. "My turn" was squealed more than any other word as Benny demonstrated how to pull himself up with his arms.

Astrid watched while Benny scooted to the end of the bed and another child took his place lying prone. Some could pull up, but most couldn't. Perhaps they should have pull-up bars for all the beds and run contests with prizes for the winners. When she suggested it to Mr. Korchensky, he shook his head. But his grin said he would think on it.

Astrid brought herself back to the letters at hand, putting the pencil and paper back in the compartments so designated. She dropped her letters off at the front desk so they could be mailed in the morning. Perhaps since there'd been no surgeries, she'd not be called to assist with anything in the middle of the night.

———

SHE WAS NEARLY finished with rounds the next morning when a surgical nurse came for her. "We have a cesarean to perform immediately."

Astrid excused herself and followed the nurse to the scrub room. "Who am I assisting?" she asked, since there was no doctor present.

"You're it for now. Dr. Whitaker is tied up in the other operating theatre, and Dr. Franck will be observing with some of the newer students."

Astrid blinked and started scrubbing. Yes, she'd assisted before, and yes, she'd been assisted by one of the other doctors. "Who will be assisting?"

The nurse named one of the other surgical students.

Taking a deep breath, Astrid continued. "All right, then, tell me the story."

"The woman has been in labor for somewhere around twenty-four hours, and when nothing was happening, the family brought her here. While she is dilated, the baby has not crowned, and—"

"Why did they wait so long? Is the fetus viable?" She could keep from thinking *live baby* if she used the technical words.

"We have a faint heartbeat."

"How fast?" She glanced at the nurse, who was shaking her head. "Let's see what we can do." *Please, God, this has to be in your hands.* She pushed through the door and stepped to the table. The woman was already anesthetized, and the nurse was holding the ether cone.

Astrid picked up the scalpel, nodded to the young man assisting her, and made the first incision. Even with the quickest work she could manage, the baby never responded. Blinking back tears, she concentrated on the mother. If she could at least keep one of them alive, she knew she would have done her best. She let the student doctor close and complimented him on a job well done. Now all she had to do was go tell the family the sad news.

"Why did they wait so long?" She fought the tears of both sorrow and anger, dumping her operating apron in the laundry.

"She's not one of ours," the nurse said, meaning one of the mothers who came to the hospital for prenatal care and training. "And the midwife thought she could handle it."

"With hips that narrow, she should have known better."

"True. That's the kind of training we are trying to offer, midwives included. They are necessary because we can't convince all the women to come here. They don't have the money, and you know that birthing units are rare in hospitals. We lead the field in our care for mothers and babies. But we cannot handle them all."

Astrid listened and nodded as she washed and changed into a clean apron and shirt. "And how many other places do cesareans?"

"Not many." The nurse patted her on the shoulder. "You did very well in there."

"Thank you. You want to go out and tell the family that?"

Dr. Franck met her in the hallway outside the door. "You did well."

Astrid bit back a sarcastic comment and let herself appreciate his comment. "Thank you. If we'd saved the baby, it would have been worth it."

"You did save the mother, however. Keep that in mind." He strode off down the hall, leaving her to go to the waiting room, where a man with two children looked up at her entrance.

"Your wife came through the surgery all right."

"And the baby?"

"I'm sorry. It was too late."

"A boy or a girl?"

"A boy."

He nodded. "Thank you. When can I see her?"

"She should be awake in an hour or so. Someone will come for you." She nodded and left the room, hearing the little girl asking where her mother was.

Lord, was there anything I could have done differently? Hurried faster? Skipped scrubbing? But then the mother might have died too, of an infection. Of course she still might. That thought made her swallow. *Please, Father, help her to live.*

Since there was nothing else on her schedule until after dinner, she returned to her room to find a letter on her pillow. From Mor. Astrid ripped open the envelope and scanned the page. She had agreed to take Benny until Rebecca and Gerald had a house without stairs, and then he would go to live with them.

Astrid read about Emaline, who still had not said a word but never left Mor's side.

She has the most expressive eyes. And she loves to play with the cat. She laughs, so we know her vocal cords work. She and Inga have become great friends, and Inga talks for both of them. No one here is at all surprised at that.

Let us know when we can come for Benny.

Love from your Mor

307

One good thing to compensate for the one bad. Astrid clutched the letter to her chest. If only she could take Benny to Blessing in time for Christmas. A wave of homesickness rolled over her, and she found herself sitting on the bed. *Almost halfway there.*

27

BLESSING, NORTH DAKOTA

*W*hat *a discussion we have going now.*

Ingeborg glanced over to see that Kaaren was praying. While her eyes were open to keep track of things, her mind was definitely elsewhere.

"Ladies, ladies." Mary Martha Solberg raised her hands, in supplication or for quiet, Ingeborg wasn't sure which. Why had Astrid sent the letter to Mrs. Solberg rather than to her or Kaaren? Thinking on it, she figured it out. Her daughter was trying to keep her mother and her aunt out of the middle.

"As if we don't give enough already!" Mrs. Valders glared around the room, her glower resting on Ingeborg. "*Your daughter* must have no idea how much we already do for those less fortunate and have done for years."

Ingeborg started to respond but kept quiet when she caught Mary

Martha's slight headshake. The emphasis on *your daughter* made Astrid sound like something newly crawled out of a muddy ditch.

"We do have a lot here," Mrs. Magron offered. "God really has blessed us all."

Ingeborg mentally applauded the usually meek woman who had always followed Hildegunn's leading. Well, not so much lately, come to think of it. Thinking back to other quilting sessions, she'd been a dissenter more than once.

Hildegunn glared at her followers. Mrs. Veiglun and Mrs. Odell could be depended on to agree with her.

"Ladies." Mary Martha stood and spoke more firmly. "We have received a perfectly legitimate appeal for assistance. And from someone who could be our window to the world. I think we need to prayerfully consider her request."

Dr. Elizabeth leaned forward. "Perhaps I could add something to this?"

Mary Martha nodded and sat down.

"Astrid and I have been dreaming of creating an outreach medical arm, sort of like a traveling clinic, where one of us would visit small towns that have no medical help. We had talked about including our local reservation. Since the Indians do not bring their ill and wounded to us, we feel we should go to them. They are part of God's family too. We are in discussion with the hospital in Chicago as to the building and staffing of our hospital here and provisioning such an outreach."

Ingeborg watched how the doctor's speech was affecting the others in the room. These were good-hearted people who would do the right thing, given some thinking time and proper leadership. Some just reacted more quickly and vociferously than the others. Now if she could control her own desire to go nose to nose with Hildegunn . . .

Remember how polite and cheerful she has been to you lately, a little voice whispered.

Pastor's lessons on forgiveness had been hitting Ingeborg in the heart region. Squirming was not a good feeling. How much easier it was to point fingers at others and not look inside herself.

No one seemed to want to look at the others. Instead they studied fingers, handkerchiefs, a spot on a skirt, anything but look up.

Mary Martha looked to Kaaren. "I think we should table this discussion and do some thinking and praying on it. Kaaren, if you will read to us as soon as we get settled into our duties. If anyone has a request for today, let her know." She glanced around the group. "We have the wedding ring quilt for Gus and Maydell on the stretcher to be quilted; that is our most critical project today. We have a wool top ready to be put together. We'll tie that one, and I know Ingeborg has a child-sized quilt that she has been working on for Emaline. Are there any other projects nearing completion that I am not aware of?"

Mrs. Geddick raised her hand. "I have the pieces cut for a three-inch nine patch, using plain blue squares in between. I am trying to make a quilt for each of my sons, for when they have their own homes."

"How many sewing machines do we have today?" Mary Martha asked. She counted the hands. "Three. Good. I put the flatirons on the stove to heat. Let's begin with prayer." She waited until all heads were bowed. "Heavenly Father, we gather here in your name to do your work, to care for each other, and to draw closer to you. We thank you for giving us a reprieve from the coming winter, for snug homes, and for an abundance of food on our tables and in our larders. Thank you for your great love for us and help us to spread that love around. In Jesus' name we pray, amen."

Like a flock of birds, they all rose, laughing and twittering, choosing where to start and settling down again in their appropriate places.

Eight women surrounded the stretcher for the wedding ring quilt. Ingeborg took charge of the ironing board. Penny and Kaaren took two machines, Mrs. Geddick the other. Rebecca and Sophie, scissors in hand, took over the cutting table.

"Where's Emmy?" Sophie asked Ingeborg.

"Helping Haakan." It hadn't taken long for Emaline to be shortened to Emmy.

"I'm surprised she let you out of her sight."

"Thorliff took Inga out there too," Dr. Elizabeth added. "She thought having a day with Bestefar would be better than coming here."

Ellie glanced over to where the small children were playing, with Addy Geddick, Mrs. Geddick's daughter, supervising. "If I'd sent Carl over there, they would have had a real party."

"You should have all brought them to my house, but with Deborah working days, Garth's sister Helga already has her hands full."

"Why doesn't she come to quilters?"

"She says she doesn't like to sew and would rather I got to go for a change." Sophie grinned. "Now if that's not the best kind of sister-in-law to have." She turned to Ellie. "Your little May looks more like you every day. I sure wish your mother could come more often. She must miss seeing the little ones something fierce."

Kaaren took her Bible and flipped it open. She raised her voice. "I'm reading from Psalms to start today. Since we are so near to Thanksgiving time I thought to start with Psalm 150." She ended with " 'Let every thing that hath breath praise the Lord. Praise ye the Lord.' "

"Sometimes it is easier to complain than to praise Him, I think." Penny stuck her finger in her mouth to keep the blood from a needle prick from staining the pieces.

"What if we all agreed to write down five things to be thankful for every day, and on Thanksgiving Day we put the lists in the offering plate?" Mary Martha looked to Ingeborg for her agreement.

"Five every day?" Sophie's voice squeaked on the words.

"We could make it ten." Kaaren rolled her lips to keep from laughing at the look on her daughter's face.

Hildegunn nodded. "What a good idea."

"Who's going to read them?"

"Why does anyone have to read them? They are an offering to God from each one of us." Penny mentally counted. "We have twelve days. Surely we can manage this for twelve days."

"Do they have to be different every day?" Ellie asked. "I haven't even had time to write to Astrid, let alone to read. Good thing Andrew reads to me every evening."

Ingeborg smiled at her daughter-in-law. How good to know that her son was following in his family's footsteps. She loved it when Haakan read to her while she sat sewing or knitting. The box she kept for Christmas presents was filling fast, but it was a good thing she had started so early. This quilt for Emmy was not bed size but cuddle size, so she would have something of her own.

Ellie turned to Ingeborg. "Don't go making a doll for Emmy for Christmas. I have one about finished. I gave the doll a tan face and dark hair so she'd look more like her."

"What a good idea. I wonder if rag dolls might be something else we could put in the barrels for the reservation children."

A *harrumph* came from the quilting frame group.

———

WHEN KAAREN AND Ingeborg got home from the quilting, Emmy flew across the floor and threw herself into Ingeborg's arms. She raised a beaming face, her eyes dancing. "Did you have a good time?" Ingeborg asked.

"Emmy likes for Grandpa to give her cookies," Inga informed them as she made sure she got her hugs too. "So does Carl."

"And you don't care for cookies?" Kaaren asked, passing around hugs too.

Inga looked at her, wide-eyed in disbelief. "I gave out the cookies. Grandpa said so."

Ingeborg looked over at Haakan sitting at the table, coffee cup in front of him and another plate of cookies on the table. "Did you have dinner?" she asked Inga.

The child nodded. "No one even spilled."

The thought of Haakan getting the two children up to the table and serving soup with bread and a glass of milk made her give her husband a raised-eyebrows look. While she had left the soup kettle on the stove and sliced the bread, she knew that getting the two taken care of at the same time took some doing.

"Inga helped," he said with a smile.

"Pa came too," Inga said, gazing up at her grandmother. "But then he left."

"After dinner?"

She nodded.

Kaaren burst out laughing. "Oh, Haakan, and here we were feeling sorry for you. I should have known better."

"Thorliff delivered the newspaper and stayed for dinner. It was only polite to ask him."

"Pa drew us kittens. We colored them."

Ingeborg glanced down at the little girl holding on to her skirt. Emmy watched and listened but still had not said a word. Yet she and Inga got along fine. How come children could play so well together even when they didn't speak and adults couldn't? She thought back to the early days when Metiz would come to visit. She always brought something along to work on, like the rabbit-skin mittens that everyone prized. Ingeborg still had a pair of the soft, fur-lined mittens. How she wished Metiz were here to bring her special wisdom and more mittens and vests. Samuel had tanned a bunch of rabbit skins. She should make some herself.

"Are we taking Inga home?"

Haakan shook his head. "She's spending the night. Carl is invited too."

"I see."

"I'm heading home," Kaaren said. "You want me to send Freda back?"

"If she wants. You think they finished the wash?"

"I see that the sheets are all hanging on the clothesline. She and Anna have made things so much easier for Ilse. This pregnancy has been hard on her."

"And she still has a month to go."

"If she makes it that long."

"Thorliff brought the mail. We have a letter from Astrid and one from Augusta."

"Wonderful. Surely you can stay to hear them?" She turned to Kaaren. "Take your things off and be comfortable. School will let out soon, and you can ride home with your bunch."

When they had their cups of coffee poured and the little ones sitting on the floor with a cookie each, Ingeborg broke the seal on Astrid's letter.

"Dear Mor and Far,

"I am so excited that Rebecca and Gerald are coming to take Benny home. Thank you for your willingness to step in and

315

help them. Gerald told me his mother is excited about Benny's coming."

Ingeborg glanced up at Kaaren. "Hildegunn didn't mention this today. Do you think she'd react with joy?"

"She took in those boys years ago, and look what a blessing it has been to her and them. She'll make a good grandmother. It'll give you two one more thing to share."

Ingeborg raised an eyebrow. This could get interesting.

"I wish I could bring Benny to Blessing myself, but all of us will be staying here at the hospital. You know he has nothing of his own except what he came in wearing. He needs a warm coat, so remind them to bring one with them. He is so game in learning to use his artificial legs, but when he wants to get somewhere fast he crawls.

"Red Hawk and I have nearly completed our dissection of our cadaver. The old man has become a hero to us as we study every bit of him. I am grateful for people who are willing to donate bodies like this. We have learned so much.

"I was at the meeting with Dr. Morganstein and her friends who are gathering information of our dreams for a hospital. Isn't it interesting that God has given them a dream for building other hospitals at the same time as we've had a dream? I told them as much as I could but suggested they need to come to Blessing and talk to people there. Mrs. Josephson's nephew asked most of the questions. She calls him her money man.

"I need to close this and get some sleep. I am hoping and praying that the women of Blessing will be willing to help those on the reservations. I know you are already doing some.

"Love from your Astrid."

Ingeborg looked up. "I do wish I could have been a mouse in a pocket at that meeting and after Astrid left. I agree with her. It is amazing to watch when God goes to work." She looked at Kaaren. "Such big dreams we have now, when all we wanted in the beginning was to prove up our land. You with the school, now a hospital, traveling clinics." She shook her head slowly, a verse trickling through her mind. *What a mighty God we serve. Mighty indeed.* With dreams far outstretching their own. "We are so blessed that God is letting us be part of all this. When I think of all He is doing right here in Blessing . . ."

She looked down to see Emmy leaning against her knee, staring up at her with her dark eyes. "What do you want, little one?"

"She wants another cookie." Inga joined her. "Me too. And Carl."

Ingeborg glanced over to see Carl sitting on his grandfather's lap, finger in his mouth, leaning against Haakan's chest, eyes at half-mast. *Now, that is the perfect picture,* she thought and leaned over to kiss each of the girls. "You go pick up your toys, and I'll see if I can find another cookie."

"What about the plate on the table?" Leave it to Inga.

"Toys first."

Emmy scampered over to pick up the blocks and wooden train Haakan had made for them. Inga followed her.

Ingeborg could tell Emmy was learning the language, at least cookies and toys and her name.

Since the lane bordered Ingeborg's yard and went on to the Knutsons', they heard the schoolchildren coming.

"I'll go tell them to stop," Kaaren said. "Anything you want sent to my house?"

"George took the cheese this morning," Haakan said, "and plenty of milk. Tell Lars we'll be butchering day after tomorrow if the cold holds. We'll start with the steers."

———

TWO DAYS LATER, as soon as the chores were finished, two rifleshots rang out, signaling the death of the two steers. Haakan made sure that when the throats were slit, the blood was caught in basins to be used for making blod klub.

"You think we have enough potatoes ground?" Freda asked.

"We'll know soon enough." Ingeborg looked up at the sound of boots on the porch. "Here comes the blood."

Using every large bowl and pan, they mixed the grated potatoes with flour, added the fresh blood, and formed balls of the dough around pieces of salt pork, the last of that in storage. Like cooking dumplings, they placed the sticky balls in boiling water and set them to simmer. When they ran out of space, they filled other bowls and sent Trygve running to Kaaren's to cook them there.

The hearts, livers, and tongues were brought in next. After setting the tongues to boiling in pickling spices, they sliced the liver for dinner. Fried liver and onions was the traditional dinner, while the blod klub would be served along with it and later heated in cream for supper.

Outside, the men salted down the hides and wrapped them in bundles to age while the carcasses were wrapped in sheets and hung in the smokehouse to age.

When the men gathered for dinner, Ingeborg looked lovingly around the extended table. Knute and Gus, George and Lars, Samuel and Trygve, Solem, Gilbert, Haakan, Andrew and Thorliff, and Hjelmer. Just like cooking for the haying or threshing crew. One would think they were having a party with all the laughter and teasing.

BY THE TIME they finished two days later, they had butchered four steers and eight hogs. Haunches, shoulders, and pork sides were brining to be smoked. Sausage was ground and patties set in crocks sealed with melted lard, which had been rendering in ovens and set in bread pans, so they now had blocks of snowy lard to keep in the cellars.

Thorliff snitched a few pieces of crusty cracklings, what was left after all the lard was rendered out of the slabs of pork fat. "You didn't salt this."

"I know. I hadn't gotten around to it yet." Ingeborg stirred a cup of the crackly pieces into the cornmeal she was setting for fried cornmeal mush in the morning. "Take some home for Thelma, along with a couple of blocks of lard."

"She has plenty. She's been rendering too."

"Where's Haakan?"

"Out at the smokehouse. There's so much meat hanging in there, he can hardly get in to feed the coals." He dug in the bowl for another cluster of the golden bits. "Good thing we're finished. I need to print the paper tonight."

"I was wishing I could get out and bag us a few of those geese we hear flying south," Ingeborg told him. "Smoked goose would taste good too."

"You think you could still hit any?"

"Thorliff Bjorklund, any time you want a shooting contest with your mother, she is more than game. In fact"—Ingeborg narrowed her eyes—"you can have tonight, but day after tomorrow I challenge you to a goose hunt, winner take all."

Thorliff backed off, hands raised as in defense. "I didn't mean anything by it, just teasing."

"Well, this will teach you to tease your mother." Hands on hips, she stared at him through half-slitted eyes.

"Just you and me?"

"So far. But when I win, you have to write an apology in your paper about making fun of your mother."

"Oh, my word, what have I gotten myself into?" Thorliff tipped his head back and looked at the ceiling. When he looked at his mother again, he wore a crafty grin. "And when I win, what kind of boon can I demand? A written apology? A new sweater? Two loaves of bread a week?" He twisted his mouth from one side to the other, stroking his chin like a diabolical villain. "I have to think on this, really think on this."

He was getting far too much pleasure out of this. What had she started? "From dawn to noon, those are the parameters. We will have dinner here at noon."

Thorliff nodded. "Agreed."

He sounded so nonchalant, but the look in his eyes said something was brewing.

———

"ARE YOU REALLY going through with this?" Haakan asked the night before the contest.

"Of course. I just wonder what that son of ours has up his sleeve." She turned to her husband. "You know, don't you?"

Guilt couldn't hide on Haakan's face.

"Men. All in cahoots."

"My, my. Such language."

"Haakan Bjorklund, you are . . . you are despicable." She had to look away so he couldn't see the glint that she was sure must be in her own eyes.

———

INGEBORG WAS DRESSED and out on the most northern of the wheat fields, where she had seen a flock of Canada geese the day before. Carrying two shotguns and hiding behind a row of low brush, she could hear them before she saw them in the dimness. When it was light enough to shoot she picked off two on the ground and two in flight. Four—not bad for five shots, but now to wait for them to come back, or where else should she go looking? Down on the riverbanks?

"Well done." She turned to see Haakan hunkered down not far from her.

"Takk." She fetched her geese, tying their legs together with leather thongs she'd stuffed into her pockets. "Would have been easier out here in britches."

Haakan took them from her and slung them over his shoulder. "Are you done?"

"No. I'll try the riverbanks." They turned at the sound of gunshots. "Thorliff?"

"No doubt. We warned all the others to not hunt this morning."

Ingeborg rolled her eyes. "What all goes on behind my back is what I want to know." She reloaded her guns and started toward the river. A flock of geese in V formation highlighted against the dawn sky caught her attention. She shaded her eyes to look. "Snow geese. Have you seen any flocks on the ground around here?"

He shook his head. "Only the Canada."

"Remember when the sky was almost black with migrating birds both spring and fall?"

"And the deer herds were so plentiful we didn't have to raise beef. I know. Times are changing."

"You're not milking this morning?" She inhaled a deep breath of crisp air. "I'm glad you are here. We don't take time to do things like this together, even just to walking out and seeing our world in the early morning or evening." They'd crossed the fields and neared the river, where thickets of Juneberries and willow provided cover for rabbits and grouse and other wildlife. She stopped at a deer trail. "Look, they bedded here last night."

"You're not hunting deer." He stretched his shoulders. "We'll watch for them." He kept his voice low, as did she.

Ingeborg stopped to listen, as she'd done several times. Surely that was geese off to the left. She turned to look back over the fields in case some had returned to their grazing. Not that she could see. They made their way along the deer trail, closer to the river. A flapping of wings, honking, and three geese thrashed over the river surface and settled to swim farther out. Without a dog or a boat, shooting them would be a waste.

Through a gap in the trees, she looked across the river to see a flock of geese grazing on the field on the Minnesota side. Too far to shoot or retrieve. Ingeborg sighed. She could wait until later and hope some had settled down or call this good. After all, she had until noon. But the hem of her skirt was heavy with water due to the dew, her stomach rumbled at the thought of breakfast, and she'd forgotten how heavy a shotgun could get with the carrying. Or perhaps she was just getting older, like she'd reminded Haakan more than once.

"Are you ready to head back to the house?"

"Any time you are. A cup of coffee sounds mighty appealing."

"You think I'll win with four?"

"No idea." He took one of the guns from her.

"Should have set the deadline for ten."

His chuckle warmed her from the inside out.

Thorliff showed up at eleven thirty, three geese in hand.

Ingeborg pointed to her four, already plucked, cleaned, and ready for the smokehouse.

Thorliff stuck out his hand. "Congratulations, Mor. I knew I should have gone back out."

"I get the down from your birds?"

"Why not."

"And an apology?"

"Painfully so."

"Good. Let's go eat. If we'd planned this right, we could have had goose livers for dinner. But then, we don't really have enough for everyone." She looked at their family gathered around. "We found a place where the deer slept. Maybe we can have fresh venison one of these days."

Inga and Emmy looked up at her with bright eyes. "We missed you," Inga said. "Emmy and I got goose feathers. Can we eat on the porch?"

"Pretty chilly out there. How about we use the table instead? You can go out to play afterwards."

Elizabeth gave Ingeborg a hug and whispered in her ear, "I'm so glad you won. He would have been insufferable."

Lord, I pray that Astrid is having good memory times. I miss her so, even more so when we are all together. She felt like a cloud had dimmed the sunshine. *Please don't send her to Africa.*

28

Smoked goose for Thanksgiving had been something new. Joshua buckled his tool belt around his hips and joined the others laying hardwood floors in Hjelmer's house. Hjelmer had promised Penny she would be in her own house for Christmas, and he was pushing hard to make his promise come true.

"Have you ever done stairs before?" Hjelmer asked.

Joshua shook his head. "That takes some special figuring, and I don't know how to do it."

"Me neither. Good thing Toby has done them before. You plan on working with him so that we have more than one man who can do that fine work."

I'd rather be building windmills. Joshua nodded his assent. Any job was better than no job, but he had to admit he was enjoying working with these men and learning new skills. If someone had told him he'd become a carpenter, he'd have thought they were running a couple eggs short of a dozen. Wouldn't his father be surprised when he told him, *if* he told him.

"Hey, Joshua, I'm ready to start. I'll draw us the diagram." Toby took the pencil from behind his ear.

Joshua shoved his hammer down into the loop on his belt and joined Toby at the table made by boards across two sawhorses. A picture of the stair design lay on the table. It had come from Sears and Roebuck along with all the other plans, which were held down by two bricks.

"See, we have a quarter turn at the landing, and the company sent us stair horses already cut to make it easier."

A stair horse? What in the world?

"See that notched two-by-twelve? There are six of them for this stairs, and we had the same for the back stairs. See, they even cut the angles for the ends. We'll cut the risers and the treads and nail them in place. You want to cut or nail?"

"Nail to start with."

"Good, let's nail this side onto the wall first."

Nail by nail and board by board, they raised the stairs to the landing in time for dinner, then to the second floor by quitting time, taking turns cutting and nailing. Joshua cut one board half an inch too short.

"You measure once, look at it, measure again. Never hurts to take time to measure even a third time. I learned that lesson same as you. We'll find another use for that board. It won't go to waste."

Joshua nodded. His father would have yelled at him for making such a stupid mistake. But he didn't need his father to do that, he did a right good job of it himself.

Penny pushed open the front door just as they were putting their tools away. She and Hjelmer strolled through the house so she could see all that had been accomplished. Stopping at the stairs, she grinned at Toby and Joshua. "Now, doesn't that look lovely. Once we get the rails and banisters up we can move right in."

"There's a lot to do before we move, so don't get your hopes up too high," Hjelmer cautioned.

"The more I keep saying it, the more certain it will happen. The Bible says to speak things into existence, like God did when creating the world. He said, 'Let there be light.' I'm saying, 'Let there be stairs, and lights and floors and . . .' " She spun and headed for the kitchen, calling over her shoulder, " 'And cupboards and shelves and . . .' Oh, look at the pantry."

Hjelmer shrugged. "Women." He turned to Joshua. "You playing for church tomorrow?"

Joshua nodded. "Trygve and Miss Deborah are singing a duet. We'll practice again tonight."

"Every year we have more musicians. Those first years were tough. Lars played his fiddle sometimes, and when the congregation sang harmony, it gave me the shivers."

Joshua stared at Hjelmer. The man continued to surprise him.

———

THE PRACTICE WENT well that evening, and after bidding Trygve and Deborah good night, Joshua walked back to the boardinghouse, thinking how more and more he felt a part of the people of Blessing. If only Astrid were here. He detoured by his hole in the ground, as he called it. For a while there had been too much snow to pour the concrete, then when that melted, it turned too cold. He'd pretty much given up his dream of working on his own house this winter. At least the basement was all dug out, and once it dried in the spring, they could get going on it. The big question: Would Astrid like the house?

The even bigger question: Could Astrid fall in love with him as he had with her? If only he had a few more letters to reread. He'd about worn out the three that he had.

————

INGEBORG GAZED DOWN at the little girl looking lost in Astrid's big bed. Emmy had been with them nearly a month, and she had yet to utter a word. Was she homesick for the tribe or for her family? What was her story? Strange that no one had come looking for her, or even to check to see if she was alive or dead. What if no one cared?

Well, somebody cares for this little one. We do. If you are God's answer to all my prayers through the years for another child, so be it. Father God, we will love her as long as you allow us to have her. She thought about that for a moment. Nobody better try to take her away.

Hands bracing on the narrow stair walls, she returned to the parlor, where Freda sat in the rocker, her knitting needles singing their simple song. Haakan held a piece of harness to the light and marked where he would hammer the awl so he could have a hole to slide the buckle in place. Fixing harnesses was indeed good winter work. Often the house smelled of horse-sweated leather. Ingeborg sat down on the kitchen chair she had pulled up to a small table covered in tanned rabbit skins. While she had knit Inga several pairs of mittens, there was nothing warmer and cozier than rabbit-fur mittens. Haakan had cut narrow strips of deer hide for her to use for sewing mittens. As Metiz had taught her, she punched the holes with a small awl and whipstitched the two pieces together. She had a smaller pair cut out for Carl.

"What are you knitting now?" she asked Freda.

Freda held up the rich blue yarn she'd purchased at Penny's store. "A jumper for Signe. She is growing so fast that the clothes we brought from Norway are getting too small. I have a sweater for Thor. I think his arms have grown three inches since we got here."

"And his legs. I have an old wool coat that we can take apart and use the material for pants for him. I must have a pattern his size in the pattern box." Through the years Ingeborg had saved the patterns she'd made for all the clothing she'd sewn, carefully labeling them with the age of the child they were for. Many of them were cut out of newspapers, and sometimes now Thorliff gave her the plain newsprint paper left over from printing the paper.

———

SNOW STARTED FALLING during church the next morning—big, fat lazy flakes that zigged and zagged so that when Inga came out the door she squealed in delight. "Snowing. It is snowing." She turned to Emmy. "Let's catch them."

Emmy stared at her, but when Inga held out her mittened hand until one landed on it, Emmy did the same. The two studied the snowflakes, then Inga touched it with her tongue and held out her hand.

Emmy did the same, and the two darted down the steps to catch more. Carl followed them until he tripped over a rut and fell plunk down on his seat. He grunted, shook his head, and using both hands, got back up.

"I hope he doesn't spend the rest of his life trying to catch up with her," Ellie said.

"Oh, he won't. One day he'll jump farther and swing higher, and either the two will be equals, or she'll be chasing him." Ingeborg held out her arms, and May reached for her grandma. Jiggling the little one on her hip, she watched as all the young children were catching snowflakes, touching them and laughing. "Isn't it amazing what can entertain children?"

"Oh, I don't know about children," Thorliff said, holding up his gloved hand and showing her his nest of snowflakes. "I remember your telling me that each one is different, but they'd always melt before I could be sure."

"Sometimes life is like that, isn't it? Beautiful, but if you try to study it, the moment is gone." Ingeborg touched her nose to May's to make her giggle. "Like these little ones. They grow so fast, and then they are gone."

"Ja. Like Grace and Astrid." Kaaren tipped her head back and caught a snowflake on her tongue. "But at least they are coming back."

"Please, God, I pray so." Ingeborg looked up when Haakan called her name. "The drivers are getting impatient." Calling the children, the families made their way to the buggies and climbed in. "Just think, pretty soon we'll be tucking the buffalo robe around our legs and heating bricks to set at our feet. While I so look forward to Christmas, I am in no hurry for winter to really get here."

"I think it is here. The reprieve is over." Haakan clucked the horse into a trot.

"I suppose." Ingeborg wrapped her arm around the little girl and drew her closer to her side.

"Tomorrow I think I'll put the bells on the harnesses, and if this keeps up, we'll clean up the sleigh so we have it ready to go. Lars is getting the sledge ready for the schoolchildren. He's thinking of putting a heater in there this year." Two years earlier Lars had built an enclosed box to fit on the wagon bed, where they had replaced the four wheels with four skids. The box had a window cut out for the driver to see and drive the team. A door opened and closed, and benches lined the inside walls. From the outside it looked similar to a house on wheels but without a sloped roof and windows. Samuel now drove all the children from the deaf school to the Blessing school so they could receive a good education.

Ingeborg glanced over her shoulder to see why Freda was so quiet. "Are you all right?"

"Ja. Thinking of Christmas just makes me homesick for Norway and our life there."

Ingeborg nodded.

"But I'll get over it. I think Solem is doing better. Haakan, has he talked to you about going farther west to homestead?"

"He mentioned it. But the land out there is not as rich as here in the Red River Valley. I know Trygve talks about doing that too. They've changed some of the rules for proving up a homestead. Now it is three years instead of five, and if you can afford to buy out your contract earlier, you are allowed to do that. I think you can buy some-one else's homestead not proved up yet, but they'd need to check on all the legalities."

"Would you go too?" Ingeborg asked Freda, concern inching higher as the pause lengthened.

"No, I don't think so. I like it here, and I like what I am doing. I would like a house of my own, is all."

Ingeborg sighed in relief. "Thank you. I cannot tell you how much I appreciate that." She looked to her husband. "Perhaps next spring we can see about building you a house."

"It needn't be big, not for one person."

"You are always welcome at our house. I hope you know that."

"Oh, I do. And I don't want it far away from the cheese house."

Haakan halted the team at the gate. By now the grass wore white frosting, and the snow was settling on roofs and roads. After dropping off women and children, Andrew and Thorliff drove the buggies to the barn and unhitched their teams to get the horses into shelter instead of waiting in the weather. Solem and Anna and their children rode with Andrew, and Gilbert came with Thorliff.

As they all gathered in the kitchen to remove coats and hats, the children headed into the parlor, where the toy box waited, the women began setting out the food, and the men, when they returned from the barn, gathered around the stove in the parlor.

Ingeborg could hear the hum of their discussions but not the gist of it. Elizabeth and Ellie were laughing about something, and Freda was handing Anna things from the pantry to put on the table. Ingeborg brought the deep kettle with the potatoes, which had simmered while they were gone, to the sink and poured the potato water into a separate crock, planning to use it in the soup she would make in the morning. Then she pulled the potato masher out of the drawer and mashed the hot potatoes, added cream and butter, salt and pepper, and mashed until the lumps were gone. She gave the contents a good whipping to lighten them up.

At the same time Freda had taken the venison haunch out of the oven and removed it from the pan. As she added flour to the drippings, Ingeborg shoved her kettle to the back of the stove to keep warm.

"You want to finish the gravy or slice the meat?"

"I'll do the gravy." She turned. "Anna, would you put the rolls in the oven to warm up?"

Haakan stepped back into the kitchen. "I asked Joshua to join us, but he had promised to help Johnny Solberg with guitar lessons, so he might be a bit late."

Ingeborg nodded. "Ellie, please set another place."

"Good thing you have such a big table."

"I know. And the children can sit on laps for now. Haakan is planning on building a lower table for the children, now that we have more of them."

As soon as they had the food in serving dishes, Ingeborg called everyone to the table. "Haakan, please lead the grace."

As silence fell, Haakan said, "I Jesu navn, gär vi til bords," with all the others joining the age-old Norwegian grace. At the amen, everyone sat but for Ingeborg and Freda, who brought the remaining plates and platters to the table. Ingeborg smiled to herself to see her three men, each with a child on a knee, dishing up their own plate plus the small one for their child. She knew that other families didn't do things this way, but when Thorliff started it, Andrew followed, and now Haakan did the same. *Thank you, Father,* whispered through her mind as she made sure all the bowls were refilled.

"You sit down now," Freda told her. "I will pour the coffee."

For a change Ingeborg did just that, dropping a kiss on Emmy's head as she sat beside Haakan. "Do you want me to take her?" she asked quietly.

Haakan shook his head. "She's fine."

She's fine. Such a short comment but so perfect. *Aren't we all fine? Healthy, happy, gathered in a house all snugged up for the winter, all together, including grandchildren, cousins, our family.* The thoughts kept floating through her mind as she filled her plate, with Haakan making sure she got some of everything. *Oh, Lord, how blessed we are. I cannot thank you enough. The only one missing is Astrid. I pray you keep her safe, and you know my opinion on where I want her to go next.*

Between bites she brought her attention back to the conversation around the table.

"If the snow keeps up, like I think it will, as soon as it is deep enough, we can use the sleighs for our Christmas tree–cutting trek."

"Where do you cut trees?" Gilbert asked, confusion in his eyes. "There are none here."

"Some of us go across the river to Minnesota. Once out of the

Red River Valley, there are plenty of pine trees. A farmer over there lets us cut trees in exchange for a wheel of cheese," Thorliff explained. "Far and Lars usually go. Not sure who else will go along. They bring back one for the church too."

"Enough for the whole town?"

"No. Some come in a railroad car."

"We used to bring one back for everyone, but now there are just too many households." Haakan set Emmy down when Inga slid to the floor. "You girls let Carl play too."

"Carl has the train," Inga said. "We have the ball."

"Ball?" Carl slid off his father's knee. "Play ball."

Ingeborg rolled her lips together. Astrid was usually the one who played with the children. Why was her name coming up so often today? Was there something going on with her? More than the every day? Or was it just that Christmas was coming and it was her first one away from home?

29

D E C E M B E R   2 0 ,   1 9 0 3

A line from Pastor Solberg's sermon this Sunday before Christmas ate at Joshua like a dog gnawing on a bone. "The one who suffers the most when you refuse to forgive someone—" there was a long pause, and he looked directly into Joshua's eyes, or so he thought—"is you." The silence shouted and echoed the comment.

Joshua stared at the man in front of the congregation. Had he really said that? At the end of the four-part series on forgiveness, all of which needled Joshua mercilessly anyway, this was hard to hear.

He played the final song on his guitar along with Elizabeth on the piano, but his mind refused to take part. Good thing his fingers knew where to go and what to do.

"Are you all right?" Dr. Elizabeth asked him when they finished playing after most of the congregation had filed out.

Joshua nodded, shook his head, and nodded again. He sighed and looked toward her. "He packs a punch, doesn't he?"

"Pastor Solberg?"

"Um-hmm." He unbuttoned the strap that looped over his shoulder. "He makes it sound so simple."

"Sound simple and be simple don't go hand in hand. Sometimes they're not even speaking."

He nodded. Good thing he had told Johnny Solberg that he couldn't give him a lesson today. "Merry Christmas, Dr. Bjorklund."

"Where's Mr. Landsverk going?" Ingeborg asked when Dr. Elizabeth joined her and Kaaren outside.

"I don't know. Why?"

Ingeborg pointed to the figure striding back toward town. "I thought he was coming to dinner."

"Perhaps he had something he needed to do beforehand."

"So are we all ready for the Christmas program tonight?" Kaaren asked.

"Far as I know the musicians are. Johnny is going to play too, for his first time."

"Guess he won't be Joseph this year, then?"

"No, and Samuel is acting like I've been beating him because I said he had to take the part," Kaaren added.

"Good thing we had a large-size male garment." Ingeborg had been in charge of sewing Christmas costumes ever since the plays began. This year she'd made a new crown for one of the kings because the other had disintegrated. "The angel wings are getting a bit worn."

"I know. And Dorothy's baby, Adam, is pretty large to be playing baby Jesus, but all will be well," Elizabeth said. "No matter what happens, we all love it. This is the third or fourth time we are using the original one that Thorliff wrote."

"I tried to get him to write another, but he said he just didn't have time. Who wrote the story he's been serializing in the paper this year?" Kaaren asked.

"He won't tell even me. Says it will be a surprise in this week's edition." Elizabeth looked around for her daughter.

"She's with Emmy. I think they are making snow angels with the big girls." Ingeborg shaded her eyes with a flat hand. "Over there by the trees."

The sun shimmering on the snow made the blue sky even bluer, if that were possible. Black fence posts wearing white top hats stuck up through the sparkling drifts, mute lines of sentinel soldiers.

Ingeborg raised her face to the sun, which had little warmth. "I am so grateful for days like this. I want to soak in the sun and trap it to take out in bits and pieces when I need it."

"Like when that old north wind is howling?" Kaaren took her arm. "The men are waiting, most likely thinking they've not been fed for a week."

———

THAT EVENING AT the church there was standing room only, as the stage in front took up extra room. Dr. Elizabeth, Joshua, Lars, Trygve, and Johnny played a medley of carols while people filed in and scooted closer so more could sit down. Kerosene lamps on wall sconces provided light, along with stair-stepped candelabras that Mr. Sam had created for the church. A pine tree dressed in angels—crocheted, carved, knit, and pieced—waited in the corner for the candles to be lit.

The players took their positions. Thorliff stepped to the podium and silence fell, that awestruck moment when the world waits for the story to be told again. A child's voice sang from the rear. "O come, O come, Emmanuel . . ."

Joshua answered. "And ransom captive Israel . . ."

The children's choir picked up. "That mourns in lonely exile here . . ."

Joshua replied. "Until the Son of God appear."

Everyone sang the chorus. "Rejoice! Rejoice! Emmanuel shall come to thee, O Israel."

Silence reigned again, and then Thorliff began reading the familiar story.

Ingeborg dabbed at her eyes, her sniff joining others.

The baby slept through the program, only one angel lost a wing, and the lamb tried to escape, but Joseph reached over and grabbed it, handing it back to the shepherd. The king's new crown glittered in the lamplight. Grace, who was so aptly named, signed for those who couldn't hear. She'd come home in time to do just that, and the smile she sent Jonathan at the piano bench left no doubt in anyone's mind as to her love for him.

And the age-old story, always new and full of promise, dug into each of their hearts and blossomed in love.

As they all sang "Silent Night," three people lit the candles on the tree while others doused the kerosene lamps so that the lighted tree was the only light.

"Oh, pretty!" Inga's voice could be heard to the corners, bringing chuckles and other comments.

The delight on Emmy's face when she was given a peppermint stick, an orange, and a wrapped package like all the other children made Ingeborg tear up again. "You can open it," Ingeborg told her.

"See, like this." Inga opened hers, as always making sure Emmy knew what to do. Inside each box was a book, thanks to Thorliff and Elizabeth, who had given the children this present ever since they came back to Blessing.

Emmy studied the orange, sniffed it, and held it out to Ingeborg.

Then following Inga's lead, she sucked on her peppermint stick, her face glowing in delight.

By the time the program was finished, the candles extinguished, the costumes in a stack by the side door, and small children asleep in their folks' arms, everyone headed for home, accompanied by sleigh bells and laughter.

"That was so beautiful," Freda said. "And when they sang some of the carols in Norwegian, why, my heart just flew home." She paused a moment. "But, you know, I think this was the best Christmas program I ever saw."

"Ingeborg says that every year." Haakan nudged his wife. "Don't you?"

"I do?" Ingeborg stared at him wide-eyed. "That couldn't be me." She glanced down at the little one nearly hidden by the buffalo robe. "She's almost asleep."

"I'm not surprised. Next year she'll be in the program too."

―――――――

THE NEXT MORNING Ingeborg found an envelope stuck in the doorframe. She opened it to read:

Dear Mrs. Bjorklund,

Thank you for the kind invitation to join your family for Christmas Day, but I am leaving on the train this morning to return to Iowa. You know my family is there, and thanks to Pastor Solberg, I have an errand to do. May you all have the most blessed Christmas ever.

Sincerely,
Joshua Landsverk

"So that was what he was about," Haakan said when he heard

her read it again later. "He told Thorliff and Hjelmer he would need to miss some work."

"But at least Penny got to move in." The move had taken two days, with everyone who could take the time helping.

"There is still much to do inside, but it is livable and the furnace works just great. I think we'll put one in here next fall."

"Along with the bathroom?"

"That comes in the spring, although I could do the inside work on it this winter." He nodded, digging at his teeth with the tip of his tongue, along with a slow nod that told Ingeborg he'd disappeared into thought land.

"Today Emmy and I are making fattigmann." Ingeborg swooped the little girl up in her arms and danced them around the kitchen.

"Again?" Freda set the last of the breakfast dishes in the pan of hot soapy water on the stove.

"I know. I saved the lard from the last ones. We should do doughnuts too. We have plenty of buttermilk."

"I thought I'd make buttermilk pies. My mor always made those for Christmas dinner."

"You better make four or five, then. The whole family will be here, and then in the afternoon everyone takes the sleighs out, and we go visiting."

"But who do you visit when everyone is out?"

"It seems to work out."

Ingeborg got out her recipe and mixed the ingredients for the fattigmann, Emmy standing on a stool beside her, a towel tied around her for an apron. "Now, when we roll these out, we cut them and you tuck the tail into the slot, and then we fry them."

Emmy nodded as if she understood every word.

Ingeborg rolled and cut the diamond shapes, a slot in the middle, and showed her helper how to tuck the tail in. They giggled together, and Ingeborg dropped a piece of dough into the lard kettle on the stove to make sure it was hot enough.

Then she slid the fattigmann into the kettle. Freda watched the cookies brown, flipped them over, and with a slotted spoon, dipped them out and laid the treats on dish towels to drain. When they'd cooled, they shook them in powdered sugar and filled the few tins they had empty.

"You have powdered sugar all over your face," Ingeborg told Emmy and held her up to see in the mirror. Emmy giggled and brushed the white spots away. She turned to smile at Ingeborg, who kissed the little cheek. "You still taste like sugar."

When Haakan returned from town, he brought an envelope from Astrid. He opened it with his pocketknife and pulled out the paper.

"Dear Mor and Far,

"I'm keeping this short, but I wanted to make sure you would be home Christmas Day. At one o'clock in the afternoon I plan to telephone you. I just have to hear your voices and tell you God Jul. Merry Christmas. And how much I love you."

Ingeborg sniffed. "Having her here would make Christmas perfect." She looked down to see Emmy staring up at her, her eyes round and face sad.

"No, I am not sad . . . well not much, little one." She bent over and hugged Emmy close. "And you make me so happy that I can't squeeze you enough."

That always made Emmy giggle.

"And one of these days, I think you are going to talk, and that will make me really, really happy too."

Haakan cleared his throat and continued with the rest of the letter.

"I dream of home and white snow, not the dirty stuff on all the streets here. Even the snow on the rooftops is an ugly gray from all the coal burning. But we are busy here. As Dr. Morganstein has said repeatedly, sickness and accidents don't take a vacation at Christmas. She also told us to prepare for more cases of family abuse. There is so much sadness at this time, when instead the whole world should be rejoicing. I better hurry. I just heard them call my name.

"Love and joy,
"Your daughter,
"Dr. Astrid Bjorklund

"P.S. I'm sorry that Mr. Josephson and Mr. Abramson decided to postpone their visit until spring, but this way perhaps I can be there too.

"A"

"She loves to sign her letters that way, I think." Ingeborg smiled at her husband. "Is it a sin to be so proud of one's child?"

"If it is, we have it together." Haakan slid the letter back into the envelope. "I could sure eat some of the fattigmann about now."

"That's why we had to make them again."

———

CHRISTMAS DAY DAWNED clear. Ingeborg scraped a spot free of ice off the kitchen window so she could see the sunrise. "Thank you, Lord, for a glorious day. No blizzard this year as there has been in the past." She thought back to the night before, when they had lighted the candles on the tree in the parlor. Inga, Emmy, and Carl had stared, oohed and aahed. Ingeborg, as always, did the same, kneeling beside the little ones and cuddling them close while Haakan read the

Christmas story. Christmas trees needed to be lit in the evening. Today would be beautiful, but not as it had been the night before.

They attended church at ten and had dinner at noon, the smoked geese having been stuffed and put in the oven before they left for church. The children danced from the tree, with the presents stacked around, to the kitchen and back to the tree while the women cleaned up the dinner and put things away.

"Presents now?" Inga asked for the thirtieth time.

"Not yet. Not until after Tante Astrid calls us on the telephone."

Inga rolled her eyes. "Cookie then?" She quickly added a "please" for good measure.

When the telephone rang two times, everyone fell silent as Ingeborg rushed to answer it. "Hello?"

"Mor, God Jul. Merry Christmas. Hold the receiver out so I can shout to everyone." And shout she did. Then they all shouted *Merry Christmas* back to her.

After quick visits with each one, Astrid said softly, "I miss you all so much."

"And we miss you." *I miss you the most.* But Ingeborg could hardly speak through the tears. "I sent you a box of Christmas goodies. Did you get them?"

"Oh, I did. Thank you so much. We had a party the other night and shared our boxes from home. Yours were the best. Well, I better let you go. Have you opened the presents yet?"

"No, I made them wait until after we talked with you. This is the best present."

"And Inga is—?"

"Being Inga. She can't wait. She's staring up at me right now, her look saying 'Hang up the telephone.' "

"Give her a kiss from me. Bye, Mor."

"Bye." She bent down and kissed Inga's cheek and then her nose. "Those are from Tante Astrid."

"We can open presents now." Inga ran into the other room. "Emmy, you sit down here by me." She patted the floor beside her. "And Carl can sit here."

Thorliff gave his mother a look and shook his head. "The queen has spoken."

Lord, I do pray that everything is going well for Mr. Landsverk. And thank you for everyone here. For all the blessings you have poured out upon us. For sending us your son. And thank you for good weather, no blizzard.

30

Astrid got comfortable on her bed and then traced her finger along her mother's handwriting before opening the envelope.

Dear Astrid,

I cannot begin to tell you how much hearing your voice meant to me—to all of us, but to me especially. I just needed to hear your voice. What a gift the telephone can be. I have decided that since the call gave us all so much pleasure, we will do it again, only not wait until the house is full of company. I wish you could have seen the look on Inga's face when you spoke to her. Her eyes lit up and she danced in place. "Tante Astrid!" she whispered. Well, you know how Inga whispers.

We had a wonderful day here. The children so loved the Christmas tree, even when the candles weren't lighted. I would find

Emmy just sitting cross-legged on the floor, staring at it, all by herself. It is the first thing she runs to in the morning. I'm not sure how we will explain it to her when we take it down. I wish I knew if she is learning English. Perhaps I need to relearn some simple Sioux words to see if that would make her answer me. I know she can hear.

When Thorliff brought in the puppy for Inga, she stroked the puppy's ears, grinned up at her pa, and said, "Really? For me?" Thorliff asked her what she would like to name her, and she stared at him, shaking her head.

We all tried to think of a name, but none has stuck yet. She is brown and white and fluffy. I don't think she'll be a cattle dog.

Emmy loved the rag doll that Ellie made for her. She used black yarn for the hair and tan skin for the face and body. Emmy hugged that doll to her chest and never let it go for the rest of the day. I was thinking we should make a papoose pack for her and skin leggings and shirt for the doll, like Emmy wore when she came. Ellie dressed the doll in a skirt, waist, and apron.

Inga, Carl, and Emmy wore the rabbit-skin mittens I made for them for the rest of the day. I need to make more of those. They are the warmest. Remember the rabbit-skin vests that Metiz used to make? I found one of Andrew's, and while it is still too big for Carl, Emmy appropriated it for herself. She was so worn out by the time everyone left that she curled up behind the stove on her quilt right along with the cat. I remember Andrew doing the same thing. This has been a year of more memories than others, I think.

Well, I better head on for bed. Both your pa and I pray for you every day, and I know God is holding you tight in the palm of His mighty hand. I know too that He will make His will clear to you at the right time, although I keep reminding Him of how much we want you to come back to Blessing.

With all my love and rejoicing in who you are,
Your mor

Astrid mopped her tears and read the letter again. While they had tried to provide a Christmas for the children on the ward, she was glad so many were able to go home. She had been hoping that Gerald and Rebecca could have come for Benny before Christmas, but sometimes even the best laid plans didn't make it. She could hardly believe they would be arriving the very next day. Containing her excitement took any extra energy she owned.

She tucked the letter into the larger fabric envelope that contained all the others and then returned to her bed with her back against the wall, contemplating her tired feet. She must have walked ten miles today. At least it felt like that. Two babies had been born on Christmas Day—both healthy, as were the mothers. An old man on the surgical floor had died that night. And tomorrow Benny would meet his new parents. They were arriving on the train before noon and would stay overnight in the hotel down the street. She had leave to join Rebecca and Gerald for supper in the dining room here at the hospital.

As she finished getting ready for bed, her thoughts got away from her. She'd not heard from Mr. Landsverk. No answer to the letter she sent him before Christmas and not even a note saying Merry Christmas.

Take every thought captive, she reminded herself. *You can't be worrying about something you have no control over. Like that man.* He was the one who asked her to write, who said he would write. *Take every thought captive. Put Jesus in my mind instead.* That was not a Bible verse but something her mother said that always made her calm down and think better. Astrid said her prayers, starting to omit Joshua and then changing her mind. *Take care of him with all the rest of my family and friends, and thank you for your Word, which does sustain me. In spite of me. I love you, Jesus.* Her amen never quite made it.

———

SHE WOKE AT the knock at her door and made her way to the washroom, where other students and nurses were in the same bleary shape as she. At least she'd been allowed to sleep through the night. One did not take that privilege lightly, she'd learned well. Down in the dining room she poured herself a cup of coffee, filled her plate, and found a place to sit with some of the other student doctors.

"So Benny goes to a home today?" one of the young men asked.

Astrid nodded. "Rebecca Baard, now Rebecca Valders, has always been one of my good friends. We grew up together, and now she and her husband are coming."

"They understand about his handicap?"

"Oh yes. I'm not worried about him going to Blessing. The whole town will become his family. Managing his crutches might be difficult in the snow, but I have a feeling someone will devise him a wagon or sled or something to make his life easier."

She glanced up to see Red Hawk taking the vacant place on her left. "Good morning."

"No, good night. I'm on my way to bed."

"Night shift?"

"Three accidents brought in. One was a woman who fell down the stairs." His sideways glance told them his opinion of that excuse.

"How bad?"

"Fracture of the right femur, broken ribs, and maybe internal injuries. She says she needs to get home to take care of her children."

"She won't be taking care of anyone for a while," another young doctor added.

"If we got rid of the booze in this town, this hospital would have a lot less patients," one of the women, well known for her views on prohibition, chimed in.

"There was a big bust at the speakeasy. Several dead and one wounded brought in here. I guess some of the other hospitals took in the rest." Red Hawk shoveled eggs and bacon into his mouth. "Saturday night in the big city."

"Who operated?"

"Jensen." Herbert Jensen, a third-year student, was staying on for more surgical training. "Two wounds actually, one in the left leg and the other in the side. Missed all the vitals. The man was grumbling about not seeing a *real* doctor."

"How did he know?" Someone down the table leaned forward. "Jensen has had more training than half the doctors practicing out there."

Astrid finished her plate and nursed her coffee for a few more minutes, half listening to the discussion waging around her. While she had come to feel acceptance within the group, she'd not developed any close friends other than Red Hawk, and she was never sure if he was really a friend or not. Perhaps he needed to retreat into himself in order to be able to endure all the close proximity of life in the hospital. She knew *she* needed to.

A nurse came through the door, heading for the coffeepot. "Benny is asking for you, Dr. Bjorklund."

"I thought he would be. I am on my way." She put her cup on the tray and headed out the swinging door. Outside the ward she paused and gathered herself, finally admitting that no matter how excited she was for Benny, she was going to miss him here. At least she would see him again in Blessing. *If you don't go to Africa,* a little voice whispered inside her.

Why was she feeling more accepting of that possibility lately? She pushed open the door to hear children laughing. Three of them were taking turns riding on Benny's cart, for lack of a better word. Mr. Korchensky down in maintenance had fashioned a flat platform with two wheels in back and one in front with a handle protruding through the base so it could be turned in either direction.

Benny sat on his bed, dressed in the new set of clothes the nurses had gone together and provided for him. The pants were long and loose enough to fit over the straps that held his prostheses in place so that when using his two crutches with his wooden legs, he looked close to normal. Scooting on the cart was much easier and faster.

"Hey, Dr. Bjorklund." He waved his crutch in the air. "Works good, huh?"

"Works very good." She stopped beside his bed. "You look all ready to go."

"Yep." He nodded so vigorously that his sand-colored curls bobbed on his forehead. "You are going to come see me, right?"

"When I get back to Blessing, I will see you for sure. Like I told you, Blessing is a small town, and everybody knows everybody else."

"And you grew up there?"

"I did, and all my family and friends live there."

"And there are cows and horses and dogs and cats."

"And pigs and tractors and sheep and chickens." She thought hard for something different. "And deer and birds and fish in the river."

"And I will go to school." He tried hard to look tough, crossed arms, hands tucked under his armpits.

"Yes, you will, and you will be so smart and learn so fast that no one can catch up with you." They'd played this game before. It was as if he needed a preview of what life would be like in his new home. She'd never asked him about his life before the hospital, but one day she hoped he would tell her.

"Now I must go see other patients, but I'll be back."

He studied the first button on his shirt. "I wish you would stay here." His whisper caught at her heart.

Astrid leaned forward and tipped his chin up so he had to look at her. "Your life is going to be good, Benny. You will have a new mother and father who will love you and make sure you have what you need. You'll have uncles and aunts and cousins and maybe even brothers and sisters sometime. I will bring your new parents to meet you when they come." She dropped her voice so he had to listen harder. "I promise you, Benny."

He sighed and sniffed, then tried to smile. He nodded one more time and rubbed his finger under his nose. "Okay."

The morning rounds flew by, and since she was not in surgery that day, she could leave when the nurse announced with a wide smile that she had company. "They are such a nice young couple. Just right for our Benny," she said as she accompanied Astrid down to the front desk.

Rebecca, dressed in a rust-colored traveling suit and hat that nearly matched her hair, stood when she came through the door. "Oh, Astrid." Arms wide, the two nearly collided in the middle of the room. Gerald, wearing a dark gray suit, a fedora in hand, waited right behind her, his smile such a taste of home that Astrid hugged him too.

"I'm so glad you could come and even more that you are taking Benny. He is such a special little boy." Astrid took both their arms. "Are you checked in to your hotel? How was your trip? Would you like a cup of coffee before we go to meet him?" When she realized she'd not given them time to answer any of her questions, she shook her head and laughed. "Pardon me. Guess I'm more excited than I thought."

"I'll answer," Gerald said, beaming at his wife. "Our train trip was good." Rebecca nodded. "And we have a room at the hotel."

Rebecca's eyes widened. "It's a huge building five stories tall. We rode in an elevator so we didn't have to climb all those stairs. Have you ridden in a little box like that?"

"Yes. It was a bit scary the first time."

"Ja, and the second too."

"And yes, we would love some coffee."

"Dr. Morganstein has prepared tea and coffee for you in her office," the receptionist announced. "She is looking forward to meeting you too." She gestured toward the door. "Dr. Bjorklund will take you there."

"Oh, of course. Help me remember my manners." Astrid led them

down the hall. She knocked at the office door and at the "Come in"
ushered them ahead of her. "Dr. Morganstein, I have the privilege of
introducing my friends from Blessing, Mr. and Mrs. Gerald Valders.
Rebecca has been my friend since we were tiny."

Dr. Morganstein met them in front of her desk and shook both
their hands. "I am delighted to meet you. Welcome to Chicago and
to our hospital. We are so excited to have you here."

"Thank you." Gerald bent his head slightly. "I . . . we have heard
so much about you through the years."

"Come, sit down, and we can visit while we have our tea, or
coffee if you prefer. I want to answer any questions you might have
regarding our Benny. I cannot begin to tell you how delighted I am
that you are willing to adopt him. He has quite stolen the hearts of
all who have cared for him."

After they sat down, Gerald leaned forward. "I have only one
real concern. Since I was a street child too, I need to be assured that
there are no parents or relatives who will come to claim him down
the road. I know there were none in my brother's and my case, but
there could be here."

"We have done all we can to find any living relatives. The last
we know of was a grandmother who died last year. Since the city of
Chicago's Missing Persons Department couldn't find any more either,
we have a signed affidavit that Benjamin Coreside, age six years and
three months, will be legally yours after you sign the papers."

Gerald slowly nodded. "I think it was easier in our case. We just
hid on the train and got off when we got so hungry we couldn't stand
it. We thought to scrounge something to eat, get back on another train,
and keep going west until we couldn't go any farther."

"I'm glad you stopped in Blessing," Rebecca said with a smile.

"Me too. And that Mr. and Mrs. Valders took us in. I know we
weren't easy to raise, especially Toby."

"I have a feeling that God has indeed brought the right parents for that little boy." Dr. Morganstein rose and returned with a sheaf of papers. "I have here a copy of Benny's birth certificate, his grandmother's death certificate, and the adoption papers you need to sign. There is a copy for you and one for the city. We will take care of filing that." She laid the papers and a pen in front of Gerald. "There is a line for each of you to sign."

Gerald signed both copies first, pressing firmly so his signature would come through clearly on the carbon copies, and then Rebecca signed and handed them back to the doctor. Gerald picked up his coffee cup and drained it. "Dr. Bjorklund told us that we would take Benny with us today to stay at the hotel. Our train leaves fairly early in the morning."

"That is correct, and if you have any questions, you can come back by or telephone us or write. We have Benny's few things packed, and the janitor here has made him a sort of wagon. I'm not sure if you want to take that or not. He cannot use it outside during the winter anyway."

"I think what we'll do is study it, and then we can make him something similar in Blessing." He turned to Astrid. "Does he mind being carried?"

"No, but we have tried to make him as independent as possible. The more he uses his crutches, the more adept he will become."

Dr. Morganstein set the papers on the desk and put the copies in another envelope. "These are for you, then. Dinner is being served in the dining room, and I have an idea there is a bit of a party going to happen. You go meet Benny, and I'll see you again in the dining room."

When they opened the door to the ward, silence fell as all the children studied them. Astrid led the way to Benny's bed, where he sat against the pillows, arms over his chest. He stared at Astrid, and she smiled back, packing all the reassurance she could muster into her smile.

"Benny, I want you to meet Mr. and Mrs. Valders, who have already signed the papers so that you can be their little boy. Your new name will be Benjamin Valders."

Rebecca nodded at the boy, then at Astrid. "You can call me Ma

353

if you like." She sat down on the edge of the bed. "We have a room at home all ready for you."

Gerald moved closer to Benny. "Do you want to be called Benjamin or Benny?"

"Benny."

"That is a good name. I have a brother named Toby. We had a good friend named Benny once."

Benny stared up at him. "You'll be my pa?"

"I am your pa." The two stared into each other's eyes, as if searching out some secret. Then Benny nodded. "Can we go now? I'm hungry."

"Do you want me to carry you, or do you want to use your crutches?"

"It's faster if you carry me."

"Then that's what we'll do." Gerald leaned forward and lifted his son in his arms. "You want to say good-bye to the others?"

"Yep." Benny turned and waved, and as they walked the center aisle, he said good-bye to each of the children, one arm wrapped around his father's neck.

Astrid and Rebecca nodded at each other, and then one took his crutches, the other his small valise and followed them. At the door Benny turned to Gerald and pointed down. "That there is my scooter."

"I see." Gerald bent over and studied the design, including moving the steering handle. When he straightened, he said solemnly, "I think we'll leave that here for the other children, and before spring, we'll build you one in Blessing that will work just the same. Okay?"

"Okay."

After dinner in the dining room, where as many of the staff as were free could join in, some bringing him presents, Benny rode out triumphantly in his father's arms. Astrid walked them to the door.

Rebecca hugged her, and she hugged Benny. "See you in Blessing," she whispered in his ear.

"Yup. At my new house."

"That's for sure. You all have a good trip home."

"We will. Oh, I almost forgot. Sophie sent you a letter." Rebecca dug it out of her bag and handed it to her.

"Thank you." Astrid put the letter in her pocket, fighting against the desire to ask about Joshua. Surely if he had come back, they would have told her. She waved again as they started down the street, then, shivering, turned and reentered the hospital.

"They sure seem like a nice young couple," the receptionist said as she started down the hall.

"Yes, they are. And they will take good care of Benny."

"Blessing is a funny name for a town. There must be a story behind that."

"There is. Remind me, and I'll tell you sometime. I better get back to work."

"Yes, that is one thing that continues here all the time. Caring for patients never ends."

Before going to bed, Astrid opened the letter from Sophie.

Dear Astrid,

I have to write this quickly so that Rebecca and Gerald can take the letter with them tomorrow when they come for Benny. By the way, they are so excited, in fact we all are. I knew you'd want to know all that has gone on.

First, Christmas was so wonderful with all the little children enthralled with the Christmas trees and the presents and all the cookies and yummy things to eat. I never dreamed I would be so delighted watching not only my children but all the children. They did so good in the Christmas program, I nearly burst with pride. The twins are growing so fast, you'd think they are racing.

The wedding made Christmas last longer with the big party at the schoolhouse after the ceremony in church. Maydell made a lovely bride, and you could hear Gus give his vows. I had my doubts for a while, but the way he looked at her, you know he really does know what love is all about now. Rebecca and Gerald stood up with them. I know I wasn't the only one wiping away tears. Why is it that weddings make us cry?

Christmas Day Jonathan annnounced the engagement of the century. He and Grace make a lovely couple, as you well know. While I still have a hard time picturing him as a North Dakota farmer, I know that those two will do great things for the deaf school. Wait until you get home and we catch up on all the plans both for the school and the hospital. I hated to see them get on the train the day after the wedding and travel to New York. I believe there will be a formal announcement there with a ball and all kinds of fancy things. Grace just smiled sweetly, yet I happen to know there is a core of steel in that twin of mine. She has needed it to overcome all she has overcome.

As I sit here in the parlor where the tree smells the best, I wish you were here too. I know you will be done with your training soon, and when you get home, I will throw a party that will be the talk of the town for months to come.

Love and chuckles from your cousin,
Sophie

———

THAT NIGHT THE clanging of fire bells woke Astrid from a deep sleep. More bells. People shouting. She leaped from her bed and into her clothes. Surely there was an emergency going on. Out in the hall she could smell smoke. Was their building on fire? No, the alarms would be going off and people shouting. An orderly ran by.

"Tenement fire. Prepare for casualties," he threw over his shoulder.

"Oh, dear Lord, save the people." Astrid rushed down to help set up—as they had practiced in an emergency drill—for fire victims.

31

Two weeks and her surgical rotation would end.

Astrid stared at the letter she'd just received. Another one from Africa. Why did it feel like the whole continent was sitting on her shoulders? A decision would have to be made—and soon. The question: Which way was the best way? Which way did God want her to go? Why couldn't He make His marching orders more clear like He had for the armies and leaders in the Old Testament? He told them where to attack, when to march, and how many were needed. Of course, if they didn't do as ordered, they died.

She set her coffee cup down on the table and sat down on the bench. She needed every bit of support she could get.

Dear Dr. Bjorklund,
Greetings from the other side of the world. I am sure you

are counting the days until you can leave the hospital and return to Blessing. I know I would be. But as Shakespeare or someone famous said, "Hope springs eternal in the human breast: man never is but always to be blessed." Maybe it was Alexander Pope. My dearest hope is that God is leading you to register for a short stint of school to prepare you for coming here for further on-the-job training.

The doctor who served this entire region had to return to the States due to declining health. We desperately need a young person, and I know of none more capable than you. What we can offer you is the knowledge that those you help here will be of eternal significance. Jesus said if you give the needy a cup of water in His name . . . Well, you know the rest.

Astrid laid the letter on the table and rested her head in her hands. Couldn't she at least take a few weeks at home to think this through? She returned to the letter.

We are in the monsoon season now. As soon as the land dries, we will be able to reach some of the far-flung villages. Many of those tribes have never seen a white person. But I can promise you will always have strong men with you on those visits to keep you safe.

Now, that certainly made her feel secure. She finished the closing and folded the letter to put away with the rest she had received from him. Maybe if she had a more adventurous personality, she would want to cross lands and oceans, but all she wanted to do was go home to Blessing. She knew she could make a difference there too.

"Dr. Bjorklund?"

"Yes?"

"Dr. Whitaker is asking for you. He's in operating theatre three."

"I'll be right there." She rose and set her half-full cup on the counter. This was supposed to be Dr. Whitaker's day off. She returned greetings from those staff members she saw on the way. In two weeks this all would be behind her.

She sniffed against the burn in her eyes that was leaking into her nose. She would miss them all.

She straight-armed the swinging door to the scrub room, where Dr. Whitaker was scrubbing up. "You're not supposed to be here," she told him.

"I know, but Dr. Franck slipped and wrenched his back. There's no way he can stand for two hours during surgery. So here I am, and now here you are, and we start as soon as we can get in there."

She donned one of the operating aprons and picked up the bar of soap and brush. "What are we doing?"

"A head wound. You've not done one of those before, as far as I know, so I thought you would find this interesting. After that we have another amputation. One of the burn victims. His foot has succumbed to gangrene. I was hoping to save it and him, but . . ." He heaved a sigh and shook his head. "I want you to do the actual amputation."

Astrid swallowed. She'd done the one in class and another on the cadaver, but this would be the first on a living human.

"Do you have any questions?"

"No, sir."

Four hours later she dragged herself to the dining room, hoping there was some food left. Dr. Whitaker had complimented her on the smooth cut through the bone, even though she had hoped to preserve more skin to cover the stump. They took the foot off right above the ankle.

The head-wound patient was still comatose and could stay that way for days or weeks or . . . The *or* was too sad to contemplate. The woman had fallen down the stairs, or at least that's what whoever brought her in had said. In her months there Astrid had seen too many injured women who'd said they fell. She now knew the signs of wife battering. And child battering.

At least in Blessing they would not have cases like these.

Another letter waited for her on her pillow, this one with well-recognizable handwriting and the stamp of Blessing. She sat on the bed to read Pastor Solberg's reply to her plea for help.

My dear Astrid,

Sometimes I feel responsible for your situation since I invited my friend Reverend Schuman to speak here at our church. I never anticipated anything but his encouraging us to donate more to missions. That is what missionaries usually do when they are home on furlough. They tell people what life there is like so more money will be sent there for support.

I have been earnestly praying for your decision, and I have to say that God has not led me in either direction. I have included some of the Scriptures I've been pondering, and all I know to do is share those with you and leave you in His mighty hands. If God is indeed calling you to Africa, He will provide for all your needs.

I know that when I heard the call to ministry—I've told this story many times—and when I finally agreed, I felt a peace that carried me for weeks. Actually for years. The knowledge that we are walking in God's will for us gives strength and wisdom, because He promised it would be so. I also know the desperate need of people who have never heard of God's plan of salvation.

I remember when you were confirmed. You looked me right in the eyes and confessed your faith. Your "Yes, by the help of God" rang so true. I know you believe aright, but I also know you have much growing up to do. I have to remind myself that God will take care of it all, no matter where He calls you.

In His loving care,
Pastor John Solberg

She read the list of verses on the back of the page. She knew most of them by heart. *Go ye therefore, and teach all nations . . .* Another was the healing of the ten lepers. Would there be leprosy in Africa? Would they teach her about the diseases endemic to that continent when she attended missionary school?

———

THE NEXT DAYS passed in a fog. She cared for the remaining burn patients, birthed babies, held a child who died in her arms, then comforted the grieving mother. The day of exodus drew closer, but still she had no answer.

Two more letters arrived one day. One from the missionary school in Georgia, saying that her place was reserved and they were looking forward to her arrival. She read it again. All she'd done was to write for information. She hadn't told them she was coming for sure. She reread the letter, finding a clause she'd missed on her first read. "If you choose."

"If I choose? I'm not doing the choosing. This is not my choice. If I do this it will be because I believe God is calling me to obedience. In this case the most painful obedience I can imagine."

She laid the letter on the small desk at the end of her bed and opened the second one. Surely a letter from Sophie would be more entertaining.

Dear Astrid,

How we miss you. I am counting the days until you return to Blessing. We had a girls' night on Friday. I guess perhaps we should call it a young women's night, but we laughed and giggled just like we have all of our lives. If you and Grace had been here, the circle would have been complete.

Rebecca and Gerald are besotted with Benny. And he with

them. Haakan has carved him new crutches that fit better, and Ingeborg and Dr. Elizabeth are figuring out better ways to pad the wooden legs. He is such a game little boy. He plays with the other children, and Inga and Emmy have taken him on as their special friend. They have not put him in school yet, but Rebecca is teaching him at home until he at least knows his alphabet and numbers.

I have a bit of news. We are expecting another child come fall. I cannot believe that I will be the mother of five children. Astrid, I am not old enough for this. Five children happen to others, not to me. But Garth is excited, and Grant is telling the others he is going to be a big brother again. Remember how we all used to play together in the barns and the woods? All these little kids are like puppies tumbling around. Speaking of puppies. Inga's puppy—she named it Scooter—is now nearly three months old and is chewing on everything. Elizabeth says he has to stay out of the surgery, that's all there is to it, and it is Inga's responsibility to keep the doors closed. I'd rather have another cat myself.

Oh, and some other news. Mr. Landsverk left for Iowa before Christmas. That's all for now. I'm sure you are too busy to write but know that we all love you and are looking forward to your coming home. There's a secret that I'm not going to tell you. Now, isn't that just like me to tease like that?

Your cousin,
Sophie

P.S. Grace did write to tell you all the details of her engagement to Jonathan, did she not? S.

P.S.S. Oops. I wrote this and forgot to mail it. Sorry. S.

Astrid finished the letter in a state of shock. Mr. Landsverk left Blessing without even letting her know. Not that he'd written often, and she couldn't complain because she hadn't either. She undressed and pulled her flannel nightdress over her head. Tonight she was not supposed to be called, so she should be able to catch up on some sleep.

Did he come back? Should she write and ask? Where could she write to? Surely someone would have his address in Iowa. Did she want to write to him? Was this just one more of the ways God was providing for her? Removing one of the stumbling blocks to her leaving?

The next afternoon she hurried to her meeting with Dr. Morganstein. While she should have been rested and refreshed, her eyes wore the grit of sleeplessness. To go or not go? A Blessing life or an African village life? *God, you have to make this clear!*

Dr. Morganstein had the tea service in place in front of the sofa and motioned her to sit down. "I have been so looking forward to our time together."

"Thank you. I have too." Astrid sank down on the sofa, then straightened her spine and sat upright like her mentor. She said one lump in response to the age-old question and shook her head at the offer of milk. She accepted her cup and saucer and picked up one of the dainty cookies trimmed in colored sugar. "These are so delicious. I should get the recipe for Mor."

"What about for you? You are going to have a home of your own soon, are you not?"

"I have a recipe box in my hope chest, along with linens and household things, but I still don't know what I am supposed to do next."

"You've heard from the missionary again?"

"Oh, several times. But I have not come to a decision."

"I would hope you will be in Blessing when we all work to build another hospital there. I know you will be a big asset, and down the road I think one of the trainers for the interns we send there."

"I think that will be more Elizabeth's job. She is an excellent teacher."

"I know. She sent us you."

Astrid shook her head. "I'm afraid I failed far more often than I thought I would. Panic is not easy to deal with." And homesickness. "I hate making mistakes."

"Now *that* I understand, but sometimes we need to make mistakes to help us learn. To develop compassion and forethought. I have your reports here. You scored a ninety-eight out of one hundred in the anatomy class."

"I did?" Surprise widened her eyes. She'd known she did well on the final, but Dr. Franck had seemed to resent her so often that she felt sure he would mark her down.

"I observed you in surgery this last week. Dr. Whitaker agrees with me that you have good hands and eyes for this branch of medicine. I would love for you to go back East for further training, like Elizabeth did when she finished here. But you have met a good many of the needs for surgery here. Because of all your experiences before coming here, you are well trained in all fields of medicine."

"Thank you." Astrid sipped her tea and nibbled a cookie.

"There are many changes coming in our field of medicine. You would be wise to get yourself back here or to other places in the East on a regular basis."

But what if I am in Africa? Astrid looked up to find Dr. Morganstein studying her.

"I have learned through the years that sometimes God seems mighty slow in acting, but He is never late."

"I hope you are right."

"You could go home for a time and continue to think on this."

Astrid nodded. *But if I go home, will I ever leave again? And if that is the case, is that my answer?*

"Do you have any other questions?"

Pausing, Astrid searched her mind. "Other than will someone please tell me what I am to do, I don't think so."

"And that, my dear, is between you and God."

Astrid swallowed. "There is a question."

"Yes?"

"What if I'm just afraid? So afraid that I cannot hear the answer?" *And how much does my answer depend on the fact that Joshua, Mr. Landsverk, might not be in Blessing like he said he would?*

"Have you thought of asking for a two-year term?"

"Yes, but I've not heard back."

"You could use the telephone if you like and receive an answer far more quickly. Do you have the number?"

"I don't know. I will check on the correspondence." Astrid set her cup down on the silver tray. "Thank you. I will do that right now."

While the operator was putting the call through, she leaned her head against the wall, the black earpiece against her ear. When someone from the school came on the line, she introduced herself, endured polite chitchat, and asked her question. "Do you have a two-year program? I can see being gone from my own practice for two years, but not for a lifetime." There, she'd said it. The picture of Grace climbing on the railroad car all by herself shot through her mind. If Grace, who was deaf, could travel the country, surely she could get on a ship and go to where she was needed.

"Yes, we do have such a program," he said. "Of course, we hope that you will reconsider and fall in love with the people of Africa, like so many of our missionaries do, and you will want to go back time and again. Our normal first furlough is after four years, but we have had some medical people sign on for two years."

Astrid sucked in a deep breath. "I will be finished here in four days and can board the train for Georgia next Monday, February twenty-ninth."

"We will have a driver meet you at the station. How much luggage will you have?"

"A trunk and a valise, along with my medical bag." Her voice should be shaking as the rest of her was. But it must have been all right, because he answered.

"That is wonderful. Have you checked on train times yet?"

"No. But I will."

"We can do that here. We look forward to meeting you. Reverend Schuman has spoken of you so highly."

"Thank you." She hung the receiver back in the pronged arms and wrapped both arms around her waist. "I am going to Africa." She paused. No, I am going to Athens, Georgia, to attend missionary school with possible plans of serving in Africa for two years. Her heart took a leap and sent a small smile to her face. She was taking the next step. All God was asking her to do right now was to take the next step. She could hear her mother's voice. *"God will guide you step by step, not mile by mile."* Why had she not thought of that before?

That night at supper Red Hawk sat down beside her. "So have you made a decision?"

"I have. I leave for the school in Georgia on Monday." Again that heart leap.

"You won't be going back to Blessing, then?"

"No." *I can't bear to.*

"I sure hope you've made the right decision."

"It's only for two years. I have decided I'll consider it more like an internship." Was that another of those decisions that leaped into her mind along with her heart?

"I've been thinking. What if you went to help my people on the reservation? I won't be finished here until next fall, and they need medical care now. What if you thought of the reservation as your Africa? Couldn't God be calling you there?"

"Hmm, that's a thought too. Maybe that will happen when I return. After all, I'll only be gone two years. Think how fast time flies. The hospital in Blessing should be built by then, and perhaps we can do a distance clinic on the reservation." That thought bred others, and the two talked until the last lights were turned out in the room.

———

MONDAY, AS SHE looked back at the hospital through a sheet of wind-driven rain, a lump caught in her throat. She was leaving one place she hadn't wanted to go to and now didn't want to leave for another that might lead to an extended journey that she wasn't ready for.

If this is really what you want, God, I will do this. But only for two years. As Far said, a young woman on a journey like this needs all of heaven's protection. Hold me tight in your hands, O Lord. I am so frightened, but I can hear you saying, "Fear not." I know you won't let go of me. You never have. Why would you start now? Even those months when I questioned you, I knew you were there. But instead of washes of the peace Pastor Solberg said you would send me, I seem to get little glimpses. Is that all right?

She boarded her train, keeping her handkerchief near in case she needed it. If only this train were bound west, the clacking wheels taking her home to Blessing . . . Sometimes obedience could be a costly thing. She took out her writing packet and began the first of the letters she should have written days before.

Dear Mor,
    The adventure continues . . .

ACKNOWLEDGMENTS

My thanks and endless gratitude to Bill and Jeannie, whose hospitality gives me time and places to hide out while writing a book, usually trying to finish it.

Thanks also to my cohort writers, Mona and Eileen. May our weeks together continue to bless you both as much as they bless me.

Thanks to my readers, many of whom offer suggestions, others who point out errors so they may be corrected, and all who cheer me on. You are why I keep writing. Besides, I love these characters as much as you do.

I thank our heavenly Father for extending us all the measures of mercy that we need and far more than we deserve. To Him be all glory forever.